About the Authors

...ie Milburne read her first Mills & Boon at age ...een in between studying for her final exams. ... completing a Masters Degree in Education she ... to write a novel and thus her career as a ...e author was born. Melanie is an ambassador ... Australian Childhood Foundation and is a keen ...er and trainer and enjoys long walks in the ...ian bush. In 2015 Melanie won the HOLT ... ion, a prestigious award honouring outstanding ... talent.

... Stephens is passionate about writing books set ... ...ulous locations where an outstanding man comes ... ...ps with a cool, feisty woman. Susan's hobbies ...e travel, reading, theatre, long walks, playing the ..., and she loves hearing from readers at her ...e. www.susanstephens.com

...Thorpe has written over seventy-five books for ... & Boon and lives in Derbyshire, along with her ...band and a huge tabby cat, Mad Max, her one son ...ng flown the coop. She is happiest when immersed ...er writing, or reading.

Latin Lovers

Latin Lovers:
The Billionaire's
Persuasion

MELANIE MILBURNE

SUSAN STEPHENS

KAY THORPE

MIX
Paper from
responsible sources
FSC
www.fsc.org   FSC® C007454

This book is produced from independently certified FSC™ paper
to ensure responsible forest management.

For more information visit: www.harpercollins.co.uk/green

Printed and bound in Spain
by CPI, Barcelona

MILLS & BOON

First Published in Great Britain 2020
By Mills & Boon, an imprint of HarperCollins*Publishers*
1 London Bridge Street, London, SE1 9GF

LATIN LOVERS: THE BILLIONAIRE'S PERSUASION
© 2020 Harlequin Books S.A.

The Venadicci Marriage Vengeance © 2009 Melanie Milburne
The Spanish Billionaire's Mistress © 2005 Susan Stephens
The South American's Wife © 2004 Kay Thorpe

ISBN: 978-0-263-29881-9

THE VENADICCI MARRIAGE VENGEANCE

MELANIE MILBURNE

To Lorraine Bleasby, Dot Armstrong and Denise Monks—my three past and present helpers who free up my time so I can write. How can I thank you for all you do and have done for me and my family? This book is dedicated to you with much love and appreciation. I want the world to know what truly special women you are.

CHAPTER ONE

'MR VENADICCI has magnanimously offered to squeeze you in between appointments,' the receptionist informed Gabby with crisp, cool politeness. 'But he only has ten minutes available for you.'

Gabby schooled her features into impassivity, even though inside she was fuming and had been for the last hour, as Vinn Venadicci took his time about whether he would respond to her urgent request to see him. 'Thank you,' she said. 'I will try not to take up too much of his precious time.'

No matter how galling it would be to see Vinn again, Gabby determined she would be calm and in control at all times and under all circumstances. Too much was at stake for her to jeopardise things with a show of temper or a tirade of insults, as she would have done without hesitation seven years ago. A lot of water had flowed under the bridge since then, but she was not going to tell him just how dirty some of it had been. That would be conceding defeat, and in spite of everything that had happened she wasn't quite ready to shelve all of her pride where Vinn Venadicci was concerned.

His plush suite of offices in the heart of the financial district in Sydney was a reflection of his meteoric rise to fame in the property investment industry. From his humble beginnings as the born-out-of-wedlock bad-boy son of the St Clair family's Italian-born house-cleaner Rose, he had surprised everyone—except Gabby's father, who had always seen Vinn's potential and had done what he could to give him the leg-up he needed.

Thinking of her father was just the boost to her resolve Gabby needed right now. Henry St Clair was in frail health after a serious heart attack, which meant a lot of the responsibility to keep things running smoothly while he went through the arduous process of triple bypass surgery and rehabilitation had fallen on her shoulders, with her mother standing stalwartly and rather stoically by her father's side.

This hiccup to do with the family business had come out of the blue—and if her father got wind of it, it was just the thing that could set off another heart attack. Gabby would walk across hot coals to avoid that—even meet face to face with Vinn Venadicci.

She raised her hand to the door marked with Vinn's name and gave it a quick two-hit tattoo, her stomach twisting with the prickly sensation she always felt when she was within striking distance of him.

'Come.'

She straightened her shoulders and opened the door, her chin at a proud height as she took the ridiculously long journey to his desk, where he was seated. That he didn't rise to his feet was the sort of veiled insult she more or less expected from him. He had always had an insolent air about him, even when he had lived on and off with his mother, in a servants' cottage at the St Clair Point Piper mansion.

In that nanosecond before he spoke Gabby quickly drank in his image, her heart giving a little jerk inside her chest in spite of all of her efforts to control it. Even when he was seated his height was intimidating, and the black raven's wing of his hair caught the light coming in from the windows, giving it a glossy sheen that made her fingers itch to reach out and touch it. His nose was crooked from one too many of the brawls he had been involved in during his youth, but—unlike many other high-profile businessmen, who would have sought surgical correction by now—Vinn wore his war wounds like a medal. Just like the scar that interrupted his left eyebrow, giving him a dangerous don't-mess-with-me look that was disturbingly attractive.

'So how is the Merry Widow?' he said with a mocking glint in his eyes as they ran over her lazily. 'Long time no see. What is it now…? One year or is it two? You look like grief suits you, Gabriella. I have never seen you looking more beautiful.'

Gabby felt her spine go rigid at his sardonic taunt. Tristan Glendenning had been dead for just over two years, and yet Vinn never failed to refer to him in that unmistakably scathing manner whenever their paths crossed. She felt each and every reference to her late husband like a hard slap across the face—not that she would ever admit that to Vinn.

She pulled her temper back into line with an effort. 'May I sit down?'

He waved a hand in a careless manner. 'Put your cute little bottom down on that chair. But only for ten minutes,' he said. 'I have back-to-back commitments today.'

Gabby sat down on the edge of the chair, hating that his words had summoned such a hot flush to her cheeks. He had the most annoying habit of unnerving her with personal comments that made her aware of her body in a way no one else could.

'So,' he said, leaning back in his chair with a squeak of very expensive leather, 'what can I do for you, Gabriella?'

She silently ground her teeth. No one else called her by her full name. Only him. She knew he did it deliberately. He had done it since she was fourteen, when his mother had been hired as the resident cleaner, bringing her brooding eighteen-year-old son with her. Although Gabby had to grudgingly admit that the way he said her name was quite unlike anyone else. He had been born in Australia but, because he had been fluent in Italian from a very young age, he made her name sound faintly foreign and exotic. The four distinct syllables coming out of his sensually sculptured mouth always made the hairs on the back of her neck stand to attention like tiny soldiers.

'I am here to discuss a little problem that's come up,' she said, hoping he couldn't see how she was tying her hands into knots in her lap. 'With my father out of action at present, I would appreciate your advice on how to handle it.'

He sat watching her in that musing way of his, clicking and releasing his gold ballpoint pen with meticulously timed precision: on, off, on, off, as if he was timing his own slow and steady heartbeat.

'How is your father this morning?' he asked. 'I saw him last night in Intensive Care. He was looking a little worse for wear, but that's to be expected, I suppose.'

Gabby was well aware of Vinn's regular visits to her father's bedside, and had deliberately avoided being there at the same time. 'He's doing OK,' she said. 'His surgery is scheduled for some time next week. I think they've been waiting for him to stabilise first.'

'Yes, of course,' he said putting the pen to one side. 'But the doctors are hopeful of a full recovery, are they not?'

Gabby tried not to look at his hands, but for some reason her eyes drifted back to where they were now lying palm down on the smoothly polished desk. He had broad, square-shaped hands, with long fingers, and the dusting of masculine hair was enough to remind her of his virility as a full-blooded male of thirty-two.

He was no longer the youth of the past. His skin was clear and cleanly shaven, and at six foot four he carried not a gram of excess flesh; every toned and taut muscle spoke of his punishing physical regime. It made Gabby's ad hoc attempts at regular exercise with a set of free weights and a home DVD look rather pathetic in comparison.

'Gabriella?'

Gabby gave herself a mental shake and dragged her eyes back to his. He had such amazing eyes. And his ink-black hair and deeply olive skin made the smoky grey colour of them all the more striking.

She had never been told the details of his father, and she had never really bothered to ask Vinn directly—

although she assumed his father wasn't Italian, like his mother. Gabby had heard one or two whispers as she was growing up, which had seemed to suggest Vinn's mother found the subject painful and refused ever to speak of it.

'Um…I'm not really sure,' she said, in answer to his question regarding her father's recovery. 'I haven't really spoken with his doctors.'

As soon as she said the words she realised how disengaged and uncaring they made her sound—as if her father's health was not a top priority for her, when nothing could be further from the truth. She wouldn't be here now if it wasn't for her love and concern for both of her parents. She would never have dreamed of asking for Vinn's help if desperation hadn't shoved her head-first through his door.

'I take it this unprecedented visit to my lair is about the takeover bid for the St Clair Island Resort?' he said into the ringing silence.

Gabby had trouble disguising her reaction. She had only just become aware of it herself. How on earth had he found out about it?

'Um…yes, it is actually,' she said, shifting restlessly in her seat. 'As you probably know, my father took out a substantial loan for the refurbishment of the resort about a year and a half ago. But late yesterday I was informed there's been a call. If we don't pay the loan back the takeover bid will go through uncontested. I can't allow that to happen.'

'Have you spoken to your accountants about it?' he asked.

Gabby felt another layer of her professional armour

dissolve without trace. 'They said there is no way that amount of money can be raised in twenty-four hours,' she said, lowering her gaze a fraction.

He began his on-off click with his pen once more, a little faster now, as if in time with his sharp intelligence as he mulled over what strategy to adopt.

'I don't suppose you've mentioned it to your father,' he said, phrasing it as neither a question nor a statement.

'No…' she said, still not quite able to hold his gaze. 'I didn't want to stress him. I'm frightened the news could trigger another heart attack.'

'What about the on-site resort managers?' he asked. 'Do they know anything about this?'

Gabby rolled her lips together as she brought her gaze back to his. 'I spoke to Judy and Garry Foster last night. They are concerned for their jobs, of course, but I tried to reassure them I would sort things out this end.'

'Have you brought all the relevant documentation with you?' he asked after a short pause.

'Um…no… I thought I would run it by you first.' Gabby knew it was the wrong answer. She could see it in his incisive grey-blue eyes as they quietly assessed her.

She felt so incompetent—like a child playing with oversized clothes in a dress-up box. The shoes she had put on were too big. She had always known it, but hadn't had the courage to say it out loud to her parents, who had held such high hopes for her after her older brother Blair's tragic death. The giant hole he had left in their lives had made her all the more determined to fill in where she could. But she still felt as if the shoes were too big, too ungainly for her—even though she had trudged in them with gritted teeth for the last seven and a half years.

Vinn leaned back in his seat, his eyes still centred on hers. 'So you have less than twenty-four hours to come up with the funds otherwise the takeover bid goes through unchallenged?' he summated.

Gabby ran the tip of her tongue across lips dryer than ancient parchment. 'That's right,' she said, doing her level best to quell her dread at the thought of such an outcome. 'If it goes through our family will be left with only a thirty-five percent share in the resort. I'm not sure what you can do, but I know my father. If he wasn't so unwell he would probably have run it by you first, to see if there's anything we can do to avoid losing the major sharehold.'

His eyes were still locked on hers, unblinking almost, which unsettled Gabby more than she wanted it to.

'Do you know who is behind the takeover?' he asked.

She shook her head and allowed a tiny sigh to escape. 'I've asked around, but no one seems to know anything about the company that's behind it.'

'How much is the margin call?'

Gabby took an uneven breath, her stomach feeling as if a nest of hungry bull ants were eating their way out. 'Two point four million dollars.'

His dark brows lifted a fraction. 'Not exactly an amount you would have sitting around in petty cash,' he commented wryly.

'It's not an amount that is sitting *anywhere* in any of the St Clair accounts,' she said, running her tongue over her lips again, as if to wipe away the residue of panic that seemed to have permanently settled there. 'I'm sure my father never expected anything like this to happen—or at least not before we had time to recoup on the investment. The markets have been unstable for several months now. We wouldn't be the first to have redeveloped at the wrong time.'

'True.'

Gabby shifted in her chair again. 'So…I was wondering what you suggest we do…' She sucked in a tiny breath, her heart thumping so loudly she could feel a roaring in her ears. 'I…I know it's a bit of an imposition, but my father respects your judgment. That's basically why I am here.'

Vinn gave a deep and utterly masculine rumble of laughter. 'Yes, well, I can't imagine you pressing for an audience with me to share your observations on the day's weather,' he said. And then, with a little sneering quirk of his mouth, he added, 'You have five minutes left, by the way.'

Gabby pursed her lips as she fought her temper down. 'I think you know what I'm asking you to do,' she said tightly. 'Don't make me spell it out just to bolster your already monumental ego.'

A flicker of heat made his eyes look like the centre of a flame as he leaned forward across the desk. 'You want me to pay off the loan, is that it?' he said, searing her gaze with his.

'My father has done a lot for you—' she launched into the speech she had hastily prepared in the middle of the night '—he paid bail for that stolen car charge you were on when you were eighteen, not long after you came to live with us. And he gave you your very first loan for university. You wouldn't be where you are today without his mentorship and his belief in you.'

He leaned back in his chair, his demeanour casual as

you please. He picked up his pen again, but this time rolled it between two of his long fingers. 'Two point four million dollars is a lot of money, Gabriella,' he said. 'If I were to hand over such an amount I would want something in return. Something I could depend on to cover my losses if things were to take a sudden downturn.'

Gabby felt a prickle of alarm lift the surface of her skin. 'You mean like a guarantee or something?' she asked. 'W-we can have something drawn up with the lawyers. A repayment plan over…say five years, with fixed interest. How does that sound?'

He gave a smile that wasn't reflected in those unreadable eyes of his. 'It sounds risky,' he said. 'I would want a better guarantee than something written on paper.'

She looked at him in confusion. 'I'm not sure what you mean… Are you asking for more collateral? There's the house but Mum and Dad will need somewhere to—'

'I don't want their house,' he said, his eyes still burning like fire into hers.

Gabby ran her tongue over her lips again, her stomach doing another nervous shuffling movement. 'Then…then what do you want?' she asked, annoyed with herself at how whispery and frightened her voice sounded.

The silence became charged with something she couldn't quite identify. The air was thick—so thick she could scarcely breathe without feeling as if her chest was being pressed down with a weight far too heavy for her finely boned ribcage. Apprehension slowly but stealthily crept up her spine, with tiptoeing, ice-cold steps, disturbing each and every fine hair on the back of her neck.

Vinn's eyes were fathomless pools of murky shadows as they held onto hers. 'How do you feel about stepping up to the plate as guarantor?' he asked.

Gabby frowned. 'I don't have anything like that amount at my disposal,' she said, her heart starting to race. 'I have a small income I draw from the company for my immediate needs, but nothing that would cover that amount at short notice.'

He tilted one of his dark brows ironically. 'So I take it your late husband didn't leave you in the manner to which you have been accustomed for all of your silver-spooned life?' he said.

Gabby lowered her gaze and looked at her knotted hands rather than see the I-told-you-so gleam in his eyes. 'Tristan's finances were in a bit of a mess when he died so suddenly. There were debts and…so many things to see to…' *And so many secrets to keep*, she thought grimly.

A three-beat pause passed.

'I will give you the money,' Vinn said at last. 'I can have it in your father's business account with a few clicks of my computer mouse. Your little problem will be solved before you catch the lift down to the ground floor of this building.'

Gabby could sense a 'but' coming, and waited with bated breath for him to deliver it. She knew him too well to expect him to hand over that amount of money without some sort of condition on the deal. Sure, he admired and respected her father, he even tolerated her mother to some degree, but he had every reason to hate Gabby, and she couldn't imagine him missing a golden opportunity like this to demonstrate how deep his loathing of her ran.

'But of course there will be some conditions on the deal,' he inserted into the silence.

Gabby felt her heart skip a beat when she saw the determined glint in his gaze. 'W-what sort of conditions?' she asked.

'I am surprised you haven't already guessed,' he remarked, with an inscrutable smile playing with the sensual line of his mouth, giving him a devilishly ruthless look.

Gabby felt another shiver of apprehension pass through her. 'I—I have no idea what you're talking about,' she said, her nails scoring into her palms as she tightened her fists in her lap.

'Ah, but I think you do,' he said. 'Remember the night before your wedding?'

She forced herself to hold his gaze, even though she could feel a bloom of guilty colour staining her cheeks. The memory was as clear as if it had happened yesterday. God knew she had relived that brief, fiery exchange so many times during her train wreck of a marriage, wondering how different her life might have been if she had heeded Vinn's warning…

The wedding rehearsal had been going ahead, in spite of Tristan calling at the last minute to say he had been held up in a meeting and might not make it after all, and Vinn had arrived at the church bleary-eyed and unshaven from an international flight, after spending the last six months in Italy where his terminally ill mother had asked to be taken to die.

He had leaned in that indolent way of his against one of the columns at the back of the cathedral, his strong arms folded, one ankle crossed over the other, and his eyes—those amazingly penetrating eyes—every time Gabby happened to glance his way, trained on her.

Once the minister had taken them through their paces, Gabby's mother had invited everyone present back to the St Clair house for a light supper. Gabby had secretly hoped Vinn would decline the invitation, but as she had come out of one of the upstairs bathrooms half an hour or so later, Vinn had stepped forward to block her path.

'I'd like a word with you, Gabriella,' he said. 'In private.'

'I can't imagine what you'd have to say to me,' she said coldly, as she tried to sidestep him, but he took one of her wrists in the steel bracelet of his fingers, the physical contact sending sparks of fizzing electricity up and down her arm. 'Let me go, Vinn,' she said, trying to pull away.

His hold tightened to the point of pain. 'Don't go through with it, Gabriella,' he said in a strained sort of tone she had never heard him use before. 'He's not the right man for you.'

Pride made her put her chin up. 'Let me go,' she repeated, and, using her free hand, scraped the back of his hand with her nails.

He captured her other hand and pulled her up close—closer than she had ever been to him before. It was a shock to find how hard the wall of his chest was, and the latent power of his thighs pressed against her trembling body made her spine feel loose and watery all of a sudden.

His eyes were burning as they warred with hers. 'Call it off,' he said. 'Your parents will understand. It's not too late.'

She threw him an icy glare. 'If you don't let me go this instant I'll tell everyone you tried to assault me. You'll go to jail. Tristan's father will act for me in court. You won't have a leg to stand on.'

His mouth tightened, and she saw a pulse beating like a drum in his neck. 'Glendenning is only marrying you for your money,' he ground out.

Gabby was incensed, even though a tiny pinhole of doubt had already worn through the thick veil of denial she had stitched in place over the last few weeks of her engagement. 'You don't know what you're talking about,' she spat at him. 'Tristan loves me. I know he does.'

Vinn's hands were like handcuffs on her wrists. 'If it's marriage you want, then marry me. At least you'll know what you're getting.'

Gabby laughed in his face. 'Marry *you?*' She injected as much insult as she could into her tone. 'And spend the rest of my life like your mother did, scrubbing other people's houses? Thanks, but no thanks.'

'I won't let you go through with it, Gabriella,' he warned. 'If you don't call the wedding off tonight I will stand up during the ceremony tomorrow and tell the congregation why the marriage should not go ahead.'

'You wouldn't dare!'

His eyes challenged hers. 'You just watch me, Blondie,' he said. 'Do you want the whole of Sydney to know what sort of man you are marrying?'

She threw him a look of pure venom. 'I am going to make damned sure you're not even *at* my wedding,' she spat back at him. 'I'm going to speak to the security firm Dad has organised and have you banned from entry. I'm marrying Tristan tomorrow no matter what you say. I love him.'

'You don't know who or what you want right now,' he said, with a fast-beating pulse showing at the corner of his mouth. 'Damn it, Gabriella, you're only just twenty-one. Your brother's suicide has thrown you. It's thrown all of us. Your engagement was a knee-jerk reaction. For God's sake, a blind man could see it.'

The mention of her brother and his tragic death unleashed a spurt of anger Gabby had not been able to express out of respect for her shattered parents. It rose inside her like an explosion of lava, and with the sort of strength she had no idea she possessed, she tore herself out of his hold and delivered a stinging slap to his stubbly jaw. It must have hurt him, for her hand began to throb unbearably, all the delicate bones feeling as if they had been crushed by a house brick.

Time stood still for several heart-stopping seconds.

Something dangerous flickered in his grey-blue eyes, and then with a speed that knocked the breath right out of her lungs he pulled her into his crushing embrace, his hot, angry mouth coming down on hers…

Gabby had to shake herself back to the present. She hated thinking about that kiss. She hated remembering how she had so shamelessly responded to it. And she hated recalling the bracelet of fingertip bruises she had worn on her wedding day—as if Vinn Venadicci, in spite of her covert word to Security to keep him out of the church, had vicariously come along to mock her marriage to Tristan Glendenning anyway.

'Just tell me what you want and get it over with,' she

said now, with a flash of irritation, as she continued to face him combatively across the expanse of his desk.

'I want you to be my wife.'

Gabby wasn't sure what shocked her the most: the blunt statement of his intentions or the terrifying realisation she had no choice but to agree.

'That seems rather an unusual request, given the fact we hate each other and have always done so,' she managed to say, without—she hoped—betraying the flutter of her heart.

'You don't hate me, Gabriella,' he said with a sardonic smile. 'You just hate how I make you feel. It's always been there between us, has it not? The forbidden fruit of attraction: the rich heiress and the bad boy servant's son. A potent mix, don't you think?'

Gabby sent him a withering look. 'You are delusional, Vinn,' she said. 'I have never given you any encouragement to think anything but how much I detest you.'

He got to his feet and, glancing at his designer watch, informed her dispassionately, 'Time's up, Blondie.'

She gritted her teeth. 'I need more time to consider your offer,' she bit out.

'The offer is closing in less than thirty seconds,' he said with an indomitable look. 'Take or leave it.'

Frustration pushed Gabby to her feet. 'This is my father's life's work we're talking about here,' she said, her voice rising to an almost shrill level. 'He built up the St Clair Resort from scratch after that cyclone in the seventies. How can you turn your back on him after all he's done for you? Damn it, Vinn. You would be pacing the exercise yard at Pentridge Jail if it wasn't for what our family has done for you.'

His eyes were diamond-hard, the set to his mouth like carved granite. 'That is my price, Gabriella,' he said. 'Marriage or nothing.'

She clenched her hands into fists, her whole body shaking with impotent rage. 'You know I can't say no. You know it and you want to rub it in. You're only doing this because I rejected your stupid spur of the moment proposal seven years ago.'

He leaned towards the intercom on his desk and pressing the button, said calmly, 'Rachel? Is my next client here? Mrs Glendenning is just leaving.'

Gabby could see her father's hard-earned business slipping out of his control. He would have to sell the house—the house his parents and grandparents before him had lived in. Gabby could imagine the crushing disappointment etched on his face when she told him she had failed him, that she hadn't been able to keep things afloat as her brilliantly talented brother would have done. If Blair was still alive he would have networked and found someone to tide him over by now. He would have had that margin call solved with a quick call to one of his well-connected mates. That was the way he had worked. He had lived on the adrenalin rush of life while she… Well, that was the problem.

She couldn't cope.

She liked to know what was going to happen and when it was going to happen. She hated the cut and thrust of business, the endless going-nowhere meetings, the tedious networking at corporate functions—not to mention the reams of pointless paperwork. And most of all she hated the rows and rows of numbers that seemed more of a blur to her than anything else.

Gabby liked to… Well, there was no point in thinking about what she liked to do, because it just wasn't going to happen. Her dreams had had to be shelved and would remain shelved—at least until her father could take up the reins again… *If* he took up the reins again, she thought, with another deep quiver of panic.

Gabby had been the last person to speak to her brother; the last person to see him alive before he ended his life with a drug overdose. Because of that she had responsibilities to face. And face them she would. Even if they were totally repugnant to her. Being forced to marry a man like Vinn Venadicci was right up there on the repugnant scale. Or maybe repugnant wasn't quite the right word, she grudgingly conceded. Vinn was hardly what any woman would describe as physically off-putting. He was downright gorgeous, when it came down to it. That long, leanly muscled frame, that silky black hair, those sensually sculptured lips and those mesmerising eyes were enough to send any woman's heart aflutter—and Gabby's was doing a whole lot more than fluttering right now at the thought of being formally tied to him.

Entering into a marriage contract with Vinn was asking for trouble—but what else could she do? Who was going to lend her that amount of money in less than twenty-four hours?

Gabby gulped as she glanced at him again. Could she do it? Could she agree to marry him even though it was madness?

Actually, it was dangerous… Yes, that was the word she had been looking for. Vinn was dangerous. He was arrogant, he was a playboy, and—even more disturbing—he had a chip on his shoulder where she was concerned.

But she had nowhere else to turn—no other solution to fix this within the narrow timeframe. It was up to her to save her family's business, even if it meant agreeing to his preposterous conditions.

'All right,' Gabby said on a whooshing breath of resignation. 'I'll do it.'

'Fine,' Vinn said, in a tone that suggested he had never had any doubt of her accepting, which somehow made it all the more galling. 'The money will be deposited within the next few minutes. I will pick you up this evening for dinner, so we can go through the wedding arrangements.'

Gabby felt herself quake with alarm. 'Couldn't we just wait a few days until I have time to—?'

His cynical laugh cut her off. 'Until you have time to think of a way out, eh, Gabriella? I don't think so, *cara*. Now I have you I am not going to let you escape.'

'What am I supposed to say to my parents?' she asked, scowling at him even as her stomach did another nosedive of dread.

He smiled. 'Why not tell them you've finally come to your senses and agreed to marry me?'

She gave him another glare that would have stripped three decades of paint off a wall. 'They will think I have taken leave of my senses.'

'Or they will think you have fallen head over heels in love,' he said. 'Which is exactly what I would prefer them to believe at this point in time. Your father's health is unstable and will be for some weeks after the surgery, I imagine. I wouldn't want him to suffer a relapse out of concern for you or for his business.'

Gabby couldn't argue with that, but she resented him using it as a lever to get her to fall meekly in with his plans. 'I was planning on going to the hospital this evening,' she said tightly. 'Will I meet you there or at the house?'

'I have a couple of meetings that might string out, so if I don't make it to the hospital I will meet you at the house around eight-thirty,' he said. 'I would like to speak to your father at some point about my intentions.'

Gabby couldn't stop her top lip from curling. 'Somehow you don't strike me as the traditional type, asking a girl's father for her hand in marriage. In fact I didn't think you were the marrying type at all. All we ever read about you in the press is how you move from one relationship to another within a matter of weeks.'

He gave her another unreadable smile. 'Variety, as they say, is the spice of life,' he said. 'But even the most restless man eventually feels the need to put down some roots.'

She eyed him warily. 'This marriage between us…it's not for the long term…is it?'

'Only for as long as it achieves its aim,' he said— which Gabby realised hadn't really answered her question.

Vinn moved past her to hold the door open for her. 'I will see you tonight,' he said. 'I'll call you if I am going to be late.'

She brushed past him, her head at a proud angle. The subtle notes of her perfume danced around his face, making his nostrils flare involuntarily. She smelt of orange blossom. Or was it honeysuckle? He couldn't quite tell. Maybe it was both. That was the thing about Gabriella—she was a combination of so many things, any one of them alone was enough to send his senses spinning. But all of them put together? Well, that was half his problem, wasn't it?

The door clicked shut behind her and Vinn released the breath he'd unconsciously been holding. 'Damn,' he said, raking a hand through his hair. 'God damn it to hell.'

'Mr Venadicci?' His receptionist's cool, crisp voice sounded over the intercom. 'Mr Winchester is here now. Shall I send him in?'

Vinn pulled in an uneven breath and released it just as raggedly. 'Yeah…' he said, dropping his hand by his side. 'I'll see him. But tell him I've only got five minutes.'

CHAPTER TWO

GABBY put on her bravest face while she visited her father's bedside. The tubes and heart monitor leads attached to his grey-tinged body made her stomach churn with anguish—the very same anguish she could see played out on her mother's face.

'How are you, Dad?' she whispered softly as she bent down to kiss his cheek.

'Still alive and kicking,' he said, and even managed a lopsided grin, but Gabby could see the worry and fear in his whisky-coloured eyes.

'Have the doctors told you anything more?' she asked, addressing both her mother and father.

'The surgery is being brought forward to tomorrow,' Pamela St Clair answered. 'Vinn spoke to the cardiac surgeon and organised it when he was here earlier. He insisted your father's case be made a priority. You just missed him, actually. It's a wonder you didn't pass him in the corridor.'

Gabby stiffened. 'Vinn was here just now?'

'Yes, dear,' her mother said. 'He's been here every day. But you know that.'

'Yes… It's just I was speaking to him this morning

and he said he had meetings to attend all afternoon and evening,' she said, unconsciously biting her lip.

Her mother gave her a searching look. 'I hope you're not going to be difficult about Vinn,' she said, with a hint of reproof in her tone. 'He's been nothing but supportive, and the least you could do is be civil towards him—especially now.'

Gabby could have laughed out loud at the irony of her mother's turnaround. Pamela St Clair had always been of the old school, that actively discouraged fraternisation with any of the household staff. She had barely spoken to Vinn's mother during the years Rose had worked at the St Clair estate other than to hand Rose a long list of menial tasks to get through. She had been even less friendly towards Rose's surly son during the short time he had lived there with his mother. And after he'd had that slight run-in with the law Pamela had tried to ban him from the property altogether, but Gabby's father had insisted Vinn be allowed to visit his mother as usual.

Gabby hadn't been much better towards Rose—which was something she had come to sincerely regret in the years since. She still cringed in shame at how inconsiderate she had been at times, carelessly leaving her things about, without a care for the person who had to come along behind her and pick them up.

But it was Gabby's treatment of Vinn that had been the most unforgivable. She had been absolutely appalling to him for most of her teenage years—teasing him in front of her giggling friends, talking about him in disparaging terms well within his hearing. She had flirted with him, and then turned her nose up at him with disgraceful regularity. She had no excuse for her behaviour other than that she had been an insecure teenager, privately struggling with body issues, who, in an effort to build her self-esteem, had tended to mix with a rather shallow crowd of rich-kid friends who had not learned to respect people from less affluent backgrounds.

On one distressingly memorable occasion, at the urging of her troublemaking friends, Gabby had left an outrageously seductive note for Vinn, asking him to meet her in the summerhouse that evening. But instead of turning up she had watched from one of the top windows of the mansion, laughing with her friends at how he had arrived at the summerhouse with a bunch of white roses for her. What had shamed her most had been Vinn's reaction. Instead of bawling her out, calling her any one of the despicable names she had no doubt deserved, he had said nothing. Not to her, not to her parents, and not even to her brother Blair, whom he'd spent most of his spare time with whenever he had visited the estate.

Gabby's father reached out a weak hand towards her, the slight tremble of his touch bringing her back to the present. 'Vinn is a good man,' he said. 'I know you're still grieving the loss of Tristan, but I think you should seriously consider his proposal. You could do a lot worse. I know he's had a bit of a rough start, but he's done well for himself. No one could argue with that. I always knew he had the will-power and the drive to make it once he got on the right path. I'm glad he has chosen you as his bride. He will look after you well. I know he will.'

Gabby couldn't quite disguise her surprise that Vinn had already spoken to her father. She moistened her dry lips and tried on a bright smile, but it didn't feel comfortable on her mouth. 'So he's spoken to you about our…relationship?'

Her father smiled. 'I gave him my full blessing, Gabby. I must say I wasn't the least surprised to hear the news of your engagement.'

Gabby frowned. 'You…you weren't?'

He shook his head and gave her hand another light squeeze. 'You've been striking sparks off each other since you were a teenager,' he said. 'For a time there I thought… Well…Blair's accident changed everything, of course.'

Gabby felt the familiar frustration that neither of her parents had ever accepted their only son's death as suicide. They still refused to acknowledge he had been dabbling with drugs—but then stubborn denial was a St Clair trait, and she had her own fair share of it.

'I'm glad you both approve,' she said, banking down her emotion. 'We are having dinner this evening to discuss the wedding arrangements.'

'Yes, he told us it wasn't going to be a grand affair,' her mother said. 'I think that's wise, under the circumstances. After all, it's your second marriage. It seems pointless going to the same fuss as last time.'

Gabby couldn't agree more. The amount of money spent on her marriage to Tristan Glendenning had been such a waste when within hours of the ceremony and lavish reception she had realised the terrible mistake she had made.

She stretched her mouth into another staged smile

and reached across to kiss both her parents. 'I'd better get going,' she said, readjusting her handbag over her shoulder. 'Is there anything you need before I go?'

'No, dear,' her mother assured her. 'Vinn brought some fruit and a couple of novels for your father to read by that author he enjoys so much. I must say Vinn's grown into a perfect gentleman. Your father is right. You could do a lot worse—especially as you're a widow. Not many men want a woman someone else has had, so to speak.'

Gabby silently ground her teeth. If only her mother knew the truth about her ill-fated first marriage. 'I'll see you tomorrow,' she said, and with another unnatural smile left.

The St Clair mansion was situated on the waterfront in the premier harbourside suburb of Point Piper, flanked on either side by equally luxurious homes for the super-rich and famous. The views across Sydney Harbour were spectacular, and the house and grounds offered a lifestyle that was decadent to say the least.

Gabby had moved back home two years ago, after Tristan's death in a car accident, and although now and again she had toyed with the idea of finding a place of her own, so far she had done nothing about doing so. The mansion was big enough for her to have the privacy she needed, and with her finances still on the shaky side, after the trail of debts her late husband had left behind, she had decided to leave things as they were for the time being.

The doorbell sounded right on the stroke of eight-thirty and Gabby was still not ready. Her straight ash-blonde hair was in heated rollers, to give it some much needed body, and she was still in her bathrobe after a shower.

She wriggled into a black sheath of a designer dress she'd had for years, and shoved her feet into three inch heels, all the time trying not to panic as another minute passed. She slashed some lipstick across her mouth and dusted her cheeks with translucent powder, giving her lashes a quick brush with a mascara wand before tugging at the rollers. Her hair cascaded around her shoulders in springy waves, and with a quick brush she was ready—or at least as ready as she could be under the circumstances. Which wasn't saying much…

Vinn checked his watch and wondered if he should use the key Henry had insisted he keep on him at all times. But just as he was searching for it on his keyring the door opened and Gabriella was standing there, looking as if she had just stepped off the catwalk. Her perfume drifted towards him, an exotic blend of summer blooms. Her normally straight hair was bouncing freely around her bare shoulders, the black halter neck dress showing off her slim figure to maximum advantage.

It had always amazed him how someone so slim could have such generous breasts without having to resort to any sort of enhancement. The tempting shadow of her cleavage drew his eyes like a magnet, and he had to fight to keep his eyes on her toffee-brown ones. She had made them all the more noticeable with the clever use of smoky eyeshadow and eyeliner, and her full and sensual lips were a glossy pink which was the same shade as that on her fingernails.

'I'll just get my wrap and purse,' she said, leaving the door open.

Vinn watched her walk over the marbled floor of the expansive foyer on killer heels, one of her hands adjusting her earrings before she scooped up a purse and silky wrap. She turned and came back towards him, her chin at the haughty angle he had always associated with her—even when she was a sulky fourteen-year-old, with braces on her teeth and puppy fat on her body.

'Shall we get this over with?' she said, as if they were about to face a hangman.

Vinn had to suppress his desire to make her eat her carelessly slung words. She meant to insult him, and would no doubt do so at every opportunity, but he had the upper hand now and she would have to toe the line. It would bring him immense pleasure to tame her—especially after what her fiancé had done to him on the day of their wedding on her behalf. The scar over his left eyebrow was a permanent reminder of what lengths she would go to in order to have her way. But things were going to be done his way this time around, and the sooner she got used to it the better.

He led the way to his car and opened the passenger door for her, closing it once she was inside with the seatbelt in place. He waited until they were heading towards the city before he spoke.

'Your parents were surprisingly positive about our decision to marry—your mother in particular. I was expecting her to drop into a faint at the thought of her daughter hooking up with a fatherless foreigner, but she practically gushed in gratefulness that someone had put up their hand to scoop you off the shelf, so to speak.'

Gabby sent him a brittle look. 'Must you be so insulting?' she asked. 'And by the way—not that I'm splitting hairs or anything—but it wasn't exactly *our* plan to get married, it was yours.'

He gave an indifferent lift of one shoulder. 'There is no point arguing about the terms now the margin call has been dealt with,' he said. 'I have always had a lot of time for your father, but your mother has always been an out-and-out snob who thinks the measure of a man is what's in his wallet.'

'Yes, well, it's practically the only thing you've got going for *you*,' she shot back with a scowl.

He laughed as he changed gears. 'What's in my wallet has just got you and your family out of a train-load of trouble, *cara*, so don't go insulting me, hmm? I might take it upon myself to withdraw my support— and then where will you be?'

Gabby turned her head away, looking almost sightlessly at the silvery skyscrapers of the city as they flashed past. He was right of course. She would have to curb her tongue, otherwise he might renege on the deal. It would be just the kind of thing he would do, and relish every moment of doing it. Although it went against everything she believed in to pander to a man she loathed with every gram of her being, she really didn't see she had any choice in the matter. Vinn had the power to make or break her; she had to remember that.

She had never thought it was possible to hate someone so much. Her blood was thundering through her veins with the sheer force of it. He was so arrogant, so very self-assured. Against all the odds he had risen above his impoverished background and was using his new-found power to control her. But she was not going to give in without a fight. He might make her his wife, but it would be in name only.

Not that she would tell him just yet, of course. That would be the card up her sleeve she would reveal only once the ceremony was over. Vinn would be in for a surprise to find his new wife was not prepared to sleep with him. She would be a trophy wife—a gracious hostess, who would say the right things in the right places, and smile and act the role of the devoted partner in public if needed—but in private she would be the same Gabby who had left the score of her nails on the back of his hand the night before her wedding.

The restaurant he had booked was on the waterfront, and the night-time view over the harbour was even more stunning, with the twinkling of lights from the various tour ferries and floating restaurants. The evening air was sultry and warm, heavy with humidity, as if there was a storm brewing in the atmosphere.

Gabby walked stiffly by Vinn's side, suffering the light touch of his hand beneath her elbow as he escorted her inside the award-winning restaurant. The head waiter greeted Vinn with deference, before leading the way to a table in a prime position overlooking the fabulous views.

'Have you ever dined here before?' Vinn asked, once they were seated and their starched napkins were expertly draped over their laps.

Gabby shook her head and glanced at the drinks menu. 'No, I haven't been out all that much lately.'

'Have you dated anyone since your husband died?' he asked, with what appeared to be only casual interest.

She still looked at the menu rather than face his gaze. 'It's only been two years,' she said curtly. 'I'm in no hurry.'

'Do you miss him?'

Gabby put the menu down and looked at Vinn in irritation. 'What sort of a question is that?' she asked. 'We were married for five years.' *Five miserably unhappy years.* But she could hardly tell him that. She hadn't even told her parents.

She hadn't told anyone. Who was there to tell? She had never been particularly good at friendships; her few girlfriends had found Tristan boorish and overbearing, and each of them had gradually moved on, with barely an e-mail or a text to see how she was doing. Gabby knew it was mostly her fault for constantly covering for her husband's inadequacies. She had become what the experts called an enabler, a co-dependant. Tristan had been allowed to get away with his unspeakable behaviour because she had not been able to face the shame of facing up to the mistake she had made in marrying him. As a result she had become an adept liar, and, although it was painful to face it, she knew she had only herself to blame.

'You didn't have children,' Vinn inserted into the silence. 'Was that your choice or his?'

'It wasn't something we got around to discussing,' she said, as she inspected the food menu with fierce concentration.

The waiter came and took their order for drinks. Gabby chose a very rich cocktail—more for Dutch courage than anything. It was what she felt she needed just now: a thick fog of alcohol to survive an evening in Vinn's company.

Vinn, on the other hand, ordered a tall glass of iced mineral water—a well-known Italian brand, she noticed.

'You'd better go easy on that drink of yours, Gabriella,' he cautioned as she took a generous mouthful. 'Drinking on an empty stomach is not wise. Alcohol has a well-known disinhibitory effect on behaviour. You might find yourself doing things you wouldn't normally do.'

She gave him a haughty look. 'You mean like enjoying your company instead of loathing every minute of it?'

His grey-blue eyes gave a flame-like flash. 'You will enjoy a whole lot more than just my company before the ink on our marriage certificate is dry,' he said.

Gabby took another gulping swallow of her drink to disguise her discomfiture. Her stomach felt quivery all of a sudden. The thought of his hands and mouth on her body was making her feel as if she had taken on much more than she had bargained for. She had held Tristan off for years—except for that one horrible night when he had... She swallowed another mouthful of her drink, determined not to think of the degradation she had suffered at her late husband's hands.

'You have gone rather pale,' Vinn observed. 'Is the thought of sharing my bed distasteful to you?'

Gabby was glad she had her glass to hide behind, although the amount of alcohol she had consumed *had* gone alarmingly to her head. Or perhaps it was his disturbing presence. Either way, she didn't trust herself to speak and instead sent him another haughty glare.

'That kiss we shared seven years ago certainly didn't suggest you would find my lovemaking abhorrent—anything but. You were hungry for it, Gabriella. I found that rather interesting, since the following day you married another man.'

'You *forced* yourself on me,' she hissed at him in an undertone, on account of the other diners close by.

'Forced is perhaps too strong a word to use, but in any case you responded wholeheartedly,' he said. 'Not just with those soft full lips of yours, but with your tongue as well. And if I recall even your teeth got into the act at one point. I'm getting hard now, just thinking about it.'

Gabby had never felt so embarrassed in her entire life. Her face felt as if someone had aimed a blowtorch at her. But even more disturbing was the thought of his body stirring with arousal *for her*—especially with those powerful thighs of his within touching distance of hers.

'Your recollection has obviously been distorted over time, for I can barely remember it,' she said with a toss of her head.

His eyes glinted smoulderingly. 'Then perhaps I should refresh your memory,' he said. 'No doubt there will be numerous opportunities to do so once we are living together as man and wife.'

Gabby had to fight to remain calm, but it was almost impossible to control the stuttering of her heart and the flutter of panic deep and low in her belly. 'When do you plan for this ridiculous farce to commence?' she asked, with fabricated quiescence.

'Our marriage will not be a farce,' he said, with a determined set to his mouth. 'It will be real in every sense of the word.'

Her eyes widened a fraction before she could counter it. 'Is that some sort of sick habit of yours? Sleeping with someone you dislike?'

'You are a very beautiful woman, Gabriella,' he said. 'Whether I like you or not is beside the point.'

Gabby wanted to slap that supercilious smile off his face. She sat with her hands clenched in her lap, her eyes shooting sparks of fury at him. But more disturbing was the way her body was responding to his smoothly delivered sensual promises. She could feel a faint trembling between her thighs, like a tiny pulse, and her breasts felt full and tight, her nipples suddenly sensitive against the black fabric of her dress.

'I'm prepared to marry you, but that's as far as it goes,' she said with a testy look. 'It's totally barbaric of you to expect me to agree to a physical relationship with you.'

'Aren't you forgetting something?' he asked. 'Two point four million dollars is a high price for a bride, and I expect to get my money's worth.'

She sucked in a rasping breath. 'This is outrageous! It's akin to prostitution.'

'You came to me for help, Gabriella, and I gave it to you,' he said. 'I was totally up-front about the terms, so there is no point in pretending to be shocked about them now.'

'But what about the woman you were seeing a month or so ago?' Gabby asked, recalling a photograph she had seen in the 'Who's-Out-and-About?' section of one of the Sydney papers. An exquisitely beautiful woman gazing up at Vinn adoringly.

He gave her a supercilious smile. 'So you have

been keeping a close eye on my love life, have you, *mia piccola?*'

She glowered at him darkly. 'I have absolutely no interest in who you see. But if we are to suffer a short-term marriage, the very least you could do is keep your affairs out of the press.'

'I don't recall saying our marriage was going to be a short-term one,' he said with an inscrutable smile. 'Far from it.'

Gabby felt her heart give a kick-like movement against the wall of her chest. 'W-what?' she gasped.

'I have always held the opinion that marriage should be for life,' he said. 'I guess you could say it stems from my background. My mother was abandoned by the man she loved while she had a baby on the way. She had no security, no husband to provide for her, and as a result she went on to live a hard life of drudgery—cleaning other people's houses to keep food on the table and clothes on our backs. I swore from an early age that when it came time for me to settle down I would do so with permanence in mind.'

'But you don't even *like* me!' she blurted in shock. 'How could you possibly contemplate tying yourself to me for the rest of your life?'

'Haven't you got any mirrors at your house any more, *mia splendida ragazza?*' he asked, with another smouldering look. 'I do not have to like you to lust over you. And isn't that what every wife wants? A husband with an unquenchable desire for her and her alone?'

Gabby swallowed back her panic, but even so she felt as if she was choking on a thick uneven lump of it. 'You're winding me up. I know you are. This is your idea of a sick joke. And let me tell you, I am not finding it the least bit amusing.'

'I am not joking, Gabriella,' he said. 'Love is generally an overrated emotion—or at least I have found it to be so. People fall in and out of love all the time. But some of the most successful marriages I know are those built on compatibility in bed—and, believe you me, you don't need to be in love with someone to have an earth-shattering orgasm with them.'

Gabby felt her face explode with colour, and was never more grateful for the reappearance of the waiter to take their meal orders.

Hearing Vinn speak of…that word…*that experience*…made her go hot all over. She had never experienced pleasure with her late husband. The one time Tristan had taken it upon himself to assert "his manly duty", as he had euphemistically called it, he had left her not cold, but burning with pain and shame.

Once the waiter had left, Gabby drained the rest of her cocktail, beyond caring that it had made her head spin. No amount of alcohol could affect her more than Vinn had already done, she decided. Her body was tingling all over with sensation, and her mind was running off at wayward tangents, imagining what it would feel like to be crushed by the solid weight of his body, his sensual mouth locked on hers, one of his strong, hair-roughened thighs nudging hers apart to—

She jerked away from her thoughts, annoyed that she had allowed his potent brand of sensuality to get under her guard. What on earth was she thinking? He was the enemy. She knew exactly what he was doing and why. He was only marrying her to get back at her for how she had treated him in the past. He knew it would be torture for her to be tied to him. Why else would he insist on it? Never had she regretted her immature behaviour more than this moment. Why, oh why, had she been so shallow and cruel?

Gabby's older brother Blair had often pulled her up for her attitude towards Vinn, but in a way his relationship with Vinn had been a huge part of the problem. She had felt *jealous* that her adored older brother clearly preferred the company of the cleaner's son to hers. Gabby had resented the way Blair spent hours helping Vinn with his studies when he could have been spending time with her, the way he'd used to do before Vinn had arrived with his mother.

When Gabby had accidentally stumbled upon the realisation that Vinn suffered from dyslexia she had cruelly taunted him with it, mocking him for not being able to read the most basic of texts. But for some reason, just as he had when she had led him on so despicably that hot summer afternoon when she was sixteen, Vinn had never spoken to her brother or her parents about her behaviour. He had taken it on the chin, removing himself from her presence without a word, even though she had sensed the blistering anger in him, simmering just below the surface of his steely outward calm.

Gabby could sense that anger still simmering now, in the way he looked at her from beneath that slightly hooded brow. Those grey-blue eyes were like mysteriously deep mountain lakes, icy cold one minute, warm and inviting the next, and they spoke of a man who had nothing but revenge on his mind.

She had seen the way women were looking at him. He had such arrestingly handsome features, and his presence was both commanding and brooding—as if he was calculating his next move, like a champion chess player, prepared to take as long as he needed to move his king, making his opponent sit it out in gut-wrenching apprehension.

Gabby felt another shiver of unease pass through her at the thought of being married to him. He had said he expected their marriage to be permanent. That meant there were issues to consider: children, for one thing. She was twenty-eight years old, and she would be lying if she said she hadn't heard the relentless ticking of her biological clock in the two years since Tristan had died. Children had not been an option while she had been married to him. She would *never* have brought children into such a relationship. She hadn't even brought a pet into the house in case he had used it against her in one of his violent moods.

'You have gone very quiet, Gabriella,' Vinn observed. 'Is the thought of having an orgasm with me too hard for you to handle?'

She gave him a withering look. 'No, in actual fact I find it hard to believe it possible,' she said. 'I can't speak for the legion of women you've already bedded, but I personally am unable to engage in such an intimate act without some engagement of emotion.'

He gave a deep chuckle of laughter. 'How about hate?' he asked, reaching for his mineral water. 'Is that enough emotion to get you rolling?'

She put down her glass and signalled for the waiter to refill it.

'Do you think that is wise?' Vinn asked. 'The amount of alcohol in that drink is enough to cloud anyone's judgement.'

Gabby put up her chin. 'In the absence of the engagement of emotion, alcohol and a great deal of it is the next best thing,' she said.

His eyes narrowed to grey-blue stormy slits. 'If you think I will bed you while you are under the influence, think again,' he said. 'When we come together for the first time I want you stone-cold sober, so you remember every second of it.'

Gabby put her glass down with a sharp little clunk. 'I am *not* going to sleep with you, Vinn,' she said, and hoisting up her chin even higher, added imperiously, 'For *that* privilege you will have to pay double.'

Vinn smiled a victor's smile as he reached inside his jacket for his chequebook. He laid it on the table between them, and the click of his pen made Gabby's spine jerk upright, as if she had been shot with a pellet from the gold-embossed barrel.

'Double, you said?'

Gabby felt her stomach drop. Her mouth went dry and her palms moistened. 'Um…I…I'm not sure. I…this…it…I…don't…*Oh, my God…*'

He wrote the amount in his distinctive scrawl, the dark slash of his signature making Gabby's eyes almost pop out of their sockets. 'There,' he said, tearing off the cheque from the book and placing it in front of her on the table. 'Do we have a deal or not?'

CHAPTER THREE

GABBY looked at the amount written there and felt a shockwave of so many emotions rocketing through her that she felt her face fire up. Each one of them stoked the furnace, although shame had by far the most fuel. But then anger joined in; she could feel it blazing out of control, and not just on her cheeks, but deep inside, where a cauldron of heat was bubbling over, making her veins hot with rage.

Vinn had deliberately made her feel like a high-end prostitute—a woman who would do anything for a price. But Gabby wasn't going to be bought. She had been a fool before where a man was concerned, allowing duty and blinkered emotions to cloud her judgement. This time things would be different. If Vinn Venadicci thought he could lure her between the sheets of his bed with a bank vault full of dollar bills, he was in for a big surprise.

With a coolness she was nowhere near feeling, Gabby picked up the cheque and, with the tip of her tongue peeping through her lips as she concentrated, she folded it, fold by meticulous fold, until she had made a tiny origami ship. She held it in the palm of her hand for a moment as she inspected it, and once she was satisfied she had Vinn's full attention she reached for the glass of full-bodied red wine the waiter had recently set down beside him. She dropped her handiwork in, watching in satisfaction as it floated for a second or two, until the density of the wine gradually soaked through the paper and submerged it halfway below the surface.

Gabby met Vinn's grey-blue gaze across the table with an arch look. 'I was going to say you could put your cheque in your pipe and smoke it, but then I realised you don't smoke.' She smiled a cat's smile and added, *'Salute.'*

Vinn's lips twitched, but even so his eyes still burned with determination. 'You might like me to swallow my offer, but I can guarantee you are going to be the one eating your words in the not so distant future, *cara*,' he warned her silkily.

She rolled her eyes and picked up her second cocktail. 'I will go as far as marrying you to save my family's business, but I am not going to be your sex slave, Vinn. If you have the urge to satisfy your needs I am sure there are plenty of women out there who will gladly oblige. All I ask is for you to be discreet.'

He leaned back in his chair and surveyed her features for a beat or two. 'Is that the arrangement you made with your late husband?' he asked. 'Or did you see to his needs quite willingly all by yourself?'

Gabby felt her heart come to a shuddering standstill, her face heating to boiling point. 'That is none of your business,' she bit out. 'I refuse to discuss my marriage to Tristan with you, of all people.'

Vinn's top lip curled in an insolent manner. 'Did he satisfy you, Gabriella? Did he make you writhe and scream? Or did he satisfy you in other ways by lavishing you with the worldly goods women like you crave?'

Gabby's hand tightened around her cocktail glass as she fought to control the bewildering combination of shame and anger that roiled through her. She hadn't thought it possible to hate someone as much as she hated Vinn. She didn't want to examine too closely why she hated him so much, but she suspected it had something to do with the way he looked at her in that penetrating way of his. Those intelligent eyes saw things she didn't want anyone to see. He had done it all those years ago, and he was doing it now.

She forced her tense shoulders to relax and, loosening her white-knuckled grip on her glass, brought it to her mouth and took a sip. 'What about *your* love-life, Vinn?' she asked, with a pert set to her mouth. 'Who's your latest squeeze? Are you still seeing that chainstore model or has she reached her use-by date?'

Vinn used his fork to retrieve the sunken boat of his cheque out of his glass before he trained his gaze on hers. 'Have you been taking extra classes in bitchiness, Gabriella, or is it that time of the month?'

Gabby knew she shouldn't do it, but even as the mature and sensible part of her brain considered the repercussions, the outraged part had already acted.

It seemed to happen in slow motion. The strawberry daiquiri in her glass moved in a fluid arc and splashed across the front of Vinn's shirt.

Time didn't just stand still; it came to a screeching, rubber burning, tyre-balding halt.

Gabby waited for the fall-out. Her body grew tense, her blood raced, her heart thumped. But in the end all Vinn did was laugh.

'Is that the best you can do, Gabriella?' he asked, still smiling mockingly. 'To toss your drink across the table like a recalcitrant three-year-old child?'

'If you are expecting me to apologise, then forget it. Because I'm not going to,' she said with a petulant glare.

He put the soiled napkin to one side. 'No,' he said, still smiling in that enigmatic way of his that unnerved her so. 'I wasn't expecting you to apologise now. I am looking forward to making you do so later, when we are not sitting in the middle of a crowded restaurant. And believe me, Gabriella, it will be a lot of fun making you do it.'

Gabby felt a moth-like flutter of apprehension sweep over the floor of her belly. She had faced numerous rages from Tristan in the past, but for some reason Vinn's cool, calm control was far more terrifying. But then Vinn had always been cool and controlled. Even when she had taunted him in the past he had taken it on the chin, looking down at her with those unreadable grey-blue eyes. Perhaps that was why he had become so successful over the years? He knew how to play people like some people played cards, and Gabby had a feeling he had just put down a hand that was going to be impossible for her to beat.

'Is everything all right, Signor Venadicci?' The *maître d'* came bustling over.

'Everything is perfectly all right, thank you, Paolo,' Vinn said with an urbane smile. 'My fiancée had a slight accident.'

'Oh, dear,' Paolo said, and quickly tried to make amends. 'Let me get the young lady another drink—on the house, of course. And send me the bill for the cleaning of your shirt. I am sure the table is rickety, or something. I have asked my staff to check, but you know how hard it is to keep track of everyone all the time.'

'It is fine—really,' Vinn said, rising to his feet. 'We are leaving in any case.'

Gabby was half in and half out of her chair, not sure what she should do. They hadn't even been served their meals and she was starving. She had missed lunch, and already she could feel a headache pounding at the backs of her eyes.

'Leaving?' Paolo said, looking aghast. 'But what about your food?'

'I am sorry, Paolo,' Vinn said. 'Could we have our meals packaged to take back to my house instead? My fiancée has had rather a tough day, and I think she needs an early night.'

'But of course, Signor Venadicci,' Paolo said, and quickly signalled to his waiting staff to see to it straight away. 'Congratulations on your engagement,' he added, smiling widely at Gabby. 'Such wonderful news. You are a very lucky woman. Signor Venadicci is…how you say in English? A big catch?'

'Yes,' Gabby said with saccharine-sweetness. 'He is a big catch. Just like a shark.'

Vinn grasped her by the arm and practically frog-marched her out of the restaurant, only stopping long enough at the front counter to collect their take-out meals.

'You can let go of my arm now,' she said, once they were on the street outside.

Vinn kept pulling her along towards his car, not even bothering to shorten his much longer stride to accommodate hers. 'You, young lady, need a lesson in manners. You have acted like a spoilt child. You didn't just embarrass yourself, but each and every person in that restaurant—not to mention Paolo, who always bends over backwards to please his diners. You should be ashamed of yourself.'

Gabby gave him a surly look as she tugged ineffectually at his hold. 'You started it.'

He aimed a remote control at his car. 'I asked you a question about your last marriage,' he said, opening the door for her. 'A yes or no answer would have done.'

She sent him a venomous glare. 'I don't have to answer any of your stupid questions, about my marriage or any of my relationships,' she threw at him.

'I can tell you one thing, Gabriella,' he said as he wrenched the seatbelt down for her with a savagery that was unnerving. 'Once we are married you will have no other relationships. Or at least none with a male.'

Gabby sat stiffly in her seat, trying to control her sudden and totally unexpected urge to cry. She had become very good at concealing her emotions. She had never given Tristan the satisfaction of seeing her break emotionally. Why she should feel so close to the edge now was not only bewildering but terrifying.

She couldn't allow Vinn to see how undone she was. He would relish in the power he had over her. He already had too much power over her—far more than Tristan Glendenning had ever had, in spite of all she had suffered at his hands. How could she afford to let her guard down even for a second? Especially given how she had treated Vinn in the past? Vinn had every reason to bring her down, to make her grovel, to grind what was left of her pride to dust. She had just enough self-respect to keep that from happening.

Not much…but just enough.

Vinn drove his powerful car across the Harbour Bridge to the North Shore suburb of Mosman. Each thrusting gear-change he executed set Gabby's teeth on edge, and another icy shiver of unease scuttled up her spine at the thought of a showdown with him on his own territory. In the crowded restaurant it had been safe to spar with him, or so she had thought. But being alone with him was something she wasn't quite prepared for and wondered if she ever would be.

He turned the car into a beautiful tree-lined street of the sort of homes owned by people with more than just comfortable wealth. Lush gardens, harbour views and stately mansions, with the mandatory fortress-like security that ensured a private haven away from the rest of the world. They indicated Vinn had made his way in the world and wasn't ashamed about taking his place in it amongst others who had done similarly—either by sheer hard work or the inheritance of a family fortune.

The driveway he turned into after activating a remote control device revealed a modern caramel-coloured mansion with a three-tiered formal garden at the front. Gabby could see the high fence of a tennis court in the background, and heard the sound of a trickling fountain close by. The heady scent of purple wisteria was heavy in the air, and so too was the more subtle fragrance of night-scented stocks, growing in profusion in a bed that ran alongside the boundary of the property.

She breathed in the clove-like smell, wondering if Vinn had somehow remembered they were one of her favourite flowers. She loved the variety of colours, the way the thick stalks didn't always stand up straight, and how the individual clusters of blossom maintained their scent right to the last. And yet perversely, if housed in a vase indoors, the water they sat in became almost fetid, as if those stately and proud blooms resented being confined.

Vinn unlocked the front door and indicated for her to precede him, which Gabby did with an all-encompassing sweep of her gaze. The marbled foyer was not in the least as ostentatious as she had been expecting. Even the works of art on the walls spoke of individual taste rather than an attempt to belong to a particularly highbrow club of art appreciation.

One painting in particular drew her eye: it was of a small child, a boy, looking at a shell on the seashore, his tiny limbs in a crouched position, his gaze focussed on the shell in his hands as if it contained all the mysteries of the world. Gabby peered at the right-hand corner of the canvas but she couldn't make out the signature.

'You don't recognise the artist?' Vinn said from just behind her left shoulder.

Gabby shivered at his closeness, but, schooling her features, faced him impassively, taking a careful step backwards to create some distance. 'No,' she said. 'Should I?'

His gaze was trained on the canvas, his mouth set in a grim line. 'Probably not,' he said. 'He was always a little embarrassed about his desire to paint. This is

the only one I managed to convince him not to destroy.'
He paused for a moment before adding, 'I believe it is
one of the last works he did before he died.'

'Oh…' Gabby said renewing her focus on the
painting. 'Was he very old?'

'No,' Vinn said. 'But then he wasn't the first and I
dare say won't be the last artist to succumb to deep-
seated insecurities about his talent. It more or less
comes with the territory. Being creative can be both a
blessing and a burden, or so I have heard people say.'

'Yes…I suppose so…'Gabby answered, still looking at the painting, which for some inexplicable reason
had moved her so much.

Perhaps it was because looking at that small innocent child made her think longingly of having her
own precious baby one day, she thought. Unlike most
of her peers, she had never been interested in pursuing
a demanding career. For years all she had dreamed of
was holding a baby of her own in her arms, watching
him or her grow into teenage, and then adulthood, just
as her parents had done with her and Blair.

'We have some things to discuss,' Vinn said, and
gestured for her to follow him to the large lounge room
off the wide hall.

Gabby took an uneven breath and followed him into
a stylishly appointed room. Two large black leather
sofas sat either side of a fireplace—the shiny black
marble mantelpiece and surround in a smaller room
would have been too much, but not in this room. An
ankle-deep rug in a black and gold design softened the
masculine feel, as did the vintage lamps sitting on the
art deco side tables. A large ottoman doubled as a

coffee table, and a state-of-the-art music and entertainment system was cleverly concealed behind a drop-down console.

'It's a nice room,' Gabby said as she perched on the edge of one of the sofas. 'In fact the whole house is lovely. Have you lived here long?'

Vinn leaned his hip against the armrest of the opposite sofa. 'Well, what do you know?' he drawled. 'A compliment from the high and mighty Gabriella St Clair.'

Gabby screwed up her mouth at him. 'Glendenning,' she corrected him, even though she loathed her married name for all it had represented. 'My surname is still Glendenning.'

Something gleamed in Vinn's eyes as they collided with hers. 'But not for much longer,' he said. 'I have already seen to the notice. Shortly we will be husband and wife and living here as such.'

Gabby got to her feet in an agitated manner. 'I don't see what the rush is for,' she said, pacing the floor. 'What are people going to think?'

'For god's sake, Gabriella,' he said, with a flash of impatience in his tone. 'You've been a widow for two years.'

She turned around to look at him. 'Yes…but to suddenly be with you seems…well, it seems…almost indecent,' she said. 'People will think it's a shotgun marriage or something.'

He came over to where she was standing with her arms folded tightly across her chest. She considered moving sideways, but as if he knew she was looking for an escape route he placed both of his hands either side of her head on the wall behind, effectively trapping her.

Gabby felt her eyes flare with panic. She wasn't used to being so close to him. This close, she could smell the tangy lemon of his aftershave. She could even see the regrowth of stubble on his jaw, making her fingers twitch to reach up and feel if it was as raspy and masculine as it looked. She could see the deep-water-blue of his eyes with their grey shadows locked on hers. The line of his mouth was firm, but soft at the same time, making her wonder if his kiss would be just as enthralling as it had been seven years ago.

'You know, Gabriella,' he said in a low velvet tone, 'we could do something about that right here and now.'

Gabby's throat tightened as his body brushed against hers. She felt the stirring of his erection, a heady reminder of all that was different between them. He was so experienced, while she was…well, perhaps not exactly inexperienced, but way out of his class. Her body was not tutored in giving and receiving pleasure. She was totally inadequate, lacking in both confidence and skill.

Gabby was in no doubt of Vinn's attraction for her. If she was honest with herself she had been aware of it for years. It was like an electric current that throbbed in the air every time they were in the same room together. She wasn't sure if other people were aware of it, although Tristan had commented on it in his scathing way more than once.

Gabby knew it was just a physical thing on Vinn's part. Men were like that. Especially men like Vinn, who were used to having any woman who took their fancy. He was only attracted to Gabby because for so many years she had been unattainable. She was the daughter of a rich man, while he was the bastard son of a strapped-for-cash house-cleaner. The only trouble was he was prepared to go to unbelievable lengths to have her, even after all this time.

And that he was determined to have her in every sense of the word was as clear as the jagged scar that interrupted the dark slash of his left eyebrow. Apparently he had received it in a drunken brawl the night before her wedding to Tristan. Though it had only been after she'd come back from their honeymoon that Gabby's mother had told her how Vinn had spent a night in hospital after becoming involved in a punch-up. Given their heated exchange that night, Gabby suspected he had gone out to get himself trashed and had ended up in a street brawl—as he had done several times during his early twenties.

'So what do you say, Gabriella?' Vinn said, one of his strong thighs nudging between hers suggestively, temptingly, and oh, so spine-tinglingly. 'We could make a baby right here and now, and then it would indeed be a shotgun marriage.'

Gabby's stomach hollowed. Her legs felt like waterlogged noodles—too soggy to keep her upright. Her heart was racing, but not with any sort of predictable rhythm. Every second beat or so felt as if it was just off the mark, making her feel light-headed. Her unruly mind was suddenly filled with images—disturbing, toe-curling images—of his body pumping with purpose into the tight cocoon of hers, nudging her womb, filling it with his life force, his cells meshing with hers to create a new life.

Somehow she managed to activate her voice, but it sounded as if it had come from somewhere deep inside

her, croaky, rusty and disjointed. 'I—I'm not interested in…having a child,' she said. 'Not with you.'

'I am not going to settle for a childless marriage,'
he said. 'I have paid a high price for you, Gabriella.
As part of that heavy financial commitment I expect a
return on my investment.'

Gabby shoved him away, both of her hands flat on
his rock-hard chest. 'Then you've bought the wrong
bride,' she flashed at him angrily. 'It's bad enough that
you want this arrangement to be permanent, but to
want children as well is nothing short of ludicrous.'

'I never said anything to suggest this wasn't going
to be a proper marriage,' he said. 'Two point four
million dollars is not pin money, Gabriella. A divorce
could turn out to be even more expensive—although I
have that covered with my legal advisors. Tomorrow
you will sign a prenuptial agreement that will ensure
the only benefit you will receive if our marriage does
for some reason fail will be an income to pay for your
manicures and the highlights in your hair.'

Gabby was almost beyond rage. Her whole body
felt as if it was going to explode with it. She wanted
to pummel him with her fists; she wanted to scratch at
his face, to make him feel some small measure of the
pain she was feeling.

Vinn made her feel like a shallow socialite who had
nothing better to do with her time that have her nails filed
and her hair bleached. But she was so much more than
that. She hadn't been before, but after the death of her
brother—not to mention the five years of her marriage
to Tristan Glendenning, had taught her how shallow her
life had been and how much she had wanted it to change.

And she *had* changed.

She had changed in so many ways. Not all of them were visible, but they were changes she was still working on daily. Taking up the reins of her father's company was something she hadn't really had much choice over, but she wasn't a quitter and would see it through—as Blair surely would have done if his personal issues hadn't got in the way.

Thinking about her brother always stirred the long-handled spoon of guilt in her stomach, its churning action making her feel sick with anguish. If only she had known about his drug use she might have been able to help him before it was too late. But he had preferred to face death than his family's disappointment, and she would always blame herself for her part in that.

She resumed her seat on the cloud-soft sofa, her trembling hands stuffed between her equally unsteady thighs, fighting not to show how close to breaking she was. No doubt Vinn would relish that. He would be silently gloating over finally breaking her spirit.

She was trapped.

The steel bars of her guilt had closed around her with a clanging, chilling finality. Vinn had all the power now, and would wield it as he saw fit. He had insisted on marriage—but not the sort of hands-off arrangement she had naively thought he'd had in mind. She had no hope of repaying the money he had put up to save her father's business. It would take her two lifetimes to scrape together even half of that amount. Vinn had known that from the very first moment she had stepped into his office. He had played her like a master, reeling her in, keeping his cards close to his chest as was his custom, revealing them only when it was too late for her to do anything to get out of the arrangement.

It *was* too late.

She was going to be Vinn Venadicci's wife; the only trouble was he had no idea what sort of bride he had just bought. He had paid a huge price, but she was going to be a disappointment.

Of that she was heart-wrenchingly sure.

CHAPTER FOUR

VINN was still leaning on the edge of the sofa, silently watching the myriad moods pass over Gabriella's face. He was well used to seeing anger, rebellion and petulance there; even the bright sheen of moisture in her toffee-brown eyes was something he was used to witnessing. But whether or not those tears were genuine was something he wasn't prepared to lay a bet on.

She was a devious little madam. He had suffered at her hands too many times to let his guard down now. He wasn't going to give an inch until the papers were signed and she was legally his wife—in name if not yet in body.

He could wait.

He had waited for seven years. He figured waiting a little longer would only increase the pleasure of finally possessing her.

As soon as he had set eyes on her all those years ago he had been struck almost dumb by how beautiful she was. He had watched her blossom from an uncertain and overweight girl of fourteen into a young woman on the threshold of full adulthood. She had grown into an exquisitely beautiful young woman by the time she was sixteen years old, with those wide Bambi eyes and her lusciously thick blonde hair a striking contrast to her darker eyebrows and sooty black lashes. Her full lips were cherry-red, and plump and soft with sensual promise. By the time she was seventeen her teasing smile and come-hither looks had tortured him by day and kept him writhing in frustration in bed at night with the thought of one day possessing her. But even though his body had throbbed with longing he had known it would take nothing short of a miracle to bring about her capitulation.

Gabriella St Clair was out of his league. Vinn had known it, although he had never really accepted it.

Blair St Clair had in his quiet, polite way gently hinted at it, and Gabriella's parents—particularly her mother, Pamela—had communicated it without pulling any punches. It had been made perfectly clear to Vinn that Gabriella's future lay with Tristan Glendenning, an up-and-coming lawyer from a long line of legal eagles, primed to be a partner in a big city firm once he settled down to marriage to his mother's best friend's daughter.

The thing that sickened Vinn the most was that he had never believed Gabriella had truly been in love with her husband—which in itself showed how shallow she was. She couldn't have been in love with Glendenning after the way she had responded to Vinn outside the bathroom the night before her wedding.

She had clung to him feverishly, her soft lips opening to the pressure of his, her tongue darting into his mouth, tasting him, teasing him, duelling with him in a totally carnal explosion of passion that had left them both panting and breathless. Vinn's hands had uncovered her breasts and shaped them worshipfully, relishing in the creamy softness of them, and she had done nothing to stop him, rather had whimpered and gasped in delight with each touch of his hands, lips and tongue.

Her hands had reached down and cupped the aching bulk of his manhood, stroking him, torturing him until he'd been fit to burst. He would have thrust her up against the nearest wall and driven into her right then and there if it hadn't been for the sound of a footfall on the staircase, and Tristan Glendenning's private academy-tutored voice calling out.

'Gabs? Are you up here? I have to get going. Sorry, babe, but I have a few things to see to before the ceremony tomorrow.'

Vinn had put Gabriella from him almost roughly, raking a hand through his hair in the hope that it would restore some sort of order to it after her fingers had clawed at him in fervent response. Although his breathing was ragged, his heart hammering and his body aching with the pressure of release denied, he had somehow held himself together—but it had taken a monumental effort on his part.

Gabriella, consummate liar and actress that she was, had simply turned with a covert straightening of her clothing and smiled sweetly at her unsuspecting fiancé, with not a single sign of what had transpired just moments ago showing anywhere on her person. Her brown eyes had been clear and steady on his, her voice smooth and even.

'You're leaving already?' she'd asked, with just the right amount of disappointment in her tone. 'But you only just got here. You missed the rehearsal and everything.'

Tristan had leaned in and lightly kissed her swollen mouth. 'I know, dearest, but I'll make it up to you on our honeymoon, I promise. Besides, it's almost midnight. Isn't it bad luck or something to see the bride before she gets to the church?'

Vinn had pushed past them, his gut churning, his fists clenched so tight he'd thought each and every one of the bones in his hands would surely crack.

'Are you off now too, Venadicci?' Tristan had asked in a condescending tone. 'No doubt you have plenty to do, helping your mother polish the silver, hey what?'

Vinn had forced his mouth into a stiff movement of his lips that was nowhere close to a smile. 'You would be amazed at how tarnished some of those St Clair silver spoons are,' he'd said, and with one last searing glance at Gabriella strode down the hall.

Gabby lifted her head after a long silence and felt her heart give a little flutter of unease when she saw Vinn's penetrating look. 'You're really serious about this, aren't you?' she asked in a voice that came out thready. 'But why, Vinn? You're a rich man now. You've made it in the world. Why insist on marrying me?'

He pushed himself away from the sofa and came and stood right in front of her, so she had to crane her neck to look up at him. 'You still don't get it, do you, Gabriella?' he said, his eyes burning into hers. 'I don't want any other woman. Not since that night when I could have taken you up against the wall outside your upstairs bathroom. You wanted it, just as much as I wanted it so don't bother insulting my intelligence by denying it.'

Shame hoisted Gabby to her feet, her eyes blazing in fury. 'That's a despicable lie! You took advantage of me,' she threw at him, knowing it wasn't strictly true but saying it anyway. 'You were always leering at me. You did it every time you visited your mother at the house.'

Vinn's mouth stretched into a sneer. 'That's how you like to recall it, isn't it, Gabriella?' he asked. 'But I seem to remember it a little differently. You liked to flirt and tease, and you used every opportunity you could to do so. You got a perverse sort of pleasure out of dangling before me what I couldn't have, like taunting a starving dog with a juicy bone. Remember all those hot afternoons by the pool, when you knew I was going to be around to mow the lawn or trim the hedges? I knew what you were up to. You wanted me to make a move on you so you could cry wolf to your father and have me and my mother evicted. That was your game, wasn't it? You didn't even want your brother spending time with me. You were jealous he'd started to prefer my company to yours.'

Gabby's face flamed as she recalled how brazen and obvious she had been. Yes, she *had* been jealous of Vinn's friendship with her brother, but it had been about much more than that. From the moment Vinn had arrived at the St Clair mansion Gabby had felt uncomfortable in a way she couldn't adequately describe. She had only just turned fourteen at the time, and certainly Vinn, although being four years older, had never given her any reason to feel under threat. He'd mostly kept to himself, keeping his eyes downcast as he went about the odd jobs Gabby's father had organised for him.

It had only been as she'd grown from a young teen into a young woman that Gabby had begun to notice the way she felt when their eyes chanced to meet. It was unlike anything she had ever felt before with anyone else—even Tristan, who everyone knew would one day be her husband.

Looking into Vinn Venadicci's startlingly attractive grey-blue eyes now was like looking into the centre of a flame. The heat came back at her, scorching her until she had to drop her gaze.

'For God's sake, Vinn, I was what? Fifteen or sixteen?' she said, in what even she realised was a pathetic attempt to belatedly right the wrongs of the past. 'Surely you're not going to hold that against me?'

He gave a coarse-sounding laugh. 'My mother was right about you,' he said, raking her with his gaze. 'She said when the highest bidder came along you would sell your soul, and that's exactly what you did. Tristan Glendenning wanted shares in your father's business, and you were the little blonde bonus thrown in for free.'

Gabby clenched her teeth, her eyes sparking with anger, her whole body shaking with it. 'That's an atrocious and totally insulting thing to say,' she tossed back. 'Tristan's mother was my mother's best friend. They were each other's bridesmaids. It was always expected Tristan and I would marry. We grew up together, and apart from when my brother and Tristan were away at boarding school we spent most of our weekends and holidays together.' She paused for a nanosecond before adding, perhaps not as convincingly as she would have liked, 'It's…it was what we both wanted.'

Vinn gave a chillingly ruthless smile. 'Did he get his money's worth, Gabriella?' he asked. 'Were you a dutiful, obedient little wife for him?'

Gabby couldn't bear to look at the unmitigated disgust on his face. It was like confronting every stupid mistake she had ever made. How had she not known what sort of husband Tristan Glendenning would turn out to be? How could she have been so blind? She had no excuse. It wasn't as if Tristan had been a perfect stranger. She had known him all her life. And yet there had been things about him she had not known until it was too late.

Gabby spun away from Vinn's harsh expression. But the too sudden movement made her stomach heave, and her face and hands became clammy as she struggled to stay upright. She reached for the nearest arm of the sofa but her hand couldn't quite connect: it flailed in mid-air, like a ghost's hand passing through solid substance, and she felt herself go down in slow motion. Her knees buckled first and then her legs folded. Her head was spinning, and her eyes were unable to stay open as the room swirled sickeningly before her…

'Gabriella?' Vinn was on his knees, cradling her head in his hands before it connected with the floor.

She made a soft sound—more like a groan than anything else. But at least it meant she was still conscious. She was like a lifeless doll—a beautiful porcelain doll with the stuffing knocked out of it. At first he wondered if she was acting. It had all seemed so staged. And yet when he placed his hand on her smooth brow it was clammy. It made him wonder if he had misjudged her. Yes, things had been stressful lately for her—the margin call and her father's illness would have knocked anyone sideways—but the Gabriella he knew from the past would have played her histrionics to the hilt. A timely swoon or faint was well within her repertoire.

'Are you all right?' he asked, frowning in spite of his lingering doubts.

'W-what happened?' she said, opening her eyes, wincing against the light.

'You fainted, apparently,' Vinn said, although he still cradled her in his arms. She was lighter than he remembered, soft and feminine, and her scent was so alluring he couldn't stop his nostrils from flaring to breathe more of her in.

She groaned again and turned her head away. 'I think I'm going to be sick…'

Vinn decided he had better not take any risks, and quickly scooped her up and took her to the closest bathroom, holding her gently as she leaned over the basin. He winced in empathy as she emptied her stomach, her slim body shuddering with each racking heave.

'Are you done?' he asked, after a moment or two of keeping her steady.

Her hands gripped the edge of the basin, her head still bent low. 'Please…leave me alone for a minute…' she said hoarsely. 'I'm not used to having an audience at times…like this.'

'I'm not leaving you until I am certain you aren't going to knock yourself out cold on the edge of the basin or on the tiled floor,' he said. 'You scared the hell out of me.'

Vinn noticed her hands tighten their hold on the basin, making her small knuckles go white. She swayed slightly again, her eyes closing against another wave of nausea. He quickly rinsed a facecloth and, lifting the curtain of her hair, dabbed it at the back of her neck, just as his mother had done whenever he was sick as a child.

Gabby finally pushed herself back from the basin. Taking the facecloth from him, she buried her face in it, conscious of Vinn's firm but gentle hand in the small of her back, moving in a circular and bone-meltingly soothing motion.

'No more cocktails for you, young lady,' he said. 'They obviously don't agree with you.'

Gabby pressed her fingers to her temples. 'Maybe you're right,' she said, turning to face him, her body suddenly feeling weak and unsupported without the touch of his warm hand on her back. 'Would you mind if I go home now? It's kind of been a long day…' She gave a jaded sigh. 'Actually, it's been a long week…'

His eyes meshed with hers for an infinitesimal moment.

'Gabriella,' he said, 'your father is going to make it. People have triple heart bypass surgery all the time, and most if not all go on to make a full recovery.'

She bit her bottom lip and lowered her eyes from his. 'I know… It's just that he's depending on me. I don't want to let him down. I can't let him know about…about…' she flapped one of her hands '…about this margin call.'

He put his hands on the tops of her shoulders. 'The resort is secure,' he said, giving her shoulders a gentle squeeze. 'After we are married I want us to go there and check out the redevelopment. People will expect us to go on a honeymoon, so it will be a perfect excuse to do both.'

He felt her tense under his hands. 'I don't want to be too far away from my parents just now,' she said, not quite holding his gaze.

'Gabriella, you have to live your own life,' he said. 'It is your mother's responsibility to support your father, not yours. You have done enough. To be quite frank, I think you've done too much.'

A glitteringly defiant light came into her eyes as they warred with his. 'I don't want to go on a honeymoon with you, Vinn,' she said. 'Do I have to spell it out any plainer than that? I'm not going to sleep with you.'

Vinn let out his breath on a long-winded stream in an effort to contain his patience, which was already fraying at the edges. 'You know something?' he said. 'As much as I would like to, I am not going to throw you onto the nearest surface and ravish you, Gabriella. I understand you will need time to adjust to our marriage. I am prepared to give you the time you need, within reason.'

She tossed her head at him. 'Oh, yes?' she said with a scathing look. 'Within reason. Whatever that might mean. What…a couple of days? A week or two? A month?'

His eyes lasered hers. 'I told you, I want our marriage to be a real one.'

She began to push past him towards the door with an embittered scowl. 'Do you even *know* what a real marriage is about? You were the child of a single mother. You have no idea how a marriage works.'

'You were married for five years,' he inserted coolly as he put his hand on the bathroom door, closing it firmly to stop her escaping. 'How about you tell *me*?'

Gabby felt as if he had kicked her in the tenderest part of her belly, where all her hurt, all her disappointment and all her guilt were contained in one gnarled mass of miserable agony. She had to fight not to double over with the pain of it. It was crippling, agonising to withstand it, but only her strength of will kept her upright.

She would *not* break in front of him.

Vengeance was his goal, but she was not going to give in to him—and certainly not with her pride as a garnish. That was what he was after. He wanted her to grovel and beg and wear a hair shirt for the rest of her life. But she was not going to allow him to humble her.

She wasn't going to do it. Not without a fight.

She stood in place, like a fountain that had suddenly been frozen. Even the bitter tears at the backs of her eyes had turned to dry ice, burning but not flowing.

'I can tell you, Vinn, that marriage takes a whole lot more work than a few fancy-sounding promises muttered in front of a minister of religion,' she said. 'What you are asking for is a commitment that no one can really guarantee, and certainly not without love. It seems to me the only motivation you have for this union of ours is vengeance.'

Vinn's top lip lifted. 'You're surely not expecting me to *love* you, Gabriella?' he asked.

Gabby briefly closed her eyes in pain, but when she opened them again she saw the same caustic bitterness glittering in his; it hadn't gone away, and it surprised her how devastated she felt to realise it was never likely to. He would always look at her with hate blazing in his eyes and revenge simmering in his blood.

'No,' she said, almost inaudibly, 'I don't expect you to love me.'

Vinn reached past her to turn on the shower head. 'Have a shower while I find something for you to sleep in tonight,' he said. 'There is no way I am going to allow you to spend the night alone at your parents' house. You can stay here with me. There are fresh towels on the heated rail.'

Gabby's hands grasped at the basin again for balance. 'I don't need a shower—and I am not sleeping in this house with—'

He ignored her and thrust a bottle of perfumed body wash into her hands. 'As much as I hate to contradict you, Gabriella,' he said, 'you have not only managed to cover yourself in your own sickness, but me as well. Now, get into that damned shower before I change my mind and get in there with you.'

Gabby threw him a fulminating glare, but she took the body wash from him with hands not quite steady. 'Has anyone ever told you what a bull-headed brute you are?' she said.

He put his hands on his hips and stared her down. 'Get in the shower, Gabriella. You're wasting water.'

Gabby stepped into the huge shower stall, clothes and all, and on an impulse she really couldn't account for lifted off the removable shower head and aimed it straight at him.

Water went everywhere—all over the marbled walls and tiled floor, but most of all on Vinn's face and upper body, before he could snatch control of it.

'Why, you little wildcat,' he growled and, stepping into the shower with her, gave her a dose of her own watery medicine.

'Stop it!' Gabby squealed as the hot fine needles of water stung her face and shoulders. 'I'm fully dressed, you idiot!'

'So you are,' he said and, hanging the shower head back up, turned off the water. 'But then so am I and these are a brand-new pair of trousers.'

Gabby stood there dripping, caught between the urge to grab back the shower head and douse him all over again, and the even more disturbing urge to pull his glistening head down so his mouth could fuse hotly with hers.

How had the atmosphere changed so rapidly? she wondered dazedly. The air was suddenly thick with sexual attraction, heavy and pulsing, especially in a silence measured through electrically charged second with a series of plops and drips that sounded like rifle-shots.

Gabby brushed a slick strand of hair off her face with a hand that shook slightly. 'I hope you're not expecting me to pay for your trousers, because I'm not going to,' she said—more for something to say to break the dangerously sensual spell.

'No,' he said, looking at her dripping mouth and chin, his own face and hair soaking wet. 'I was thinking more along the lines of you paying a penalty in another currency entirely.'

Gabby licked the droplets of water off her mouth, trying to control the hit-and-miss beat of her heart. 'I'm n-not sure what you mean…' she said, stepping back as far as the shower cubicle would allow. But it wasn't far enough. For that matter Perth, on the other side of the continent, wouldn't be far enough.

She felt the cold hard-marbled wall at her back, and when Vinn stepped closer she felt his wet shirt and trousers come into contact with her sodden black dress. Never had the expensive designer fabric of her outfit seemed so thin, Gabby thought. She could feel Vinn's belt buckle pressing into her belly, and not only his buckle but his growing erection as well. It was rock-hard, and so close to the aching pulse of her body she couldn't breathe.

'What about it, Gabriella?' he asked in a smoulder-ingly sexy tone. 'What say we strip off and finish this properly? That's the game you want to play, isn't it? It's just like the game you wanted to play in the past. Let's get Vinn all hot under the collar so he acts like a rutting animal, right? That's what you want, isn't it?'

Gabriella was shocked at how much she wanted to rise to his challenging statement. She did want to rip his shirt from his broad chest and press her mouth on each of his flat male nipples in turn. She did want to unfasten his belt and expose his engorged male flesh to the exploration of her fingers, to feel the strength and power of his blood pulsing through him. She wanted to have him press her back against the marbled wall of the shower, his hands cupping and kneading her breasts, his mouth moving moistly over each tight nipple, until every thought flew out of her head.

But that was the trouble. Her head and all the thoughts inside it. The swirling, torturous thoughts that reminded her in that taunting, unrelenting tone how useless she was at seduction. She was a novice at lovemaking. Her own husband had found her body a total turn-off, so disgusting he had sought the company of other women.

'Gabriella?' Vinn tipped up her chin, a frown bringing his brows together. 'Are you cold? I'm sorry—I didn't notice how much you were shivering. Here, let me turn the water back on.'

Gabby was shaking. Not from cold, but from the effort of keeping a lid on her emotions. Never had she felt more outmatched, outmanoeuvred and totally powerless. Vinn had her in the palm of his hand, and if she didn't find an excuse to get him out of the bathroom within the next few seconds she knew she was going to fall apart completely.

Somehow having him witness her at her lowest point was too much to bear right now. How he would gloat and mock her for all she had represented. She could hardly blame him; she had been such a fool, a silly little insecure fool, who hadn't for a moment considered his feelings. He had every right to hate her, to want to avenge all the petty wrongs of the past. That was why he was marrying her—to bring her under his control, to humble her, to gloat over his possession of her.

'N-no, I'm not c-cold,' she said, although she was shivering. 'B-but I would like to be alone.'

Vinn adjusted the water to make it slightly warmer before he stepped out of the cubicle. 'I'll get you something to wear,' he said, and reached for a towel to dry off before he left her.

He came back to stand outside the bathroom door a few minutes later, with a tracksuit which was at least four sizes too big for her. Although the shower was now turned off, he could hear the muffled sound of Gabriella sniffing, as if she had been crying. Something pulled in his chest, like a string tied to his heart, but he staunchly ignored it. Tears and tantrums were some of the many tools in Gabriella's arsenal: she used them interchangeably to get her way. How many times in the past had he been fooled by carefully orchestrated tears? He was no such lovesick fool now—no way. He had wised up and wised up well. Gabriella had a lot riding on maintaining his goodwill right now, and he was going to make the most of it.

When she finally came out, after he had handed her the tracksuit through a crack in the door, there was no sign of distress on her face. Her eyes were clear, and if anything characteristically defiant. And he had to admit, dressed as she was in his clothes, she looked like a small child. She had rolled up the arms and the legs, but with her hair still wet and hanging about her shoulders she looked tiny and fragile and totally adorable.

Vinn felt a momentary tug at his heart again, but just as quickly ignored it. This was not the time to go all soft on her. They had a deal, and he was going to make certain she fulfilled her side of it.

'Maybe I will take you home after all,' he said gruffly. 'As your father's surgery has been rescheduled for tomorrow morning. Let's get past that hurdle before we deal with the next.'

'Thanks, Vinn…' she said, in a whisper-soft voice, her eyes lowering from his. 'This has all been such a terrible shock to me…'

Vinn wanted to ask what she was referring to: his

demand for marriage or her father's health scare? But he didn't, because he already knew the answer.

The Gabriella St Clair he knew would take her father's heart attack in her stride. But being forced to marry the bastard son of the St Clair house-cleaner was something else again.

CHAPTER FIVE

GABBY chewed her nails one by one as she'd waited with her mother in the relatives' lounge for news of her father's condition. It had been a long wait, for although Henry St Clair had been first on the list, the procedure usually took anything up to three or four hours, as veins were harvested from the lower legs to relocate in the chest as heart valves.

Finally the surgeon came out with good news. Everything had gone extremely well, and Henry was in recovery. He would be there for quite some time, before being transferred to Intensive Care, and then to the high-dependency unit a few days later.

'When can we see him?' Gabby asked, holding onto her mother's hand and squeezing it tightly.

'As soon as he is transferred to the ICU I will have someone inform you,' the surgeon said. 'Try not to be too put off by all the machines and drips attached to him. It all looks a lot scarier than it really is, I can assure you. He is one of the luckier ones. He hasn't smoked in years, and his weight is within the normal range. A family history of heart disease is, of course, unfortunate, but with the right lifestyle changes he should make a very good recovery, as long as his stress levels are kept down during rehabilitation.'

Gabby couldn't have heard more convincing words. The pre-nuptial agreement papers she had signed first thing that morning sent via express courier had been worth it. She was committed to marrying Vinn Venadicci in front of a marriage celebrant in a registry office. They would be leaving for a short honeymoon at the St Clair Island Resort later the same day.

Gabby tried not to think too much about it all, and was almost glad she had her father to worry about instead. It gave her a focus, supporting her mother, who didn't cope well even with breaking a nail or her roots showing, let alone a crisis of this sort. Her mother's reaction to Blair's death had been part of the reason Gabby had agreed to marry Tristan Glendenning, even though she had been having doubts for months. Tristan had assured her a big wedding to plan was just the thing to get her mother out of bed each day, and off the strong and highly addictive sedatives the doctor had prescribed.

Gabby's concern over her mother's health and well-being had more or less sealed her own fate. She had been so distracted by her parents and their heart-wrenching grief she had more or less had to ignore her own, and in so doing had set in motion years of hell.

Now she was doing it all over again. She was marrying a man she didn't love in order to protect those she loved with all her heart.

But for some reason Gabby didn't feel Vinn would be in quite the same category of husband as Tristan. Perhaps that was why she was feeling so unsettled.

Vinn was a mystery to her. In many ways he always had been. That was what she found so intriguing about him; she didn't know him because she suspected he didn't want to be known.

Gabby didn't think he would raise a hand to her. God knew he'd had plenty of reason to in the past, but he had never struck back at her in any way at all—apart from that kiss, of course. She had always secretly admired him for his self-restraint. She had been such a bitch towards him. How he had tolerated it still amazed her. So many young men in his position would have sought their revenge at the time; instead he had waited seven long years in order to do so…

Gabby gave a shiver and turned her attention back to her mother, who was crying into yet another crumpled tissue.

'It's OK, Mum,' she said gently. 'You heard what the surgeon said. Dad's going to be just fine.'

Pamela St Clair blew her nose. 'I know, darling, but I just wish Blair was here,' she said. 'With your father out of action for God knows how long, what will happen to the business? Your father never tells me anything about what's going on. Are you sure it's all going well? You haven't said anything about it for ages, and I can't help worrying that…well, we could lose everything we've worked so hard for. If we were to lose the house… Oh, God, I just couldn't bear it!'

'Mum, stop worrying right now,' Gabby said, hugging her mother close so she couldn't see the deceit in her eyes. 'The resort is doing just fine. I spoke to the Fosters only yesterday. Everything is fine. They've had almost full occupancy for the last month. We're making a profit, just as we hoped and planned. Everything is safe and secure.'

'I'm so glad,' Pamela said, stepping back and wiping at her tears. 'I'm also glad about you marrying Vinn. I want you to know that, Gabby.'

Gabby met her mother's tawny-brown gaze. 'I always thought you didn't like him, Mum,' she said, trying not to frown. 'You always gave the impression he and his mother were beneath you.'

Pamela gave a wincing look. 'I know… It seems so…dreadfully hypocritical of me, thinking about it now,' she said. 'But I guess it was because I was so ashamed of my own background.'

Gabby allowed her frown purchase this time. 'What do you mean?'

Her mother blew her nose again and, tucking away the tissue, faced Gabby squarely. 'Darling, your father married me against his parents' wishes. We never spoke of it to you or to Blair, and thank God your grandparents when they were alive didn't mention anything either. But I was from the wrong side of the tracks, if you know what I mean.'

Gabby could barely believe her ears. She stood silently staring at her perfectly groomed mother, with her perfect diction and rounded vowels, and wondered if she had ever known her at all.

'Vinn's mother Rose reminded me of my own mother,' Pamela explained. 'She was an unwed mother too, with no skills to speak of, and at the mercy of whoever employed her. I was shunted from place to place for most of my childhood, never making friends long enough to keep them. As a result I dropped out of school and had to rely on my looks to get me where I wanted to go. I met your father at a function where I was waiting on tables. That's where I met Janice— Tristan's mother. Her parents owned the restaurant. She was so lovely to me, and we became close friends… The rest, as they say, is history.'

Gabby swallowed. 'You did love Dad when you married him, though, didn't you?' she asked, unconsciously holding her breath.

Pamela let out a long sigh and shifted her gaze. 'I didn't at first,' she confessed. 'The thing is I got pregnant with your brother. I was stupid and naive, and I didn't factor in the risks when we first started seeing each other. Your father insisted we marry, and so we did—against all the objections thrown at us.'

Gabby didn't say a word. Her voice seemed to be locked somewhere deep inside her throat.

Her mother's reddened eyes came back to hers. 'But over time I grew to love him. I don't have to tell you he is a good man, Gabby. He doesn't always get it right, any more than I do, but he's all I've got now apart from you. I just wish Blair h-hadn't…' She took a deep, uneven breath and continued, 'I just want you to be happy, Gabby. Janice, Tristan's mother, wishes it too. I was just talking to her last night. She and Gareth think the world of you. You were such a wonderful wife to their son.' She began to sob again, and buried her face into another wad of tissues.

Gabby felt sick. Guilt assailed her, almost overwhelming her already fragile control. Tristan's parents, like hers, had never known the full story. How could she have told them what had occurred behind closed doors? How could she have ruined so many lives by telling them the sordid truth?

She had felt so alone.

She *still* felt so alone.

Did anyone understand what it was like to carry such a burden of guilt and shame and regret? Would her life always be marked by the dark stains of her mistakes? How could she clear her slate and start afresh? Was it even possible?

Gabby became aware again of her mother's renewed bout of tears, and gathered her close. 'Don't cry, Mum,' she said softly. 'Things will work out. I know they will. Vinn and I will sort things out between us.'

Pamela brushed at her eyes as she removed herself from Gabby's embrace. 'Do you love him, darling?' she asked, looking at her intently.

Gabby felt her heart drop inside her chest. How could she lie to her own mother? Hadn't she already told so many lies? 'Um… Mum…' she faltered, shifting her gaze a fraction. 'What sort of question is that? Why on earth would I be marrying him if I didn't feel like…that for him?'

Her mother smiled a watery smile and, grasping Gabby's wrists, gripped them warmly. 'Then you will be a better wife to him than I was to your father in those first years of our marriage,' she said. 'At least you're not marrying Vinn because you feel you have to. You are marrying him because you love him and can't imagine living your life with anyone else. Apart from Tristan, of course. You were soul mates—everyone knows that—but life throws up other paths, which is just as well, don't you think?'

Gabby stretched her mouth into a smile that felt as if it had been stitched in place. 'Of course,' she said. 'That's exactly what I think.'

When Gabby finally got home to Point Piper, Vinn arrived within minutes. As she checked his tall figure via the security camera, she wondered if he had been parked somewhere outside waiting for her.

He had called in at the hospital briefly, halfway through the afternoon, but hadn't stayed long. Just long enough to kiss her on the lips—a soft press of warm sensual flesh against her trembling mouth—before he turned and smiled at Gabby's mother. Gabby had listened to him chat about her father's condition with one ear while her heart had skipped and hopped all over the place and she'd surreptitiously swept her tongue where his mouth had just been. She had been able to taste him—a hint of good-quality coffee, a touch of mint, and a massive dose of sexy, full-blooded male.

Her belly had given a little quiver as she'd stood close to his side, his arm slipping around her waist in a possessive but strangely protective manner. She hadn't quite been able to control the instinct to move in even closer. He had felt so tall and strong, like a fortress.

Gabby had only suddenly realised her mother had left them to return to her father's bedside in ICU, where only one visitor was allowed at any time. She'd felt Vinn's arm drop from her waist and had quickly rear-ranged her features so he couldn't see how he had affected her.

'Do you think that kiss was necessary?' she asked, in a deliberately testy tone, taking great care not to glance at that sensual mouth, focussing on his grey-blue eyes instead.

His eyes contained a glint of amusement. 'Actually, I was thinking about slipping my tongue inside your mouth as well, but I thought your mother might be uncomfortable with such an obvious and very public display of my affection for her daughter.'

Gabby lifted her brows in twin arcs of cynicism. 'Affection?' she said. 'Is that what you call it? It's animal attraction, and you damn well know it.' She took a little heaving breath and added, 'And it's totally disgusting.'

He gave her a lazy smile and brushed the back of his hand down the side of her face—a barely touching caress, but it set off every nerve beneath the skin of her cheek like electrodes set on full voltage. 'Ah, but you feel it too, don't you, *mia piccola?*' he said. 'And soon we will be doing something about it, hmm?'

Gabby glowered at him even as she tried to ignore the flip-flop of her heart behind her breastbone. 'Not if I can help it,' she said stiffly, and crossed her arms tightly over her chest.

His smile widened and, leaning down, he pressed a soft-as-air kiss to her forehead before she could do anything to counteract it. 'Keep stoking that fiery passion of yours,' he drawled, in a low and sexy, knee-wobbling tone. 'I get turned on by the thought of you fighting me every step of the way, even though you want what I want. It's what you've always wanted.'

'I want you to burn in hell,' she bit out, practically shaking all over with rage.

He winked at her, and without another word turned

and walked with those long easy strides of his down the corridor to the lifts.

Gabby stood watching him, annoyed with herself for doing so, but for some reason unable to get her body to move. The lift doors opened and she saw Vinn smile as two nurses came out, each one doing a swift double-take as he stepped into the lift. The doors whooshed shut behind him.

The nurses' voices carried as they came up the corridor towards Gabby. 'Wasn't that Vinn Venadicci?' the dark-haired one asked her red-headed companion. 'You know…the hotshot property investment tycoon?'

'Sure was,' the red head said. 'I heard a rumour he's just got engaged. His future father-in-law's just had open heart surgery. I wonder how long *that* marriage will last? Vinn Venadicci is a bit of a player, or so the gossip mags say.'

'I wouldn't mind a bit of a play with him,' the dark-haired nurse admitted with a grin. 'God, those eyes of his, and that smile would be enough to melt anyone's moral code.'

Gabby spun away in disgust and, pushing open the nearest female conveniences door, locked herself inside a cubicle until she was sure the nurses had moved on.

And now she had to face her nemesis all over again, Gabby thought sourly, as she opened the door of her parents' home to let Vinn in. She stepped well back, in case he took it upon himself to repeat his mode of greeting earlier that afternoon.

'Why are you here?' she asked in a clipped tone.

Vinn reached into the inside pocket of his suit jacket and handed her a black velvet box. 'This is for you,' he said, with an inscrutable expression. 'If you don't like the design you can exchange it for something else. It makes no difference to me.'

Gabby took the small box with an unsteady hand, desperately trying not to come into contact with his long fingers. But even so she felt the zap of his touch as one of her fingers brushed against one of his. She opened the lid and stared down at the classically designed solitaire diamond ring. The brilliance of the gem was absolutely breathtaking.

She looked up at him, her voice coming out slightly husky. 'It's…it's beautiful… It must have cost you a fortune.'

He gave her a wry look. 'Not quite as much as the margin call, but certainly close.'

Gabby pressed her lips together and looked at the diamond again, her mind reeling at the thought of how much he had paid for her to be his bride. Even though she had grown up with the sort of wealth and privilege most ordinary people never saw in a lifetime, she still couldn't quite believe the lengths Vinn was prepared to go to in order to secure her hand in marriage.

It made her realise yet again how difficult it was going to be for her to get out of the arrangement. She had already endured one miserable marriage, every day a torture of secrets and lies and betrayals. How would she cope with years of Vinn's philandering? He was sure to do so, since he had done little else since he had left the St Clair estate all those years ago.

'Of course you will have to remove Glendenning's rings first,' Vinn said into the silence.

Gabby looked down at her left hand, at the diamond

cluster and the wedding band she had wanted to remove so many times over the last two years since Tristan's death. She'd felt unable to face the comments from her parents if she had done so.

'Yes…yes…of course,' she said, and began to tug at them.

One of Vinn's hands closed over hers, the other taking the velvet box out of her hand and putting it on a hall table next to him. 'Allow me,' he said. And, holding her left hand in the strength and warmth of his left one, he removed each of the rings, his grey-blue gaze not once leaving her startled brown one.

Gabby could feel her heart picking up its pace, and the way her breathing was becoming shallow and uneven. Her body felt hot inside and out—especially her hand, which was still enclosed in his. She took a tiny swallow as he reached for the ring he had bought her, and then her breathing stopped altogether as he gently eased the circle of white gold with its brilliant diamond along the slim length of her finger to its final resting place.

'It is a perfect fit,' he said with an enigmatic smile. 'How about that?'

Gabby couldn't account for her scattered emotions, but she felt as close to tears as she had the previous evening. It made her feel vulnerable in a way she resented feeling in front of someone she disliked so intensely.

'A lucky guess,' she said in an off-hand tone, and stepped back from him.

A flicker of annoyance momentarily darkened the blue in his eyes. 'Are you going to invite me in for a drink to celebrate our impending marriage?' he asked.

'If so, I think I might remove my shirt right now, in case you take it upon yourself to throw the contents of your glass at me again.'

Gabby tightened her mouth like the strings of an evening purse. 'I promise not to throw anything at you if you promise to keep your insulting suppositions to yourself,' she said, with an elevation of her chin.

'And what would some of those suppositions be, I wonder?' he mused.

She stalked towards the large lounge overlooking the harbour, tossing over her shoulder, 'What would you like to drink? We have the usual spirits and mixers, wine and champagne—French, even, if you so desire it.'

'I think you know very well what I desire, Gabriella,' he said, as he came to where she was standing in front of the bar fridge and drinks servery.

Gabby sucked in a sharp little breath as his hands came down on the tops of her shoulders. The heat of his touch was like a brand, even through the layer of her cotton shirt. She felt the solid presence of him at her back, and wondered what it would feel like to lean back into his hardness, to feel the hard outline of his body against the softness of hers, to feel his hands move from her shoulders to cup her breasts, to feel the slight abrasion of his fingers skating over her erect nipples…

She might not like him, but Gabby was starting to realise she would be lying to herself if she said she didn't desire him. He had a magnetism about him that was totally enthralling. Even now she felt an over-whelming compulsion to turn around and lock gazes with him, to see if his need was anything like her own.

'What's that perfume you are wearing?' he asked, moving in a little closer.

Gabby felt her spine give a distinct wobble as his chest rumbled against her back as he spoke. 'Um…I'm not sure… I can't remember… Something I've had for ages…' She couldn't seem to get her scrambled brain to work. It seemed to be short-circuited by all her body was feeling with him so close.

'It reminds me of warm summer nights,' he said against the shell of her ear. 'Frangipani and jasmine and something else.'

Gabby wondered if the 'something else' was the scent of her desire for him. She could feel silky moisture gathering between her thighs, the secret and hollow ache making her feel even more unguarded around him. She had always been able to hold him off with her caustic tongue. That had been her protection in the past. But what if her body totally betrayed her now? Could he sense how close she was to responding to the temptation of his closeness?

Vinn turned her around to face him, his hands sliding down the length of her slender arms, his right thumb rolling over the bump of the diamond ring on her finger, back and forth, as he watched the way her expression became shuttered, as if his touch didn't affect her one iota. But he could feel the slight tremble of her hands in his, and see the flare of her pupils, making her toffee-brown eyes darken, and the way the point of her tongue darted out to deposit a fine layer of moisture over her soft lips.

He wanted to kiss her, to taste the sweetness of her, to feel her tongue war with his until he tamed it. He wanted to press her back against the nearest wall and bury himself in her, to feel his hard body surrounded by her silky warmth, to thrust himself to paradise and take her writhing and screaming with him.

But instead he released her hands and stepped back from her. 'I have changed my mind about that drink,' he said. 'I have another engagement this evening, and since I drove myself here instead of using a cab, I don't want to end up with a drink-driving charge.'

A frown pulled at her smooth brow. 'You don't have a driver?' she asked.

'Not a full-time one,' he said. 'And nor do I have a live-in housekeeper, so I hope it's not going to be a problem for you pitching in occasionally to help keep things running smoothly at home.'

Her frown deepened, and a fiery light came into her eyes as they narrowed slightly. 'Is this some sort of sick joke?' she asked.

'It's no joke, Blondie,' he said. 'I do my own cooking, and I expect you to do the same.'

'B-but you're a multi-millionaire for God's sake!' she spluttered. 'In fact, aren't you close to being a billionaire by now?'

'So?'

'So you get people to do stuff for you,' she said, flapping her hands for effect. 'It's totally crazy, spending your time on menial tasks when you could employ someone else to do it for you so you can concentrate on what you're best at doing.'

'I happen to enjoy cooking,' Vinn said, relishing every second of their exchange. She was so pampered she hadn't a clue how the real world worked, and it would do her good to learn. It would teach her to think twice about treating those less fortunate than her with her customary disdain.

'If you think for one minute I'm going to wash your socks and fold your underwear then you are even more deluded than I thought,' she tossed at him heatedly.

'The only thing I expect you to do with my underwear is peel it off me—preferably with your teeth,' he returned with a deliberately lascivious look.

Her eyes flared and he saw her hands go to tight little fists by her sides. 'I will do no such thing!'

He gave a chuckle of laughter and, before he was tempted to kiss that pouting mouth of hers, turned on his heel and left.

Gabby stormed up and down the lounge after he had driven away, her anger duelling with her disappointment that he hadn't stayed for a drink.

No, that wasn't quite the truth, she decided on her pace back towards the sofa. What she had really wanted him to do was to stay long enough to kiss her. She had been expecting him to turn her around in his arms and smother her mouth with his. Her whole body had been screaming out for it. But he had left her high and dry. She hated him for it. She hated him for toying with her like a cat with a mouse, taunting it, teasing it mercilessly, just waiting for the best moment to make that final devastating pounce.

She hated him.

OK, so that wasn't quite the truth either, Gabby thought as she scraped her fingers through her hair. That was the whole problem. She didn't know what the hell she felt for Vinn Venadicci, but one thing was certain: it was not as close to hate as she wanted and most desperately needed it to be.

CHAPTER SIX

'DARLING,' Pamela St Clair said to Gabby as soon as she arrived at the hospital the following morning. 'Please tell me this…this…' she thrust the morning's newspaper in Gabby's hands '…this scandalmongering isn't true!'

Gabby looked at the page the newspaper was folded open to and felt a knife-like pain jab through her. There was a photograph of Vinn with his arm around a young and very beautiful brunette, who was smiling up at him adoringly. The couple of paragraphs accompanying the picture declared Vinn Venadicci was rumoured to be getting married to widowed socialite Gabriella Glendenning, nee St Clair, and the journalist was quite adamant the young woman with him was not his fiancée but a mystery date he had been seen with once or twice before.

'Well?' Pamela St Clair was practically wringing her hands. 'For God's sake, Gabby, if your father hears or sees this it could cause another heart attack.'

'Mum…' Somehow Gabby located her voice, but it sounded slightly strangled. 'Of course it's not true. You know what the press are like. They make this stuff up all the time. It's probably an old photo.'

Pamela's eyes narrowed. 'Are you sure?' she asked. 'Are you absolutely sure?'

Gabby had never felt more uncertain in her life, but she was not going to admit that to her mother. With an acting skill she had no idea she had possessed until now, she relaxed her tense features into a smile and handed back the paper with a surprisingly steady hand. 'Mum,' she said, holding out her left hand, 'do you think Vinn would give me this and then go off gallivanting with someone else the very same evening?'

Her mother gasped as she held Gabby's hand up to the light. 'Oh, my God, it's gorgeous,' she said. 'It must have cost him an arm and a leg.'

Gabby took her hand back. 'Yes, it did,' she said, unconsciously fingering the diamond. 'But apparently I'm worth it.'

Pamela looked past Gabby's shoulder. 'Oh… Vinn…' She cleared her throat delicately and continued, 'We were…er…just talking about you.'

Gabby had to summon even more acting ability to face Vinn with any sense of equanimity. 'Hi,' she said, and reached up on tiptoe to plant a brief kiss on his cheek, with the intention of landing it close enough to his mouth for her mother to be fooled. However Vinn had other ideas. He took control of her mouth in a deep, bone-melting assault on her senses that left her totally out of kilter once it ended.

'Hi yourself, *cara*,' he said, before turning to face Gabby's mother, who was trying to hide the newspaper behind her back but failing miserably. 'I hope you weren't upset by that article? I have already spoken to my legal advisors about lodging a defamation claim against the journalist concerned.'

'Oh…' Pamela said, smiling broadly. 'No…no, of course not, Vinn. I wasn't upset at all, and neither was Gabby. Were you, darling?'

Gabby smiled stiffly. 'I am well used to the mudslinging that goes on in the press, having been subjected to it myself once or twice in the past.'

Vinn smiled as if butter wouldn't melt on his skin, let alone in his mouth, Gabby thought resentfully.

'So how is Henry doing today?' he asked, addressing Pamela.

'He's resting just now, but he's had a good night,' Pamela answered with visible relief. 'The surgeon is pleased with everything so far. It's just important we keep him quiet and free from stress.'

'Yes, of course,' Vinn said, reaching for Gabby's hand and pulling her closer. 'We'll let you get back to him while we have a coffee together. Can I get you something before we go?'

Pamela blushed like a schoolgirl. 'Oh, no, I'm fine, thank you, Vinn,' she said and then started to gush like one too. 'You're so kind. You've been absolutely marvellous. Gabby's so lucky to have someone like you. I really mean it. And that ring! Why, it's practically the Hope Diamond!'

Vinn gave a low rumble of laughter. 'Not quite— but she's worth it, don't you think?'

Pamela beamed from ear to ear. 'Well, she's my daughter, so I have to agree, don't I? But she *is* worth it—although it would please me to see her smile a bit more. Come on, darling.' She swung her gaze to

Gabby. 'I must say for someone who is supposed to be madly in love you don't seem all that happy.'

'Um… I'm just worried about Dad, that's all,' Gabby faltered. 'It's been such a trying time and…'

Vinn's arm snaked around Gabby's waist. 'I promise you, Mrs St Clair, you won't know her when I bring her back from our honeymoon,' he said. 'She will be smiling from ear to ear. I guarantee it.'

Pamela blushed again. 'Oh, my, but you have turned into such a charmer, Vinn Venadicci. And you really must call me Pamela now that you're to be part of the family.'

'Thank you, Pamela,' he said, with an easygoing smile.

Gabby pulled herself out of his hold once her mother had gone back to be with her father. 'Who is she?' she threw at him icily.

'Who is who?' Vinn asked, as he began leading the way down the corridor towards the lifts.

Gabby had to trot to keep up. 'That woman in the picture,' she said, glancing around to see if anyone was listening. 'She's your mistress, isn't she?' she hissed at him in a hushed tone. 'Don't bother denying it, because I just won't believe you.'

He pressed the 'down' button. 'Then I won't waste my time denying it,' he said. 'What would be the point, if you're not going to believe me either way?'

Gabby glared at him as they stepped into the lift, but couldn't fling a retort his way due to several other passengers in the lift. She stood stiffly by his side, her anger towards him going upwards even as the floor numbers went downwards.

The lift delivered them on the ground floor, and

Vinn placed a hand beneath her elbow to guide her out of the busy hospital foyer to where his car was parked.

'Where are we going?' Gabby asked, flinging him a churlish look.

'We are going to have a coffee together,' he said, and opened the passenger door for her. 'Get in.'

She threw him another furious glare. 'Don't order me about as if I'm a child.'

'Then don't act like one,' he returned, and repeated his command, this time with an implacable edge to his tone. 'Get in the car.'

'I don't see why we have to drive somewhere to have a coffee when there's a perfectly good cafeteria back there in the hospital foyer,' she tossed back, with a shrug of her shoulders.

Vinn's eyes challenged hers. 'You know something, Blondie?' he said. 'You are really starting to annoy me—and that is not a good thing.'

'Yeah, well, you're a late starter then, because I've been annoyed with you from the moment I met you,' she threw back, her brown eyes flashing at him.

Vinn put the brakes on his temper with an effort. 'Listen,' he said, 'I have nothing against hospital food and drink, but right now I want us to be alone. We have things to discuss.'

She gave him a contentious look. 'Like your mystery lover?'

Vinn silently ground his teeth. 'She is nothing of the sort. She's a…friend.'

Her brows lifted cynically. 'A friend, huh?' she said. 'What do you take me for, Vinn? Do you think I'm so naive I would fall for that old line?'

Vinn set his mouth. 'Quite frankly, right at this minute I don't give a damn *what* you think,' he bit out. 'I have a huge list of things to see to today because I'm going to be away next week, and I can do without this infantile behaviour from you—especially considering the money I've handed over without a single word of thanks from you.'

'You expect me to *thank* you for blackmailing me into marriage?' she asked in an incredulous tone.

'If you're not happy with the conditions you can hand back the money and the ring,' he said, locking his eyes on hers. 'Right here and right now.'

Gabby tussled for a moment with his challenging and annoyingly confident look. There was no point calling his bluff because there was no way she could find an alternative source of funds to keep the resort safe. 'You know I can't do that…' she mumbled.

'Then let's go with Plan A and get on with it,' he said and nodded his head towards the passenger seat.

Gabby got in the car with uncharacteristic meekness, her spirits sagging. Her head was starting to pound from the tension in her neck and shoulders that had been building all morning. She pressed her fingers to the bridge of her nose, her eyes scrunched closed to avoid the stab of bright sunlight coming through the windscreen.

'Hey…' Vinn's deep voice was almost as soothing as the warmth of his palm at the back of her neck, the gentle massaging of his fingers untying the knots of tension like magic. 'You have a headache, yes?'

She bit her lip and gave a tiny nod. 'I didn't sleep well, and I skipped breakfast…'

She heard him mutter a curse, but his fingers didn't stop their soothing action. She rolled her head and shoulders to make the most of his touch, her breath coming out in a long, easy stream as the tension gradually eased.

'Feeling a bit better?' he asked.

She opened her eyes and turned to look at him, her heart stalling like an old engine. There was concern in his grey-blue gaze, and his mouth had lost its grim set. He was now looking as sensually tempting and irresistible as ever. She couldn't seem to stop looking at him, at the way his mouth tipped up at the corners as if he always had a smile at the ready, the fuller bottom lip hinting at the potent sensuality of his nature.

Then there was the dark stubble that peppered his jaw, in spite of his early-morning shave, making him so essentially masculine she wanted to place the palm of her hand on his face and feel the texture of his skin, feel the abrasion of it against her softer one. She could imagine herself kissing her way all over his face, over each of the dark slashes of his eyebrows, his eyelids, and down the length of his crooked patrician nose until she got to his lips.

Gabby felt her eyelids begin to lower as his mouth came inexorably closer, his head tilting to accommodate the contours of their faces. The slow-motion brush of his lips against hers was soft, like a feather floating down to land on top of a smooth surface. Her lips tingled from the brief contact, each nerve springing to life in anticipation of a follow-up kiss.

But instead he sat back in the driver's seat and started the engine with a throaty roar. Releasing the handbrake, he sent her a smile before turning back to the task of driving out of the car park.

Gabby rolled her lips together, to see if it would stop them tingling, but all it did was make her hungry for more of his drugging kisses. Was he doing it on purpose? she wondered. Day by day ramping up her desire for him, so she would not be able to resist him when he decided it was time to consummate their marriage. Her belly quivered at the thought of him making love to her, his hands on her body, touching her, stroking and caressing her until she was boneless with need.

She fidgeted in her seat, her body hot and bothered, and that secret place between her thighs pulsing and aching and moist with want.

Would she disappoint him? In spite of her marriage to Tristan she had never experienced pleasure, only pain and shame. She mentally cringed as she recalled the filthy insults her late husband had flung at her, making her feel so worthless and unattractive the little self-esteem she had possessed had been obliterated completely.

Gabby suddenly became aware of where they were heading as Vinn took the exit to Mosman off the Harbour Bridge. 'We're going to your house?' she asked, swivelling to look at him.

'Yes,' he said, concentrating on the traffic. 'We could have gone to a café in the city, but you obviously need some peace and quiet—not to mention a couple of painkillers.'

Gabby turned back to look at the road ahead, her brow creasing slightly. The caring, solicitous Vinn was a change from the teasing, taunting one, but she wondered if he was trying to divert her attention away from his mystery lover by acting out the role of thoughtful fiancé. Jealousy gnawed at her insides like hundreds of miniature hungry mouths nipping at her tender flesh, making her feel sick with despair.

She didn't want to feel such intensity of emotion.

She didn't want to feel vulnerable.

She suddenly realised with a little jolt of surprise she didn't want him to want anyone else. She wanted him to want her and only her.

Vinn parked the car in the driveway and strode around to help her out of her side. She looked pale, and there were dark bruise-like shadows under her eyes. Her mouth had a downward turn to it. It was obvious she was burning the candle at both ends, spending long hours at the hospital as well as juggling her father's business affairs.

He was all too familiar with the worry over an ill parent. Watching his beloved mother die had been one of the toughest things he had ever faced, made all the harder when he had received the news of Blair St Clair's suicide. Vinn hadn't been able to leave his mother's bedside and travel to the other side of the globe to attend Blair's funeral. Nor had he been able to offer much in the way of support to Blair's parents and Gabriella, even though he had dearly wanted to.

The news of her engagement a few weeks after Blair's death had been another blow he had struggled to deal with. He had never particularly liked Tristan Glendenning; there had always been something about him that irked Vinn the more he got to know him. He'd been too smooth, too self-assured, and not one bit in love with Gabriella. Of that Vinn was sure. But in spite of his warning she had married Glendenning anyway. And the bruisers Tristan had engaged to work him over had certainly kept him away from the wedding, as Gabriella had requested. Vinn had put up a tough fight, but four against one was asking too much—even of someone with his level of physical fitness.

Vinn escorted her inside the house and straight to the kitchen, where he pulled out a stool for her. 'Sit,' he said. 'I'll make you some scrambled eggs and toast.'

For a moment or two she looked as if she was about to refuse, but then she gave a little sigh and wriggled onto the stool. 'Don't make too much,' she said. 'I'm not really very hungry.'

'When was the last time you ate?' he asked as he placed a knob of butter in the pan and set it on the cooktop.

'I don't know... I can't remember,' she said. 'Lunch yesterday?'

He rolled his eyes as he reached for a carton of eggs in the fridge. 'If you get any slimmer you'll have to wear snow skis in the shower to stop you going down the drain.'

She gave him a droll look. 'Very funny.'

Vinn cracked some eggs into a bowl and began to whisk them. 'How are you the handling work at the office since your father's been taking a break?' he asked, in a casually interested tone.

The momentary silence made him glance at her over his shoulder. 'Not so good, huh?' he said.

'What makes you think that?' she said with a defensive set to her features. 'You think I'm not capable of handling things on my own?'

He gave the eggs a good grind of pepper before responding. 'My gut feeling is you only do it because you feel you have something to prove. Your heart's not in it. It's never been in it.'

Her silence this time was a fraction longer. Vinn could almost hear the cogs of her brain ticking over, trying to find some way of justifying herself.

'It's a family business,' she said at last.

'So?'

'So family members usually take up some sort of role in the company.'

'Yes,' he said. 'But it helps if they're suited for it. And it helps even more if they enjoy it and get some sort of satisfaction out of it.'

He turned to see her slip down off the stool, her arms going across her chest in that classic defensive pose. 'I do enjoy it,' she said, but her eyes skittered away from his.

'Perhaps. But I still think there are things you would enjoy more.'

'Oh, really?' Gabby said, flashing her gaze back to his. 'Since when have you become such an expert on what would satisfy me?'

His eyes gave her that look—the look that made Gabby's legs feel weak and watery and her belly start to flutter as if tiny wings were beating with excitement inside her. And then her colour rose as she realised she could have phrased her question with perhaps a little less propensity for a double meaning.

'Because I know you, Gabriella,' he said. 'You have no head for business. And I'm not the only one who thinks so.'

Gabby stiffened as she looked at him. 'What?' she said, narrowing her eyes in suspicion. 'You mean you've been talking to someone in the company about me?'

He leaned back against the bench in an indolent manner. 'I just poured two point four million dollars into the company. Did you think I wouldn't do a bit of research before I committed myself so heavily?'

'What sort of research did you do?' Gabby asked with a guarded look. 'It's not like you had much time. I came to see you practically at the last minute, and you—' She stopped, her heart beginning to pound as the truth began to dawn. 'You went snooping around well before then, though, didn't you? My God, but you have some gall, Vinn Venadicci. How dare you undermine me like that?'

'I was concerned about your father's health way before he had the heart attack,' he said. 'I had lunch with him a couple of months ago and it became clear to me he didn't have his finger on the pulse of the business any more. He had lost that fire in his belly. Quite frankly, I think he was relieved to leave you in charge because he was feeling so worn out. It's my bet that once he recovers he'll change his mind about retiring and want to get back at the helm—which is why I have organised a business manager to take your place until he does. He starts tomorrow.'

Gabby's eyes went wide in outrage. 'You did *what*?'

'I want you to take a break from the business,' he said, dishing up the eggs. 'Take a few months to think about what you'd like to do. You might find you'd prefer not to work at all and just enjoy being a wife and mother.'

She gave him a livid glare. 'You've got it all worked

out, haven't you, Vinn? You expect me to give up everything just to be a breeding machine. God, I can't believe there are still men like you around. I thought they died out with the dinosaurs.'

He set the plate of eggs and toast on the bench between them. 'Sit down and eat that before it gets cold,' he said.

In a fit of temper Gabby shoved the plate back towards him, with more force than she had really intended. The plate slid off the bench and shattered on the floor at his feet, eggs and toast going everywhere.

Her eyes flew to his in apprehension. 'I—I'm sorry,' she said. 'I didn't mean to do that…'

'Sure you didn't.' He stepped back from the mess, his eyes hard on hers, his mouth pulled into a tight line of simmering anger.

Gabby took an unsteady step backwards. 'I'll c-clean it up,' she said, in a voice that was scratchy and uneven. 'If you'll just show me where the dustpan and broom are…'

'Leave it,' he said tersely. 'I'll see to it myself. In any case, you probably wouldn't know one end of a broom from the other.'

She compressed her lips, struggling to keep the tears back but in the end failing. One by one they slipped past the shield of her lashes and silently flowed down her cheeks.

Vinn paused on his way back from the utilities cupboard with the dustpan and broom. 'It's just a plate of eggs,' he said, his anger fading at the sight of her tears. 'It's not the end of the world.'

She choked back a sob and covered her face with

her hands, her shoulders shaking as she began to cry in earnest.

He let out a little curse, directed at himself rather than her, and, putting the pan and broom to one side, gathered her in his arms. 'Are you *sure* it's not that time of the month?' he asked.

She shook her head, buried against his chest, and sobbed and sniffled some more.

He stroked his fingers through the silky strands of her blonde hair, enjoying the feel of her soft and pliant against him. Her sobs gradually died down until she was silent, her head turned sideways, so her cheek was pressed close to his thudding heart.

His body was getting harder by the second, and the rush of blood to his groin was making him ache to grind his pelvis against hers. He could feel the softness of her breasts pressing against his chest, and her arms had somehow snaked around his waist, bringing her lower body just that little bit closer to his.

He felt a tremor of awareness go through her, like little ripples over the surface of smooth water, and then she lifted her head and met his gaze, her lips so soft and inviting that he brought his head down and covered them with his own.

CHAPTER SEVEN

GABBY totally melted under the blowtorch of his kiss. His lips were hard and then soft, firm and demanding one minute, gentle and cajoling the next. It was a heady repertoire, making all her senses shiver in response.

She returned his kiss with a level of passion that was almost frightening in its intensity. She was on fire for him, every part of her longing to feel him touch her all over, to bring her body to the highest peak of pleasure. She felt the stirring of her intimate muscles, the liquid warmth that seeped from deep inside her to prepare her for the thick invasion of his body. She could feel how aroused he was—so very hard, so intoxicatingly male.

With his mouth still locked on hers, Gabby felt his fingers working on the tiny buttons of her cotton top, undoing them one by one as his tongue danced a sexy tango with hers. He didn't bother undoing her bra; he simply shoved it out of the way and bent his mouth to her breast. She gasped in delight as his tongue circled her nipple a couple of times, before he began to suckle on her with a gentle drawing-in motion that made her knees start to buckle. He moved to her other breast, increasing the pressure of his mouth, using his teeth in tiny tug-like bites that sent shooting sparks of need right through her core. Waves of pleasure rolled over her, making her mind empty of everything but how he was making her feel.

He brought his mouth back to hers in a scorching kiss of passionate urgency, his pelvis jammed so tightly against hers she felt the throb and thunder of his blood beneath his skin.

'You taste so damned good,' he said, just above her swollen lips. 'I want to taste all of you—every beautiful inch of you.'

Gabby reconnected her mouth to his, her tongue stroking and curling around his, tasting the maleness and fiery heat of him. Her heart-rate went through the roof as he nudged her thighs apart, rubbing one of his own against her feminine mound. Her body exploded with sensation, the deep hollow ache intensifying until she was whimpering, soft little mewing sounds that came from the back of her throat.

'Come upstairs with me,' he said, lifting his mouth again to look down at her, his grey-blue eyes as dark as she had ever seen them. 'We don't have to wait until Friday. I want you now.'

Gabby felt herself wavering. Her body was tilting her one way while her brain was trying desperately to send her back the other. He had a mistress, she reminded herself. He was a playboy. He was only marrying her for revenge. There was no love in the arrangement—not even mild affection. This was about lust. He had wanted her for a long time and had gone to extraordinary lengths to have her. He would use her, and when he grew tired of her she would be left, trapped in a going-nowhere marriage, until he decided if or when it was to end.

Her body put up an equally powerful argument. It was still throbbing with need, every pore of her skin sensitised to his touch, every nerve-ending buzzing. Her lips were as swollen as the folds of her feminine cleft, the silky moisture between them making it even harder to ignore the need he had awakened in her.

'Or what about we do it here?' Vinn said, spinning her round so her back was against the kitchen bench. One of his hands lifted her skirt, his fingers searching for her moist heat.

'No!' Gabby thrust both hands against his chest.

He cocked one brow at her, his hand stilling on her thigh. 'No?'

She pressed her lips together, trying to control her breathing, trying to tame her wild needs, trying to gather some sense of decency and self-respect.

'No…' she said, releasing a tightly held breath. 'I can't…'

'You certainly weren't giving me that impression a few seconds ago,' he pointed out, with more than a hint of wryness. 'May I ask what changed your mind?'

Gabby moved out of his hold, rearranging her clothing with as much dignity as was possible, considering her breasts were bare and still damp from the ministrations of his mouth.

'I don't want to sleep with you before we get married,' she said, saying the first thing that came into her mind.

'For God's sake, Gabriella, you've been married for to another man, so it's not as if you're some sweet virgin saving yourself for your wedding night.'

Gabby could hear the frustration in his voice, and felt guilty and ashamed for allowing things to go as far as they had. 'I'm sorry… I know it's hard for you…'

He gave a rough bark of laughter. '*Hard* being the operative word.'

She felt colour storm into her cheeks and bit down on her lip. 'This is not easy for me,' she said, still fumbling with her buttons. 'It's…it's been a long time since I…you know…was intimate with…with—'

He placed a finger over her lips, his eyes a steely grey. 'Let's not keep bringing your late husband into the conversation, hmm? Every time I think of you with him I want to punch something.'

She stood there, her mouth sealed with his fingertip, the desire to push her tongue out to meet it almost overwhelming.

After a tense moment his finger dropped from her lips. 'Was he your first lover?' he asked.

Gabby gave a tiny nod, mentally grimacing as she recalled the one and only time Tristan had forced himself on her. She had never thought it would be that painful—but then he had not done anything to prepare her. She had been used like a whore and left torn apart, both physically and emotionally.

'Has there been anyone since?' Vinn asked, after another short but tense silence.

She shook her head. 'No… No one…'

He wondered whether or not to believe her. She certainly hadn't grieved the way everyone had expected her to grieve. Her husband had wrapped himself around a telegraph pole on his way home from work on the night of their fifth anniversary, dying instantly—or so the coroner had found. The press had captured Gabriella numerous times in the first few weeks after Glendenning's death, carrying on as if nothing had happened. She had shopped, got her highlights and nails done, with nary a hint of sadness etched on her beautiful face. Vinn had often wondered if the rumours he had heard around town were true. Word had it she'd had numerous affairs during her marriage, and that Glendenning had chosen to turn a blind eye rather than jeopardise the alliance of the two well-to-do family empires.

'Did you love him?' Vinn asked.

'I thought you didn't want me to talk about him?' she said, with an ironic glance over her shoulder.

'It's a simple question,' he said. 'And, like most simple questions, a yes or no will suffice.'

'Why do you want to know?' she asked, turning to face him. 'It's not as if you have any feelings for me other than lust. Or are you not telling me something I should know?'

Vinn had to admire her talent for the quick comeback. She was good at getting the focus off herself. The funny thing was, he wasn't exactly sure what he felt about her. For years he had simultaneously desired and hated her. She had been such a toffee-nosed bitch to him in the past, and while he could forgive those misdemeanours on the basis of her youth at the time, he could not forgive her for the way she still looked down her nose at him now. To her he was still the house-cleaner's son—not worthy to hold a door open for her let alone touch her until she screamed his name in ecstasy as he was so determined she would do.

'That would suit you, now, wouldn't it, Gabriella?' he said. 'To get me to confess undying love for you? Sorry to disappoint you, but my feelings are much more basic. Lust is a good word. Perhaps a little coarse for someone from your rather cosseted background, but it more or less sums it up.'

She gave him a haughty glare.

He smiled as he picked up his car keys. 'You might want to rebutton your top, Blondie, before I take you back to the hospital to see your father. The last button doesn't seem to have found its correct hole.'

Gabby looked down at her shirt and felt her face fire up. She looked as dishevelled and as ravished as she felt—but, even worse, Vinn had yet again got in the last word. She felt as if he had her pride in the palm of his hand and with just one small clench of his fist he could totally destroy it. She was going to fight tooth and nail to stop that from happening, but with each kiss he subjected her to she realised she was drifting further and further out of her depth and into totally unchartered waters.

She had always thought marrying Tristan Glendenning had been the biggest mistake of her life, but she could see now that falling in love with Vinn Venadicci would more than likely surpass it in spades.

Gabby stood by Vinn's side in front of the marriage celebrant and listened to herself mechanically repeat the vows that under the circumstances were nothing short of meaningless.

Vinn's clear and deep voice, however, made them sound much more convincing, she thought. The way he spoke with such firm conviction sounded as if he did indeed love her, and would treat her with honour and respect for the rest of their lives.

She turned when the celebrant said it was time for him to kiss the bride, and, tipping up her face, closed her eyes as Vinn's mouth sealed hers with a kiss that had a hint of possessiveness about it. Each movement of his lips on hers seemed to say, *You are mine now, body and soul.* And Gabby knew if Vinn had his way that could very well be the case within a matter of hours.

Their flights had been booked for their trip to the St Clair Island Resort, and they were due to leave within just over an hour. Their luggage was already in Vinn's car, and once the marriage certificate was signed he escorted Gabby out to where it was parked on the street outside.

Gabby found it hard to think of something to say on the way to the airport. She was conscious of Vinn's muscled arm occasionally shifting gears near her thigh. He had already taken off his jacket and peeled back his shirt cuffs due to the increase in temperature. The ink-black springy hairs on his forearms made her feel a mixture of trepidation and excitement to feel his touch on her bare skin.

There would be plenty of opportunity to do so on the tropical island resort, she reminded herself, with another little quiver of nervous anticipation. She had looked at next week's weather forecast, and with temperatures in the late twenties and low thirties predicted on the island, she knew her bikini and sarong would be the most she would be wearing during the day. She didn't dare think what she would be wearing at night. If Vinn had his way she was sure she would be naked.

'How long has it been since you were last on the island?' Vinn's voice cut across her thoughts.

Gabby had to think for a moment. 'I flew up earlier in the year,' she said. 'February, I think it was. I went up to check over the new refurbishment, but I only stayed a couple of nights.'

He didn't say anything in response, but Gabby wondered if he thought she should have visited more often, to keep a closer eye on things. The new business manager he had appointed had already found a few mistakes in her records, which had increased Gabby's feelings of incompetence, although Vinn had not made a big issue of it at the time. He had simply told Mark Vella that things had been very stressful recently. with Gabriella's father's health issues, and Gabby had found herself hoping he was doing it for the sake of her feelings. But she had realised in a saner moment he had probably been playing the part of supportive fiancé again, and her feelings had not been a consideration of his at all.

She was not quite ready to admit it to Vinn, but since she had stopped going into the office she had felt as if a huge weight had been lifted off her shoulders. Even her parents had not been the least bit concerned when she had stepped down from the board. Instead they had both communicated how much they trusted Vinn's judgement in handling the business side of things while Henry was out of action.

'Anyway,' her mother had said with a coy smile, 'it won't be long before we hear the patter of tiny feet, I am sure. Right, Gabby? After all, you are getting on for thirty. You don't want to leave it too late to have children, otherwise you might miss out altogether.'

Vinn had smiled as he'd placed his arm around Gabby's waist. 'Don't worry, Pamela,' he'd said. 'We'll get working on it right away.'

Gabby had blushed to the roots of her hair, but had forced a stiff smile to her face. She had, however, given Vinn's arm a hard pinch, and sent him a reproachful glare when her parents hadn't been looking. But all he had done was wink at her, which had made her already simmering blood start to boil.

Vinn drove into the valet parking area at the airport, and within in a few minutes they were checked in and waiting to board.

Once they were on their way the flight gave Gabby the perfect opportunity to close her eyes and feign sleep. But after what seemed just a few minutes she opened her eyes to find herself leaning against Vinn's shoulder.

She straightened and blinked a couple of times. 'Sorry…I must have fallen asleep,' she said. 'I hope I didn't crease your shirt too much.'

His smile was easy and relaxed. 'No, it's fine. I enjoyed listening to you snore, actually.'

Gabby pursed her lips. 'I do not snore.'

'How would you know?' he asked with the arch of one brow. 'You haven't had a lover since your husband passed away, or so you said.'

She frowned at him. 'Don't you believe me?'

He looked at her for a lengthy moment. 'You cannot be unaware of the rumours that circulated during your marriage.'

Gabby felt her stomach drop. 'W-what rumours?'

His gaze continued to pin hers. 'Rumours about all the lovers you took.'

Gabby felt her cheeks grow warm under his piercing scrutiny. 'I find it rather ironic that you apparently take on board everything you read in the press when you insisted that the woman you were photographed with was not your mistress when everything pointed to her being so.'

'So you are saying the rumours about you were unfounded?' he asked, still looking at her unwaveringly.

Gabby wondered if she should tell him what had really gone on during her marriage. But two things stopped her. One was the fact they were sitting on a plane surrounded by other people, and the other was her pride. Vinn had been the one to warn her not to marry Tristan, and she had ignored that warning and paid for it dearly. She couldn't risk him rubbing her nose in it every chance he could. She had suffered enough. In some ways she would always suffer for that mistake. Her life had taken on a trajectory she could never have anticipated.

'I am saying you shouldn't believe every bit of gossip you hear,' she said. 'There are always two sides to every story.'

'I have heard there are three,' he said with an enigmatic smile. 'The wife's version, the husband's version, and then there's the truth.'

Gabby was relieved when the flight attendant announced they were preparing to land at that point, so she didn't have to continue the conversation. She pushed her handbag back under the seat in front and, tightening her seatbelt, looked out of the window at the azure blue of the ocean below.

Various other tourist islands were dotted around St

Clair Island, but to Gabby none of them seemed as beautiful and tranquil. She had fond memories of coming to the island as a child. She had spent so many magical days with her brother, beachcombing, making sandcastles and sand sculptures, going for walks to all the private beaches away from the main one at the front of the resort restaurant and bar area.

A wave of nostalgia came over Gabby as the plane touched down. She felt tears spring to her eyes, and had to blink rapidly to make them go away. Blair had loved the island as much as she did. Even after all this time it was still hard to imagine he would never come here again, and walk with her along the sandy shore to pick up a shell or two to add to his collection.

Vinn's hand reached for one of hers, where it was clasped tightly in her lap, his long fingers curling around her smaller ones. 'Everything all right?' he asked.

Gabby gave him a forced smile. 'Of course. It was just a bumpy landing, that's all.'

He gave her fingers an almost imperceptible squeeze. 'I miss him too, *cara*. He was a good friend,' he said softly.

Gabby's throat thickened, but she somehow managed to speak in spite of it. 'You were like a brother to him. I was so jealous of how well you got on. It seems so petty and childish now…'

'You *were* a child,' he said, releasing her fingers. 'And a rather spoilt one at that. I am not going to hold it against you.'

Gabby surreptitiously massaged her fingers where his touch had set off a tingling reaction beneath her skin, all the time wondering if what he had said was true. Wasn't that the whole point of their marriage?

Retribution.

Revenge.

Vengeance...

She gave a little involuntary shiver as the last word and its well-worn biblical phrase reverberated in her head.

Vengeance is mine...

CHAPTER EIGHT

THE resort managers, Judy and Garry Foster, gave Vinn and Gabby a warm welcome. Garry took their luggage ahead, and, after a little tour of the resort for Vinn's benefit, Judy led the way to their deluxe penthouse-style unit overlooking its own private beach.

There was a plunge pool and a spa and sauna, and an outdoor shower with twin shower heads set in a tropical garden that was totally private. The exotic fragrance of frangipani was heavy in the warm air, and each of the bright splashes of colour from the hibiscus blooms reminded Gabby of crushed silk.

'If there is anything you need, just dial one,' Judy said as she made to leave.

'Thank you, Judy,' Vinn said with an easy smile as he held the door open for her.

The door closed once Judy had left, and Gabby felt a shiver run up her spine when Vinn's grey-blue gaze sought hers.

'How about a swim to cool off?' he asked.

'Um… OK…' She turned to where her bag was, on the luggage rest beside Vinn's, her belly a nest of nerves at the thought of sharing this penthouse with him. It was very spacious, but it was also incredibly secluded.

Not only had she never shared a bed with Tristan, she hadn't even shared a bathroom with him. He had insisted on having his own—the reason for which Gabby hadn't found out until a few months before his death. She had gone in there in search of more soap for her own bathroom and had seen the telltale traces of white powder and the rolled-up twenty-dollar bill lying on the marble benchtop.

It had not been so much of a shock to find out her husband was regularly snorting cocaine. What had been the biggest surprise was how she hadn't until then guessed it. His erratic moods, his almost manic behaviour at times and his lugubriousness at others, she'd realised in retrospect, were all signs of a drug habit slipping out of control. Just like her parents' inability to accept Blair had been struggling with an addiction, Gabby had not wanted to face the fact her husband was a drug-user. Along with his numerous affairs it had remained yet another dirty secret—another lie to live with.

'I will leave you to get changed,' Vinn said from the door. 'I'm going to have a look at the gym set-up.'

Gabby clutched a bikini and sarong against her chest as she looked at him. 'Oh…right…thanks…'

The door closed on his exit, and she let out a breath that rattled all the way past her lips.

The beach outside their apartment was about two hundred metres long, before an outcrop of rocks cut it off from the next bit of shore. Gabby swam back and forth in a leisurely fashion, enjoying the feel of the water against her skin. When she opened her eyes underwater she could see thousands of colourful tropical fish darting about beneath her. The sandy bottom made the water as clear as glass, and even when she swam out further to sea the clarity was unaffected.

She was quite far out from the shore when a dark shape appeared, seemingly out of nowhere. She gave a startled gasp, her heart pounding like a jackhammer, but then she realised it was Vinn.

'You really shouldn't come out this far without someone with you,' he said, treading water in front of her. 'It could be dangerous.'

'I'm a strong swimmer,' she said, trying not to look at the water droplets clinging to his dark lashes, making them thick and spiky.

'Strength and fitness have very little to do with safety when it comes to getting cramp or being stung by a jellyfish,' he pointed out.

'You don't seem to find it a problem, being out of your depth,' she returned with spirited defiance.

He came up closer, every now and again one of his long legs brushing against hers beneath the water. 'That's because it's rare for me to be out of my depth.' His grey-blue eyes dropped to her mouth as he added, 'In any situation.'

Gabby's tongue flicked over her lips, tasting salt, and her own need clawed at her from inside with long-taloned fingers. He was too close, but she hadn't moved away—even though she had the width of the beach to do so. The brush of his thighs stirred her blood, making it rush through her veins at breakneck speed.

When his head came down she had already lifted her face to meet his, and their lips came together in a hardened press that contained the potency of frustration, urgency and deep-seated passion.

Gabby whimpered with delight when his tongue found hers, tangling with it, seducing it, and then ruthlessly subduing it. She faintly registered she was no longer keeping herself afloat; his arms were wrapped around her, holding her so close their near-naked bodies were almost as one. She felt his erection pressing with such strength and power against her that the breath was pushed right out of her lungs. Desire licked through her, long-tongued and feverish, making every nerve in her body zing with sexual energy.

Vinn lifted his mouth from hers. 'You don't know how close I am to thrusting myself into you right here and now,' he said, in a tone gravel-rough with need.

Her caramel-brown eyes flared in excitement—the same excitement he could feel in every delicious curve of her body pressed so tightly against him. She sent her tongue out to her lips, driving him wild with longing, and her smooth legs tangled with his.

'Do you think that's such a good idea, out here in the open?' she asked in a breathless voice. 'Someone might see us.'

'Right now I couldn't care less who sees us,' he said. 'But for the sake of decency perhaps we should take this indoors.'

She shivered in his arms, but not from cold. She felt warm and vibrant, and pliable with desire. It was immensely satisfying for him to feel that from her, even if so far it had only been physical, not verbal. She wanted him as much as he wanted her. And, God, did he want her. Every throbbing part of him was aching to sink into her, to feel surrounded by her honeyed flesh. He had dreamed of it for years, hating himself for his weakness where she was concerned, but knowing he would never be truly satisfied until he had taken her. It was a fever in his blood; it ran like a turbulent flood beneath his skin, a pounding river of need, desperate to burst from its confines.

He led her out of the water, his eyes drinking in the sight of her clad only in a red string bikini. Her slim limbs were golden and smooth, her beautiful breasts protesting about the tiny triangles keeping them in place, and the shadow of her cleavage making his imagination run riot.

There were so many things he wanted to do to her, he thought as he took her hand and led her towards the penthouse apartment. He wanted to kiss every secret place, brand her as his in every position possible, so she would no longer think of anyone but him when they made love. He wanted to pump himself into her, to make her swell with his seed, to stake his claim on her in the most primal way of all—as the father of her children. She would think twice about walking away from him if they shared the bond of a child—a child he would love with his whole being, sacrificing everything for it, just as his mother had done for him.

The penthouse was blessedly cool after the heat down on the beach, but Gabby still felt as if she was on fire. As Vinn closed the door she stood before him, trembling all over with anticipation. He had stoked her desire to an unbearable level. She could no more say no to him now than walk on the water they had just left. It was an inevitable outcome of their union—something they had both wanted for longer than perhaps she was prepared to acknowledge. And his longing was more than obvious.

It might not be dressed up in pretty words, such as those said to her by Tristan Glendenning to get her to marry him, but somehow Gabby suspected Vinn Venadicci was not going to be the disappointment in bed her late husband had been.

Sexual potency practically oozed from Vinn's olive-toned pores. He had no doubt bedded many women, done things to them she had never even thought of, and yet he was here with her now, tied to her, aroused by her and reaching for her.

Her bikini top was the first thing to go. Her breasts fell free, the achingly tight nipples soon soothed by the hot, moist cavern of his mouth. It was mind-blowing to feel the rough abrasion of his jaw on her tender flesh. And it was knee-buckling to feel him reach for the strings that held her bikini bottoms in place. They fell to the floor in a silent puddle of red fabric, her body totally exposed to him in a way it had never been before.

'You are beautiful,' he said, in that same roughened tone he had used down on the beach. His gaze ran over her. 'So stunningly beautiful.'

Gabby felt her breath hitch as his eyes came back to hers. 'I want to see you too.' *Was that what she had just said?* she wondered in amazement. Had she openly admitted how much she wanted him?

He held his arms up, as if in surrender. 'I'm all yours,' he said. 'I'll give you the honours.'

Gabby needed no other inducement. She reached out with fingers not quite steady and peeled back the black Lycra covering him, her throat almost closing over as she saw how he was made. He was big, far bigger than she had expected, even though she had been pressed up against him so intimately several times. He was as nature intended him—fully male and fully aroused.

Her fingers skated over him, like a light-footed dancer going through a complicated routine, taking her time, rehearsing, going back over the same part again and again to get it right.

'God, that feels so good,' he said, as he captured her hand and held it aloft. 'But I don't want to arrive ahead of schedule.'

Gabby felt her belly quiver like a not-quite-set jelly. She was not used to this extended routine. This strung-out torture of the senses, the screaming of desires begging to be fulfilled. Her body ached for him as it had never ached before. Silky fluid moistened her intimately, swelling her feminine folds with longing. Her breasts were tight and tender at the same time, and her mouth was already missing the heat and fiery conquering of his.

So she did what any aroused woman would do under the circumstances. She pressed herself up against him, her mouth taking his in a hot, wet kiss that showed him how much she wanted him.

He responded just the way she'd wanted him to. He pressed her to the bed behind her, his weight coming over her, his body piercing her in one thick urgent thrust that should not have hurt but somehow did.

Vinn felt her flinch and stilled his movements, raising himself up on his arms to look down at her. 'Am I going too fast for you?'

She gave her head a little shake. 'No…it's just been…a long time…'

Vinn hated being reminded of who had taken her first. It made his blood almost singe his veins to think of that silver-tongued creep having her night after night, pleasuring her the way *he* wanted to pleasure her. He would make her forget him. He would do everything in his power to make her forget, to have her scream his name when he took her to paradise.

'I'll slow down,' he said, pressing a soft kiss to her bow of her mouth. 'Relax for me, *cara*, go with me, don't tense up.'

He moved slowly, relishing the tight warmth of her, but still conscious of her hesitancy. He could feel it—the way her muscles locked as if she was frightened he would hurt her.

'That's it,' he soothed as she started to pick up his slow but steady rhythm. 'You're doing great, Gabriella, just great. Come with me, nice and slow.'

Gabby started to feel the slow melt of her bones. He was so gentle, and yet so powerful. She could feel the latent strength of him sliding inside her, each slow thrust going a little bit deeper. She felt the tremors begin, but they were not enough to satisfy the ache she felt so deep inside. She writhed beneath him, desperately seeking what she was looking for—something extra, something that would tip her over the edge of oblivion and make her his for all time.

He moved his hand down between their tightly

locked bodies, searching for the tight pearl where all her need seemed to be concentrated, and began a gentle but rhythmic stroking. Sensation after sensation flowed through her. She felt herself climbing a steep cliff; she was almost there, the plunge over the edge was so close she could almost taste it, but she kept pulling back, too frightened to finally let go.

'Come for me, *cara*,' Vinn said, kissing her mouth into soft malleability. 'Don't hold back. Let yourself go.'

She concentrated, trying so hard to keep those other dark images out of her mind, her breathing coming in quick sharp bursts. 'I can't…' she gasped, almost close to tears, annoyed at herself for being such a failure. 'I'm sorry… I just can't…'

He slowed his movements, giving her a break from the caressing of his fingers as if he sensed how fragile she felt. 'It's all right,' he said softly. 'We don't have to rush this. Take your time. I can hold on. Only just, mind you, but I can hold on.'

Gabby looked at him with shame colouring her cheeks. 'I can't do this…' she said. 'I've never been able to do this…'

A frown pulled at his brow, and she felt his whole body tense above and within hers. 'What are you saying, Gabriella?' he asked in a raspy tone.

Gabby pressed her lips together, hoping she wouldn't dissolve into tears, but still perilously close all the same.

'Are you saying you have *never* had an orgasm?' he asked after a moment.

She gave a small nod, silent tears making their way down her cheeks.

Vinn recalled her hesitancy, the flinching as if she had expected him to be rough with her. His heart began to pump—hard, out-of-rhythm pumps against his breastbone—as dark thoughts assembled themselves in his head.

His one short sharp curse cut through the air like a switchblade. 'Did that bastard hurt you?' he asked.

She didn't answer, but he saw all he needed to know in the wounded caramel-brown of her eyes, in the way her bottom lip trembled ever so slightly. His gut clenched, tight fists of anguish punching at his insides, making him see red dots of rage behind his eyes.

He moved away from her as gently as he could. 'I'm sorry, Gabriella,' he said huskily. 'I would never have taken things this far and this soon if I had known.'

She reached out a soft hand and touched him on the arm. 'It's all right, Vinn,' she said. 'I want to know what it's like. I want you to pleasure me. I was so close… I'm sure I can do it…with you…'

Vinn wavered for a moment. His mind was all over the place. She had been married for five years and apparently not once experienced the ultimate pleasure of physical union. What was he to make of that? He'd already suspected she hadn't loved Glendenning, but she had responded to *him* without restraint. He didn't want to think too much about that. He wasn't prepared to examine his own feelings, much less hers.

'I don't want to hurt you,' he found himself saying, even as his body sought the silky warmth of hers, sliding back in with a shiver of goosebumps lifting the entire surface of his skin as he felt her accept him smoothly. 'Tell me how fast, how slow, what you need.'

She gripped his buttocks tightly in her hands. 'I just need you,' she said. 'No one has ever made me feel like this before.'

She gave a breathy sigh as he began to move, slowly building up the tempo, caressing her, testing how much or how little she needed, gauging her reaction by feeling the pulse of her body and watching the flitting emotions on her face.

He knew when she was coming close. He could feel it in her body, wrapped so tightly around his, and he could see it in the contortion of her features, in the agony and the ecstasy played out on her face. He felt the first ripple course through her, heard her startled cry, and then the aftershocks as wave after wave consumed her, tossing her about in his arms, triggering his own response with a force that was beyond anything he had ever experienced. He felt himself spill, and that delicious moment or two of nothing but intense pleasure. Shockwaves reverberated through him, inducing a lassitude that made him slump over her almost helplessly, like a bit of flotsam tossed up by a very rough surf to the sandy shore.

When he finally had the energy to lift himself above her, Vinn saw that she was crying. Not noisy sobs, just silent tears that tore at him like nothing else could.

He brushed the hair back from her face, his thumb lingering over the soft swell of her bottom lip that her perfect white teeth seemed so determined to savage. 'You were amazing,' he said. 'Truly amazing.'

Her eyes couldn't quite make the full distance to his. 'I didn't realise how…how intense it could be…'

He pressed a soft kiss to her brow. 'It gets better when

you know what your body needs. I am still learning about yours—how it responds, what it wants, what it doesn't like, how soft, how hard, that sort of thing.'

She looked at him with an open vulnerability he had never seen in her gaze before—or at least not to that extent. 'Did I pleasure you?'

He frowned as he saw the deep-seated insecurity in her gaze. 'How can you doubt it, *cara*?'

She began to finger the scar that slashed his left eyebrow in two. 'I've always felt such a failure... physically,' she said, her voice so soft he had to strain his ears to hear it. 'Tristan never touched me during our engagement...apart from kissing and holding hands. He told me he wanted to wait until we were married...' She took a deep breath and added, 'I didn't realise he was having affairs. They went on for most of our marriage.'

Vinn frowned as he absorbed the information. Somehow he had thought Gabriella had turned a blind eye to Glendenning's affairs for the sake of the prestige of being his wife. Had he got it wrong?

'When did you find out about it?' he asked.

Her eyes moved out of reach of his. 'Just after our wedding. I found him in a rather...er...compromising situation.'

His gut tightened. 'How compromising?'

Her cheeks were cherry-red, her voice unsteady, and still her eyes would not meet his. 'He was being...' She winced as if she didn't like using the word. 'Serviced by his secretary...'

Vinn let out another curse as he got off the bed. He whipped a towel around his waist and began to pace.

'For God's sake, Gabriella, why the hell didn't you tell anyone? The marriage could have been annulled. Even then it wouldn't have been too late.'

She swallowed tightly, her eyes glistening with tears. 'My parents had been through so much,' she said. 'I didn't want to cause another scandal. I could just imagine the scene. Mum was so proud of the wedding—how she had dragged herself out of her depression and come off the tranquilisers. How could I do that to her? They had already been through so much. I just couldn't do it.'

Vinn frowned. 'I swear to God if I had been there I would have stopped it. But you made sure I wasn't there, didn't you?'

She bit her lip. 'I didn't want a scene, Vinn,' she said. 'I didn't want Mum and Dad upset.'

His top lip curled. 'Didn't your husband tell you he was the one who gave me this?' He pointed to the slash of the scar on his eyebrow.

She went white, her mouth dropping open. 'No… *No*…'

'He got his thugs to hold me down—all three of them,' he said, bitterness heavy in his tone. 'And then he shoved the heel of his shoe on my face, telling me it was a gift from you.'

CHAPTER NINE

GABBY thought she was going to faint. In fact she felt as if the vicious assault Vinn had just described had hit *her* full in the face.

She flinched away, her shocked gasp tearing at the dry ache in her throat. She couldn't speak, no matter how hard she tried; the words were stuck behind that boulder-sized restriction in her throat. Vinn had been brutally assaulted, and for all this time he had thought *she* had orchestrated it. Yes, she had spoken to her father's security head Tony Malvern on the phone, asking him to not admit Vinn Venadicci into the church the following day. But she had not told him to use any sort of violence. Besides, Tony was not that sort of man. He was a loving husband and father—a bit tough on the outside, but never would she believe him capable of being party to such a cowardly and vicious attack on another person. All Gabby had done was to tell him to inform Vinn he wasn't welcome to attend the ceremony in case he took it upon himself to disrupt it, as he had threatened.

'N-no… *No!*' Gabby cried. 'I didn't ask anyone to

hurt you! You have to believe me, Vinn. Why would I do such a thing?'

His eyes were diamond-hard, the cast to his features as if carved from granite. 'You resented me from the moment I walked through the gates of your family estate. You looked down your nose at me with increasing disdain as the years went on. Don't you remember how much you enjoyed taunting me, Gabriella? Setting me up just so you could giggle behind the bushes with your empty-headed friends?'

Gabby could feel her shame in the slow burn of her cheeks. 'I know I was a bitch towards you,' she said. 'I've explained it already…how I was jealous of you cutting in on my relationship with Blair. He had no time for me whenever you were around.'

'You didn't seem to mind his relationship with other people,' he commented. 'Your late husband being a case in point.'

'That was different,' she said. 'Blair and Tristan had been at school together. Also, Tristan was my mother's best friend's son. He had been coming to our house even before I was born. I was used to sharing my brother with him. It was all I knew.'

His eyes were still trained on hers—hard, unreachable, and unrelentingly angry. 'Do you deny you asked Glendenning to keep me away from the wedding?' he asked.

Gabby compressed her lips, releasing them after a moment. 'Of course I deny it. I admit I spoke to Tony Malvern, my father's chief of security, but only to ask him to refuse you entry to the church. But I never said a word to Tristan about it.'

Vinn studied her for several tense moments, weighing up whether or not to believe her. Although Tony Malvern no longer worked for Henry St Clair, since taking early retirement due to a chronic health condition, Vinn had never found him to be anything other than a hard-working and decent family man, who was paid to keep an eye on the various St Clair's business properties after hours.

'Did anyone overhear your conversation with Tony?' he asked.

She gave him a flustered look. 'I don't know… I was upset. I wasn't looking around corners to see if anyone was listening.'

'No doubt your husband was.'

Her frown deepened. 'You went out drinking,' she said. 'That's what I was told when I got back from my honeymoon. They told me you got drunk, and then got into some sort of brawl and ended up in hospital. But if you were assaulted as you said by those thugs, including Tristan, why didn't you press charges?'

'And drag your parents through a very public scandal, with their beloved daughter at the centre of it?' he asked with a sardonic lift of one brow. 'I might be a bit rough for your tastes, Gabriella, but I am not without feeling or a sense of honour.'

Gabby dropped her shoulders, her thoughts in turmoil. He had hated her for all these years for what she had supposedly done, and yet he had protected her family and therefore her as well. He had not once spoken of it to her parents, of that she was sure. Instead his anger towards her had quietly simmered in the background, as he'd waited patiently for the chance to have his revenge. By going to him for financial help that day she had unwittingly handed him one on a platter.

She brought her gaze back to his hardened one. 'That's what this marriage you've forced on me is all about, isn't it?' she said. 'You wanted to make me pay for the attack you think I ordered by locking me into a loveless marriage with you?'

His expression was unapologetic. 'I told you my reasons for wanting this marriage to take place,' he said in a gritty tone.

'Oh, yes,' she threw at him resentfully. 'You've been lusting after me for years and you just couldn't wait to get your hands on me.'

His eyes burned into hers, with a satirical glint lighting them from behind. 'I didn't hear you saying no just a little while ago,' he said. 'In fact I seem to recall you *begging* me to make love to you.'

Gabby swung away from him in fury, unable to bear his mockery of her desperate need of him. As angry as she was, she still felt the thrumming pulse of blood in her veins, the heady awareness of him and how he had made her feel. Her body was still damp from him. If it wasn't for the fact she was on the pill to regulate her cycle she might have even conceived the child he had bought and paid her to bear for him.

The thought of her belly ripe with his seed made her knees weaken unexpectedly. He might not have married her for the right reasons, but she had no doubt he would make a wonderful father. He had loved his mother more than any other son she had ever known, putting his own life on hold to nurse her through the last months of her too-short and too-hard life.

'Nothing to say, Gabriella?' he asked. 'No feisty comeback to insult me or put me in my place?'

Gabby let out a rattling breath and faced him. 'I'm sorry, Vinn, for what happened to you that night,' she said, taking her pride in hand. 'I know you don't believe me…might never believe me…but I had nothing to do with it. Tristan may have overheard my conversation with Tony, but even if he didn't he had good enough reason to stop you from coming to the wedding.'

'What was that?' he asked, holding her gaze with steely intent.

Gabby chewed at her lip, her eyes falling away from his. 'I'm not sure if he saw us kissing that night… I've often wondered…'

'He was jealous that you responded to me in a way he could never get you to respond to him,' he said. 'I don't blame him. I have revisited that kiss a thousand times in my head, and no one has come close to making me feel the way I did with your mouth on mine.'

Gabby felt warmth flow through her at his words. It was like warmed honey flowing through her veins. He had revisited that kiss so many times—as she had done over the years. What would he say if she were to tell him how often she had thought of how she had responded to him that night? How alive her senses had been, as if he had flicked a switch on in her body no one else had access to?

She had been attracted to him for so long but had stoically denied it.

She had always been in love with him, but too terrified to admit it.

Once the admission was out, Gabby felt it rush

through her like the cleansing tide of saline in grit-filled eyes.

She was in love with him.

She had felt that tug of attraction from the moment her female hormones had switched on in her youthful body. She had somehow recognised him as her match, the one person who could meet her needs, but she had pushed him away out of fear, out of insecurity, and out of misplaced pride.

Would her parents have really objected if she had told them all those years ago she loved Vinn instead of Tristan? They had lately accepted the news of her hasty marriage to Vinn without a ripple of disapproval. Even her mother, who had been so toffee-nosed towards him and his mother in the past, had practically wept as she had welcomed him into the bosom of the St Clair family…or what was left of it, Gabby thought with a painful ache, as a vision of her brother flitted into her brain.

Blair had adored Vinn. They had been mates from the word go—comrades, confidantes, all the things good friends should be.

And yet Blair had ended his life…

While his best friend was several thousand kilometres away, nursing his mother on her deathbed, Gabby realised with a stun-gun jolt of awareness.

'Is something wrong?' Vinn's voice sliced through her reverie. 'You look pale.'

'I'm fine…' she said, mentally shaking her head to get her thoughts into some sort of order. 'I'm just thinking…trying to make sense of it all…'

'What happened back then doesn't have to affect us

now,' he said. 'If you say you had nothing to do with the assault, then I will have to accept that.'

She looked at him again, swallowing against the lump of uncertainty in her throat. 'How can you ever know for sure I wasn't behind it? You don't trust me; you have no reason to trust me.'

He leaned back against the wall, his arms folded across his broad chest, his eyes still holding hers. 'As long as I am certain you were not party to it, I will be happy,' he said. 'I would not like our future children to think that at one point their mother was intent on bringing about my demise.'

Gabby felt her knees give another distinctive wobble. 'You seem in rather a hurry to land yourself an heir,' she said. 'What if I prove to be infertile?'

'Have you any reason to suspect you might be?'

'Have you any intention of releasing me from this arrangement if I am?' she countered.

His grey-blue eyes tussled with hers, bringing hers down in a submission she resented but couldn't for the life of her control. 'No,' he said. 'If you can't give me an heir naturally, then we will pursue the other options available.'

'What if I don't want to have a child right now?' Gabby asked, and then, after a carefully timed interval, added, 'What if I don't want to have children at all?'

The silence that ensued grew teeth that seemed to gnaw at the space that separated them.

'Do you have a particular aversion to motherhood?' he finally asked.

'Not really…' She waited a moment before continuing, 'I guess what I have an aversion to is being forced to deliver according to someone else's schedule, not mine.'

'Having a child should ideally be a joint decision,' he said, still honing in on her with those unreadable grey-blue eyes of his. 'If you are not ready, then we will wait until you are.'

'You don't even like me,' she said, frowning at him in irritation. 'How can you possibly think of fathering a child with me?'

His eyes ran over her sheet-wrapped form in one sweeping, all-encompassing movement that had possession and arrogant control written all over it. 'Because I have always wanted you, Gabriella,' he said. 'You are my nemesis, my other half, my completion. It was confirmed when we came together physically. I always knew it would be like that between us. I just had to wait until you were willing to see it.'

Gabby felt the need to keep some level of distance. 'What if Tristan hadn't died?' she asked. 'Would you have continued with this vendetta?'

He raised one broad shoulder in shrug. 'That would have entirely depended on you,' he said. 'I was testing the waters the night before your wedding. I was convinced you were no more in love with Glendenning than he was with you, and it seems I was right. No woman in love with another man would have responded the way you did to me.'

'So…kissing me was some sort of experiment?' Gabby asked, with reproach heavy in her tone.

'Kissing you was a temptation I could not resist,' he responded, stepping towards her, holding her in place with his hands on the tops of her shoulders. 'Like it is now, *cara*. I want to feel the tremble of your lips beneath mine, the way your tongue so shyly meets mine. I want it all, Gabriella. I want all of you.'

Gabby would have pushed him away, but he had already brought her too close to the tempting heat of his near-naked body. With only a towel loosely slung about his hips, she was left in no doubt of his arousal. Her body was just as eager behind its flimsy shroud of a sheet. Her nipples were clearly outlined, pert and aching for his touch, and her body was swaying towards him. Her mouth opened just as his was lowering to commandeer hers.

The kiss was like two combustible fuels meeting. Explosions went off in her brain, sending a fiery trail through her veins, making every nerve stand to attention. Her tongue snaked out to meet his in a sexy tangle of duelling need. Hers was igniting slowly but surely; his was at the ready, urgent, pressing, and totally, intoxicatingly, irresistibly male.

'You know I want you again, don't you?' he murmured against her mouth, as his hands skated so very skilfully over her, removing the sheet as if it was a layer of tissue wrap.

Gabby's hands had already dispensed with his towel, and were now shaping him, relishing in the tilted engorgement of him that so matched her body's intimately designed contours.

'I want you too,' she said, pressing kiss after kiss to his mouth. 'I want to feel it all again. Make me feel it all again.'

Vinn didn't need her to beg or plead. He wanted it as much as she did—the magic, the mindlessness of it, the total exhilaration of the senses that shoved aside every other rational thought. He didn't want to think just now. He wanted to feel. He had unlocked in her a treasure chest of sensuous pleasures, and he wanted to lay each and every precious piece out for his indulgence. The way she shivered when his hands touched her in the lightest of touches. The way her eyes flared when he looked at her with unwavering desire. The way her mouth softened, as if preparing for the hard descent of his, her lips parting to accept the searching thrust of his tongue.

God, had any woman done this to him in the past? With her he seemed to be always fighting for control, holding back the urge to spill, his need so great he had trouble reining it in to ensure she was not rushed, not hurt the way she had been in the past.

'Vinn?' Her soft voice was against his neck, her lips brushing his flesh.

He stroked the back of her head, his fingers splayed to feel the silky softness of her hair, to anchor him to her, to keep her where she was—close, so very close, so he could feel every beat of her heart.

'Don't talk, *mia piccola*,' he said, cupping her face to look deep into her eyes. 'Just feel.'

Gabby's eyelashes fluttered closed as his mouth came down to reclaim hers, the intimate contact so consuming she felt her mind spinning out of control. His kisses were so drugging they made her forget the past. They made her think only of the here and now, of how he made her feel, of how her body responded to him, of how it came alive in a way it had never done before. She could feel the echo of his kiss resounding in the rest of her body. It made her aching need for him all the more intense. It throbbed in her belly, low and deep, it swelled in her breasts, making them eager for his touch, and it trembled in her fingertips as she continued to explore him.

His hand pulled hers away from his hardened body, holding it above her head as he ravaged her mouth with his lips and tongue. Gabby laid her head back against the wall as he subjected her to a conflagration of the senses, her heart pounding inside her chest, her legs barely able to keep her upright.

He lifted his mouth off hers long enough to guide her back to the bed, his hands shaping her breasts, his mouth bestowing hot, sucking kisses to each one until she was twisting and turning beneath him as he pinned her with his weight.

'I have thought of doing this to you for so long,' he groaned against her right breast. 'I don't think there is a man alive who has wanted a woman more than I have wanted you.'

Gabby knew his attraction for her was only physical. He had said nothing of other feelings. At least he wasn't lying to her, as Tristan had done, but still she felt achingly disappointed her love for him was not returned. Was she destined to be tied to men who wanted to exploit her? Was she never to feel loved for who and what she was? She longed for security, for the warm protection of a love that would not die in spite of the passage of years. And yet into this loveless arrangement Vinn wanted to bring children—their children—a mingling of their blood and DNA. How could she agree to such a scheme without the assurance that he felt something for her other than lust?

'Vinn?' she said, touching his face with the flat of her palm, her fingers splaying over his stubbly jaw before she could stop them.

He turned his head and pressed a kiss into the centre of her palm. 'Do we have to talk right now, *cara?*' he asked, his eyes heavy-lidded with banked-down desire.

'Do you still hate me?'

His grey-blue eyes opened fully, and then focussed on hers. 'No,' he said on an expelled breath. 'Hate is not what I feel for you.'

Gabby drew in a ragged breath and held it. 'You…you don't?'

His eyes were unwavering on hers. 'I would not be here now, doing this to you, if I hated you, Gabriella,' he said.

'But you don't love me,' she said. And, waiting a beat, added, 'Do you?'

The distance between his brows narrowed slightly. 'That seems to me to be a rather loaded question,' he mused. 'Is that a prerequisite for allowing me access to your body? Showering you with empty words and phrases just so I can have my physical needs met?'

Gabby felt a stirring of resentment at his words. 'I am not entirely disconnected from my feelings, and I don't believe you are either,' she said. 'You make love to me as if you worship every inch of the space I take up, and yet you won't admit a modicum of affection for me. How am I supposed to make sense of it all?'

He eased himself up on his elbows, his weight still pinning her, pelvis to pelvis, stomach to stomach. 'Do you want me to tell you I love you?' he asked. 'Is that it? Is that what you want? For me to pretend to have feelings for you?'

Gabby blinked back tears. 'No, I don't want you to pretend to love me,' she said, trying to keep her voice steady. 'That's not what I want at all.' *I want you to love me for real.*

'Why is what I feel or don't feel suddenly so important to you?' he asked.

She frowned at the harshness of his tone. 'Because almost every woman wants to be assured the man she is involved with is not just using her physically. It's so degrading, so emotionless and…and dehumanising.'

He lifted himself off her, the sudden rush of cooler air on her chest and stomach making her feel not just physically abandoned, but emotionally as well.

She watched as he reached for the towel she had peeled off him just moments ago, wrapping it around himself almost savagely.

Anger flickered in his grey-blue eyes, and his body was whipcord tense as he faced her. 'Is that what you think I am doing?' he asked. 'Slaking my lust with no regard whatsoever for who you are and what you might need? Didn't the last half-hour prove *anything* to you about who I am as a person?'

Gabby pressed her lips together to keep them from trembling. 'You married me to possess me,' she said. 'I am the highly prized trophy you missed out on in the past. You know I would not have married you for any other reason than money, so you swooped as soon as the opportunity arose.'

'I am not denying I have wanted you for a very long time,' he clipped back. 'But don't let's confuse the issue with pretending things we don't feel. You have looked down your nose at me for as long as I can remember. Sure, we just had great sex—better even than I thought it would be—but that doesn't mean either of us has to pretend things we don't feel in order to feel better about the level of desire we just experienced and will no doubt continue to experience.'

Gabby pulled the sheet up to her chin. 'I don't think you would admit to loving someone even if you did,' she said. 'You wouldn't want to let anyone, particularly a woman, get the upper hand—and certainly not me.'

He gave a mocking laugh that chilled her blood. 'Is that what you think? That I've been pining away all these years with unrequited love for you, but I won't admit it in case you get the chance to use it against me in some way?'

Gabby didn't know what to think. She was confused, so very confused, and suddenly feeling more vulnerable than she wanted to be. She was making a fool of herself. She knew it, and it made her feel all the more exposed. She was practically begging him to confess feelings for her he clearly didn't have and never had. She was a fool, a romantic fool, crying for a moon that was never going to rise on her horizon.

She curled up in a tight ball on the bed, dragging the rest of the sheet over her to cover herself. 'I would like to be left alone,' she said in a toneless voice.

Vinn hesitated. He didn't really want to leave her like this, she was upset and very probably close to tears, but he just couldn't stay.

The first heady rush of love he had felt for her when she was younger had very quickly been replaced by a deep loathing for all she represented. The way she had always carried herself with that cold air of condescension, ridiculing him at every opportunity, had fuelled that hatred to boiling point. But now her adamant denial of having anything to do with his assault had made him rethink everything.

Revenge had been at the forefront of his mind for so long he needed time to re-examine his feelings. Up until a few hours ago she had hated him with an intensity that had glittered in her brown eyes every single time they clashed with his. Yet she had fallen apart in his arms, her body responding to his in a whirlwind of passion. There could be many reasons for that, he thought cynically. Two point four million of them, for starters. Anyway, she hadn't come right out and said it. She had just hinted at having feelings for him. But what if it was his wealth she was really in love with?

OK, he had saved her skin and given her a taste of what her late husband had denied her. Women were funny like that; one earth-shattering orgasm and suddenly they were madly in love with you. How many times had he heard other women say it to him, only to move on when the first wave of lust died down?

Vinn dragged on his bathers. 'I'm going for another swim,' he said. 'I guess I'll see you later.'

There was a muffled sound from beneath the tightly wrapped sheet that sounded as if she didn't care either way—which was probably no more than he deserved, Vinn thought as he softly shut the door as he left.

CHAPTER TEN

GABBY woke to semi-darkness and to a feeling that someone was in the room with her. She pushed herself upright, brushing the hair out of her eyes as she saw the shadow of Vinn's figure sitting on a chair close to the bed.

'What time is it?' she asked, trying for a cool, calm and collected tone, even though it was far from what she felt.

'Just gone nine.'

'Oh…'

'We can still have dinner in the restaurant, or order in some room service—whichever you prefer,' he said, rising to his feet and stretching.

Gabby wondered how long he had been sitting there, silently watching her. 'I need a shower,' she said. 'Do you think the restaurant will stay open long enough for me to freshen up?'

He switched on the master switch, which activated all the lamps in the suite. 'You are part-owner of this resort, Gabriella,' he reminded her. 'If you want the restaurant to remain open for you, then you only have to issue the command.'

Gabby held the sheet she had gathered around

herself up close to her chin. 'Don't mock me, Vinn,' she said. 'Please…not after this afternoon.'

'Is that what you think I'm doing?' he asked, frowning.

She gave him a surly glance. 'Look, I know I haven't got the best business head in the world, but at least I've tried my best to fill the gap my brother left.'

'Is that why you put your hand up for the job?' he asked. 'To fill in for Blair? Even though it was never what you wanted to do?'

Gabby tightened the sheet around her body rather than meet his eyes. 'We do what we do,' she said stiffly. 'There's no turning back.'

'What is that supposed to mean?'

She faced him squarely. 'My parents depend on me, Vinn,' she said. 'Do you think for a moment I would have come of my own volition to see you about the margin call? I only did it for them. I am only here now for them. I am all they have left.'

'So you sacrificed yourself?'

She lifted one shoulder. 'Your words, not mine.'

'But that's how you see it, isn't it?' he asked in an accusing tone. 'You, the Princess, have agreed to marry the peasant to save your family from financial shame.'

Gabby flinched at the weight of bitterness in his tone. 'I don't see you as a peasant, Vinn,' she said. 'I have never thought of you that way.'

His top lip curled. 'Nice try, Blondie. You nearly had me there. You sound so convincing, but we both know you will always see me as the cleaner's son. You married down, sweetheart, *way* down. How does it feel?'

Gabby held his fiery look for a beat or two before

slowly lowering her gaze. 'It certainly feels a whole lot better than my previous marriage,' she said, and then, meeting his eyes once more, added, 'That is unless you are going to add to your repertoire of accusing me of being a bitchy snob with the occasional slap or punch to bring me to heel.'

The silence began to pulse, each drawn out beat increasing the tension to snapping point.

Vinn stared at her, his eyes twin pools of stormy grey and blue. 'You mean to tell me that…he *hit* you?'

She nodded grimly. 'Not all the time, but often enough to keep me terrified he would do it again. It was a power thing. I wasn't the woman he really wanted. His parents would never have accepted any of the women he was having affairs with, so he used me as a punching bag now and again to keep me in line. I soon learned to keep my head down.'

Vinn's stomach churned. His hands felt numb even though he was clenching and unclenching them. 'Why didn't you say something?' he asked. 'For God's sake, Gabriella, you took years of that from him?'

She hugged her arms across her chest. 'I wanted to tell so many times,' she said. 'But I would have hurt people. My parents adored Tristan—he was like a second son to them. He had been so good when Blair died—he'd helped organise the funeral, and he even gave the eulogy.' She released a breathy sigh and continued. 'And then there were his parents—his well-connected parents, with a legal pedigree longer than your arm. Appearances are everything to them. How do you think they would have reacted to a spousal abuse claim against their beloved son lodged by me?'

Vinn swallowed tightly. He could see she had been in an impossible situation. The legal powerhouse the Glendenning family represented would have made anyone think twice about coming forward with such a claim against one of their blue-blooded heirs. She had gone through a living hell, each day a torture of being tied to a man who had treated her appallingly. Glendenning had even used her as a shield, making Vinn believe for all these years she was responsible for the attack on him the night before the wedding.

'I'm sorry,' Vinn said through a throat that felt as if he had swallowed a handful of razorblades. 'I wish I had known what had been going on. I wish you had felt you could have turned to me for help.'

'You were the last person I could turn to, Vinn,' she said, giving him a despondent look. 'You tried to warn me about Tristan and out of stubborn pride I refused to listen. Then, when I realised what a stupid mistake I'd made, I didn't want to hear you say *I told you so*. I just couldn't bear it.'

He scraped one of his hands down his face. 'Everyone is entitled to make a few mistakes in life,' he said. 'God knows I've made plenty. But thanks to the support and direction of people like your father I have been able to turn things around.'

'Some things can never be turned around,' she said blowing out a sigh. 'After Blair's suicide I felt so guilty… I felt like I had to do something to bring my mother out of her deep depression. My father threw himself into his work, but Mum had nothing…just me. I wanted to give her a new focus—a wedding, grandchildren in the future, that sort of thing. But I didn't stop to examine how I really felt about Tristan, or—even more stupid of me—how he felt about me.'

Vinn took one of her hands and brought it up to his mouth, pressing his lips softly to the back of her knuckles. '*Cara,* don't punish yourself any more,' he said gently. 'You were in no way responsible for your brother's death. He had an addiction problem. He didn't get the help he needed. There was nothing you could have done.'

Vinn's words were like an arrow in Gabby's heart. She would always feel there was something she should have done. That was the pain she had to live with—the regret that she hadn't seen what was right under her nose.

Vinn brushed his lips over her fingers again. 'We all wish many things, Gabriella,' he said. 'Things we would have done differently if we knew then what we know now.'

Gabby felt her breathing start to shorten. 'Does that mean you want to end our marriage?' she asked.

He looked down at her for a long moment. 'Is that what you would like?' he finally asked. 'To be free?'

She couldn't hold his intense gaze, for she was sure he would see the longing and desperation reflected in hers. 'I'm not sure what the press will make of it if we end our marriage on the very day it was formalised,' she said. 'Then, of course, there are my parents to consider.'

'I was thinking the very same thing,' he said in a sombre tone. 'Your father has been through major surgery and is still a long way from being in reliable health. We can hardly fly back to Sydney and announce our separation.'

Gabby brought her eyes back to his, craning her

neck to do so. 'So…' she said, moistening her lips with the tip of her tongue. 'What do you suggest we do?'

He gave her another long, studied look. 'I told you the day you came to see me about the margin call that I believed marriage to be a permanent commitment. That has not changed.'

Gabby searched his features, hoping, praying for some clue to how he felt about her. But his expression was unfathomable. She began to toy with the idea of telling him she had fallen in love with him—openly this time, instead of hinting at it as she had done earlier. She even went as far as having the words mentally rehearsed; she could see them inside her head in capital letters: I LOVE YOU.

But something stopped her. He was still coming to terms with all he had learned about her this evening. The dark secret she had kept hidden for so long was finally out, which she could see had not only shocked him but had summoned his pity. She didn't want his pity. She wanted his love and his respect. But it would take more time to secure the latter, and the former she had no control over whatsoever.

All she knew was that he desired her, and had done for as long as she could remember. She had treated his attraction for her with disdain in the past, rejecting him in order to marry a man who had not only exploited her in the worst way possible, but orchestrated a vicious attack on Vinn that had left a lifelong scar— and not just the one on his eyebrow.

Gabby loved Vinn for who he was now just as much as she loved him for who he had been before. He had tried to rescue her from a disastrous marriage. He had done the responsible thing by coming to her as soon as he possibly could and asking her to reconsider. He had even offered himself as a substitute groom to save her pride on the day, and yet she had been too proud to listen.

Gabby thought back to that moment when Vinn's mouth had been sealed to hers. The flames of mutual desire had leapt between their bodies like an out-of-control forest fire, with every sense of hers tuned into his and his into hers, as if they had been programmed from birth to respond to each other in that heady, earth-shattering way.

Had Tristan come up the stairs just at that moment and seen them locked in such a passionate embrace? Or had he been lurking about in the shadows even earlier? Perhaps overhearing the start of Vinn's warning? Not wanting to allow Vinn the chance to besmirch him any further, he had come up in that charming, laid-back way of his and lured Vinn away from the house with a request for a private man-to-man chat that had led to Vinn spending a night in hospital, with no hope of bringing a halt to her marriage from hell?

'Gabriella?' Vinn's voice brought her thoughts back to the present moment. 'You've gone very quiet. Do you not agree we should keep our marriage as it is? For the time being at least?'

Gabby tried to smile, but it contorted her mouth, giving it an unnatural feel. 'I still can't work out why you wanted to marry me in the first place. It seems to me you have paid a heck of a lot of money for a bride who doesn't quite fit the bill of what you were expecting.' She gave him a rueful look. 'You've been short-changed, Vinn, and yet you don't seem to be the least bit annoyed about it.'

This time he took both of her hands in his, squeezing them gently. 'If I am annoyed about anything it is about my own ignorance of your circumstances.'

'It is not your fault,' Gabby said, looking up at him. 'You did the right thing by coming to me, but I was too proud to heed your advice.'

Should she tell Vinn of Tristan's cocaine addiction? Gabby wondered. The thought danced in her mind on tentative feet, like a ballerina on damaged toes, trying to convince the judges at an important audition she was worthy of the role. Every step of the process hurt unbearably, with pain and shame, and also the niggling fear that Gabby might have been partly to blame for Tristan going to such desperate measures. There had been no sign of drug use before their ill-fated marriage, but that didn't mean it hadn't been going on.

'Vinn…' she began. 'Did you know Tristan had a cocaine habit?'

'When did *that* start?' he asked, frowning heavily. 'Before or during your marriage?'

'I'm not sure,' she answered. 'I had never noticed anything untoward before, but then I didn't know he was having affairs either—so who am I to be certain one way or the other?'

'Have you considered Tristan might have been the one to get Blair involved in drugs?' he asked. 'That Tristan was perhaps his supplier?'

Gabby felt her heart slip sideways in her chest. 'Oh no…'

Vinn's expression was grim. 'You were a pawn in his game, *cara*. I am sure of it. He had to use you as a screen to keep things on the level. Especially after Blair died.'

It all made sense now Gabby thought about it. Tristan had intensified his attentions not long after her brother's suicide, insisting on their marriage even though she had been having doubts for months.

'Did you ever consider speaking to my parents the night before the wedding?' she asked.

He closed his eyes for a nanosecond. 'Yes,' he said, scoring a pathway through his hair. 'I did consider it, and I have tortured myself ever since that I didn't seek a private audience with them first. But I guess I felt at the time it was better to start with you, to somehow get you to see the mistake you were making before I approached them. After all, it was your decision. You claimed to be in love with Glendenning, and even though I doubted it I had no way of proving it either way. Other than that kiss.'

That kiss.

The kiss he had revisited so many times, Gabby thought with a delicate flutter of her insides. She looked at his mouth, at the sensual contours of it, the full lower lip her teeth longed to nibble at and her tongue longed to salve with soft moist sweeps and strokes, until he took control in that masterful but spine-loosening, gentle way of his.

His head came down and the kiss became real, exhilaratingly real, as their tongues mated, their lips suddenly hot and wet with mutual need. Gabby pressed herself closer to the turgid heat of his body, her arms going around his waist, then lower. She dug her fingers into the tautness of his buttocks to bring him up against the increasingly urgent pulse of her body.

'It's too soon,' Vinn groaned against her mouth.

'For you?' Gabby asked in mild surprise, nibbling at his lower lip, her lower body rubbing against his rock-hard erection.

'God, no.' He gave a little laugh and nibbled back. 'For you, *cara*. You will be tender inside. You were practically a virgin. You are so small, and I am—'

'So big—and I want you now,' Gabby said with a boldness she had never known she possessed. 'Right now.'

His eyes glittered with need. 'Are you sure?' he asked, stroking the side of her face with one tender hand. 'I can pleasure you instead. There are other ways of releasing the tension without hurting you.'

Gabby felt her heart swell at his concern for her. Didn't that prove he loved her? Why wouldn't he admit it? Did he think she would use it against him? Oh, how much she adored him! Why had she spurned and ridiculed him all those years ago?

'Vinn…' she said, summoning up the courage to tell him how she felt. 'There's something I want to tell you…'

Vinn kissed the side of her mouth, working slowly but steadily towards its throbbing centre. 'You have this rather endearing but no less annoying tendency to want to talk when I want you to feel,' he said. 'What could be more important right now than feeling this…?' He kissed her deeply, and then after a few breathless seconds moved his mouth to the side of her neck, making the sensitive skin there and all over her body lift in a prickly pelt of goosebumps. 'And this…?'

Gabby had no verbal answer. Everything she wanted to say, her body said for her. She squirmed with desire in his arms, desperate to feel his electrifying touch on every part of her. Her breasts swelled with need, her nipples hard as pebbles, aching for the sweep of his tongue or the primal scrape of his teeth to soothe their ache. She pushed herself against him brazenly, throwing her head back, her insides clenching and cramping simultaneously with the anticipation of assuagement.

Vinn's mouth was on her collarbone, his tongue laving a pathway over its fragile scaffold to the sensual flesh of her breasts which he had uncovered. They seemed to swell in his hands, the softness of them like silk and cream, and the tight points of her nipples drew his mouth like a magnet, each stroke of his tongue evoking another sweet gasp of surprise and delight from her lips. She was so keen, and yet he was so hesitant. He didn't want to hurt her. And he *would* hurt her if he drove in without careful regard to her lack of experience.

He eased back, trying to control his breathing, trying to control the thundering roar of the blood in his veins, but her shy fingers searched for him and found him, the work of her fingertips sending arrows of sharp need from his groin to his toes and back, leaving him breathless and out of reach of common sense. He wanted to feel her mouth on him, the wetness and velvet softness of it taking him in, her tongue playing with him, teasing him until he exploded.

He clamped his eyes shut as his dream came alive. She was doing it by the script he had formed in his head. She was shaping him with her hands, discovering his hard length, exploring the detail of it, the moist tip of his need, the stickiness of his essence, banked up and waiting to be summoned by the honeyed grip of her body or the lick or slide of her tongue.

His back arched as he felt her soft, moist mouth close over him, and the shyness of it was part of the overwhelming allure. She didn't know what she was doing, but she was going on instinct—and everything she was doing was right. His blood surged, his pulse raced, his heart rate soared and his breathing all but stopped as she drew on him, her lips a soft but insistent caress, her tongue a teasing temptress, luring him out of the realms of control into the dark, swirling abyss of release.

Suddenly he was there, the force of it taking him by surprise. He pumped, he spilled, he shuddered—and she accepted it all, not for a moment shrinking away from the rawness of it, not for a second repulsed or shocked by how he had responded to her. Instead she smiled as she came up for air, licking her soft lips as if she had just sampled the elixir of heaven, before pressing a soft kiss to the left of his chest, right where his heart was pounding out of control.

Vinn placed his still shaking hand on the back of her silky head, stroking it absently as his breathing gradually slowed. He couldn't find the words to describe what he was feeling. She had left him stunned, not just physically but emotionally. He had had so many lovers, and not one had moved him as Gabriella had done. And not just then, but before, giving herself to him when she had been so frightened, so terrified he would use her without respect…without love.

Love was a strong word—a word he liked to shy

away from, an unfamiliar word to him. Or at least it always had been in the context of sex.

Vinn had loved his mother; he seriously doubted any son could have loved a mother more. And he loved his half-sister—not that he was at liberty to claim her as such. Lily Henderson had sought him out after an exhaustive search, trying to make sense of her place in the world as the love-child of Hugo McCready, a prominent mover and shaker in the corporate world who, even after all this time, obstinately refused to acknowledge the living, breathing harvest of the wild oats he had sowed—Vinn included.

Hugo McCready thought it his worldly privilege to seduce the young housemaids who came to clean up after him, under the nose of his long-suffering wife and three legitimate children. But Vinn suspected that, unlike him, Lily was intent on blowing McCready's cover once and for all. Vinn was primarily concerned that it would hurt her rather than their conscienceless father, and so he had done and would continue to do what he could do to protect her—even if the press consistently misinterpreted their relationship.

Paying off this loan was part of Vinn's plan to outsmart his father and his takeover bid, and it had all gone according to plan—with the added bonus, of course, of securing Gabriella St Clair as his wife. He had denied feeling anything for her but desire, but even while his body ached and throbbed for her there were other feelings he had still to make sense of in his head.

She seemed intent on prying an admission of love out of him, but he still wasn't certain of her motives. Money had a habit of inciting deep feelings in many of the women he had associated with in the past. Why else did women in their twenties marry men old enough to be their grandfathers? The press was full of such cases, where rich old men had adoring, beautiful young women draped on their arms, claiming to love them.

Gabriella St Clair had been used to a certain life-style, which she had thought was going to be ripped from beneath her, so she had laid herself at the mercy of the one man she had claimed to dislike intensely for as long as Vinn could remember. For her to suddenly turn around and claim to love him was something Vinn found a little hard to believe, even though they shared a powerful physical chemistry.

But he was starting to realise, irrespective of what she did or didn't feel for him, that perhaps Gabriella had a right to know a little more of his past than she currently did. But telling her about Lily was something he wanted to clear with his half-sister first. Lily was a very sensitive girl of just twenty. Just one year younger than Gabriella had been when she had married Tristan Glendenning. And, like Gabriella, Lily didn't know what she wanted; she was confused and looking for an anchor. Vinn was determined to be that anchor for as long as he needed to be, and to protect her from the unscrupulous man who had fathered her.

Vinn looked down at Gabriella; she was his wife now, in every sense of the word, and his blood surged at the realisation. *She was his wife.* He had made her so, not just in word and at the stroke of a pen, but in the union of their bodies—a union he could still feel buzzing in his veins.

A union he wanted again and again.

CHAPTER ELEVEN

OVER the next few days Gabby was almost able to fool herself her honeymoon with Vinn was as perfect as any other lovestruck bride's could ever be. She felt herself blooming as each lazy sun-filled day passed, with hot, sweaty nights writhing in Vinn's arms, leaving her panting and breathless and even more hopelessly in love. She spent hours watching him, her eyes drinking in every smile he cast her way, her spine melting at every light touch he gave her as they explored the various sheltered coves and beaches and rainforest walks all over the island.

Her body felt so different—so energised and alive. Which she knew had nothing to do with the light golden tan she had developed, or the delicious cuisine she had consumed, which had already gone a long way towards softening the sharp edges of her frame. It was because every nerve was tuned into him, every pore of her skin aware of him, as they lay on secluded beaches on sand as soft as finely ground sugar. He had only to look at her with those smoky grey-blue eyes of his and she would turn to him, opening her mouth for the descent of his, her legs entwining with his hair-roughened ones as he began a sensual exploration of every curve and indentation of her body until her cries of release flew up on the air like those of the wild seabirds around them.

It was the second to last day of their visit to the resort, and Gabby and Vinn had walked to the most remote part of the island, where few of the guests fancied taking a four-hour return journey to access its pristine privacy. Vinn had organised a picnic with the kitchen staff, and had carried a pack with beach towels and extra drinks for the trek back.

After a mouthwatering lunch of tandoori chicken roll-ups and a selection of cheeses and fruit, and a crisp bottle of French champagne, they had made love on the outstretched towels until every part of Gabby's body felt as if it had been refashioned into molten wax. She lay in his arms after the storm of release was over, catching her breath, her eyes closed against the sun, listening to the sound of the gentle lap of water against the shore as Vinn's fingers played idly with her hair.

Their lazy movement gradually stilled, and his breathing was so slow and even she realised he had fallen asleep. She propped herself up on one elbow and looked down at him, her heart swelling inside her chest at how magnificently male he looked, so tanned, so muscular and yet so lean.

She trailed her fingertips over the relaxed curve of his mouth, leaning forward to press a soft-as-a-breeze kiss to his mouth. His lips gave a little shifting movement, as if even in the depths of his slumber he still registered her touch.

She eased herself out of his light hold and wandered

down to the water, wading in to thigh depth before slipping under the surface and swimming out at a leisurely pace, enjoying the feel of the salt water on her sun-kissed skin. She had never skinny-dipped until now, and the freedom was totally liberating, not to mention deeply erotic. The water caressed her, making her even more aware of how much pleasure her body could give and receive.

It thrilled her how much Vinn wanted her. He might not claim to love her, but there was every indication he no longer held the angry vengeful feelings of the past. He was tender towards her, protective and considerate of her every need. At first she'd thought he was doing it for show, for the resort staff were often serving drinks by the pool and moving around the grounds, but he acted exactly the same way when they were totally alone. She liked to think he was falling in love with her, but after her mistake with Tristan she didn't trust her judgement.

When Gabby came out of the water a little while later, Vinn was sitting upright on the beach, watching her, his eyes flaring with desire as she walked towards him. She felt a delicious shiver of anticipation run up under her skin as the brush of his gaze set her alight with longing all over again.

'You look like a mermaid, *cara*,' he said as he got to his feet. 'A beautiful mermaid who has risen from the depths of the sea to seduce this mere mortal.'

Gabby's eyes were like twin magnets, drawn to his groin where his erection was already stirring in response to her. Her belly gave a little shuffle-like movement as she came up close—close enough to feel the hard ridge of him pressing against her.

'Some mermaid I must look, without any make-up on and my hair in sandy knots,' she said with a self-effacing grimace.

He smiled and brushed the wet hair back off her face with a gentle hand. 'I don't think I have ever seen you look more exquisite than right now,' he said, placing his hands on the curve of her bottom and drawing her into his heat.

She looked into his eyes and felt her insides turn over. She could feel the pulse of his blood, the thickness of him making her legs turn to water. Her breasts were crushed against his broad chest, the masculine sprinkling of hair there tickling her, tantalising her, and making her nipples tighten.

She drew in a hitching breath as his head came down, the hard urgency of his kiss in perfect tune with hers. Her hands dug into his buttocks to hold him close, her tongue tangling with his, darting and duelling, until she could think of nothing but how much she wanted him to drive deep inside her until she was shuddering and convulsing beneath him.

He pressed her back down on the towels, his mouth moving from hers to attend to each of her breasts, drawing on her until her spine was arched and her body wet and aching for the completion she knew only he could give her.

His first thrust was deep, evoking a gasping cry of delight from between her lips as her body slickly embraced him. He moved with an ever-increasing rhythm, his fingers delving between their rocking bodies to maximise her pleasure. There was no hesitancy about her responses now. Her body responded to him every time with explosive force. It felt as if every part of her shattered into a million tiny pieces for that mindless moment or two when she was tossed in the rolling waves of ecstasy, only coming back to one piece as she felt him finally lose control. She loved the feel of him at his supreme moment—the way he suddenly tensed, the way he sucked in his breath before letting it go, sometimes with a groan, other times with a harsh gasp, or, like now, with a raw, primal-sounding grunt that sent a shower of goosebumps over her skin to think she had made him experience such an intense release.

Gabby stroked her fingers up and down his back, lingering over each knob of his vertebrae, feeling his chest rise and fall against hers, his warm breath dancing against the sensitive skin of her neck.

'That feels nice,' he murmured against the tiny dip near her collarbone.

'I like touching you,' she said, still stroking him.

He propped himself up on his elbow and looked down at her. 'I like touching you too, *cara*,' he said huskily. 'I don't think I will ever get tired of doing so.'

Gabby rolled her lips together and lowered her gaze to his stubbly chin. 'So what happens if some time in the future you do?' she asked, her fingers unconsciously stilling on his back, along with her breath in her chest.

'There will be no divorce, Gabriella,' he said, forcing up her chin so she had to meet his gaze. 'You know the terms.'

She tried to push aside her resentment, but it came flooding back. 'So I suppose if I no longer please you,

you'll just hot-foot it to one of your many mistresses and let her see to your needs?'

His grey-blue eyes warred with hers. 'Is that really the sort of man you think I am?' he asked. 'Have you learned nothing about me over the last few days?'

She bit her lip, trying to rein in her emotions. 'I know you like sex, and lots of it,' she said. 'But, as you said before we were married, it is my body you want, that you lust after.'

Vinn eased himself off her and got to his feet. 'Yes, well, things are different now,' he said, turning to dust the sand off his thighs.

Gabby pulled one of the towels around her body. 'How do you mean?'

He turned to look at her, but the angle of the sun made it hard for her to see what was written in his expression. 'You are not the woman I thought you were when I married you,' he said. 'I have had to make certain adjustments since.'

Gabby moistened her mouth. 'Would one of those adjustments be learning to *like* me instead of hating me?'

'I have never hated you,' he said, and then, blowing out a breath, grudgingly admitted, 'Well, maybe I thought I did once or twice in the past, but certainly not now.'

She stayed silent, hope building a rickety scaffold around her thudding heart.

'Gabriella…' He shifted so the shadows were off his face. 'I have always kept my sex-life separate from my emotions. This is the first time I have felt something other than desire for a woman.'

'Are you telling me you…you love me?' she asked in a whisper.

He gave her a teasing smile. 'If love is an almost unbearably tight feeling in your chest every time you see the person you are married to, then, yes, perhaps I am in love with you. Or perhaps I need to see a cardiac surgeon. What do you think?'

Gabby was up on her feet and in his arms, pressing hot, passionate kisses all over his face. 'I think you are the most wonderful person I have ever met,' she said. 'I love you so much. I didn't realise how much until just recently.'

'Enough to get rid of those contraceptive pills you've been taking?' he asked, with a distinct twinkle in his eyes.

Gabby gave him a sheepish look. 'You know about those?'

He kissed her forehead lightly. 'If you need more time, then we will wait,' he said. 'But I would like a family. It is something I have wanted for a long time. I guess growing up as an only child with a single mother has made the yearning all the greater.'

'I will throw my pills away,' she promised. 'I want to bear your children, Vinn. I want to be a wonderful wife for you, to make up for all the awful things I did to you in the past.'

He cradled her against him, resting his chin on the top of her head. 'We are different people now, Gabriella. The past should not dictate our future.'

Gabby tipped her head back to look up at him again. 'Why do you always call me Gabriella?' she asked.

His thumb rolled back and forth over the softest part of her chin, just below her bottom lip. 'It is a beautiful name,' he answered. 'It is also Italian. But if you would like me to call you Gabby then I will try to remember to do so.'

'No.' She smiled. 'I like the way you say my name. No one says it quite like you do. It sends shivers up my spine—always has.'

'Oh, really? Now, that *is* interesting,' he said with a smile. 'Here I was thinking for all these years you loathed the very sight of me.'

Gabby gave him a twisted smile in return. 'I think it might be true what they say about love and hate being two sides of the same coin,' she said. 'I think I was always so mean to you because I was frightened of the way you made me feel—even as young as I was when you first came to my family's home.'

He cupped her face in his hands. 'Are you still frightened of how I make you feel, *mia piccola?*'

'You make me feel safer than anyone else I know,' she said, gazing up at him devotedly. 'I never thought I would learn to trust another man after Tristan, but in these last few days you have somehow managed to sweep away every single fear I ever experienced.'

His eyes contained dark shadows of regret as they held hers. 'I wish I had been able to protect you from his hands,' he said, his jaw tightening over the words. 'If I had known what was going on I would have had him thrown in jail—but only after I gave him a dose of his own medicine. He only picked on you because he knew you couldn't defend yourself. It's a wonder he didn't…' He visibly flinched. 'God, I don't want to think about what else he could have done to you.'

Gabby pressed one of her palms to his unshaven

jaw. 'I don't see myself as a victim any more,' she said. 'I did before, but not now.'

He kissed her softly, almost worshipfully. 'We should head back,' he said as he lifted his mouth from hers. 'We have a long walk ahead, and I don't want you to be too tired for what I have in mind for later tonight.'

Gabby sent him a sultry glance as she reached for her bikini, lying on the sand next to the towels. 'You mean I have to wait until tonight to see what it is?'

He gave her a smouldering look and grabbed her by the waist, bringing her naked body up against his, turning her so his front was to her back, every plane and ridge of his body fuelling her desire like gasoline thrown on a flame.

'Maybe we could reset the timetable just a little,' he said, his teeth starting to nip at her earlobe.

'Fine by me,' Gabby said, on the tail-end of a blissful sigh as his erection probed her from behind.

Was there no end to his mind-blowingly sensual repertoire? He constantly surprised her with what he could do with his hands and mouth and body, and it constantly surprised and shocked her how hers responded. She could feel the pressure building even now, the need so insistent she thought she would die if he didn't plunge into her right there and then. But he made her wait, stringing out the torture until she was almost sobbing for the release she so desperately craved.

'Be patient, *cara*,' he said as he teased her tender, sensitised folds with the erotic promise of penetration. 'You will enjoy it much more if you have to wait for it.'

'I want it now!' Gabby said, pressing herself back into him. 'Don't make me wait any longer.'

He gave a chuckle of laughter and began to probe her—just enough to separate her, but not enough to fill her.

'Tell me what you want, Gabriella,' he growled close to her ear. 'Tell me what you want me to do to you.'

'You know what I want you to do,' she gasped, rubbing up against him wantonly.

'Do you want me to do this?' he asked, and slid inside her in one thick, slow thrust that lifted every hair on her scalp.

'Oh, God, *yes…*' She clutched blindly at his thighs, trying to keep her legs from collapsing beneath her.

'And this?' He began to move inside her, deep and far too slowly.

Gabby felt every nerve ending scream for more friction, more speed, more depth and more urgency. 'Yes…*yes…*' she let out, on a panting breath of rampant need.

He held her hips and drove deeply, gradually increasing the pace until she felt her tension building to the point of no return. She fell over the edge, freefalling into an abyss of cascading sensations, the ripples and contractions of her body sending her into a tailspin of feeling that went on and on and on.

Finally it was over, and the aftershocks like tiny rumbles deep down in her body, but then it was Vinn's turn. Gabby felt every carnal second of it—the way his legs braced themselves for the final plunge, the way his breath sucked in deep in his chest, and the way he suddenly pitched forward, the pumping motion of his body filling her, delighting her, making her feel a feminine power she had never felt before as he spilled the essence of himself into the warm cocoon of her body.

Vinn held her in place, trying to get his breathing to settle, but it was difficult. She had the amazing ability to totally unhinge him, to shatter every sense of control he had fooled himself he still possessed. He had put himself out on a limb, an unusual and totally uncharacteristic position for him, but there it was. He loved her as—he had always done.

He had been fooling himself for years that he felt otherwise, but the truth was he had always wanted only her, had only ever loved her. She was the other half he had been searching for all his life. The trouble was he had found it too early, frightening her off with his single-mindedness, virtually pitching her headlong into another man's arms because she had been scared by the intensity of what he had so clumsily communicated to her.

Vinn cupped her breasts, still reluctant to release her, his body relaxed now, but still encased in hers.

'Do you think you could find your way back in the dark?' he asked. 'You know this island better than I do.'

She slowly turned in his arms and linked her arms around his neck. 'Would it matter if we stayed out here all night?' she asked. 'I don't want this magic moment between us to end.'

He gave her a wistful smile. 'We have to fly home tomorrow, *cara*,' he reminded her. 'Back to the real world.'

'I guess… But I don't want anything to change,' she

said. 'I want to be the best wife in the world for you. I don't want to disappoint you.'

He smiled and hugged her close. 'You will not disappoint me, Gabriella,' he said. 'Of that I am sure.'

CHAPTER TWELVE

GABBY sat beside Vinn on the flight back to Sydney, her hand linked with his, her head resting against his shoulder. But her heart was still back on the island.

She had almost cried as she had packed her bag. She had wanted the magic of their honeymoon to go on and on. The blissful sense of security had settled about her shoulders like a shawl, but ever since they had got on the plane it felt as if someone had ripped it away from her, leaving her shivering in uncertainty.

Vinn was mostly silent on the journey back. He kept fidgeting with his watch, as if it was the most fascinating thing in the world, when only hours earlier Gabby's body had been his entire focus.

'Are you OK?' she asked at one point.

He turned to look at her, his expression shuttered. 'Sorry, Gabriella, did you say something?'

'I said, are you OK?' Gabby squeezed his hand but after second or two he pulled out of her hold and reached for the in-flight magazine instead.

'I'm fine,' he said, flipping a few pages, his brow furrowing.

'Have I done something wrong?' she asked after another pause.

He gave her a quick on-off smile. 'No, of course not, *cara*,' he said, patting her hand. 'I have a lot on my mind right now. Business doesn't take a holiday, I'm afraid.'

Gabby felt a twinge of remorse that she hadn't once asked him about his work. She knew so little of what he did, other than he had first made a fortune on a development project in an outlying suburb which had suddenly taken off after a change of council zoning. He had reinvested the profit into more developments, astutely keeping one step ahead of the market so he could maximise his profits.

'Is there anything I can do to help?' she asked.

He shook his head and briefly touched her nearest cheek with his fingertips. 'No, Gabriella. I want you to concentrate on producing me an heir,' he said. 'Your parents need you too, right now. Your father is doing well, but seeing you happy and contented will aid his progress like nothing else can. And a grandchild will be something wonderful for both of them to look forward to.'

Gabby settled back in her seat, smiling to herself as she thought of how she had flushed every one of her contraceptive pills down the sink at the resort apartment. Her hands crept to the flat plane of her belly, wondering what it would feel like to have Vinn's child growing there. Even though she knew it was probably unlikely, since she had only just ceased her protection, she wondered if she was already pregnant. She had been on a low-dose pill, more for convenience than contraception, and the failure rate was a lot higher than other brands…

She reached for his hand again, stroking her fingers up and down his long fingers. 'Thank you, darling, for everything you did to make the last week so special for me,' she said. 'It was a perfect honeymoon.'

He covered her hand with his and gave her another smile, but Gabby couldn't help feeling it looked forced this time. 'It was my pleasure, *cara*,' he said.

'I love you,' she said, stretching across to press her mouth against his.

'I know you do,' he said, still with that not-quite smile.

Gabby started to feel the stealthy creep of doubt; like ghostly fingers tickling the fine hairs on the back of her neck. Why, when she told him how much she loved him, did he not say he loved her too? In fact, when she backtracked through their loving exchange the afternoon before on the beach, she couldn't remember him saying he loved her at all. He had hinted at it, but not openly spoken of his feelings. But then he hadn't had to, she reminded herself ruefully. She had raced in headlong and confessed her love for him, then recklessly thrown away her pills, promising him the heir he so dearly wanted.

But what if that was all he wanted from her? What if, when she gave him the child or children he desired, he decided he no longer had a need for her in his life? He kept saying there would be no divorce, but that didn't mean he wouldn't change his mind some time in the future. After all, he had insisted she sign a pre-nuptial agreement. Didn't that suggest he had no plans or indeed no confidence that the marriage would continue indefinitely?

Everything had happened so quickly. Her father's heart attack, the takeover bid, and the sudden margin call had sent her into a tailspin, tossing her into Vinn's orbit where, two weeks later, she was still spinning.

Gabby didn't get much of a chance to speak with Vinn in private again, for as soon as they got off the plane a driver was waiting to collect them.

They called in to the hospital to see her father briefly, and then Vinn instructed the driver to drop him off at his office, before telling him to take Gabby to his house in Mosman.

Vinn gave her a brief, impersonal kiss before he got out of the car, and within moments he was striding away, his mobile phone already up to his ear.

Gabby sat back with a sigh as the driver nudged back out into the traffic. She had secretly hoped Vinn would do all the traditional things, like carry her over the threshold—perhaps carry her all the way upstairs and make love to her in the bed they would share as man and wife. But he was back to business as if the last seven days hadn't happened. He hadn't even given her a second glance as he had walked through the doors of his office block.

Gabby busied herself with unpacking once the driver had left, after carrying in the luggage for her. She put on a load of washing and while it was running wandered outside to look around the garden. The lawn had been recently mown, but there was no sign of a gardener about the place, for which she was grateful.

She needed time to settle into Vinn's house without the speculative gaze of his household staff.

Vinn had arranged the delivery of her car and her clothes on the day of their wedding. All of her things were neatly hung or folded in the walk-in wardrobe off the master bedroom—she assumed by Vinn's housekeeper, although there was no sign of anyone having been in the house for the last few days. The house was clean and tidy, certainly, but there was no fresh food in the refrigerator, so Gabby decided to drive up to the closest shops for some basic supplies.

When Gabby got back to the house Vinn was on the harbourside deck leading off the lounge, his back towards her as he spoke into his mobile phone. The hushed urgency of his tone was what made her step closer on silent feet, and her heart came to a skidding halt in her chest when she heard his words, carrying on the still afternoon air.

'No, *cara*,' he said. 'Trust me. This is not the right time to announce to the world our true relationship.'

Gabby felt as if a knife had been plunged between her ribs, but somehow she remained upright, coldly, determinedly upright, as she listened to the rest.

'I know,' he said, blowing out a sigh. 'I love you too, and I want the world to know how much you mean to me, but do you know what the press will make of this? It's too dangerous. I have a lot in the pipeline—this takeover bid for one thing. I don't want anything to jeopardise that until it is totally secure, which won't be until the end of next week at the earliest.'

There was a pause as he listened to whoever was on

the other end, and Gabby's heart thudded painfully as each second passed, in case he turned and saw her standing there, listening to every damning word.

'Look, *cara*,' Vinn went on, raking a hand through his rumpled hair, 'I spent a lot of money on securing this deal. I don't want anything to compromise it at this stage. We have to tread carefully. There are other people to consider in all of this.'

Another pause as he listened to the other person.

'I will have to tell her at some stage,' he said. 'She has a right to know. She is my wife now. But let's leave it a week or two longer, hmm? Just keep your head down, and I will send you some money to tide you over. *Ciao*.'

Vinn closed his phone and turned—to come face to face with the shell-white face of Gabriella.

'*Cara,*' he began. 'I didn't hear you come in.'

Gabby clenched her hands into fists. 'Don't you "*cara*" me, you two-timing bastard,' she bit out in blistering fury.

He took a step towards her. 'Gabriella, you don't understand. I was—'

'Oh, I know what you were doing,' Gabby shot back. 'You were talking to *her*, weren't you? Your mistress—your mystery lover. The woman you love. I heard you say it.'

'You have misinterpreted everything,' he said. 'You heard one side of the conversation and are jumping to conclusions.'

'Oh, for God's sake!' Gabby was shrieking at him and couldn't seem to stop, her voice getting shriller with each word she threw at him. 'What sort of fool do you take me for? I heard you tell her about the takeover bid. *You're* the one behind it, aren't you? You were behind it the whole time and never let on. You let me make a complete and utter fool of myself that day when I came to you for help. All the while laughing behind my back at how you'd not only got the majority share of the St Clair Resort but me as a bonus.'

He looked as if he wanted to deny it, but at the last moment changed his mind. He shoved a hand through his hair again and, tossing his phone to one of the sofas, rubbed the back of his neck with his hand, as if to release the tension there.

'There are things you don't know that I was not at liberty to tell you,' he said, in a weighted tone.

'The truth is always a good place to start,' Gabby inserted coldly.

'The truth is, Gabriella...' Vinn paused, searching for the right words. 'I have been on a vendetta of sorts, but it really has nothing to do with you.'

She gave him a flinty glare. 'Oh, please,' she said. 'Don't let the highlights fool you, Vinn. I'm not really as blonde as I look.'

'I mean it, Gabriella,' he insisted. 'The person I have been targeting is no one you know, and I would like to keep it that way. He is not the sort of person I want anyone I care deeply about coming into contact with.'

She rolled her eyes in scorn. 'So you've decided you *do* actually care about me now, have you?' she asked. 'Why? Because I've caught you out? Or because I was surprisingly good in the sack?'

'Don't cheapen yourself like that,' Vinn said, his jaw so tight his teeth ached.

'I'm hardly what you could call cheap,' she tossed back. 'Two point four million dollars is a heck of a lot of money to pay for sex. I hope you were happy with what you got, because that's all you're getting. It's over, Vinn.'

Vinn drew in a harsh breath. 'You would compromise your father's health just to spite me?'

Her eyes went wide with anger. 'You talk to me of compromising my father?' she spat. 'What gall you have! You've just done the dirtiest deed in business—swiping away his life's work behind his back.'

'It wasn't behind his back.'

Gabby stared at him, her mind reeling so much her head was starting to pound. 'W-what did you say?'

'Your father approached me about the takeover bid a couple of days before his heart attack,' he said. 'He suspected who was behind it, and he came to me for advice. I assured him I would do whatever I could to keep the St Clair Island Resort safe.'

Gabby opened and closed her mouth. Not able to speak, hardly able to think. Her father had *known*? He had already approached Vinn for help? Then why…?

'Henry was well aware of the rumours going about, and he knew he couldn't raise the funds if a margin call was activated,' Vinn said. 'I had already helped him secure the house, and—'

Her eyes went wide as she choked, 'The house? You…you own my parents' *house*?'

He pushed his hand through his hair again. 'On paper, yes, but not on principle.'

She gave him a cynical glare. 'What is that supposed to mean?'

'It means I would never take their house from them,

no matter how much money they owed me,' he said, holding her gaze.

Gabby struggled to contain her see-sawing emotions. There was so much she didn't know—*hadn't* known. She felt like a pawn in a chess game, moved about with no will or choice of her own.

'I am in no doubt that the stress of the business was what caused your father's heart attack,' Vinn continued. 'And then, of course, his worst nightmare actually did happen. The lenders suddenly wanted their money.'

Gabby swallowed a couple of times to clear her tight throat. 'So…so you had already agreed to help my father?' she said, still trying to make sense of it all.

'Of course I had,' he said. 'Your father stood by me when I was on the skids. He was the only one who ever believed I had potential. I found it hard, growing up without a father. My mother did her best, but I was heading down a pathway to disaster when your father took me aside and told me how it was up to me to turn it all around. He sponsored me through university and organised special coaching on campus to help with my dyslexia. There is no amount of money I wouldn't put out for him.'

'So…what you're saying is…the resort was never in any danger?' Gabby asked, frowning.

He met her questioning gaze without flinching. 'It was never in danger, Gabriella,' he said heavily. 'Your father is still the major shareholder, and as long as he wants to be he will remain so.'

She ran her tongue over her lips, surprised at how dry and cracked they felt. 'I'm not sure I am really following this…' she said. 'Why did you involve me? Why force me into marriage?'

He looked at her for a lengthy moment, his grey-blue eyes dark and unfathomable. 'I cannot think of a time when you were not a part of my dream for success,' he said. 'I have always wanted you. I can't explain it other than to say my life and my quest for success did not feel complete until I had you.'

'So I am some sort of status symbol, am I?' she asked churlishly. 'Like a top-model sports car to show the world you've really made it?'

'That is not quite how I would put it.'

She gave him another flinty look. 'How *would* you put it, Vinn?' she asked. 'You've already got a mistress. What on earth do you want with a wife—especially one like me?'

'I do not have a mistress,' he bit out. 'Do you really think I am that low?'

Gabby scored her fingernails into the soft bed of her palms. 'How can you stand there and lie to me like that?' she asked incredulously. 'I just heard you tell her you loved her.'

There was a long, tense silence.

Vinn let out his breath. 'All right,' he said. 'I will break my word to her and tell you.'

She arched her brows. 'What's this? A last-minute twinge of conscience, Vinn?'

He gritted his teeth and tried to be patient. 'The young woman I was talking to is not my mistress,' he said. 'She is my half-sister.'

She gave him another raised-brow look, which communicated cynicism along with disgust. 'Then why not clear up that little misunderstanding with the press?' she asked. 'Why go along with the story of her being your mystery lover?'

'I want to protect her,' he said. 'She doesn't have any idea of the sort of man her father is, or the lengths he will go to in order to keep his reputation intact.'

Gabby frowned. 'So…let me get this straight… this half-sister of yours is your father's child, not your mother's?'

'Of course she is not my mother's,' he said. 'My mother would have loved other children—she would have loved to have had a husband to bring them up with her. But the man she fell in love with was already married. He tricked her into a relationship, and then when she got pregnant put her out on the streets, threatening to destroy her if she ever told who the father of her child was. I only found out the day she died who he was. I will not rest until I bring him down for what he did to her.'

Gabby was having trouble following it all. 'Your father is a dangerous man?' she finally managed to ask.

His look was grim. 'Very,' he said. 'He has underworld connections—drugs, organised crime, that sort of thing. He found it amusing to try and swipe away your father's business because he found out about my connection to your family, but fortunately I have contacts who informed me of it so I could take evasive action.'

'Oh, Vinn…' she said. 'I don't know what to say… I feel so confused.'

He came up to her and held her by the shoulders, locking her gaze with the grey-blue intensity of his. 'Listen to me, Gabriella,' he said. 'I love you. I have loved you since the first day I set eyes on you, when you were fourteen and thinking yourself all grown up. I loved you when you *did* grow up. I even loved you when you married that scum Glendenning, because I felt deep down that one day we would be together.'

Gabby blinked back tears. 'Oh, darling, we would have been together so much earlier than this if I hadn't been too proud and stubborn to listen to you that night.'

'I blame myself,' Vinn said, dropping his hands from her shoulders as he began to pace the room. 'I handled it all wrong. I had not long landed back in the country when I heard Glendenning was playing around on you. I blame myself for Blair's death too. I should have seen that coming, but I didn't.'

Gabby shook her head and took a step towards him. 'No, no—you mustn't say that. It wasn't your fault. How can you think that?'

He gave her a grim look. 'Let me finish, *cara*, please,' he said, his voice rough with emotion. 'I was away too long. Blair had come to me for advice about his career before I left to take my mother home to Italy to die. He didn't want to take up a position in your father's business, but he was too afraid to admit it. He was ashamed of not being what your parents wanted him to be. He wanted to study art. He had a gift, a rare gift he should have felt free to explore, but he didn't want to let your parents down.'

'The painting in your foyer…' Gabby said, her heart swelling with pride and a host of other emotions she knew she would have to pick over later. 'Blair did it, didn't he?'

Vinn nodded. 'He was so talented, Gabriella. But he

didn't believe in himself. I think that's why in the end he turned to drugs. He wanted to block out the insecurities he felt—the insecurities all of us feel at times. But for him they were like demons, gnawing away at him relentlessly. I tried to help him, and I felt I was making some headway, but then my mother was diagnosed with cancer. She desperately wanted to mend the rift she had made in her family by succumbing to my father's charm and having a child out of wedlock. I felt I owed it to her to take her home, to nurse her until the day she died. It seemed fitting. She was there at the moment I drew my first breath. I was there when she drew her last.'

Gabby stumbled towards him, wrapping her arms around him, loving him, adoring him, worshipping the man he was—the man he had always been.

'I can't tell you how much I love you,' she said. 'I am not worthy of you. I don't deserve your love. I think that's why I was so reluctant to believe you actually loved me. Deep down I know I don't deserve someone as wonderful as you. But somehow you have loved me through it all.'

Vinn tucked her in close, holding her against his heart. 'You do deserve to be loved, Gabriella,' he said. 'You are more than worthy of love, and no one could love you more than me. I am sure of it.'

She looked up at him with tears of happiness shining in her eyes. 'So the honeymoon is not quite over?'

He smiled and lifted her up in his arms. 'Just as soon as I carry you out of the house and back over the threshold it is going to get a second wind—so you had better prepare yourself for it.'

'I'm prepared,' Gabby said, shivering all over in anticipation. 'Or at least I think I am.'

He gave her a smouldering look. 'Let's put that to the test, shall we?' he said, as he carried her towards the door.

And not too much later Gabby passed with flying colours.

THE SPANISH
BILLIONAIRE'S
MISTRESS

SUSAN STEPHENS

For all my long-suffering friends. You know who you are. I couldn't do it without you.

CHAPTER ONE

'COME here—come closer so we can see you,' the male voice commanded.

Cursing softly under her breath, Zoë Chapman slithered down to the ground and straightened up. Uncomfortable but invisible, or so she'd thought, she had been wedged into a smooth crevice between two giant rocks, discreetly observing the activity around the campfire.

She had located the flamenco camp and chosen her hiding place before anyone arrived. Her unique and popular cookery shows depended upon the co-operation of special interest groups, but the fact that she worked on a TV programme didn't make her welcome everywhere. She had wanted to observe the dancing before she introduced herself, just to make sure it was as good as was rumoured in the village.

The man speaking now had arrived shortly after she had. Back turned, he had stood gazing out across the valley. She had seen nothing more than an aggressively tall male figure, a shock of inky black hair and a wide sweep of shoulders—in fact, everything she had vowed to avoid since gaining her freedom.

As more people had joined him, she'd realised he was the leader of the group. Why hadn't she been surprised? She had wondered who he was, wondered about the quivers running through her as she stared at him. It had made her angry to think she had learned nothing since her divorce. She was still drawn to dangerous men.

Now, walking up to him, she saw he was everything she had expected: strikingly handsome, arrogant, and angry that she was here uninvited. If this hadn't been work she would have done the sensible thing, and left.

During the course of her television series she searched out interesting people from all walks of life. Local people in whichever country she chose to film were the seasoning in her shows, the magic ingredient that lifted her above the competition.

Generally she enjoyed the research. This time she had to put her personal feelings to one side and hope the dancing started soon. She couldn't let some local brigand put her off. Forget the man! This was her target group. The only thing that mattered was persuading someone to perform flamenco on her programme.

Dance was Zoë's passion outside of work. She knew she would never make a professional, but part of her climb-back after the divorce had been to join a jazz dance exercise group. It had proved the best therapy she could have chosen—though right now it looked as if all her good work was being undone.

She could not have prepared for this, Zoë reminded herself. She had not expected to run up against such a strong character again quite so soon.

'Well, what are you waiting for?'

He beckoned her forward with a short, angry gesture, and his voice was cold. It brought back memories she didn't need, but she was like a terrier with a bone when it came to work, and she focused her concentration easily. They were attracting a lot of attention. Perhaps one of the people around the mountain hut would agree to audition for her programme?

The man held up his hand to stop her coming any closer. It was close enough for Zoë, too. He was quite something. Along with the aura of power and brute strength, she had to admit he had style. Why did she have to find such a man irresistible when she knew he had danger carved into the stone where his heart should be?

Somewhere between thirty and thirty-five, he was around

six feet two or three, and his build was every bit as impressive as she had thought from some distance away. Everything about him was dark: his eyes, his hair…his expression.

'Why have you come here?' he demanded.

'I heard this is where flamenco enthusiasts gather, and I want to learn more about flamenco.'

'So you can go home to England and show off to your friends?' He made a derisive sound and clicked his fingers, mimicking the worst of the shows she had seen down on the coast.

'No, of course not. I…' His steely gaze remained fixed on her face, but she couldn't let that get to her. 'I am genuinely interested in flamenco.'

'Are you alone?'

'I am at the moment—'

He cut her off. 'At the moment?'

'I know this looks bad—'

'What do you mean, you're alone at the moment?'

'I'm working with a television crew. They're not here right now.'

Could his expression darken any more? She tried to explain, but her voice came out as a croak. Unconsciously, her hand flew to her throat. She should have brought some water with her. She had been at the mercy of the sun all afternoon, and now she was desperate for a drink.

'Do you think I could have some water?' She gazed around.

'What do you think this is? A café?'

But people were drinking all around her. 'I'm sorry, I—'

'Did you think this was one of those cheap tourist places where you get a free drink along with your *paella* and chips?'

'No!' She calmed herself. 'No, of course not—'

He straightened up and moved a menacing pace towards her, and all her courage drained away. Lurching backwards, she nearly stumbled. She was only saved by the sheer bulk of a man behind her. He was carrying a stone flagon and some pottery beakers. He didn't understand when she started to apologise, and poured her a drink.

She didn't want it. She just wanted to get away—back down the mountain to safety, to where people barely looked at her, where no one knew who she was or where she had come from.

But the man with the flagon was still smiling at her, and the situation was bad enough already. *'Gracias, señor.'*

Keeping watch on the brigand, Zoë took the beaker from the older man and gratefully drank from it.

It was delicious, and tasted harmless—like fruit juice and honey laced with some spice she couldn't name. The beaker felt cool, and she was so thirsty she didn't protest when he offered her more. The golden liquid gleamed in the light as it flowed from the flagon, and the elderly man filled her beaker to the brim.

'Salud!'

The alpha male's voice was harsh and unfriendly. Handing the beaker back to the man with the flagon, Zoë raised her chin. She felt better now, bolder. 'Delicious,' she said defiantly, staring her unwilling host in the eyes. 'What was that drink?'

'A local speciality, brewed here in the village.'

'It's very good. You should market it.'

'On your recommendation I'll certainly consider it.'

His sarcasm needled Zoë, but it also renewed her determination to go nowhere until she got the feature for her programme. At any cost?

At the cost of a little charm, at least. 'I really should introduce myself.'

'You really should.'

Brushing a strand of titian hair from her face, Zoë stared up and tried to focus. She hadn't realised the drink was so strong. On an empty stomach, she was suddenly discovering, it was lethal. She was in no state to object when he reached forward to steady her.

His grip on her arm was light, but even through an alcohol-induced haze she could feel the shock waves radiating out from his fingertips until every part of her was throbbing. He led her away out of earshot, to where a wooden hut cast some shade.

'So, who are you?'

'Zoë—Zoë Chapman. Could I have a glass of water, please?'

Rico thought he recognised the name, then brushed it aside. It hardly mattered. She had damned herself already out of her own mouth: a television crew! He might have known. He grimaced, catching hold of her again when she stumbled.

'I think you'd better sit down.' He steered her towards a bench, and once she was safely planted turned and called to two youths. 'José! Fernando! *Por favor, café solo—rápido!*' Then, turning to her again, he said, 'Welcome to the Confradias Cazulas flamenco camp, Zoë Chapman. Now you're here, what do you want?'

'It's good to meet you too—'

'Don't give me all this nonsense about flamenco. What do you really want? Why have you come here? Are you spying on me?'

'Flamenco isn't nonsense.' She reeled back to stare at him. 'And I'm not spying on you. I'm researching.'

'Oh, of course. I see,' he said sarcastically.

No, he didn't, Zoë thought, shading her eyes with her hand as she tried to focus on his face. Her head felt so heavy. It bounced instead of simply moving. Squeezing her eyes together, she struggled to follow his movements—he seemed to be swaying back and forth. 'So, who are you, then?' Her tongue was tied up in knots.

'Rico. Rico Cortes.'

They were attracting attention, Zoë noticed again. Peering

round him, she gave a smile and a little wave. He moved in closer, shielding her from his companions. 'I'm very pleased to meet you, Rico.' As she put her hand out to shake his, it somehow connected with a coffee cup. Raising the cup to her lips, she drank the coffee down fast. The hot, bitter liquid scalded her throat, but it couldn't be helped. She had to pull round from this fast. The last couple of programmes based around flamenco were supposed to be the crowning feature of her series.

'Here, drink some more.'

His voice was sharp, and then he made a signal to the boy with the coffee pot to fill her mug again.

'Leave it here, José, *por favor*.'

He sounded different, warmer when he spoke to the youth, Zoë registered fuzzily.

'We're going to need every drop,' he added.

And he was back to contempt when he turned to look at her! It wasn't the best start she'd ever had to a programme.

This time, once she'd drained the strong black coffee, it was Zoë who asked for more. The second she had finished, the questions started.

'If you're with a television crew I take it you're after an exclusive. I'm right, aren't I? That's why you were spying on us, sneaking about.'

Thanking the boy, Zoë gave him back her empty cup. Her head was clearing. She felt better, much more focused. She might still be a little under par, but she had no intention of being bullied by Rico Cortes—by anyone.

'I'm here to see if flamenco will make a suitable item for my television series. Nothing more.'

'*Your* television series?'

'It's my programme. I have full editorial control. I own the company that produces the programme.'

'So, it's you.'

'Me?'

'Staying at the Castillo Cazulas.'

'Yes, my company has taken a short-term lease on the castle—'

'And it's there you're going to create your masterpiece?'

'I beg your pardon?' She couldn't keep the chill out of her voice now. Could he have been more disparaging? She had worked long and hard to raise her programme above the rest, to make it different and special. She had brought a great team together, and she was proud of what they had achieved.

'Flamenco for Spain, opera in Italy, fashion when you shoot a programme in France—is that how it goes? Skimming over the surface of a country, using the name of art just to make money?'

'I make money. I won't deny it. How would I stay in business, pay the wages of the people who work with me, otherwise? But as for your other assumptions—frankly, they stink.'

'They do?'

His voice was faintly amused now, and he was looking at her in a whole different way. She wasn't sure if she liked it any better. Her thundering heart told her it was dangerous. 'Look, Rico, if you're not the person I should be speaking to about the dancing, then perhaps you could find me someone who will listen to what I have to say.'

'And allow you to trample over my privacy? I don't think so.'

'*Your* privacy? I wasn't aware that my programme was going to be made around you.'

His look was cynical. 'It's time you went back to your film crew, Ms Chapman.'

'Are you asking me to leave?'

'It's getting dark—I'd hate for you to lose your way.'

'Don't worry, I'll go. Just as soon as I finish my business here.'

'You *have* finished your business here.'

'Why are you so touchy about my being here? I'm not doing you any harm!'

'People have a right to space.'

'And this is yours?' Zoë gestured around.

'If you like. I don't have to explain myself to you.'

'Correct,' Zoë said, standing up to face him. 'But I wasn't aware that there were any private estates up here in the mountains. I've got as much right to be here as you have. And, for your information, I have never had a single complaint from a guest on my show. I treat everyone with respect.'

He shifted position and smiled. It was not a friendly smile. It was a 'don't mess with me' smile.

'I give you my word,' Zoë insisted. 'Nothing in my programme will invade your privacy—'

His short bark of laughter ran right through her, and his derision made her cheeks flame red.

'You really believe that?'

'Yes, of course I do.'

'Then you're dreaming.'

'Perhaps if you'd allow me to explain how everything works—'

'You still couldn't come up with anything to reassure me.'

This was her most challenging project yet. But she had never failed before. Not once. No one had ever refused to take part in one of her programmes, and she wasn't going to let Rico Cortes start a trend.

'Have the effects of that drink worn off yet?'

He couldn't wait to get rid of her, Zoë guessed. 'Yes, they have.' Hard luck. She was firing on all cylinders now.

He turned away. Evidently as far as Rico was concerned their discussion had come to an end. He couldn't have cared less about her programme—he just didn't want her blood on his hands when she tumbled over a cliff after drinking the local hooch at his precious flamenco camp. 'We haven't finished talking yet!' she shouted after him.

'I have.'

As he turned to stare at her Zoë wondered if he could sense the heat building up in her. His slow smile answered that question, and she wasn't sure if she was relieved or not when he walked back towards her. 'Please, let me reassure you. I don't pose a threat to you or to anyone else here. I'm just trying to—'

'Find out more about flamenco?'

'That's right.'

As their eyes met and locked Zoë shivered inwardly. Rico was exactly the type of man she had vowed to avoid. 'It's getting late.' She looked hopefully at the sky. 'Perhaps you are right. This isn't the time—'

'Don't let me drive you away,' he sneered.

She was painfully aware of his physical strength, but then something distracted her. A broken chord was played with great skill on a guitar, so soft it was barely discernible above the laughter and chatter—but this was what she had come for. Silence fell, and everyone turned towards a small wooden stage. Lit by torchlight, it had been erected on the edge of the cliff, where it could catch the slightest breeze from the valley.

'Since you're here, I suppose you might as well stay for the performance.'

Rico's invitation held little grace, but she wasn't about to turn it down.

He cut a path through the crowd, and Zoë followed him towards the front of the stage. She could see the man with the guitar now, seated on a stool at one corner of the stage, his head bowed in concentration as he embraced the guitar like a lover. Then an older woman walked out of the audience and went to join him. Resting her hands on her knees to help her make the steep ascent up the wooden steps to the stage, she looked her age, but when she straightened up Zoë saw an incredible transformation take place.

Giving the audience an imperious stare, the woman

snatched up her long black skirt in one hand and, raising the other towards the sky, she stamped her foot once, hard.

A fierce energy filled the air as the woman began her performance. Zoë had no idea that Rico was watching her. She was aware of nothing outside the dance.

'Did you feel it?' he murmured, close to her face, as the woman finished and the crowd went wild.

'Did I feel what?' she said, moving closer so he could hear.

'*Duende.*'

As he murmured the word she looked at his mouth. '*Duende.*' Zoë tasted the word on her own lips. It sounded earthy and forbidden, like Rico Cortes. She sensed that both had something primal and very dangerous at their core.

'You wanted real flamenco,' he said, drawing Zoë back to the purpose of her visit. 'Well, *this* is real flamenco. This is wild, impassioned art at its most extreme. Are you ready for that, Zoë Chapman?'

She heard the doubt in his voice. Perhaps he saw her as a dried-up husk, incapable of feeling passion of any sort—and why not? He wouldn't be the first man to think that. 'I'm just really grateful to have this chance to see flamenco at its best.'

'You don't see flamenco. You feel it.'

'I know that now.' He thought of her as a tourist out for a cheap thrill, Zoë realised. But she was a long way from the tourist trail here. She was a long way from her old life too—the old Zoë Chapman would have backed off without a fight, but there was no chance of that now. She knew what she could achieve, with or without a man at her side. And she hadn't come to Spain to be insulted. She had come to make a programme, a good programme. She wasn't going to let Rico Cortes distract her from that goal. 'Can you explain this word *duende* to me?'

'You'll know it when you feel it.'

'What—like an itch?'

'Like an orgasm.'

Zoë's mouth fell open. Not many things shocked her. OK, so she'd been less than reverent in response to his cutting remarks, but it had been a serious question. She had been right about him. Rico Cortes was a man of extremes—a man who was looking at her now with a brooding expression on his face, no doubt wondering if his shock tactics had been sufficient to scare her off.

'An emotional orgasm, you mean?' She was pleased with her composure under fire.

'That's right.'

There was a spark of admiration in his eyes. It gave her a rush—maybe because there was passion in the air long after the woman's performance had ended. Vibrations from the flamenco seemed to have mixed with his maleness, taking her as close to *duende* as she would ever get. She held his gaze briefly, to prove that she could, and found it dark and disconcerting. Her body was trembling with awareness, as if an electric current had run through her.

'So, you have taken a summer lease on Castillo Cazulas,' he said, staring down at her as if he knew what she was feeling. 'And you want to make a programme about flamenco. Why here, of all places? Hardly anyone outside the village knows about the Confradias Cazulas flamenco camp.'

'People who know about flamenco do. And I enjoyed the walk.'

'But how will you find your way back again? It's almost dark.'

He was right, but she was prepared. 'I have this.' Digging in her pocket, Zoë pulled out her flashlight. Suddenly it didn't seem adequate. She should have remembered how fast daylight disappeared in Spain. It was as if the sun, having blazed so vigorously all day, had worn itself out, and dropped like a stone below the horizon in minutes.

They both turned as some more dancers took the stage. They were all talented, but none possessed the fire of the first woman. She had already found her guest artist, Zoë realised, but she would still need an introduction.

Glancing up, she knew that Rico was her best chance. But there were man waves coming off him in torrents, and he smelled so good—like pine trees and wood smoke. His sexual heat was curling round her senses like a blanket. *And lowering her guard!* She hadn't come to Spain to indulge in an adolescent fantasy over some arrogant stud. Her interest in flamenco was purely professional. Work was all she cared about; a new man figured nowhere in her plans.

By the time the stage had cleared again it was pitch-dark, with no moon. Quite a few people had come by car, parking in a clearing not too far away. Zoë watched with apprehension as their headlights glowed briefly before disappearing into the night.

'You really think that little light of yours is going to be enough?' Rico said, as if reading her mind.

Zoë glanced at him. 'It will have to be.' Shoving her hands in the pockets of her track suit, she tilted her chin towards the stage. 'Was that the last performance for tonight?'

'You want more?'

'How much would it cost to hire someone like that first performer—the older woman?'

She saw an immediate change in his manner.

'All the money on earth couldn't buy talent like that. *You* certainly couldn't afford it.'

Zoë bit back the angry retort that flew to her lips. This was no time for temperament: everyone was leaving—the woman too, if she didn't act fast. Their gazes locked; his eyes were gleaming in the darkness. This man frightened her, and she knew she should turn away. But she couldn't afford to lose the opportunity.

'I'm sorry—that was clumsy of me. But you can't blame me for being carried away by that woman's performance—'

'Maria.' His voice was sharp.

'Maria,' Zoë amended. She felt as if she was treading on eggshells, but his co-operation was crucial. She generally made a very convincing case for appearing on the show. Right now, she felt like a rank amateur. There was something about Rico Cortes that made her do and say the wrong thing every time. 'Maria's performance was incredible. Do you think she would dance for me?'

'Why on earth would she want to dance for *you*?'

'Not for me, for my show. Do you think Maria would agree to dance on my programme?'

'You'd have to ask her yourself.'

'I will. I just wanted to know what you thought about it first.' Zoë suspected nothing happened in Cazulas without Rico's say-so.

'It depends on what you can offer Maria in return.'

'I would pay her, of course—'

'I'm not talking about money.'

'What, then?'

A muscle worked in his jaw. 'You would have to win her respect.'

Did he have to look so sceptical? 'And what do you think would be the best way to do that?'

They were causing some comment, Zoë noticed, amongst the few people remaining, with this exchange, conducted tensely head to head. It couldn't be helped. She had to close the deal. She wasn't about to stop now she had him at least talking about the possibility of Maria appearing on the show.

'You'd have to bargain with her.'

An opening! Maybe not a door, but a window—she'd climb through it. 'What do you suggest I bargain with?' She smiled, hoping to appeal to his better nature.

'Are *you* good at anything?' Rico demanded.

Apart, that was, from joining the hordes who spied on him and the idiots who thought an important part of his heritage had the same value as the cheap tourist tat along the coast.

She had manoeuvred him into starting negotiations with her, though. She was sharper than most. He should have got rid of her right away, but his brain had slipped below his belt.

He shouldn't have stayed away from Cazulas for so long. He should have kept a tighter hold on who was allowed into the village. But he had trusted such things to a management company. He wouldn't be doing that again.

'I don't just make programmes,' she said, reclaiming his attention. 'I present them.'

'I apologise.' He exaggerated the politeness. 'Apart from your ability to make programmes and present them, what do you have to bargain with that might possibly interest Maria?'

'I cook.'

Removing her hands from her pockets, she planted them on her hips. She smiled—or rather her lips tugged up at an appealing angle while her eyes blazed defiance at him. Her manner amused him, and attracted him too. 'You cook?'

'Is there something wrong with that?'

'No, nothing at all—it's just unexpected.'

'Well, I don't know what you were expecting.'

Just as well. He had been running over a few things that would definitely make it to the top of his wish list, and cooking wasn't one of them. Outsiders were practically nonexistent in the mountains. It was a rugged, difficult terrain, and yet Zoë Chapman, with her direct blue-green gaze and her wild mop of titian hair, had come alone and on foot, with a flashlight as her only companion, to find—what had she expected to find?

Rico's eyes narrowed with suspicion. In his experience, women made careful plans; they didn't just turn up on the off chance. 'We'll discuss this some other time. I'll have someone see you home.'

'When I've spoken to Maria.'

Her mouth was set in a stubborn line. He liked her lips. He liked her eyes too—when they weren't spitting fire at him.

She was about five-five, lightly built—but strong, judging from her handshake. The rest was a mystery beneath her shapeless grey track suit. Maybe it was better that way. There were very few surprises left in life.

But this was one mystery parcel he had no intention of unwrapping. The gutter press could use subtle tactics to succeed. Zoë Chapman might be working for anyone—how did he know? The television company, even the programme she was supposed to be making, could all be a front. Cazulas was special—the one place he could get some space, some recreation—and no one was going to spoil that for him.

'So, you'll introduce me to Maria?'

She was still here? Still baiting him? Rico's jaw firmed as he stared at Zoë. The sensible thing to do would be to cut her, blank her out, forget about her. But she intrigued him too much for that. 'It's not convenient right now—'

'Who says so?'

'Maria!' Rico turned with surprise. 'I didn't hear you coming.'

'That is obvious.' The older woman's eyes were bright and keen as she stared curiously at Zoë. 'But now I am here why don't you introduce us, Rico?'

'She won't be staying—'

'I will!'

Maria viewed them both with amusement.

'I didn't think you would be interested in what Ms Chapman had to say,' Rico said with a dismissive shrug.

'So now you are thinking for me, Rico?'

There was a moment when the two of them stared at each other, unblinking, and then Rico pulled back. 'Maria Cassavantes—allow me to present Zoë Chapman to you.'

'Zoë,' Maria repeated, imbuing Zoë's name with new colour. 'I have heard rumours about your television programmes and I would like to talk to you. Forget Rico for a moment. Perhaps we can come to some arrangement?'

It was everything Zoë had hoped for—but forget about Rico? That was asking a bit too much. She saw him tense and she couldn't resist a quick glance of triumph.

Rico was seething. What was Maria thinking of? They knew nothing about this Zoë Chapman—nothing at all. What set her apart from all the other female sharks, with their bleached teeth and avaricious natures? Maria hadn't a clue what she was letting herself in for—she was playing with fire…

'We should know more about your cookery programme before Maria agrees to do anything.' He took a step forward, deliberately putting himself between them. 'I don't see how flamenco could possibly be relevant.'

'If you'd only let me explain—'

'How can I be sure you're not wasting Maria's time?'

'I said I don't mind this, Rico.' Maria put a restraining hand on his arm. 'I would like to talk to Zoë and hear what she's got to say—'

'I promise you, Maria,' Zoë cut in, 'I'm not in the habit of wasting anyone's time, least of all my own. And if you need me to prove it to you—'

'I really do.' It was Rico's turn to butt in.

Maria was forgotten as they glared at each other. Then Zoë broke eye contact, allowing him a brief moment of satisfaction.

'I'll make everyone in the village a meal,' she declared, gesturing extravagantly around the clearing. 'How does that suit you, Rico?'

Now he was surprised. 'That's quite an offer.' There was just enough doubt in his voice to provoke her, to brighten her green eyes to emerald and make her cheeks flare red.

'I mean it.'

'Fine.' He lifted up his hands in mock surrender, then dipped his head, glad of the opportunity to conceal the laughter brewing behind his eyes. Somehow he didn't think Ms

Chapman would appreciate humour right now. But there were about one hundred and sixty souls in the village. She would never pull it off.

Ms Chapman. Who knew what was behind a name?

Rico's gaze flew to Zoë's hands. Clean, blunt fingernails, cut short, but no ring, no jewellery at all. He drew an easing breath. That was all he needed to know. It gave him the freedom to overlook his vow never to court trouble on his own doorstep again. 'I shall look forward to it, Ms Chapman.'

'Rico,' Maria scolded him, 'why don't you call our new friend Zoë, as we're going to be working together?'

'So we *are* going to be working together, Maria?'

She sounded so excited. Rico ground his jaw and watched with concern as the two women hugged each other. Zoë Chapman wouldn't win *him* round so easily.

'I have never appeared on television,' Maria exclaimed.

'I'm going to make it special for you, Maria.'

Zoë's promise grated on him. If she let Maria down—

'I think we'll make a good team.' Maria looked at him and raised her eyebrows, as if daring him to disagree.

For now it seemed he had no choice in the matter. Zoë Chapman had won this round, but he would be waiting if she stepped out of line. Maria might have been taken in, but he wasn't so easily convinced. The thought of an artist of Maria's calibre appearing on some trivial holiday programme with a few recipes thrown in made him sick to his stomach.

As far as he was concerned, *Ms* Chapman had identified her quarry and had stopped at nothing until she got her own way. She was no innocent abroad. She had all the grit and determination of the paparazzi. That wary look he had detected in her eyes when she looked at him didn't fool him for a minute. It was all an act. She was as guilty as hell. But Maria was right. He wouldn't presume to make decisions for Maria Cassavantes, though in his experience third-rate television companies only dealt in plastic people; treasures like Maria were out of their league.

If he had to, he would step in to protect her from Zoë Chapman. But for now he was sufficiently intrigued to give Ms Chapman enough rope to hang herself. He would watch her like a hawk, and the first time she tried to cheapen or trivialise what Maria Cassavantes stood for both she and her television cameras would be thrown out of Spain.

CHAPTER TWO

'CAN we talk business now, Maria?'

'That sounds very formal,' Rico cut in.

He was suspicious of her motives. She had to curb her enthusiasm, take it slowly, Zoë reminded herself. She usually got to know people first, before talking business. Building confidence was crucial. Contrary to popular opinion, not everyone wanted to appear on television. Usually she was good at choosing the right moment, but having Rico in the picture was making her edgy, making her rush things.

'I know it's late—I won't keep you long.' She glanced at Rico. 'Perhaps if Maria and I could talk alone?'

'It's all right, Rico,' Maria said soothingly.

'I'd rather stay.'

Zoë looked up at him. 'It's really not necessary.'

'Nevertheless.' He folded his arms.

For Maria's sake Zoë tried to bite back her impatience, but she was tired and stressed and the words just kept tumbling out. 'Really, Rico, I can't see any reason why you should stay. Maria and I are quite capable of sorting this out between us—'

'It's better if I stay.'

She could see he was adamant. 'Are you Maria's manager?'

'They call him El Paladín,' Maria cut in, interposing her not inconsiderable body between them.

'El Paladín?' Zoë repeated. 'Doesn't that mean The Champion?' She only had a very basic knowledge of conversational Spanish to call upon. 'What's that for, Rico? Winning every argument?'

'Rico is everyone's champion,' Maria said fondly, patting his arm.

That seemed highly unlikely—especially where she was concerned, Zoë thought. 'Champion of what?' she pressed.

'Zoë likes her questions,' Rico observed sardonically, 'but she's not too keen on giving answers about why she's really here in Cazulas—'

'And Zoë's right about you,' Maria cut in. 'You don't like losing arguments, Rico.'

'I like to win,' he agreed softly.

Lose? Win? Where was all this leading? Zoë wondered, suppressing a shiver as she broke eye contact with Rico. 'We're never going to win Rico's approval, Maria, but I believe we can make great television together.'

'What have you been telling this young woman, *malvado*?' Maria demanded, turning her powerful stare on him.

'Nothing. If you want to dance and she wants to cook, that's fine by me. Only problem is, we know *you* can dance.'

'Rico!' Maria frowned at him.

'My third television series says I can cook!'

'There—you see, Rico,' Maria said, smiling at Zoë.

'And the connection between dancing and cooking is what, exactly?' He raised his shoulders in a shrug as he stared at Zoë.

He would never go for her idea, but at least she had Maria's support. She had to forget Rico's insults and build on what she had. But he was one complication she could do without. He probably crooked his finger and every woman around came running. Well, not this woman.

Turning to Maria, Zoë deliberately cut him out. 'This is the connection, Maria: the people around me inspire the food I cook on television. In this part of Spain the influence of flamenco is everywhere.'

'So cooking isn't just a hobby for you?' Rico said.

Zoë stared up at him. He refused to be cut out. 'No, Rico, it's a full-time career for me.'

'Along with your television company.'

Maria stepped between them again. 'So you would like me to dance on your television programme to add some local interest to the dishes you prepare? Is that right, Zoë?'

'Exactly.' Zoë's face was confident as she flashed a glance at Rico. 'I'll cook, you'll dance, and together we'll make a great team.'

'*Bueno,*' Maria said approvingly. 'I like the sound of this programme of yours. Of course, any payment must be donated to the village funds.'

'Absolutely,' Zoë agreed. 'Whatever you like.'

Maria smiled. 'Well, that all sounds quite satisfactory to me.'

But not to Rico, Zoë thought. At least he was silent for now. 'I have never seen anyone dance like you, Maria. You are fantastic.'

'*Gracias*, Zoë. And you are very kind.'

'Not kind, Maria, just honest.' Zoë stopped, hearing Rico's scornful snort in the background. What did she have to do to convince him?

She turned to look at him coldly. There were a couple of buttons undone at the neck of his dark linen shirt, showing just how tanned and firm he was. She turned back quickly to Maria. 'When you appear, I just know the programme will come to life…' Zoë's voice faded. She could feel Rico's sexual interest lapping over her in waves.

'Don't worry, Zoë,' Maria assured her, filling the awkward silence. 'It will be fine—just you wait and see.'

Zoë wasn't so sure, and she was glad of Maria's arm linked through her own as the older woman drew her away from Rico, towards the bright circle of light around the campfire.

'Have you offered Zoë a drink?' Maria said, turning back to him.

'She's had more than enough to drink already.'

'Surely you didn't let her drink the village liquor?'

'It's all right, Maria,' Zoë said hastily. She could see the hard-won progress she had made winning Maria's trust vanishing in the heat of a very Latin exchange. 'Thank you for the kind offer, but I've already had some coffee.'

Rico was staring at her almost as if he was trying to remember why she made him so uneasy. But they couldn't have met before. And he couldn't know about her past; she was anonymous in the mountains. Television reception was practically non-existent, and there were no tabloid papers on sale at the kiosk in the village.

'So, Zoë, when do I dance for you?' Maria said, reclaiming Zoë's attention.

'How about Tuesday?' Zoë said, turning back to thoughts of work with relief. 'That gives us both time to prepare.'

'Tuesday is good for me.' Maria smiled broadly as she broke away. 'On Tuesday you cook, and I dance.'

'Are you sure you know what you're taking on, Zoë?'

Rico's words put a damper on their enthusiasm.

'Why? Don't you think I'm up to it?'

'It's *what* you're up to that I'm more interested in.'

'Then you're going to have a very dull time of it,' Zoë assured him. 'I'm going to cook and Maria is going to dance. I don't know what you're imagining, but it really is as simple as that.'

'In my experience, nothing is ever that simple.'

Zoë's gaze strayed to his lips: firm, sensuous lips that never grew tired of mocking her.

'Today is Saturday—no, Sunday already,' Maria said with surprise, staring at her wristwatch. 'It is well past midnight. I have kept you far too long, Zoë.'

'That's not important,' Zoë assured Maria, turning to her with relief. 'All that matters is that you're happy—you're the most important person now. I want to make sure you have everything you need on the night of your performance.'

'Such as?' Maria said.

'Well—would you like to eat before or after you dance?'

'Both. I need to build up my strength.' She winked at Zoë. 'Some people don't need to build up strength, of course.' She shot a glance at Rico. 'But you had better feed him anyway. I'm sure he'd like that.'

'I'm sure he would.' Zoë's gaze veered coolly in Rico's direction. She might find him a few sour grapes.

'Don't take me for granted, Zoë,' he said, 'I might not even be there.'

'Don't worry, Rico. Where you're concerned I won't take anything for granted. I'll expect you at the castle around nine?' she confirmed warmly with Maria.

'And I will dance for your cameras at midnight.'

Zoë felt a rush of pleasure not even Rico could spoil. She had accomplished her mission successfully, and there was a bonus—she had made a new friend in Maria. She just knew Maria would have what they called 'screen magic', and the programme in which she featured would be unique.

'Rico, would you make sure that everyone in the village knows they are welcome to come and eat at Castillo Cazulas and celebrate Maria's performance on Tuesday night?' Zoë said, turning to him.

For a moment he was amazed she had included him in her arrangements. He had to admit he admired her guts—even if she did annoy the hell out of him. He should be there, just to keep an eye on her.

In fact, he could take a look around right now if he drove her back to the castle. Time to turn on the charm.

'Don't worry, no one loves a party more than we do in Cazulas—isn't that right, Maria?' He looked at Zoë. 'You'll be calling in extra help, I imagine?'

There was something in Rico's eyes Zoë didn't like.

Something that unnerved her. 'There's no need. I'm not alone at the castle, Rico. I have my team with me—and don't forget that cooking is what I do for a living.'

Turning away from him, she said her goodbyes to Maria, all the time conscious of Rico's gaze boring into her back. He might as well have gripped her arms, yanked her round, and demanded she give him her life history. She could only think that having a woman set both the rules and the timetable was something entirely new to him.

'How are you going to get home tonight, Zoë?' Maria said.

'I'll drive her back.'

'I'll walk.'

Maria frowned, looking from Rico to Zoë and back again. 'Of course you will drive Zoë home, Rico.' She put her arm around Zoë's shoulder. 'It is too dangerous for you to walk, Zoë, and you will be quite safe with Rico—I promise you.'

There was something in Maria's eyes that made Zoë want to believe her. But as she walked away Zoë could have kicked herself. Why hadn't she just asked if she could take a lift with Maria?

'Are you ready to go?' Rico said.

'I thought we'd already been through this.' Digging in her pocket, Zoë pulled out her flashlight again.

'Oh, that's right. I had forgotten you were an intrepid explorer.'

'I'll only be retracing my steps—'

'In the dark.'

'Well, I'd better get going, then.'

She moved away, and for one crazy moment hoped he would come after her. When he did she changed her mind. 'I'll be fine, Rico. Really.'

'What are you afraid of, Zoë? Is there something at the castle you don't want me to see?'

'Is that what you think?' She ran her hand through her hair

as she looked at him. 'I can assure you I have nothing to hide.
Come around and check up on me if you don't believe me.'

'How about now?'

'I'd rather walk.'

'Well, I'm sorry, Maria's right. I can't let you do that. It's
far too dangerous.'

Maria hadn't left yet. Her friend's truck was still parked in
the clearing. She might just catch them. But Maria moved as
fast as she had on the stage. Climbing into the cab, she
slammed the door and waved, leaving Zoë standing there as
the truck swung onto the dirt road leading down to the village
and accelerated away.

'Don't look so worried.'

*Don't look so worried? I'm stuck at the top of a mountain
in the middle of the night with a flashlight and the local brig-
and—who happens to have a chip on his shoulder labelled
'media-types/female'—and I shouldn't worry?*

'Like I said, I'll drive you back.'

'No way!'

'You can cut the bravado, Zoë—there's no moon, hardly
any path, and this stupid little light won't save you when
you're plunging down a precipice.'

'Give that back to me now.' Zoë made a swipe for her
flashlight, but Rico was too quick for her.

'It's no trouble for me to drop you at the castle.'

'Thank you, I'll walk.'

She got as far as the rock-strewn trail leading down to the
valley before he caught hold of her arm and swung her
around.

'You are not going down there on your own.'

'Oh, really?'

'Yes, really.'

Their faces were too close. As their breath mingled Zoë
closed her eyes. 'Let go of me, Rico.'

'So you can mess up a rock? So you can cause me a whole

lot of trouble in the morning when I have to come looking for your mangled body? I don't think so, lady.'

'Your concern is overwhelming, but I really don't need it! I know these mountains—'

'Like the back of your hand? And you've been here how long?'

'Nearly a month, as a matter of fact.' That silenced him, Zoë noted with satisfaction.

As long as that? Rico ground his jaw. Another reason to curse the fact he had stayed away too long. He couldn't let her go—he didn't want to let her go—and he wanted to find out what she was hiding. 'You don't know these mountains at night. This path is dangerous. There's a lot of loose stone, and plenty of sheer drops.'

'I'll take my chances.'

'The road isn't half bad.'

Somehow he managed to grace his last words with a smile.

She stopped struggling and looked at him, her bright green eyes full of suspicion.

'Come on, Zoë, you know you don't really want to walk.' Charm again? New ground for him, admittedly, but well worth it if she agreed. If he took her back he could take a look around. He knew her name from somewhere—and not just from the television. But how did she affect him? Was she a threat? 'It's only a short drive in the Jeep.'

'OK,' Zoë said at last.

She was relieved she didn't have to walk back in the dark. But as Rico dug for his keys in the back pocket of his jeans she wondered if she was quite sane. If it hadn't been for Maria's reassurances she would never have agreed to anything so foolish. She didn't know a thing about Rico Cortes, and the day her divorce came through she had promised herself no more tough guys, no more being pushed around, mentally or physically.

'Don't look so worried. You'll be a lot safer going down

the mountain in the Jeep with me. Are you coming or not?' he said when she still hesitated. 'I've got work tomorrow.'

'Tomorrow's Sunday.'

'That's right—and I have things to get ready for Monday morning.'

'What things?' Maybe he *was* the local brigand, and Monday was his day for mustering the troops. And she had agreed to take a lift home with him…

Zoë frowned as he opened the passenger door for her. Rico Cortes was as much a mystery now as ever, and it wasn't like her. She was an expert at winkling out information. It was the secret of her success—or had been in the past.

The moment he swung into the driver's seat beside her he fired off another question. 'What keeps you in this part of Spain?' He was larger than life, which went with the dramatic scenery, but he didn't fit into the small-town scene at all.

'I have many interests.'

'Such as?'

He didn't answer as he gunned the engine into life. The noise was supposed to distract her, she guessed. He was dodging her questions like an expert—almost as if he was used to dealing with the media.

Local reporter, maybe?

No way! And better not to ask—better not to get involved. She had only just won her freedom from an unhappy marriage. Divorce had come at a high price, even if the break had been like a cleansing torrent that washed most of her insecurities away. And she didn't want them back again. Ever. So why had she agreed to take a lift back to the castle with a man she didn't know? The only answer was that Maria liked him, and she liked Maria.

Was that enough? It had to be, Zoë realised as they pulled away.

Maria had said he was a fighter. El Paladín. Was fighting

his profession? Zoë felt a quiver of apprehension run down her spine as she flashed a glance at him.

No, it couldn't be. Not unless he was the luckiest pugilist alive. He was built like a fighter but his face was unmarked, and his hands, as she had already noticed, were smooth. And in spite of his casual clothes, and his life up in this remote mountainous region, he had polish. But then quite a few boxers did too…

'Seen enough, Zoë?'

'I'm sorry, was I staring? I'm so tired I hardly know what I'm doing.'

Rico could feel the sexual tension between them rising fast. Any other time, any other woman, he might have swung off the road and fixed it for them both. But he had to know more about a woman before he got involved. He wasn't about to commit some reckless indiscretion Zoë Chapman could broadcast to the world.

He had learned not to court disaster on his own doorstep. She was luscious, but she would keep, and she backed off every time he looked at her. If she had kept her legs crossed all this time she would wait a little longer.

What if she was innocent? It seemed unlikely, but— No. Life wasn't like that. Fate never dealt him an easy hand.

Guilty, innocent—it hardly mattered which. He would still go slow until he'd worked out what made her tick… Go slow? So he *was* going somewhere with her?

Rico smiled. He could feel Zoë looking at him. Life got too easy at the top of the mountain. He hadn't had anything approaching a real challenge to deal with in quite some time.

Normally Zoë was a confident passenger, but Rico Cortes scared the hell out of her driving back down the steep track. He really did know the mountains like the back of his hand. And the speed he took the road, it was just as well—because the only faster way would have been over a cliff.

She was relieved to arrive back in one piece at the castle,

and even more relieved when she talked him out of staying. He'd wanted to look around, but he couldn't argue when she pointed out how late it was and that they would wake everyone up. But he would be back on Tuesday for the party—he made that clear.

This mess had to be sorted out before then.

Zoë groaned as she looked round the set. She had discussed the layout with her chief designer. But, according to the note she'd found propped up on the kitchen table, Carla had been called home to attend a family emergency and her young assistant had stepped in.

Zoë couldn't be angry with him; she could see he had tried. But he had fallen a long way short of achieving the authentic look she had decided on with Carla. How could she expect Maria to take part in a show that featured a fake Spanish kitchen decorated with imitation fruit? It might look real enough through a camera lens, but it would never pass close scrutiny, and it would only reinforce Rico's misconceptions about her work.

Why should he barge into her thoughts? She had more important things to consider—like rescuing the programme from disaster! Men like Rico Cortes were no good—great to drool over, maybe, but worse than lousy in real life.

Planting her hands on her hips, Zoë looked round again, but things didn't improve on closer inspection.

Posters brashly proclaiming the title of her latest bestselling cookery book were tacked up everywhere, while garish bunting was strung overhead. The exquisite marble-tiled floor had been hidden beneath a hideous orange carpet, and in the centre of the shag-pile the open-fronted area where she would be filmed sat in all its plywood and plastic glory. Hardly any attempt had been made to mask the fact that it was blatantly fake. There was lurid fake greenery draped around the top, with plastic fruit tacked in clumps to the backdrop.

It would all have to come down, but it could wait until the

morning. She couldn't concentrate while she was so tired. She couldn't concentrate while her thoughts kept straying back to Rico Cortes. A good night's sleep would help her get over him, and then she would get down to work.

As soon as it was light Zoë leapt out of bed. The crew were due on set at nine for a technical rehearsal. That was when the lights, camera angles and sound levels would be decided upon. The best she could hope for was that they would sleep in. She didn't have much time to strip the set and redress it, but it was important she had an authentic set in place for the rehearsal so there would be little or no change when she recorded the programme. She didn't like surprises when the red light went on.

Half an hour later she had picked fruit straight from the trees and brought in a basket full of greenery from the shady part of the castle gardens. Each time she'd visited the market in Cazulas Zoë hadn't been able to resist buying another piece of the local hand-painted pottery, and she now laid out her hoard on a working table along with the fresh produce.

She stared up at the plastic bunting.

Balancing halfway up a ladder wasn't easy, but, working quickly, she got the bunting down, then moved to the 'fishing net' on the back wall of the set to flip out some more tacks. Then she still had to tackle the plastic castanets pinned up with the plastic fruit on the same wall. Proper wooden castanets were miniature works of art. They came alive in the hands of an artist like Maria. These plastic efforts were about as Spanish as chop suey!

Sticking the screwdriver she had found in a kitchen drawer into the back pocket of her jeans, Zoë glanced at her wristwatch and made a swift calculation. If she could get the rest of them down without too much trouble, she might just finish in time.

'Talk about a relief!'

'Are you speaking to me?'

'Rico!' Zoë nearly fell off her ladder with shock. 'What are you doing here?' Her knuckles turned white as she gripped on tight. She watched transfixed as he swooped on the clutch of castanets she had just dropped to the floor.

'Very nice,' he said, examining them. 'Which region of Spain do these represent?'

'Bargain basement,' Zoë tried lightly, trying to regulate her breathing at the same time. How could any man look so good so early in the morning after hardly any sleep? It just wasn't human. 'How did you get in?' she said, as it suddenly struck her that she would never have gone to bed and left the front door wide open.

He ignored her question—and her attempted humour. 'What is all this rubbish?'

Coming down the ladder as quickly as she could in safety, Zoë faced him. 'The set for my television show.' Her appreciative mood was evaporating rapidly. She had never seen such scorn on anyone's face.

'I gathered that.' He stared around with disapproval.

OK, so it was a mess—but it was her mess, and she would sort it out. Zoë could feel her temper rising. According to the lease, at this moment Castillo Cazulas belonged to her. She could do with it what she liked. And if plastic castanets were her style, Señor Testosterone would just have to put up with it.

Reaching out, she took them from him. 'Thank you.' His hands felt warm and dry. They felt great. 'Can I help you with anything?' Her voice was cool, but she was trembling inside.

'Yes, you can. You can get all this trash out of here.'

'Trash?'

'You heard me. I want it all removed.'

'Oh, you do?' Zoë said, meeting his stare. 'And what business is it of yours, exactly?'

Ignoring her question, Rico paced the length of the set, shoulders hunched, looking like a cold-eyed panther stalking its prey. 'You can't seriously expect an artist of Maria's calibre to perform in this *theme park*?'

'No, of course I don't—'

'Then get all this down! Get rid of it! Do whatever you have to do to put it right—just don't let me see it the next time I'm here.'

'Next time? There doesn't have to be a next time, Rico,' Zoë assured him with a short, humourless laugh.

'Oh, forgive me.' He came closer. 'I thought you invited me here for Tuesday.'

'If you feel so bad about all this—' Zoë opened her arms wide '—there's an easy solution.'

'Oh?'

'I'll just withdraw my invitation, and then you won't have to suffer another moment's distress.'

'That would be too easy for you.'

'Easy?' Zoë rested one hand on her head and stared at him incredulously. What the hell was easy about any of this? As far as she was concerned, nothing had been easy since she'd run up against Rico Cortes.

'If you want Maria to dance, I'll be here.'

'Oh, I see,' Zoë said sarcastically. 'You own Maria. You make all her decisions for her—'

'Don't be so ridiculous.'

'So what do you think is going to happen here, Rico? As far as I know we'll be making a television programme. I'll be cooking, Maria will dance, and everyone in the village will have a great time at the party. Is that so terrible?'

He made a contemptuous sound. 'You make it sound so straightforward.'

'Because it is!' What was he getting at? Why didn't he trust her?

They glared at each other without blinking, and then Rico

broke away to stare around. His expression hardened. 'You don't seriously expect me to allow my friends to come to a place like this on Tuesday night.'

'Oh, so now you own the whole village? I didn't realise the feudal system was alive and well in Cazulas. I suppose it's never occurred to you that my neighbours might be capable of thinking for themselves?'

'Your neighbours don't know what you plan to do here.'

'What *do* I plan to do, exactly?'

'You don't respect them.'

'How do you know that?'

'You don't respect their culture.'

'How dare you say that?'

'How dare I?' Rico's voice was contemptuous as he glared down at her.

He was close enough for her to touch—or attack—but she would never lower herself to that. She wasn't about to lose control, like every man she had ever known, and let Rico add that to her long list of shortcomings.

'You come here to Cazulas—Cazulas, of all the flamenco villages in Spain! And you try to tell me it's just a coincidence? And then you bring Maria into it. Another coincidence? I don't think so.'

She'd had enough. She wasn't going to stand by and let him rant. 'You're right, Rico. Bringing Maria into my plans was no coincidence. The reason I asked her to appear on my programme is because she is easily the best dancer I have ever seen. She is certainly the best performer in Cazulas. That's no coincidence; it's a fact.' Zoë couldn't be sure if Rico had heard her or not. He was so tense, so angry—like a wound-up spring on the point of release.

'You come here with your television cameras and your questions.' He gazed around the half-finished set contemptuously. 'You throw together some cheap items and pass it off as a Spanish setting. You really think that's going to convince me that you're putting together some worthy programme about cultural influences on Spanish cooking? You must think I'm stupid.'

'You're certainly mistaken.' But she could see that he might think she was putting up the plastic rubbish, rather than taking it down.

He was so still, so keyed up, he reminded her of a big cat before it pounced. Zoë was beginning to ache with holding herself so stiffly. She sagged with relief when he pulled away from her with a jerk.

'I'll be back to check up on you later. If this rubbish isn't removed by then you can forget Tuesday. Maria will not be dancing for you.'

'Doesn't Maria have a mind of her own?'

Rico was already striding towards the door. He stopped dead. He couldn't believe that she would still dare to challenge him. 'Yes, of course Maria has a mind of her own. She will take one look at this mess and refuse to dance.'

'Oh, get out!'

As he wheeled around he saw the local produce—fresh fruit, greenery, even some attractive pieces of hand-painted pottery. His lips curled in a sneer of contempt. Someone had planned to do something classy for the programme, something appropriate to the area. What a shame Zoë Chapman didn't have any taste.

She really was no better than the rest. Even if she didn't work at the gutter end of television, he would not stand by and see her discard Maria the moment her usefulness was at an end. Maria was too soft-hearted for her own good. It was up to him to protect her from people like Zoë Chapman.

Zoë jumped as the door slammed. Contempt for the disastrous set was about where her dial was pointing, too. But that didn't give Rico Cortes the right to come storming in, ordering her about.

Snatching a plastic parrot down from his perch, she tossed

it into the bin bag with the rest of the rubbish. She hated being caught on the back foot, hated leaving Rico Cortes with the impression that this was all her doing. Most of all she hated the fact that he was coming back to check up on her later. Who the hell did he think he was?

But it would have been far worse still if he hadn't planned to come back at all.

CHAPTER THREE

IT WAS all Rico could do to stay away from the castle. It was barely noon. He had planned to return around late afternoon, but every moment since leaving the castle had been torture.

He had never witnessed such desecration in his life. That was the only reason he was pressing his heel to the floor now. He ground his jaw with satisfaction as the Jeep surged forward. Zoë wouldn't expect him until later, and a surprise visit always revealed more than a planned return. With any luck he would catch her unawares.

Maybe she wasn't the type of tabloid journalist he loathed, but she was still as shallow as the rest, still ignorant of the precious heritage Maria carried forward in the village.

Before he'd left the castle that morning he'd found a member of the television crew, who had assured him they would still be in rehearsal at midday. The youth had also confessed that he was responsible for the set design.

What type of television company used boys fresh out of college for such responsible work? If she owned a decent television company, why didn't she have a proper set designer? Plastic parrots! What the hell did she think she was filming? *Treasure Island?* And what kind of programme had sets dressed with garish rubbish? He could think of a few cable channels that might have gone down that route, and none of them was respectable.

He'd seen Zoë up a ladder dressed in figure-hugging jeans and a skimpy top, instead of her shapeless track suit—and he'd heard her harangue him. He knew now she could play angel or vamp with equal zest.

Glancing at his watch, Rico smiled grimly. He had timed

it just right. The rehearsal should have started. He would check out what line of entertainment Zoë Chapman was really in. Anticipation surged through him. Even through the red mist of his rage this morning she'd looked sensational. Pin-thin women weren't his style, and there was nothing pin-like about Ms Chapman. What would she wear to play her plastic castanets? She had curves that would have done credit to a Rubens.

Slowing the Jeep as he approached the ancient stonework, Rico picked up speed as he hit the long main drive. Accelerating down the avenue of cypress trees, he gave a final spin of the wheel and turned into the familiar cobbled court-yard.

Leaning back with his arms folded against a door at the far end of the Great Hall, he didn't announce his presence, just stood watching in silence. No one noticed him in the shadows. All the focus was on Zoë, in front of the camera.

Even he had to admit the transformation to the set was marked. In place of the fairground bunting and fake castanets there was a plain wooden butcher's block upon which she appeared to be chopping a mountain of herbs. She had a col-lection of wine bottles at her side, and from their shape he recognised a couple as coming from pretty decent cellars.

Rico began to feel increasingly uncomfortable as he watched Zoë working—and he never felt uncomfortable. But then, he had never misjudged anyone quite so badly before.

She couldn't possibly have thrown all this together in a few minutes. It had to be how she always worked—she was too familiar with everything around her for it to be a sham. Brass pots gleamed brightly on the cooking range, and the imple-ments suspended from an overhead rail were all steel, with not a single gimmick in sight. There were wooden bowls close to hand on the counter where she was working, as well as several white porcelain saucers—bearing a selection of spices, he supposed. Next to them a large, shallow blue and white ceramic bowl overflowed with fresh vegetables. Maybe there were a lot of other things he couldn't trust about her, but this was real enough. He had to give her credit for that.

Zoë worked quickly and deftly, her small hands moving instinctively about the necessary tasks as she addressed herself cheerfully to camera. She had charisma as well as beauty, Rico thought, and he felt a sudden longing to harness her smiles and turn them in his own direction.

But how was he supposed to believe she had turned up in Cazulas by chance? If he could talk her into having dinner with him, maybe he could find out. But it wouldn't be easy after their ill-tempered exchange that morning… Easing away from the door, he decided to go. He had seen all he needed to see.

In between takes, Zoë's glance kept straying to the door. Half of her wanted to see Rico again, while the other half dreaded him walking in unannounced. But she needn't have worried because her director, Philip, had just wrapped the day's filming and there was still no sign of Rico. Empty threats, Zoë presumed. Rico's Spanish pride had taken a hit when she'd stood up to him. Or maybe she was just beneath contempt. That was probably it. His face when he'd seen the apprentice set designer's attempts to recreate a 'typical' Spanish setting had said it all. He'd thought she meant to trivialise everything he held dear.

And what was the point of trying to explain when he never listened? But he might have let her know if the others still planned to come on Tuesday night. If he had put them off… She would have to make sure he hadn't talked Maria out of appearing on the programme or she would be facing disaster. Perhaps she should go back to the mountains and find out what was happening?

Zoë was still frowning when one of the girls in the crew asked if she would like to eat with them in the local café that evening. 'I'd really love to come with you,' she said honestly, 'but there's something else I have to do first.'

Was all this totally necessary for a trek into the mountains? Zoë asked herself wryly as she craned her neck to check her rear view in the elegant console mirror. Of course she could always take off the snug-fitting jeans and replace them with a dirndl skirt... *No way!* And what about the blouse: ever so slightly see-through, with just one too many buttons left undone? OK, so maybe that was going a step too far. She fastened it almost to the neck. Reaching for a lightweight cotton sweater from the chair, she checked her hair one last time and then added a slick of lipgloss and a spritz of perfume.

Her eyes were glittering like aquamarine in a face that seemed unusually pale, Zoë noticed—apart from two smudges of red, high on each cheekbone. That was thanks to excitement at finally bringing the programme together. It was the culmination of a year of hard work. It had nothing at all to do with the fact that she might be seeing Rico Cortes again.

She had come to him. Rico subdued the rush of triumph before it had time to register on his face. 'Ms Chapman,' he said coolly. 'To what do we owe this pleasure?'

Leaning back against a gnarled tree trunk, arms folded, he watched Zoë's approach through narrowed eyes. Her unaffected grace was so like that of the dancers she admired, and she looked great in casual clothes. She wore little make-up, and her skin was honey-gold from her time in the sun. She was beautiful—very different from the glamorous women he was used to outside Cazulas, but all the more beautiful for that. The light was slipping away fast, and the sky behind the snow-capped mountains was more dramatic than any he had seen for a while: a radiant banner of violet and tangerine— the perfect backdrop for their latest encounter. The night breeze was kicking up, rustling through the leaves above his head as she walked up to him.

'You said you would come back to the castle.'

Her blunt statement took him by surprise—a pleasant one. 'I did come back, but you were working.'

That rather took the wind out of her sails, Zoë thought, but her heart was still thumping so violently she felt sure Rico would be able to hear it. 'I see.' She was relieved to sound so cool. 'I trust the changes I made met with your exacting standards?'

He gave a short laugh and relaxed. 'You did a great job, Zoë. Can I get you a drink?'

'Nothing stronger than orange juice!'

'Fine by me.'

He gestured that she should follow him, and his impressive rear view led her to silently praise the inventor of close-fitting jeans.

It was too early for the campfire to be lit, but there were still quite a lot of people around. Most of them were waiting for the children to finish their dance class. This meeting place served a number of functions, Zoë realised. There was the social side, and the performance opportunities, as well as the very valuable teaching that went on to preserve tradition.

She could see the youngsters now, tense with excitement and anticipation as they clustered around their dance teacher, listening to what she had to say. In another area a couple of the boys were sitting at the feet of the guitarist who had played for Maria, watching engrossed as his agile fingers rippled across the strings.

Pouring them both some juice from a covered jug that had been left for the children on a trestle table, Rico handed a glass to Zoë and then took her to sit with him on a flat rock out of the way. Crossing one leg over the other, he rested his chin on his hand as he listened to the music.

The low, insistent rhythm of the solo guitar was the perfect

soundtrack for Rico Cortes, Zoë thought, glancing at him surreptitiously as she sipped her drink. Dressed in simple black
jeans and a black top, he made her heart judder, he looked so
good. The close-fitting top defined every muscle and sinew
across the wide spread of his shoulders, and the jeans moulded
thighs powerful enough to control a wild stallion, or a
woman…

'You're far too early to see any of the adult performers
dance, you know,' he said, his gaze lingering on Zoë's face
as the guitarist picked out a particularly plangent arpeggio.

'I haven't come to see them,' she said, meeting his gaze
steadily.

'Oh?' A crooked smile tugged at one corner of his mouth.

'Or you,' she said immediately. 'I hoped I might find
Maria.'

'Well, you will—but you can't talk to her yet. So you might
just as well settle back and enjoy the children rehearsing for
our fiesta.'

'Fiesta? That must be fun.' Zoë turned to watch them.
'Does everyone take part in the fiesta?'

'Why don't you come along and see for yourself?'

She wanted to. She really wanted to feel part of Cazulas.
Since the moment she'd arrived in the village she had felt an
affinity with the area, and with the people. Rico made it sound
so easy for her to become part of their way of life, but she
wouldn't be staying that long.

'When will everyone else arrive?' Zoë looked around.
There were a few cars parked already, notably Rico's rugged
black Jeep.

'Most people take a long, lazy siesta in the afternoon, when
the weather gets hot.'

'So Maria's still in bed?' Zoë could feel the blood rushing
to her cheeks. Where was she going with *this* line of questioning?

'Many people are still in bed—but Maria is not one of

them.' Standing up, he beckoned to Zoë to follow him, and, walking ahead of her, he made for the stage where the children were still learning their steps.

Once again, he reminded Zoë of a big black panther. He had the same grace and stealth of a big cat, and made her feel very small by comparison. It was impossible not to imagine how it might feel to be enclosed in his arms and held safe. Or to be pinned down by those long, hard-muscled legs, and— *Stop it! Stop it now!* This was dangerous.

'Zoë?'

'Maria!' Zoë exclaimed, throwing her brain into gear. 'I'm sorry, I was daydreaming. I didn't realise it was you dancing with the children. It's good to see you again.'

'Why have you come here? Not to see the children, I think,' Maria said, tapping the side of her nose.

'No—no, of course not,' Zoë said, recovering fast. 'I came to see you.'

'Ah,' Maria said, staring at her keenly.

'I wanted to make sure you hadn't changed your mind.'

'Changed my mind? About dancing on Tuesday, you mean?' Maria said. 'Why would I?'

'Oh, I don't know,' Zoë said, suddenly embarrassed at the weakness of her supposed mission. She was conscious of Rico watching them, arms folded, with the same brooding look that made her quiver. 'I just wanted to be sure no one had put you off the idea.' She stopped, thinking frantically for something to explain her visit. 'After all, you don't know me—'

'Stop worrying,' Maria insisted. 'I will be there for you on Tuesday, Zoë. Your television programme will be made, and everything will turn out for the best in the end.'

Would it? Zoë wondered. There were moments when she wished she had never come to Spain. A fresh start was supposed to be just that—not a rerun with a matching set of characters that just happened to have different names.

Was she overreacting? She really hoped so. Men like Rico

had always been her downfall: big, powerful men like her ex-husband. Men who oozed testosterone through every pore; men who made her believe she could be desirable and might even find sexual fulfilment with them.

Unconsciously, Zoë made a small sound of despair. She was a sexual oddity—and likely to remain so. She was frightened of sex, it always hurt, and she wasn't sure how to improve the situation. Her husband had grown tired of her excuses. She had made him hate her. Small wonder they had divorced.

But that was behind her now. She had rebuilt her life. She couldn't allow anyone, especially Rico Cortes, to fan her past insecurities into flame…

'Zoë?' Maria asked softly. 'What is the matter?'

'Nothing.' Collecting herself, Zoë spoke firmly and smiled. 'Now,' she added quickly, before Maria could probe any deeper, 'I'd like to discuss my outline plan for the programme in which you're to appear. I want to be quite sure you're happy with everything.'

'*Bueno,*' Maria murmured softly, frowning a little as she allowed Zoë to lead her away from Rico.

The two women remained deep in conversation for some time. They were both on the same wavelength, Zoë realised. Maria was only too pleased to have the opportunity to bring genuine Spanish culture to a wider audience, and Zoë liked to present her food in context, rather than offering individual, unconnected recipes. This was her definition of lifestyle TV— a show that was genuine in every single respect—and now she had control over the content of her own programmes it was exactly what she delivered.

It was going to be really good, she realised with a sudden rush of excitement. Maria's talent would imbue the show with her own special quality. Rico had correctly identified it as something that no amount of money could buy.

Glancing around, Zoë looked for him. But he must have left while she was talking to Maria.

'Don't look so sad,' Maria insisted, chucking her under the chin. 'I know what we will do,' she added, getting to her feet.

Once again Zoë was struck by the difference in mobility between the Maria who had been sitting next to her and the Maria who performed on the stage—the one so fluid and graceful, the other showing definite, if gracious, signs of her age. 'What will we do, Maria?'

'We will dance together.'

'Oh, no, I can't—'

'You can walk, you can run, and you can jump?'

'Well, yes, of course—'

'Then you can dance,' Maria told her sternly. 'But first we must find you some clothes. Those will not do,' she said, eyeing Zoë's slim-fitting jeans and top. 'You look like a boy. I want to make you look like a woman.'

Zoë's eyes widened. She was too polite to argue. And far too curious to see what Maria meant to refuse.

Now she knew the secret of the wooden mountain house around which people congregated. It was packed to the rafters with the most spectacular clothes: rows of shoes, boxes of hair ornaments, cascading fringed shawls, and dresses by the score in every colour under the rainbow.

'You're so lucky to take performing under the stars for granted.' Zoë peered out of one of the small windows at the darkening sky. Someone had lit the campfire, and flames were just beginning to take hold. It was such a romantic scene, like something out of an old musical film. The children were still rehearsing—not because they had to now, but because they wanted to. Their heads were held high, faces rapt, their backs were arched and their hands expressive. 'The children are a credit to you, Maria.'

Maria paused as she sorted through the dresses packed tight

on the rail. 'They are a credit to themselves and to each other,' she corrected Zoë gently. 'And if they can do it, so can you.'

'Oh, no, really—I can't—' Her dancing was confined to her classes.

'Who said you can't? Here, try these on.'

Maria brought her an armful of clothes and Zoë's face broke into a smile. Maria was like a gust of fresh spring air behind a heavy rain cloud. It was impossible to be hooked by the past when she was around.

'The colour of this dress will look good on you.'

Zoë exclaimed with pleasure as she gazed at the beautiful lilac dress. Maria's confidence was infectious.

'You can put the dress on over there.' Maria pointed across the room. 'That's where the children get changed—behind that screen. When you have it on, come out and choose some shoes to fit you from this row here. Don't worry—I will help you to finish fastening the dress, and then I will do your hair.'

For once it was a pleasure to do as she was told. Zoë knew she would dance, because Maria would give her the confidence to do so. She was excited at the prospect of trying something new, especially now Rico had gone. She wouldn't have wanted to make a show of herself if he'd still been around.

Maria was right; the low-cut lilac dress did look good against her titian hair. It moulded her figure like a glove down to her hips, where it flared out, and then was longer at one side than the other. She was showing quite a bit of leg, Zoë saw in the mirror, raising the skirt with a flourish. Just wearing the dress made her stand straight and proud, made her want to toss back her hair with the same defiant move she had seen Maria perform on stage.

Dipping her chin, Zoë tried out her expression, staring fiercely into the mirror through a fringe of long lashes. A poster on the wall behind her caught her attention. The dark-haired young woman was incredibly beautiful. Passion blazed from her eyes as she glared straight into the camera. She had the sinuous frame of a top model, though was more striking than any model Zoë had ever seen. Her full lips were slightly parted and a strand of her long ebony hair had caught across them, giving her flamenco pose a sense of movement. There was a single word stretched across the top of the fiery background: Beba.

'*Bueno!*' Maria said with approval when Zoë finally emerged from behind the screen. 'That dress really suits you. I knew it would. Let me just finish the hooks and eyes at the back for you. They are hard for you to reach.'

'I feel different. It's ridiculous, but—'

'It's flamenco.' Maria laughed happily and stood back to look at Zoë. 'Now you feel proud and confident, like a woman should. Come, I will arrange your hair for you. And then we dance!'

Taka taka taka tak tak tak…taka taka taka tak… She was doing it! They had practised for about an hour on the dusty ground, and now Maria had deemed Zoë ready for the stage where, working together, the heels of their shoes made a crisp, satisfying sound on the hard wooden floor.

Breathing hard, her face fierce with concentration, Zoë thrust her head back as Maria had directed. One arm sweeping behind her back, she raised the other hand stiff, in a defiant pose, as if calling up some invisible energy…

'*Olé!*'

'Rico!'

'Don't stop now,' Maria ordered sharply.

But Zoë suddenly felt exposed and foolish. 'I'd much rather watch you,' she said, moving to the back of the stage. 'You haven't danced a solo yet.'

'I'm saving myself,' Maria said sardonically. 'Whereas you, Zoë, are hiding yourself.'

'That's not true…'

'Isn't it?' Maria demanded as Rico approached the stage.

'Why did you stop?' He stared up at Zoë.

'I'm very much a beginner—I'm not ready to perform in public.' Her heart lurched at his assessing look.

'But from what I have seen you have potential—don't you agree, Maria?'

'*Mucho* potential,' Maria agreed, but she made a disapproving sound with her tongue against the roof of her mouth when she looked at Rico, as if she sensed some double meaning behind his words.

'So, will you dance for me, Zoë?'

Rico's question had an alarming effect on Zoë's senses. It was like every seduction technique imaginable condensed into a few short words. She would love nothing more than to dance for him, with this new and abandoned feeling rushing through her. Just the thought of being so uninhibited in his presence was tempting. She felt strong, and in control, and highly sexual—as if the dance had enabled her to plunge head first into a world of sensuality for the first time in her life. Sucking in a deep, shuddering breath, Zoë realised she loved the feeling. It was intoxicating—and extremely dangerous.

'I'm waiting for your answer,' Rico reminded her.

Zoë glanced around, but Maria had melted away, lost in the crowds already gathering for that night's performance.

'Come down from there.'

She looked at him and hesitated.

'Please, Zoë?'

She was surprised. His voice had gentled.

'I don't bite, and—'

'Are you apologising to me?' Zoë said, cocking her head to one side as she looked at him.

'Me?' Rico half smiled at her as he touched one hand to his chest.

His eyes were different now, she noticed. Darker, still a

little guarded, but warmer—definitely warmer. 'Yes, you. Who else has doubted my motives in Cazulas, Rico?'

And he still doubted her motives. But he could handle it. He could handle her too. 'So, you're too timid to dance for me?'

'I don't do private exhibitions.'

'That's a pity.'

'Is it? Would you really think more of me if I made a habit of dancing for men? I don't think so. You've already shown your contempt for me—I can just imagine what you would make of that.'

'I admit we've got off to a bad start—'

'That's putting it mildly.'

'So, here's our chance to start again.'

'Should I want to?'

She saw his mouth quirk at one corner, as if he wanted to smile.

'I hoped you might.'

Zoë half turned away, lifting her chin as she considered his words. 'I'm not so sure,' she said, turning back to him again with a frown. 'Why should I? I don't need the aggravation.'

'Who said anything about aggravation, Zoë? Come on—come down from there and let's talk.'

She couldn't stand up on the stage all night. People were beginning to stare at her. She would have to do something soon—dance a solo or get off the stage. Picking up her skirt, she walked briskly down the steps.

'Zoë, please.'

She looked down at Rico's hand on her arm. 'This had better be good.'

'I hope you think so.'

She gasped when he drew her in front of him. 'Rico, what—?'

'I think I've behaved rather badly.'

'Yes, you have.' It was harder than she had thought to meet his gaze this close up.

'I can understand why you don't feel like trusting me now.'

'Can you?' She didn't trust herself either when he was around.

'Will you let me make amends? Have dinner with me.'

Zoë stared at him. Was he serious?

'Zoë?'

She had to get herself out of this somehow. 'I've got an idea.'

'Which is?'

He seemed amused. But hopefully this would get her off the hook. It was the only challenge she could think of that Rico wouldn't want to take up. 'If you cook for me, I'll dance for you.'

'*Bueno.*' He didn't waste any time over his answer. 'Shall we say later tonight?'

'Tonight?' All the breath seemed suddenly to have been sucked out of her lungs.

'We eat late in Spain.' Rico was quite matter-of-fact about it. Did he think her hesitation was due to ignorance of local customs? 'Shall we say ten o'clock?'

'Ten o'clock?' Zoë repeated, staring up at him blankly.

'Yes, let's say ten. That will give you enough time to pre-pare.'

To prepare what? She bit her lip. Unaccountably, her brain stalled, and not a single word of refusal made it to her lips.

'Then it's agreed,' Rico said with satisfaction. 'We will meet again, later tonight, at Castillo Cazulas.'

CHAPTER FOUR

THIS was the last thing she had expected to be doing, Zoë thought, as she tested the small four-wheel drive she had just hired to its limits. Rico had said he would follow her back to the castle later, to cook the meal and watch her dancing. She could only hope he was joking. The idea of dancing for him already seemed ridiculous.

Glancing in the driver's mirror, she saw the bundle of clothes Maria had insisted she take with her, assuring her that she would feel more comfortable dancing in them than jeans. More comfortable? Maybe—until Rico saw her wearing the flimsy low-necked blouse and ultra-feminine practice skirt!

She knew she was playing with fire, but where Rico Cortes was concerned it seemed she couldn't resist courting danger. Fortunately the film crew would be out partying until late, so no one would even know what she planned to do—or what kind of fool she made of herself.

As she pulled into the courtyard she thought about cancelling. But she didn't know how to get hold of Rico—and why should she pull out? She was more likely to dance than he was to cook. It was an opportunity to redress the balance between them…he would never doubt her will again.

The heavy iron knocker echoed ominously through the long stone passages as Zoë hurried to open the front door. Prompt at ten o'clock, Rico had said, and he was bang on time, she saw, glancing up at the tall grandfather clock on the turn of the stairs.

She was shivering all over with excitement and apprehension, and, reaching the hallway, she made herself slow down. She didn't want to appear too keen.

But as she walked her hips swayed beneath the ankle-length skirt, and as the swathes of fabric brushed her naked legs she knew the clothes Maria had given her to wear made her move quite differently. Even the simple peasant blouse was enough to make her want to throw her head back and walk tall. No wonder the women of Spain looked so magnificent when they stepped onto a stage when all their clothes were designed to make the most of the female form.

'Zoë.'

She could feel her face heating up as Rico stared at her. She tried for cool and unconcerned as she stood aside to let him pass. 'Welcome. How nice to see you.'

Nice! Zoë felt as if a furnace had just roared into flame somewhere inside her. She felt weak, she felt strong, and her legs were trembling uncontrollably beneath her skirt. She registered the flash of a dark, imperious gaze, and then he was gone, walking past her towards the kitchen.

He seemed to know his way—but then he would. Who knew how long he had been hanging around the castle earlier that morning? And so far he seemed to be keeping his side of the bargain: he had a box of provisions, as well as a guitar case slung over his shoulder.

'That was absolutely delicious,' she said, some time later.

'You seem surprised.'

She was, Zoë realised. Not only had Rico kept to his part of their bargain, he was an excellent cook. 'I am.'

'Because I can cook?'

Zoë smiled. It was hard to concentrate on anything apart from Rico's face as he stared at her. It wiped her mind clean, made her long to know him better. Physically, he was everything she knew to avoid. But they were alone together, and she wondered if she had misjudged him. He was still proud, male and alpha, but he had a sense of humour too—something she hadn't anticipated. 'I'm not surprised you can cook. I'm just surprised that you can cook so well.'

'Is there any reason why I should be incapable of feeding myself?'

'Of course not. It's just that most men—'

'Most men?'

She loved the way one of his eyebrows tilted a fraction when he asked a question. She'd been thinking of her ex, sitting at the table waiting for his meal after they had both put in a long day at work. He'd only commented on her food when it hadn't been to his liking. She had never received a compliment from him for her cooking.

'Most men wouldn't know their way around a warm barbecued vegetable salad with anchovies.'

'*Escalivada amb anxoves?*' Rico translated for her. 'It's a great dish, isn't it? My mother is a fabulous cook, and she taught all her children how to prepare food. It is no big deal.' He got to his feet to collect their plates.

'Your mother?' Instantly Zoë was curious. Either Rico ignored her interest, or he didn't notice. But she noticed the fact that he was clearing up after them. He wouldn't even allow her to help, just pushed her gently back down in her chair again.

'Save your strength for the dancing.'

His eyes were glinting with humour again. Not mockery, humour—humour shared between them. Feeling her confidence returning, Zoë smiled back. 'You know your way round a dishwasher too. I'm impressed.'

'You must have known some very strange men in your time, Zoë.'

Zoë smiled faintly. *You don't want to know how strange.*

Rico insisted on doing everything—even wiping down the surfaces and clearing the condiments from the table. Only when the kitchen had been returned to its former pristine condition did he turn to her.

'Now it is time for you to dance, Zoë.'

His eyes, she noticed, were already dancing—with laughter and with challenge. But somehow it gave her courage. He gave her courage.

'I'm ready. After that meal I've got a lot to live up to, so I'd better limber up before I begin. I would hate to disappoint you.'

'I will tune my guitar while you prepare.'

How long would that take? she wondered. Not long enough for her to be ready to dance for him, that was for sure!

As fast as Zoë's courage had returned, it vanished again. She wanted to impress Rico, and doubted she could. She wanted his gaze to linger on her, to bathe her in his admiration. She wanted him to want her as much as she wanted him.

She wanted to know more about his mother, Zoë corrected herself fiercely.

'Why don't we have pudding first, and talk a little longer?'

'You can't put it off all night. Are you having second thoughts, Zoë?'

'Not at all.'

'Then no more delaying tactics,' Rico said, reaching for his guitar. 'Sweet things come later, when we have earned them.'

How good his command of English was! His few words had set her on fire. She hadn't given a moment's thought to *later*, but clearly Rico had.

Subduing a rush of apprehension, Zoë led the way into the Great Hall. Rico sat on the stool she had placed there for him, and began adjusting the strings of his guitar.

'You have a beautiful guitar.' Under Rico's hands it had come to life, producing sounds that were rich and lovely.

'It's a flamenco guitar, made of spruce and cypress.'

'So it really does represent the music of the region?'

'Absolutely,' he murmured.

Zoë looked away first.

While Rico strummed some chords, testing them for clarity and tuning, Zoë centred herself, bending and stretching before the dance began.

Rico seemed to sense when she was ready to begin, and turned his head. With a brief nod, she walked to the centre of her improvised performance space in the centre of the vast square hall.

At first she was stiff and self-conscious, but Rico second-guessed her every move. She had never danced with such a sympathetic accompanist before—in fact she'd never danced with a real live accompanist before, and certainly not one who made her thrill even more than the music.

Rico made no allowances for the fact that she was new to flamenco, and in truth she didn't want him to; after just a short time she didn't need him to. Their partnership was as tight as Zoë could have wished, and after a few minutes all her tension disappeared.

There were some large ornate mirrors in this part of the hall, which was why she had chosen it. She could see Rico sitting cross-legged on his stool. He appeared lost in the music, but then he looked up and Zoë was lost in his eyes.

Instead of hesitating, Rico picked up the pace, his gaze boring into her as he drew rhythms hotter and more powerful than Zoë had ever thought possible from his guitar. His fingers moved at speed across the fretboard, producing an earthy sound that throbbed insistently through her. She could feel herself growing more abandoned with every step, until she was whirling in time to a rhythm of Rico's choosing. Then, abruptly, he slowed the tempo so that it rose and fell in waves of sound that dropped at last to a low and insistent rumble.

The sound was so faint Zoë could barely hear it. She might not have known he was still playing had it not been for the fact that she could still feel the music in every fibre of her being.

'That's enough for tonight,' he said suddenly, damping the strings with his hand.

She had been so absorbed in the dance, so lost in the sound he was creating, it took her a moment to come round and realise that Rico had stopped playing. She watched him prop his guitar against the wall, and was still in a sort of trance when he walked across the floor to her.

And then she came to with a bump, realising she was so aroused that her nipples were pressing tautly against the fine lawn top. Instinctively she lifted her hands to cover herself, but she could do nothing about the insistent pulse down low in her belly.

'I think you enjoyed that, Ms Chapman…and you're very good.' He stopped a few feet away, and made no attempt to close the gap.

Zoë licked her lips. Rico knew she was aroused. She could feel his response to that arousal enveloping her. He might as well have undone the ties on her blouse and exposed her erect nipples. Or lifted her skirt high above her waist and seen her there… He could arouse her as easily as that—without even touching her. And now she didn't want him to stop or turn away. This could be her one and only chance to push past arousal and see if she could handle the next stage…

'I think it's time for our dessert, Zoë.'

Zoë tried to hide her disappointment when Rico held out his hand to her. Her face was on fire at the thought she had made such a fool of herself. 'Dessert? Yes, of course.'

'Spanish-style.'

She saw the look in his eyes and felt a rush of heat flood through her as she realised that the last thing on Rico's mind was a return visit to the kitchen. *Oh.*

Her gaze fixed on his hand. He was waiting for her to clasp it. Was this what she wanted? Could she go ahead with it? Wasn't it better to stop now, before she proved to herself as well as Rico that as far as sex went she was one big disaster area? She didn't want to spoil the evening—which was what would happen if she allowed things to go any further.

For some reason the young flamenco dancer on the poster in the mountain hut flew into Zoë's mind. Beba was a proper woman, a sexual woman... But then Rico's arms closed around her and it was too late.

Zoë shuddered with desire as his mouth brushed her lips. She felt so small, so dainty—and desired. This far was fine—it was as far as she could ever go: a kiss, a light caress... She closed her eyes as he applied a little more pressure, his firm lips moving over her mouth until she softened against him.

Could so much pleasure come from a simple kiss? But there was nothing uncomplicated where Rico was concerned.

He felt her tense, and stroked her back with long, light strokes until she eased into him again. He tugged lightly with his teeth on her bottom lip until the tremors rippling through her reached her womb. She whimpered, wanting more, and, teasing her lips apart, he deepened the kiss.

Zoë accepted the pace Rico set just as she had accepted the music he had played for her—music that had begun so gently, so calmly... It was like that now. He was so strong she could sense the powerhouse contained beneath his tracing fingers and wonderfully caressing hands. His touch was as light as the softest chord on the guitar, and as if she was his instrument now the vibrations through her body went on and on.

As their kisses grew more heated she was swept up in the need to rub against him, to feel the hard bristle on his face scoring her cheeks, rasping her neck. Their breathing was hectic and there were sounds welling from deep inside their throats as the pace quickened like the fiery rhythms of flamenco. Need was overwhelming them. They were as rough now, and as mindlessly passionate, as the final furious torrent of demanding chords.

Then a flash of reality intruded, brutal and strong. She didn't know if she could stop him. He frightened her. She frightened herself. Things were getting out of control. What the hell was she doing?

Zoë tensed as the floodgates of the past gave way beneath the weight of ugly memories. 'No, no! Stop it! I can't—' She tried desperately to push him away.

'What do you mean, you can't?' Rico said sharply, holding her fast as he stared intently into her eyes.

'I just can't,' Zoë said, snatching her face away from his as she struggled to break free.

But he wouldn't let her go, and, cupping her chin, brought her back to face him again. 'What can't you do, Zoë? Answer me.'

She knew he sensed her fear.

'Tell me, please.'

His voice was gentle, and when she looked up at him their faces were almost touching.

'Tell me what's wrong, Zoë. Is there someone else?'

'I can't tell you what's wrong.' Zoë pressed her lips together. That was true. How could she? Where were the words to explain how some giant switch had simply turned off inside her, so that all she felt now with him was fear and apprehension?

'Has someone hurt you? Or do you already have a man? Did he do something to you? Did he hurt you?'

'No!' Zoë covered her ears with her hands, protecting herself against the barrage of questions, trying to shut out the ugly scenes replaying in her mind. She wasn't ready for this. Would she ever be ready?

But none of it was Rico's fault. Her gaze flew to his face, and she knew he saw the answer in her eyes.

'Zoë…Zoë.' He brought her close. 'Why didn't you tell me?'

'We don't know each other.' Her voice was muffled against his chest.

'I'd like to change that.'

She wanted to believe him. She wanted desperately to be-lieve him, to think he might be different. But her past kept on insisting she was wrong. 'Can we change the subject?' She straightened her hair. 'What about if I make the pudding?'

'Zoë—'

'I don't mind.'

'Stop it, Zoë.' Pulling back, Rico held her in front of him.

'It won't take me long.' She couldn't look at him.

'Not tonight.'

There was a sharp note in his voice that drew her gaze, and she saw his face was serious and troubled.

'All right, you make the pudding,' she said.

She was determined to stick to the mundane, Rico realised. That way she could pretend it had never happened. He stared at her, wishing she would tell him everything, knowing that would never happen. 'OK. I did promise to cook for you tonight.'

He could feel the relief radiating from her, but the easy atmosphere they'd shared earlier had gone; they both knew it. He had opened an old wound, and he shuddered to think what that wound might be.

Rico occupied Zoë's mind throughout most of that night. She couldn't sleep and she couldn't think about anything apart from him. She had gone cold and he had gone—no surprises there. His bright golden fritters dressed with fresh lemon juice and vanilla sugar had been a surprise. They'd been truly un-forgettable—as had his swift departure the moment he had bolted them down!

He hadn't been able to get away fast enough. She couldn't blame him. They had shared one lovely evening, thanks to Maria. And now, with The Kiss out of the way, at least he knew she wasn't interested in that sort of thing.

She had laid her cards out in front of him. She couldn't be like other women—women who took their right to enjoy physical love for granted. Women like the flamenco dancer on the poster. It was better Rico knew that.

Her ex had been right. She was frigid. And it wasn't that she didn't try—she felt sexy, and she hoped she looked at least a little bit appealing, but as soon as things turned hot she went cold. That was what had happened tonight. No one could change what she was—not even Rico. Thumping her pillows into submission, Zoë settled down to sleep.

Zoë's hands flew to her face. The stinging slap had jolted her whole frame. She could never beg; that was her problem. She could never ask for forgiveness, for understanding, when she didn't know what she had done wrong.

She backed away, stumbling in the darkness, feeling for the furniture to guide her. Finally there was nowhere else to go. She was pressed back against the cold, hard door. She could only stand now, and wait for her punishment. There was no escape. The door was locked. She knew that too, without trying the handle. She knew it just as surely as she knew what was coming next.

She looked at him then, but his face was shadowed and she couldn't be sure who it was. She searched her mind desperately, trying to think of something that would make him change his mind, make him listen to her. But he was already taking off his belt.

This was always the worst part—the waiting. She could hear herself whimpering as she held up her hands to shield her face…

'Oh!' Zoë lurched up into a sitting position, reeling with shock. It took her a few minutes to get her bearings and realise she was safe in her bed at the castle.

Steadying her breathing, she looked around. Of course there was nothing unpleasant in the room. It was quite empty. The castle was completely still. She had heard several doors slamming when the film crew came back from their evening at the café, but it was the middle of the night now; everyone was sound asleep.

Glancing at her wristwatch on the bedside table, she saw that it was three o'clock in the morning. Slipping out of bed, she pulled back one side of the heavy curtains and gazed out to where the castle walls were tipped with silver in the moonlight. Where was Rico now? Where was he sleeping? Was he alone? He had never told her where he lived, and she had never asked. Did he live with anyone? Was he married?

A bolt of shame cut through her. She would never hurt anyone as she had been hurt—yet she knew none of the answers to these questions. She had let Rico kiss her without knowing anything about him, and then she had gone on to betray her innermost fears to him.

Zoë pulled away from the window. Unwelcome details of the nightmare were slithering back through the unguarded passages in her mind. She couldn't shut them out. She had tried that before, but they always, always came back. Rico didn't know anything about her, about her past. How would she bear the shame when he found out? His rejection tonight would be nothing compared to the scorn and contempt he would feel for her then.

In her mind's eye Zoë could already see his face; it was cold and unforgiving. But even that was better than revisiting the dark side of her memories. She could only be grateful that by filling her mind with Rico Cortes she had finally found a way to blot the worst of them out.

Was this how it was always going to be—her ex-husband haunting her for ever?

Yes—if she allowed him to, Zoë realised.

Opening the window as far as she could, she leaned out, drinking in the healing beauty of the mountains.

The moonlight was like a blessing on her face. Closing her eyes, she inhaled deeply. There was a faint scent of blossom on the air.

CHAPTER FIVE

ZOË was up shortly after dawn on Monday. She was skilled at putting the dark shadows behind her, and, though she was tired after her disturbed night, her mind was full of the party the following day. She was determined to have everything ready in good time.

The local producers took a well-earned rest over the week-end, and Monday was the only day the market opened late. That played into her hands, giving her a chance to draw up a schedule and get organised before she went shopping for in-gredients. She enjoyed supervising everything—even down to which flowers she would have on the tables.

Taking a glass of freshly squeezed orange juice with her onto the veranda, she perched on a seat overlooking the cy-press grove to make her list. It was still cool, and she had taken the precaution of wearing a cosy sweater over her py-jamas. Her hair was still sleep-tangled round her shoulders and for a while she just sat idly, soaking up the view. The air was quite still, apart from the occasional flurry of early-morning breeze, and there were few sounds to disturb her tranquil state other than the birds chorusing their approval of another bright new day.

Closing her eyes, Zoë relished the touch of the sun on her freshly washed face. She breathed deeply and smiled as she inhaled the same scent she had enjoyed the previous night. The cicadas were just kicking off with a rumba. The perfume of the blossom was overlaid with the warm, spicy aroma of Spain. She couldn't have been anywhere else. She didn't want to be anywhere else. Feeling a sudden rush of joy, she stretched out her arms towards the sun—then another sound intruded.

Opening her eyes, she straightened up and looked around, and saw a horse and rider coming towards her at speed. Shading her eyes against the low, slanting rays of the sun, she could just make out the shape of a man crouched low over the neck of his horse. He was galloping flat out towards her, down the tree-lined grove, using the mile-long stretch like his own private racecourse.

'Rico?' Zoë murmured, getting to her feet. Her heart was pounding, and for a moment she panicked. Only an emergency could have brought him to the castle at such a pace.

But then he slowed abruptly, when he was still some yards from the entrance to the courtyard.

Almost as if he knew he was close to water, the horse pricked up his ears and pranced towards the trough located right beneath the veranda where Zoë was standing. The sound of his hooves on the cobbles made her smile. Did everyone dance to the rhythm of flamenco in Cazulas?

The black stallion and his rider were a magnificent sight. Rico was so much a part of his mount it was difficult to tell who made the decisions, and Zoë smiled again in admiration as she raised her hand in greeting. She could ride—but not like that.

Reining in beneath the veranda, Rico smiled up at her.

Zoë was surprised he looked pleased to see her. Had he forgotten what had happened between them the previous night? She had made a fool of herself. So why was he here? What had he come for?

'Buenos días, señorita!' Rico bowed low over the withers of his horse. 'I trust I find you well this morning?'

His uncomplicated greeting bolstered Zoë's determination not to slip back into her old ways. He wasn't being scornful or cruel, he was just saying good morning.

'*Buenos días, señor.*' Planting her hands on the veranda rail, she smiled down at him.

'You look tired,' Rico observed as he sprang down to the ground. Swinging the reins over the horse's head, he tethered him to a pole.

'Do I?' Zoë put a hand to her cheek. She had no intention of telling him why. 'I haven't had a chance to put my make-up on. That must be it.' Then she remembered her shabby old pyjama bottoms, flapping in the breeze beneath her rumpled sweater.

'You don't need make-up.' He took the steps two, three at a time. 'But you do look tired.' Pulling off his soft calfskin riding gloves, he slapped them together in the palm of one hand. 'That juice looks good.'

'It is. I'm sorry, would you like one?'

'Thank you, that would be nice.'

The jug of juice was in the refrigerator in the kitchen. And he would need a glass. She would have the chance to slip out and change into a respectable outfit. 'Please, sit down. I'll go and get the juice for you.'

'I'll come with you.'

'No, that's—' Pointless arguing with him, Zoë thought wryly, leading the way inside.

Every tiny hair rose on the back of her neck at knowing Rico was behind her, and as he held the door for her she could picture his muscles flexing beneath the close-fitting riding breeches, the turn of his calf beneath the long leather riding boots. And that was before she considered the wide spread of his shoulders, the powerful forearms shaded with dark hair, the inky black waves caressing high-chiselled cheekbones, slightly flushed beneath his tan after the exertions of his ride.

She could picture everything about him—his mouth, his lips—she could feel the scrape of his bristle on her cheeks, and she could remember all too clearly that she had pushed him away when he had wanted to kiss her.

Because she was frigid.

It was no use, Zoë realised as they walked into the kitchen. She would never be able to relax with a man like Rico. She would never know what it felt like to be properly kissed by him. But that didn't stop her wanting to.

'The work for this meal isn't proving too much for you?' He looked around when she had given him a glass of fresh juice. 'You seem to have made enough for an army already.'

'I'm never happier then when I'm cooking.' She stared at him as he went to wash out his empty glass at the sink. She was so used to clearing up after people she knew she would never get used to this.

When he had finished, Rico turned back to her. He slipped one thumb into his belt-loop, and before she knew what she was doing Zoë had followed the movement. Feeling her face flame red, she redirected her gaze into his eyes.

'It all smells wonderful.' Rico smiled.

'Thank you.' Zoë's throat seemed to have closed up. The riding breeches moulded him precisely, revealingly—terrifyingly. 'Why are you here?' Her voice sounded faint, and she was glad there was a table between them.

'It's such a beautiful morning I thought you might like to ride out with me—if you're not too busy…'

She could hardly pretend to be when she had been lazing on the veranda when he arrived. 'I've thought about riding lots of times since I got here, but—'

'But?'

'Well, I can't ride like you.'

'There are plenty of quieter mounts than mine to choose from in the stables.'

'I'd really like that.' Zoë frowned. 'But I'd have to change.'

'Go right ahead. I'll wait for you.'

'All right, then.'

Closing the door behind her, Zoë leaned against it for a moment to catch her breath. What was she doing? She closed her eyes. She couldn't let her old life get in the way. She had fought her way out; she wasn't going to slip back now. There was nothing wrong in riding with Rico. She could do with the exercise. The rest of the day was for shopping and cooking, so an hour's recreation would be perfect. In fact, it was just what she needed.

Zoë changed her clothes quickly, putting on jeans and a shirt. When she returned to the kitchen Rico was gazing around at the changes she had made.

'I trust you approve?' Zoë hoped she didn't sound too defensive. He put the pottery dish he had been examining back on the shelf. The changes were small, but it made the place feel like home—and that was no easy task in a castle.

She spent so much time in the kitchen it had to feel right. It was where she prepared everything, painstakingly testing each dish any number of different ways long before the cameras rolled on set. So she had hung some new blinds at the windows to control the flow of light while she worked, and there was a row of fresh herbs lined up in terracotta pots along the window-sill. She loved the local pottery. It was precious in a world where everything was growing more and more alike.

'Wouldn't it have been easier to do the filming in here?'

'Yes, but my director felt there was more space in the hall, so I gave in to him on that point.'

'Your director? He works for you?'

'For my production company.'

'I'm impressed.'

'No need to be. It's not unknown in the television world for people to take the independent route.'

'So whose fault was the set dressing?'

'Mine,' Zoë said quickly. 'I own the company. The buck stops here.'

Rico's lips pressed together as he stared at her, then curved as if he was amused. 'Are you ready to go?' He glanced towards the door.

As he held it open for her, and she walked past him, Zoë felt a tingle race down the length of her spine. The heady scent of saddle soap and leather laced with warm, clean man was overwhelmingly attractive, and her thoughts turned wilfully to what was beneath Rico's breeches. She had never indulged in erotic thoughts before, always dreading where they might lead. But there was something about Rico Cortes that made it impossible to think about anything else.

Daydreaming was a dangerous game…

Once they were outside in the fresh air Zoë knew that at least for the next hour or so she was going to put every negative thought from the past out of her mind.

They stood on the veranda side by side for a few moments, enjoying the view. They were standing very close, close enough to brush against each other, but then Rico's stallion scented his master's presence and squealed with impatience.

'I think he's trying to tell us that he's been kept waiting long enough,' Zoë said.

'We had better go down,' Rico agreed, 'before he pulls that post out of the ground.'

She followed him down the steps.

'We should find you a horse.' Rico tipped his chin towards the stables. 'Before Rondeno breaks free.'

'Rondeno?'

'A native of Ronda. My stallion is named after the most famous of all the White Towns in Andalucia. Ronda is surrounded by rugged mountains that once sheltered bandits and brigands.'

'How very romantic.' And how perfectly suited to Rico, Zoë thought, looking up at him. He would have made a very good pirate, with his swarthy, dangerous looks. Had Rico's career taken a similar path to her own, she could see him as a leading man, breaking hearts on the small screen as well as the large. There was always a hunger for new talent. 'Have you ever thought of acting as a career?'

'Never.' He slanted her a look. 'I prefer reality to fantasy every time.'

'Flamenco, cooking, riding…' She smiled. 'Is there no end to your talent?'

'You haven't even begun to scratch the surface yet.' He laughed. 'Come on, let's get you that horse.'

At a gentle canter, and with the warm wind lifting her hair, Zoë began to wonder if she had ever felt so carefree before. The countryside was bathed in a soft, golden light, and the sky was as clear a blue as she had ever seen.

In this part of Spain the ground was well fed by a fast-flowing river, but now it was approaching the hottest months of the year the water was little more than a sluggish trickle. The pastures in the shadow of the mountains, however, were still green, and provided the perfect ground for riding over.

'We'll stop over there by the bridge.' Rico had brought his stallion alongside her horse, and was keeping pace at an easy canter. 'There should just be enough water for the horses to drink.'

As she cantered ahead of him, Zoë couldn't believe she hadn't ridden one of the horses stabled at the castle before. She had assumed they were in livery for any number of local riders, and therefore not included in her lease. Not so, Rico had explained. They all belonged to the same person—someone he knew, presumably. He knew the horses, and had chosen a quiet gelding for her to ride, saying Punto was perfect for her.

And he was, Zoë thought, patting the horse's dappled neck. Punto was just the type of horse she liked: he was kind, and willing, and wore an American-style high saddle, which was a lot more comfortable than the English saddle she was used to.

Rico's stallion moved ahead as he scented water. Urging her own horse forward, Zoë caught him up by the slow-moving stream. She allowed the reins to fall loosely on Punto's neck and gazed around. Apart from the gurgle of water and the sound of the two horses drinking there was utter silence. Lifting her face to the sun, Zoë closed her eyes, allowing the light to bathe her in its warmth.

'It's so beautiful here.'

'I agree,' she heard Rico murmur.

She longed for him to lean over in his saddle then, and kiss her as he had kissed her before. This time she wouldn't pull back. No bad feelings could intrude here, on such a beautiful day.

But Rico didn't kiss her. He didn't even try to touch her. He just sat patiently, waiting for their horses to finish drinking.

Of course he wouldn't kiss her. Men couldn't stand women who pulled away at the last minute. It was every man's idea of a turn-off. *There were only so many knocks to his pride a real man could take.* Wasn't that what her ex-husband had told her? He was right, and this was the proof.

She collected up the reins. 'I'd better get back to the castle. There's still so much to do. I have to get to the market before all the best produce is sold.' She turned Punto away from the water.

'You don't have to do that,' Rico insisted. 'Why don't I get someone to collect what you need?'

The breeze flipped Zoë's hair from her face as she turned to him. 'That's very kind of you, Rico, but I prefer to choose everything myself.'

'Force of habit?'

'That's right.'

They began to trot, and then the horses broke into a canter.

'So, are you still coming tomorrow?' She had to yell to make him hear.

'Try and keep me away. Shall we race back to the castle?'

The challenge excited her. Urging Punto on, Zoë loved feeling the wind in her hair and hearing the sound of Rondeno's hooves pounding after her. She knew Rico had to be holding back, and, snatching a glance over her shoulder, she laughed with exhilaration. Rondeno was far more powerful than her own mount, but she could almost believe Punto was enjoying this as much as she was.

The control Rico exercised over his mighty stallion was the biggest turn-on of all, and Zoë's heart was thundering louder than the combined sound of both horses' hooves. The friction of the saddle as she brushed back and forth was something new to her. She had never taken notice of it before, but now she was intensely and electrifyingly aroused. Leaning low over Punto's neck, she begged the horse to speed up and carry her away from Rico—and away from temptation.

He had to dig his heels into Rondeno's side to catch up with her. His laugh of pleasure and surprise was carried away on the wind because they were moving so fast. She was quite a woman. He liked her spirit. In fact he liked Zoë Chapman—a lot, Rico realised, easing up so they were galloping alongside each other.

Her lips were parted to drag in air, and there was a faint line of pink along the top of her cheekbones that had not been put there by the wind. Her lips were moist where she had licked them, and when she flashed him a glance he saw that her exquisite eyes had darkened to the point where only a faint rim of turquoise remained.

She was not leading him on even a little bit—she was sexually unawakened. The realisation sent arousal streaking through him like a bolt of lightning. So much sexuality packed into one woman with everything to learn about the art of love. Even if he'd cared nothing for her, he would still have had to find that a turn-on. But after Zoë's fearful response to him sorting her out in the sex department was starting to feel more like a crusade. Her frustration was obvious—something had to give. And he wanted to be around when that happened.

As they approached the castle they both reined in, but Zoë kept the lead. She laughed, and smiled across at him in triumph.

The change in her was striking. Where was the cool professional businesswoman now? Where was the frightened girl who had pushed him away? Right now she radiated confidence. The grey cloud that sometimes hung over her had vanished; he hoped it stayed that way.

She wanted to feel this good for ever, Zoë thought as she sprang down from the saddle. 'Thank you.' She turned to Rico, smiling. 'That was the best time I've had for—'

'Ever?' he suggested.

'I should definitely try to ride more frequently. Perhaps I will, now I know I can take one of the horses from the stables here.'

'The groom will always pick one out for you, or just tell him you prefer to ride Punto.'

'I will.' Zoë rested her cheek against Punto's neck for a moment. 'He's the best—aren't you, Punto?'

'Don't ride unaccompanied until you know the lie of the land better.'

Zoë's pulse began to race as she gazed up at Rico. 'I won't.' It was such an easy promise to make. With Rico riding next to her she would be in the saddle every spare moment that came her way.

'The groom will ride with you if you ask him.'

Somehow she kept the smile fixed to her face. 'That would be great.'

'*Adios*, Zoë!'

'*Adios*, Rico.' He was too busy holding his black stallion

in check to note her sudden lack of enthusiasm, Zoë saw thankfully. 'I appreciate you taking me out.'

'Don't mention it.' He wheeled Rondeno away.

I wouldn't dream of mentioning it, Zoë thought, smiling to herself as Rico cantered away.

Turning, she viewed the elderly bow-legged groom with wry amusement. Riding was definitely crossed off her 'must-do' list for now.

CHAPTER SIX

TUESDAY was almost too busy for Zoë to give much thought to anything apart from cooking—cooking and Rico. Now she knew for sure he was coming, everything had gained an extra impetus. She wanted to make Maria feel she was part of something special, something that gave the exceptional flamenco dancer the recognition Zoë believed she deserved.

She was in the kitchen by nine, having been up at dawn to go to market to find the freshest ingredients for those dishes that could not be made in advance. On her return she had laid everything out on the counter to make one last check. But, however many times she looked at them, she couldn't get past the feeling that there was still something missing.

She had decided upon a menu of clams *à la marinara*, in a sauce of garlic, paprika and *fino* sherry, with an alternative of *zoque*, the popular gazpacho soup made with red peppers and tomatoes. But for the main course she had called upon her secret weapon—a wise old man from the village who seemed to be everyone's *tio*, or uncle. Zoë had been debating over the best recipe for *paella*, and the *tio* was the only person who could advise her properly, according to Maria, who had unexpectedly appeared at her side at the market.

Thanks to the introduction from Maria, the elderly expert uncle had approved Zoë's choice of ingredients, after turning them over and sniffing for freshness. He had even demanded a heavy discount from the stallholders, reminding them, as Zoë would never have dreamed of doing, that they would be eating the food they had just sold to her when they came to the castle for the party that night.

'Locals care more about the rice than the rest of the meal,' the *tio* had said, patting his nose with one finger just as Zoë had seen Maria do. 'It must be well washed if you want the grains to separate, and then the rice must be cooked in fish stock—never water—water is for soup. You must have *caldo*—sorry, broth—for your rice. And the yellow colour of *paella* comes as much from the *noras*—you would call them peppers—as it does from the strands of saffron you add to the broth. Did you enjoy your ride?'

Cooking methods and Rico in the same breath! Zoë knew her astonishment must have shown on her face.

'It's a very small village,' the *tio* had explained with a smile, tapping his nose once again.

So it was, Zoë had thought, as she thanked him for his kindness.

Armed with quite a lot more local knowledge than she had bargained for, she had returned to the castle to prepare the main dish.

Balancing a cheap pan the size of a bicycle wheel on the counter, Zoë laid out pieces of chicken and squid, clams, scampi and *rojas*—large red prawns—with all the precision of a stained-glass window on top of a bed of rice, onion, garlic and peppers. Finally she added three types of beans and then some seasoning. Now the dish was almost ready for the oven.

She paused, inhaling the faint salty tang of the sea rising from the cool, fresh ingredients, her mind straying back to the earlier events of the day. How had the *tio* known she had been riding with Rico? Did everyone in the village know? Was it coincidence that Maria had found her at the market?

Suddenly Zoë wasn't sure of anything. Had she imagined she could ride out with Rico, bathe in his glamour, and get away with it? Frowning, she turned back to her cooking. She had already made some rich fish stock laced with strands of deep red saffron, and she poured that over the raw ingredients. Standing back, she had to admit she was delighted with the finished product.

The *tio's* last piece of advice had been to wrap the *paella* in newspaper once it was cooked. Then the finished dish should be left for ten minutes for the rice grains to separate. But wouldn't the newsprint spoil the striking colours?

Newsprint. Banner headlines. Zoë actually flinched as she turned away.

The icy fingers of the past were with her again, clutching at her heart. *Star Sells Sex.* Three words that damned her for ever in her own mind, even though they were lies. As far as the world at large was concerned, the story had brought her to wider public notice, and, in the topsy-turvy way of celebrity, had actually boosted her career. Going along with public perception had actually helped her to get through things. Keeping a smile fixed to her face had become such a habit that gradually the reality that lay behind the headline had been consigned to the back of her mind like a sleeping monster.

The Zoë Chapman who didn't appear on the television screen or at book signings was careful never to wake that monster—but she knew it would stir if she allowed herself to feel anything too deeply again. The shame, the failure, the brutality that lay behind it—all of that would rise up and slap her down into the gutter, where her ex-husband thought she belonged. So far she had frustrated his attempts to see her eat dirt, but it had been a long road back.

But she *had* made it back, Zoë reminded herself, and that was all that mattered. Every time the past intruded she pictured herself as a cork being held down in the water—she *always* broke free; she *always* bobbed up again. It was only men with brutally strong characters she had a problem with now. Men like Rico Cortes.

She had to get over this—get over him. She had to force her thoughts back on track. Perhaps she would wrap the *paella* in one of her huge, freshly laundered cloths when she removed it from the heat, and allow it to settle that way…

*   *   *

She could relax at last. The *paella* looked great on camera. It had been filmed at each stage of its preparation, and she had been sorry for the film crew, who had had to carry the loaded pan back and forth between the set in the Great Hall and the kitchen, where she was working.

Philip, her director, was demanding, but he was the best—which was why she had hired him. She trusted his judgement, and his decision to do things this way had kept everyone out from under her feet. Her own 'to camera' shots would be added later, when make-up and wardrobe had been let loose on her. It wasn't easy to cook and appear as cool as a cucumber at the same time.

Now she had finished the *paella*, Zoë's thoughts turned to pudding, which was her favourite part of any meal. She planned to serve a chocolate and almond ice cream, garnished with her own *guirlache*, which was crushed and toasted almonds coated with a sugar and lemon juice toffee. And there would be hot orange puffs dusted with sugar, as well as *figuritas de marzapan*, marzipan shaped into mice and rabbits for the children.

She concentrated hard, loving every moment of the preparation. Cooking was an oasis in her life that offered periods of calm as essential as they were soothing. She counted herself fortunate that her love of food had brought her success.

Resisting the temptation to sample one of everything she had made, Zoë finally stood back, sighing with contentment. It all looked absolutely delicious.

Someone else thought so too—before she knew what she was doing Zoë had automatically slapped Rico's hand away as he reached for a marzipan rabbit.

'Rico!' She clutched her chest with surprise. 'I thought it was one of the crew! I didn't realise it was you...' And then all she could think was that her chef's jacket was stained and her face had to be tomato red from the heat in the kitchen. 'I didn't expect you until tonight.'

'It is tonight.' He gazed past her through the open window.

'I must have got carried away. What time is it?'

'Don't worry. Not time to panic yet.'

Not time to panic? So why was her heart thundering off the chart? Zoë tried to wipe her face on her sleeve without Rico noticing. 'What brings you here so early?'

'I thought you might need some help. It looks like I was right.'

'I'm doing fine.'

'I brought drinks.'

'Drinks… *Drinks!* That was what was missing!' She turned to him. 'I've made some lemonade to pour over crushed ice for the children, and for anyone who doesn't drink…'

'That's fine, but you should have plenty of choice. It's going to be a long night.' Going to the kitchen door, he held it open and a line of men filed in. They were loaded down with crates of beer, boxes of wine and spirits, and soft drinks.

'*Cava*, brandy, sherry, and the local liquor…' Rico ticked them off, shooting an amused glance at Zoë as a man bearing a huge earthenware flagon marched in.

'Oh, no—not that!'

'You don't have to drink it,' he pointed out, smiling when he saw her expression.

'You're far too generous. Of course my company will pay for everything—'

'We'll worry about that later.'

'The crew will drink everything in sight, given half a chance.'

'Not tonight. Just worry about getting the white wine and *cava* chilled.'

'What do you mean, not tonight? Once they've filmed Maria, and taken a couple of crowd shots, the crew will join in the party—'

'Haven't I told you not to worry?' Rico slipped the lead man some banknotes to share around as tips.

'You don't know the crew like I do. I don't want to spoil it for them, but, bluntly, with all this drink around—I just can't face the mess in the morning.'

'Let me assure you that your crew are going to be far too busy to get into any mischief. You have my word on it.'

'Rico, what are you talking about?'

'Your director has arranged for another feature to be filmed tonight. Hasn't he told you yet?'

'No…' Zoë frowned. How could that happen when they always discussed everything in advance?

'He is very enthusiastic.'

'That's why I hired him.' She resigned herself. It had to be something good. She couldn't imagine the man who was the mainstay of her team asking everyone to work late unless it was really worthwhile…

'He's got everyone's agreement to work overtime,' Rico added.

'Can you read my mind?'

'From time to time.'

Zoë looked at Rico, looked at his lips, then dragged her gaze away. 'It must be an excellent feature.'

'Last minute.'

'Yes, I guessed that.' She couldn't be angry with Philip, though she was curious. She welcomed suggestions from anyone in the team. The strength of her company was that they worked together, with no one person riding roughshod over another. She knew from bitter experience that those tactics never worked. 'Do you know what it is?'

'A typical sport of this region.'

'A sport?' Zoë looked doubtful.

'Something colourful and authentic for your programme.'

'Don't tease me, Rico. Tell me what it is.'

'I'm going to get some extra glasses out of the Jeep.' Before Zoë could question him further he added, 'And by the way, *señorita*, your *figuritas* are delicious.'

So what was this surprise feature? Zoë flashed a glance at the door. Rico should have told her. He made her mad, and he made her melt too—a dangerous combination, and not something she should be looking for in a man. She wasn't looking for a man, Zoë reminded herself firmly.

'Tell me about this sport,' she insisted, the moment Rico came back.

Putting the case of glasses down on the counter, he turned to look at her. Zoë tried not to notice the figure-hugging black trousers and close-fitting black shirt moulding his impressive torso, or the fact that there was something wild and untamed about him. It lay just beneath the sleek packaging, telling her he would never settle down. Men like Rico Cortes never did.

'Wrestling.'

'Wrestling!' And then it all fell into place: El Paladín!

She shuddered inwardly. 'Will you be taking part?'

'Perhaps.' He shrugged. 'I've arranged for people to come and wash these glasses for you, and to serve tonight, so that after you finish filming you can have fun too. My people will clear up after the crew. You don't have a thing to worry about. You should kick back a little, enjoy yourself for a change.'

'Thank you,' Zoë murmured, her good manners functioning on automatic pilot. Her brain was working on two levels: the first accepted the fact that she needed help on the practical side because she had promised the crew they could join the party after work; the second level was dragging her down to a place she didn't want to go. Anything that smacked of violence, even a sport, made her feel queasy.

'Wrestling is hugely popular in this part of Spain. When your director asked me about it, I knew I could help him.'

'El Paladín?' Zoë's voice came out like a whisper, and she tried very hard not to sound accusing. It *would* make a good feature. If the programme was to reflect the area properly, it was just the type of thing she would normally want to include.

'I'm always looking for authentic items to bring the programmes to life…'

'It doesn't get more authentic than this.' Rico smiled at her on his way out of the door. 'See you later, Zoë.'

Zoë watched with mixed feelings as the raised square wrestling ring was erected in the middle of the courtyard. A beautiful day had mellowed into a balmy evening, and there was scarcely the suggestion of a breeze. Wrapping her arms around her waist she knew she had to pull herself together and stop fretting. Half-naked men would definitely be a bonus for her viewers. She could do this. She had to do this. How hard could it be?

The ring was almost finished, and people were starting to arrive. Soon it would be showtime. Surely it couldn't be that bad? She wouldn't have to watch it all—though she would have to be in shot for at least some of the time.

Firming her jaw, Zoë took a final look through the ropes at the empty ring. She still had to take a shower and prepare for the programme. Turning back to the castle, she hurried inside.

By the time she returned to the courtyard it was packed. Men had come from all over the region to test their strength. She guessed it was something of a marriage market too, judging by the flirtatious glances several groups of girls were giving their favourites.

The thought of Rico stripping off and stepping half naked into the ring was enough to make anyone shiver. Zoë tried hard not to react when she spotted him at the opposite side of the courtyard, surrounded by a group of supporters. At first she thought he was just greeting friends and she relaxed, but then he stepped away from the others and she saw he was naked from the waist up. Maria and the wise old *tio* from the village were standing with him; it seemed every soul in

Cazulas had come to support him. They were a good-natured group, and cheered him on as he strode to the ringside.

Zoë turned away, but then she guessed Rico must have vaulted over the top rope, because the applause around her was suddenly deafening. She looked up. She couldn't help herself. She had to see him for herself.

He was everything she found attractive in a man—and everything that terrified her too. It was impossible to believe that any of the other men had a physique to equal Rico's, or could match the fierce, determined look in his eyes. He was, after all, the champion. Rico Cortes was El Paladín.

Zoë fought down the panic struggling to take control of her mind. He was about to become a guest on her programme—no one said she had to sleep with him. She shivered, feeling fear and excitement in equal measure as she watched him flex his muscles in the ring. The woman standing next to her shouted something in Spanish, and then grabbed hold of her arm in her enthusiasm.

All the women wanted Rico, Zoë saw when she glanced around. For one crazy moment she felt like climbing into the ring and laying claim to him herself. And then the television lights flared on and she was working.

Smiling for the viewers, Zoë looked properly for the first time at the ring. She had to observe everything carefully so she could provide an appropriate voiceover for the film.

Clinging to her responsibilities certainly helped her through. But how to describe how she really felt at the sight of Rico's smooth, bronzed torso without turning her cookery programme into something for late-night viewing?

His belly was hard and flat, and banded across with muscle, whilst the spread of his shoulders seemed immense from where she was standing. And she couldn't stop her gaze tracking down to where his sinfully revealing wrestling shorts proved that it wasn't just the spread of his shoulders that was huge.

She wanted to look anywhere but at the ring—but how could she when she knew the camera would constantly switch between her and El Paladín? She had to stare up at Rico Cortes, and she had to applaud enthusiastically along with the rest of the crowd.

As the evening wore on the temperature began to rise. Rico was red-hot.

She would see it through because she had to. It was only a sport, after all, Zoë told herself. But by the time the bell rang and the first bout was over she was shaking convulsively from head to foot.

Making her excuses over the microphone to Philip, she eased her way through the crowd and went back into the castle, where she hurried up the stairs to her bedroom. Sinking onto the chair in front of the dressing-table, she buried her face in her hands.

How could she go back? Lifting her head, Zoë stared at her reflection in the mirror. She was pallid beneath her tan, and her hands were still shaking. She tried to apply some fresh lipgloss, and gave up. She couldn't risk a smudge of red across her face. And why was she trying to make herself look appealing? Did she want to attract trouble? Was she *asking for it* again, as she had done in the past?

When the shuddering grew worse, Zoë sat with her head bowed until she'd managed to bring herself back under control. She had to go back outside again eventually. She couldn't let everyone down—not Maria, not the *tio* who had helped her so generously, nor the film crew. And, most of all, she couldn't let herself down. She had fought hard to get her life back. She had to get over this.

There was a soft knock on the door. Marnie, the girl in charge of Wardrobe, had brought her a fresh top to change into. It was identical to the one she was wearing—low-cut and sexy—and the brash cerise looked good with her jeans. It was meant to stand out on camera when she was in a crowd.

It certainly did that, Zoë thought as she viewed herself critically in the mirror. The colour was identical to the skintight flamenco dress the girl named Beba wore on the poster at the mountain hut.

'I'm going to change.' She started tugging off the top.

'You can't, Zoë. What about continuity?'

'I don't care. I'm going to put on a shirt. If we have to reshoot, so be it.' Zoë saw Marnie's expression, but nothing was going to change her mind.

'Do you need me for anything else?'

'Marnie, I'm really sorry. This isn't your fault. Just tell Philip I insisted.'

'Well, it's your programme,' Marnie pointed out.

'Before you go, could you redo my lips?'

'Sure.' Marnie smiled at her.

Marnie applied the lipgloss expertly, with a steady hand. Zoë knew it was more than she could have done. She checked in the mirror. 'That's great. Thank you. I'm sorry to have dragged you up here just for that.'

'As long as I'm back in time to see Rico Cortes in action—' Marnie winked at her '—I'll forgive you.'

Zoë felt a chill strike through her composure, but forced a laugh as Marnie left the room.

She looked fine for the camera. The ice-blue of the shirt looked good against her tan, and complemented her red-blonde hair. She looked far more businesslike. She didn't look sexy at all. It was much, much better.

The shots on set inside the castle went smoothly—too smoothly, Zoë thought, cursing her professionalism. They didn't need a single retake.

'The change of clothes is fine for in here,' Philip advised her. 'But of course you'll change back into that cerise top again for ringside?'

'No, Philip.' Zoë shook her head. 'I'm keeping this shirt on. We'll just say the second half of the competition took place on another day—I don't care, I'm not changing.' She could tell by his face that Philip was taken aback. It wasn't like her to be difficult or unprofessional.

The competition was in its final stages by the time Zoë returned to the courtyard. The noise, if anything, had grown louder. Philip had to cut a path for her through the crowd. Then she realised that he meant her to stand right up at the front, as close to ringside as possible.

'Is this my punishment for changing clothes without warning you?' Zoë had to grab Philip's arm and yell in his ear above the roar of the crowd. She even managed a wry smile. But the moment he left her to return to his cameras Zoë's throat dried.

Philip's voice came through on Zoë's earpiece, testing the sound levels.

'You OK, Zoë? You sound as if you're getting a cold.'

'No, I'm fine—absolutely fine.'

'Then it must be the excitement at seeing all those muscles up close. You can't kid me,' he insisted, 'I know you love it—just like all the other women.'

That was the point. She wasn't like all the other women. *She wasn't normal.*

It was surprising how well you could know people, and yet know nothing about their private lives, Zoë thought, remembering that Philip had once worked for her ex-husband. He had been surprised when she had called time on their marriage, having thought them the perfect couple.

'Do you want me in shot for the presentation of the prizes?' she said into her microphone, clinging to her professionalism like a life raft.

'I'll want a reaction shot. You should have chosen something more glamorous to wear than that shirt. You look so plain!'

Perfect, Zoë thought.

'Never mind. It's too late to do anything about it now. I'll stick to head shots.'

She felt guilty because Philip sounded so grumpy, but it couldn't be helped. She was more concerned about getting through the next few minutes.

Women on either side of her were clutching each other in excitement as they stared into the ring. One of them turned to her, gesturing excitedly, and Zoë looked up. Rico was standing centre stage.

The television lights drained everything of colour, but Rico's torso still gleamed like polished bronze. The ghosts were hovering at Zoë's shoulder as she stared at him. But he was laughing good-naturedly with one of his defeated opponents, and then, leaning over the ropes, he reached out to help the elderly *tio* of Cazulas into the ring.

Zoë frowned. She hadn't expected that. Drawing on other times, other trials of strength, she had expected a grim face, a hard mouth and cruel eyes. But those trials of strength had been no contest. How could there be a physical contest between a woman and a powerful bully of a man?

Watching her elderly friend take Rico's hand and raise it high in a victory salute, Zoë tried to piece together what the *tio* was saying with her very basic knowledge of Spanish. Finally she gave up, and asked the woman standing next to her if she could translate.

'Our *tio* is announcing the prize,' the woman explained, barely able to waste a second of her awestruck gaze on Zoë.

A heavy leather purse changed hands between Rico and the *tio*. 'What's that?' Zoë shouted as cheers rose all around them.

'A purse of gold,' the woman shouted back to her.

But now Rico was passing it back to the *tio*. 'What is he doing?' Zoë said, looking at her neighbour again.

'It is the same every year,' the woman explained, shouting above the uproar. 'El Señor Cortes always returns the purse of gold to the village.'

'And what are they saying now?' Zoë persisted, but the excitement had reached such a fever pitch she couldn't hear the woman's reply. After several failed attempts her neighbour just shrugged, and smiled to show her it was hopeless.

Rico was staring at her, Zoë saw, going hot and cold. What did he want?

Holding her gaze, he walked quickly across the floor of the ring, leaned over the ropes, and held out his hand to her.

Zoë glanced around. No one could tell her what was happening because everyone was cheering and shouting at the top of their voices.

Rico held up his hands and silence fell. Everyone was staring at *her* now, Zoë realised. She couldn't understand it, but then Rico leaned over the ropes again and her face broke into a smile. She reached out to shake his hand, to congratulate him on his win. The next thing she knew she was standing beside him, with the spotlights glaring down on them both, and the *tio* was beaming at her while the crowd cheered wildly.

Rico's mouth tugged in a grin and he held up his hands again to call for silence. After he had spoken a few words in Spanish the cheering started up again. 'I choose you,' he said, staring down at Zoë.

'Me?' Zoë touched her chest in amazement. 'What for?' Her heart was racing out of control. She couldn't think what he meant. She couldn't think—

'You will find out.' Humour warmed his voice.

Zoë laughed anxiously as she stared up at him. She could still feel the touch of his hands around her waist— Her thoughts stalled right there. She might have weighed no more than a dried leaf in his arms. Shading her eyes, she tried to read his expression, but he drew her hand down again and enclosed it in his own.

Taking her into the centre of the ring, he presented her ceremoniously to the *tio*, and Zoë forced herself to relax.

What could happen with the *tio* standing there? She found a smile. These pictures would be flashed around the world. The last thing she wanted was to cause offence to an elder of Cazulas—a man who was her friend.

The *tio* seemed delighted that Rico had 'chosen' her, and embraced her warmly.

'What's all this about, Rico?' Zoë asked the moment the *tio* released her and turned away to address the crowd. Someone handed Rico a black silk robe and she waited while he put it on.

'You're part of my prize,' he said, when he had belted it.

'I'm *what*?'

Before Rico could answer, the *tio* turned around. Television cameras were angled to capture every nuance in Zoë's expression, and she cared for the *tio's* feelings, so she forced a smile.

'Do you understand our tradition?' he said to her warmly.

'I'm not sure.' She didn't want to look to Rico for answers.

'Allow me to explain.' The *tio* made a gesture to the crowd, begging their indulgence. Then, taking Zoë's hand, he led her out of the spotlight.

'It is our tradition. Having won the competition, Rico may choose any woman he wants. He chooses you.'

Incredible! Antiquated! Totally unacceptable! But the *tio* was looking at her so warmly, so openly, and he made it sound so very simple.

'Don't I have any say in the matter?' Zoë was careful to keep her voice light.

'Don't worry—the custom is not open to the same interpretation it might have been fifty years ago, when I was a young man.'

Zoë managed a laugh. 'I'm pleased to hear it.' She smiled at him, and then glanced at Rico. The expression in his eyes suggested he would have preferred sticking to the old ways.

Waves of panic and bewilderment started threatening to engulf her.

'It is a great honour to be chosen,' the *tio* coaxed. 'Look how disappointed you've made the other women.'

Zoë gazed around to please him, but whichever way she turned she saw Rico.

'All you have to do,' the *tio* explained persuasively, 'is to spend one night with him.'

'What?'

'I mean one *evening* with him,' he corrected hastily. 'My English is…' He waved his hands in the air with frustration, making Zoë feel worse than ever.

'I'll do it for you—of course I'll do it. Please don't worry.' This wasn't about her own feelings any more, or just work. It was about showing loyalty to an old man who was only trying to uphold the traditions of his youth. 'I won't let you down.'

Zoë allowed the *tio* to lead her back into the centre of the ring. She wouldn't let him down, but she was damned if she was going to play some antiquated mating game with Rico Cortes. She smiled tensely while the official announcement was made.

'Don't worry, I'll take a shower before I come back for you,' Rico murmured, the moment the applause around them subsided.

'Let's get one thing straight, Rico,' Zoë said, turning to face him. 'I'm grateful you took me riding, and helped me out here with staff for tonight. But I don't like surprises—especially not surprises that affect my work. The television lights are off now, the *tio* has gone to join his friends, and as far as I'm concerned the show's over.'

'And?' His eyes had gone cold.

'And I have no intention of becoming another of your trophies!'

'*Bravo*, Ms Chapman,' he murmured sardonically.

'Why don't you go and take that shower now? There are plenty of bathrooms in the castle.'

Rico's expression hardened as he looked down at her—and who could blame him? Zoë hadn't meant to sound so harsh, but there was an engine blazing away inside her, and a voice in her head that said, *Drive him away.*

What had happened tonight—all the fighting, the sounds, the tension, Rico overpowering everyone... It was just too close to her nightmares. She tried telling herself that all his strength was directed into sport. She had seen him ride; now she had seen him fight. But another side of her said: This is Rico Cortes, El Paladín, the man who conquers everyone with his strength... Her mind was fogged with fear. Unreasonable fear, maybe, but she couldn't shake it off.

The only thing she could latch on to in a world that was slipping away beneath her feet was the thought that she must not let the *tio* down. She would keep her promise to him, spend the rest of the evening with Rico. But first she had to go and seek some space, some cool, quiet place where she could get her head together.

She should fix somewhere to meet up with Rico before she did that. 'When you come back, Rico, I'll be—'

'I'll find you,' he said coldly, swinging a towel around his neck.

He vaulted over the top rope, dropped to the ground, and strode away from her without a backward glance.

CHAPTER SEVEN

THE meal was everything Zoë hoped it would be. The *tio* stood up and told everyone that the *paella* was the best he had ever tasted.

Rico was sitting next to her at the top table. He turned when she sat down after accepting the enthusiastic applause. 'Congratulations, Zoë. This has been a huge success for you.'

He was polite, but then, since he'd decided to trust her he was always polite. She wanted more. 'It's all thanks to the *tio* of Cazulas—' But Rico had already turned away to continue his conversation with the young Spanish beauty seated on his other side.

Zoë's smile faded. Rico had been cool ever since they'd sat down. It was understandable after her behaviour in the ring. But she couldn't tell him why she'd felt so bad after the wrestling. The *tio* of Cazulas had embroiled her in some ancient fertility rite that had fallen flat on its face.

She had kept her part of the bargain, staying with Rico throughout the evening, though he preferred the company of the vivacious young woman sitting next to him. His back had been half turned to her for most of the time.

Zoë noticed people were still smiling at her and raising their glasses. She smiled back, raising her own glass, but it was a hollow victory. She was thrilled everyone had enjoyed themselves, but the one person whose enthusiasm really mattered to her was otherwise occupied. She had thought of changing tables, but it would only cause comment—and Maria would be dancing soon.

There were about twenty people seated around each of the long tables set at the edges of the courtyard. The tables were laden with food, as well as countless bottles of beer, still water, and jugs of wine. She had used red and white gingham tablecloths to add a splash of colour, and placed lofty arrangements of brilliantly coloured exotic flowers on every one. Strings of lights swung gently in the night breeze overhead, twinkling like tiny stars, and waves of conversation and laughter were flowing all around her.

Resting her chin on her hand, she saw Maria's guitarist place his stool in a corner of the performance area. Sitting down, he began to strum some popular tunes. It was all perfect. She had asked to sit at the end of the table so that she could get up easily to supervise the food when necessary. Her plan had worked well—brilliantly, in fact. Though she might as well have stayed in the kitchen. Why hadn't Rico chosen the ebony-haired beauty as his trophy in the first place?

Zoë was distracted from her thoughts by Maria's entrance, and sat up. Straight away it was incredible. The air was charged with energy the moment she appeared. Framed in the doorway of the castle, Maria stood with one hand pointing towards the stars, calling up whatever mysterious energy fuelled her performance. Even Rico had turned to watch, forgetting, at least for a moment, the young beauty at his side.

The guitarist picked out an arpeggio, filling each note with incredible weight and passion. Maria stood unmoving until the last vibration from the strings of the guitar had faded away, and then she stepped proudly into the full glare of the television lights. Hovering like an eagle for an instant, she suddenly moved forward with all the grace of a much younger woman, crossing the courtyard with swift, precise steps.

She came into the centre of the performance area, raised her chin, and stared at some far distant point only she could see. The expression on her face was one of defiance, great pride, and anger, but there was pain and compassion too. Sweeping her crimson skirt off the floor in one hand, she made a powerful gesture with the other, and at the same time struck the floor one sharp blow with her foot.

Philip was by Zoë's side minutes after Maria had finished her performance. 'This programme will go down in history. That woman is superb—they're saying she's even better than Beba—though she's old enough to be Beba's mother.'

'I'm sure you're right.' Zoë frowned, tuning out for a moment. She had never heard of this Beba before in her life, and now she was haunted by the woman.

Philip dashed away before she could ask him anything, and then Maria had another surprise for them. She came back into the centre of the courtyard and invited everyone to join her in a dance.

Strictly speaking, this was country dancing, the *tio* said when he came over to explain what was happening to Zoë. All Zoë knew was that Rico's seat, as well as the one next to him, was empty, and what he and his young partner were doing on the dance floor was more dirty dancing than country dancing.

'Rico is good, eh?' the *tio* said, following her interest keenly. 'But the girl is too obvious. No subtlety.'

No subtlety at all, Zoë agreed silently. The young woman was like a clinging vine, all suckers and creeping fingers.

'Why don't you dance?'

Zoë turned to smile at the *tio*. 'With you?' She started to get to her feet.

'No, not with me!' The *tio* pressed her down in the seat again. 'I mean you should dance with Rico.'

'Rico is already dancing with someone,' Zoë pointed out, trying her best to sound faintly amused and casually dismissive.

'Here, in this part of Spain,' the *tio* told her slyly, 'women do not wait to be asked.'

Zoë turned to stare at him, wondering if she'd heard correctly, but instead of explaining himself the mischievous old man drew his shoulders in a wry shrug.

There were a million reasons why she could not—should not—do as the *tio* suggested, Zoë thought as she stood up. This was insane, she told herself as she walked towards the dance floor. Rico Cortes would simply stare at her and turn away. As for his young partner—Zoë could just imagine the look of triumph on her face when Rico told her to get lost. She was about to make a fool of herself in front of the whole village—the whole world, if you took the television cameras into account. But she just went on threading her way through the crowds on the dance floor.

'*Brava, Zoë! Eso es!*'

'Maria!'

'You should have worn your performance dress,' the older woman whispered in her ear before melting back into the crowd.

Too late for that now—jeans and a tailored shirt would have to do. She couldn't stop to think about it, Zoë realised as she reached her goal. She tapped the young Spanish beauty lightly on the shoulder. 'Excuse me. I'm cutting in.'

'*Qué?*'

The girl couldn't have looked more shocked. Zoë almost felt sorry for her. Almost. She didn't have a chance to see the expression on Rico's face; the next thing she knew she was in his arms.

'Well, this is a surprise.'

She could feel his breath warm against her hair. 'A pleasant one, I hope?'

'Unexpected, certainly.'

He had changed into casual clothes for the party: blue jeans, shirt with the sleeves rolled up and the collar open at the neck. He smelt divine, and he felt…

Zoë shivered as the music slowed to a sensuous rumba rhythm, as if responding to her mood. She saw that the young girl had quickly moved away to dance with some people of her own age, and didn't seem too upset—though right at this moment Zoë had decided to be selfish. She only cared how *she* felt. And she felt wonderful.

Having so many people around them gave Zoë the confidence to relax in Rico's arms. As they brushed past people smiled with approval. Whether that was to show their appreciation of the party or because she was in Rico's arms, Zoë didn't know, and right now it didn't matter. Even with the difference in their size they fitted together perfectly. They were dancing as one, as if they had always danced like this, and the planes and curves of his body invited her to mould against him.

Rico had an innate sense of rhythm, and Zoë could only be grateful that Maria had given her the courage to dance in a way that made her feel seductive and desirable. Nothing existed in her universe outside of Rico as they danced on to the haunting music, and Zoë barely noticed when one of his powerful thighs slipped between her legs, bringing her closer still. She only knew that it felt right, essential to the dance, and now they were one—moving as one, breathing as one, and dancing as one…

He let her go when the melody turned to something lively. Zoë realised that they had been the centre of attention, and that now couples were turning to their own pleasures again. It was true, she had been so deeply and sensually aware of Rico she had forgotten for the space of their dance that they were not alone.

She trembled as Rico stared down at her. The tempo of the music had increased, but they were both oblivious to it. Nothing existed outside the ambit of his gaze, and as she watched his lips tug up in a smile Zoë realised she was hoping for something more.

'Shall we?' He tipped his chin in the direction of their empty places at the table.

She dropped back into the real world. Of course Rico didn't want to dance with her all night. People were staring. The music had stopped again, and she was still standing on the dance floor like a fool.

'I'll…go and see if there's any pudding left. Someone might be hungry.'

Rico didn't try to stop her as she struggled to make her way through the whirling couples, but then she realised he was beside her, shielding her with his arm. When he stopped to talk to an old acquaintance she slipped away, making for the door to the kitchen. But she hadn't even had a chance to close it when Rico came in behind her.

'What's wrong with you, Zoë? Why are you running away from me?' He leaned back against the door, and she got the impression he wasn't going anywhere until she explained.

'Nothing.'

'Nothing?' His voice was flat, disbelieving. 'I think it's time you told me what all this is about, don't you? You were fine when we were out riding together, and then tonight you turn on the ice.'

'You haven't spoken to me all night!'

'Do you blame me?'

Truthfully, she didn't.

'Then you come up to me and want to dance. And then you run away again.' Rico made a sound of exasperation as he spread his arms wide. 'Are you going to tell me what all this is about?'

'I can't—'

'You can't?' He shook his head. 'Why not, Zoë? You've never been short of opinions in the past.'

'I can't explain because you'll just think I'm being ridiculous.'

'Try me.'

She met his gaze, and this time neither of them looked away.

'Violence frightens me.' Her voice was just a whisper.

'Violence?' Rico frowned and straightened up.

'Of any kind. I know how that must sound to you—and I do know wrestling's just a sport—'

'Are you saying I'm a violent man?' His eyes narrowed, and she could see she had offended him deeply.

'No—not you…' Zoë's voice dried. She looked away.

'Are you saying I remind you of someone who was violent in your past?' He looked stricken. 'That's it—isn't it, Zoë?'

'I can't help it.' She made a weak gesture with her hands.

'Do you have any idea how insulting that is?'

She saw his hand tighten on the door handle until his knuckles turned white, and took a step towards him. 'I'm sorry, Rico. I haven't even congratulated you—'

He made an angry gesture, cutting her off. 'I don't know what shocks me the most—the fact that you can mention violence in your past as if it were nothing, or the thought that you could possibly confuse me with some snivelling bully who preys on women and others who are weaker than himself.'

'I just don't want tonight to be all about me. This is your night too, Rico.'

'What you've just said overrides anything else.'

'We can't talk about it now. I can't just abandon my guests.'

'Forget the damned party!'

'How can I?' Zoë said, moving towards the door. 'It's wrong of me to keep you so long like this, Rico. Your young companion—'

'Will do perfectly well without me.' He caught hold of her arm as she tried to move past him. 'You can't leave it like this, Zoë. If you are protecting someone—someone who's hurt you—'

'I'm not,' she said steadily, meeting his eyes. 'I promise you, Rico, it's all over now.'

'Is it?'

'Yes,' she said, holding his gaze. 'Yes, it is.'

He shook his head, and his eyes were full of concern. 'Know this, Zoë: I am not and never have been a violent man. I have never raised my hand in anger to anyone. When you have great strength the very first thing you must learn is control. Strength has not been given to me to use against a weaker person, or some helpless creature. It has been given to me to help other people when I can, and for me to enjoy. Nothing more.'

And before she could say another word, he added in a fierce undertone, 'And don't you ever confuse me with some other man again.'

Rico opened the door for her and stood aside to let her pass, and the happy noise and bustle of the courtyard claimed her.

'*Señorita?*'

Zoë looked round to see that he had followed her out. It took her a moment of recovery after their highly charged exchange for her to realise what he meant to do.

Sweeping her a formal half-bow, he offered her his arm. 'May I escort you back to the party, Señorita Chapman?'

The rest of the night passed in a blur of laughter and dancing for Zoë. By the time people started drifting away her feet were aching. She had joined in every traditional dance of the region—men, women and children, all on their feet, colourful skirts flying and proud hands clapping the irresistible syncopated rhythms.

Now she was exhausted, and more grateful than ever to Rico's efficient staff, who had cleared away absolutely everything from the hall, leaving her with nothing to do there.

'Why are you back in the kitchen?'

'Rico—you caught me.' Zoë turned, embarrassed that he had seen her stealing her own *figuritas*. Now it was her turn to get her hand slapped—the only difference was, Rico's slap was more of a caress, and then he raised her hand to his lips. 'You have earned a break, Zoë.' He looked around. 'My people are only too happy to clear up—I told them they could take anything that was left home with them.'

'Oh, I'm sorry.'

'Don't be. I'm sure they can spare you one marzipan mouse.'

'Why are you frowning?'

'I just don't have the knack of dismissing the things you told me—as you seem to have.'

'Have I spoiled the party for you?'

'Don't trivialise what you said, Zoë. You can't keep everything locked inside you for ever.'

Why not? She'd been doing a pretty good job up to now. 'Let's not talk about it tonight,' she said, forcing a bright note into her voice. 'We're both tired—'

'Are we?'

Heat flared up from Zoë's toes to scorch her cheeks. 'Is it a deal? Can we just leave all the other stuff for another time?'

Pressing his lips together, he frowned. He didn't look keen. 'If that's what you want. I don't want to spoil the night for you.'

'You could never do that.'

The suggestion of a smile tugged at his lips.

They broke eye contact at a knock on the door. She couldn't have given a better cue herself, Zoë realised as Rico's helpers trooped in. It was impossible to talk about the past now. 'Shall we go back to the party?'

'Not for too long.'

There was something in the way he said it that made Zoë blush. 'Why?' She looked up at him, and immediately wished she hadn't.

Dipping his head close as he opened the door for her, he

whispered in her ear: 'I'm tired of playing games, Zoë. Can't you see how much I want you?'

It was so unexpected. She couldn't imagine anyone other than Rico even saying the words. No man had ever admitted to wanting her—he was the first. She didn't know how to answer him. She didn't know what was expected of her. 'I don't want to talk about—'

'Who said anything about talking? And you have my word I won't make you do anything you don't want to do.'

Rico drew her out of the bustling kitchen through a door that led into the silent hall. 'That's better,' he murmured, pulling her close to drop a kiss on her brow. 'I like to see you smile. I don't want to see you tense and unhappy ever again.' Nudging her hair aside, he planted a second tender kiss on the very sensitive place below her ear.

When he rasped the stubble on his chin against her neck Zoë gasped, and allowed him to draw her closer still. It was so easy to slip beneath Rico's seductive spell. She could have broken away at any time; but his hold on her was so light there was no reason to try.

She parted her lips, welcoming the invasion of his tongue, but he teased her gently, pulling away until she locked her hands behind his neck and brought him back again. And then their mouths collided hungrily, and it was Rico's turn to groan as she moulded into him.

She was in a dream state as Rico led her swiftly by the hand through the castle. Every part of her was aching for his touch. His hand was firm and warm, and she went with him willingly through the archway that led to the luxury spa.

'I haven't been down here before,' Zoë admitted as Rico let go of her for a moment to close the door. She couldn't bear the loss, and reached for him.

'Not yet,' he warned, his fingertips caressing her cheek.

'Why not?'

'Because it's better this way.'

She followed him down a short flight of marble steps.

'Are you sure you have never been down here before?' Rico stopped at the bottom and turned to look at her.

'Never.'

'Then you're about to get a very pleasant surprise.'

Zoë watched Rico punch a series of numbers onto a panel on the wall. A door slid behind them. 'What are you doing?'

'I've changed the code so we won't be disturbed. Zoë?' Rico touched her face with one fingertip when he saw the expression on her face. 'The code is twenty-one, twelve—my birthday. Don't look so worried. You can leave any time you want.'

'I just thought if there was an emergency—and I needed to get out in a hurry—'

'An emergency?' Rico smiled. 'What? You mean something like this?'

And then somehow she was in his arms again, and he was kissing her so tenderly, so thoroughly, Zoë wondered how she remained standing. Heat flooded through her veins, and when his tongue tangled with her own a soft moan came from somewhere deep in her chest, showing him how much she wanted him to kiss her.

When he pulled back, she reached up, wrapping her arms around his neck to mesh her fingers through his hair and draw him close again. When Rico kissed her she felt no fear. She wanted him to know how she felt, that she was ready for him: moist, swollen, hot. But then she remembered…

'First ice, and now fire?' Rico murmured, looking down at her.

He was so tender, so caring—but how could she be sure he wouldn't be shocked or disappointed when she experienced the painful spasm that had always made fully penetrative sex impossible for her? She had to be sure she wouldn't stop, Zoë thought as her hand strayed to his belt buckle…

Rico moved her hand away, bringing her fingers to his lips

to kiss each tip in turn. Zoë's eyes filled with hot tears of failure.

'You need to slow down, Zoë.'

Glancing up uncertainly, she saw his lips were curving in a smile. She started to try and say something, to explain herself, but, putting one firm finger over her lips, Rico stopped her.

'I'm going to find you something to wear in the hot tub.' He broke away. 'And then I'll order some refreshments for us from the kitchen.'

Something to wear? Food from the kitchen? She was so naïve! She had expected to be naked, feeding on him.

'And then we'll sample the hot tub together.'

Better.

She gazed around. The ancient walls had been sandblasted in this part of the castle until they were pale yellow. The floor was a mellow golden marble, and all the tiles and fittings had been selected with a view to nothing startling to the eye or the senses. The temperature was perfect, the silence complete.

Rico reached inside a beautiful old oak chest and brought out some fluffy caramel-coloured towels, then black swimming trunks for himself and a swimming costume the same shade as her eyes.

'That's a lucky find.'

'Or good planning,' Rico said.

'You know your way around here pretty well.'

'I should. The castle belongs to a very good friend of mine. Do you want to go and change now? Music?' he added, handing her the costume.

'Why not? Something gentle and soothing would be nice.'

'I'll see if I can accommodate you.' His voice was ironic as he moved to select a CD.

A sinuous melody started weaving its spell around Zoë as Rico took hold of her hand again, and she went with him, deeper into the spa.

The hot tub in the centre of the floor was illuminated by hundreds of flickering candles. Zoë gasped. 'How—?'

'You ask too many questions. Just accept you're going to be pampered for a change.'

There were a million questions she would have liked to ask him, but for once in her life she bit them back.

They changed in beech-lined changing cabins, and she covered her costume with one of the white towelling robes hanging on the back of each door.

'To think I didn't even realise this place existed!'

'The hot tub is kept locked up for most of the time.'

'Your friend must like you a lot to let you use it.'

Loosening the belt on his robe, Rico let it drop to the floor. Zoë kept her gaze strictly confined to his face, but to her relief saw the black bathing trunks in her peripheral vision.

'Aren't you going to take your robe off?'

'Yes…yes, of course I am.'

Zoë waited until she was up the steps of the hot tub and had one leg in the water before slipping off the robe. Then she was in like a flash, submerged beneath the water before Rico had even climbed in.

There were tiny lights above her head, winking on and off in a deep blue ceiling decorated with puffs of smoky cloud to give it the appearance of a night sky. 'This is unbelievable.' Zoë sighed, stretching out her arms along the top of the tub to keep her balance in the swirling water. She leaned her head back, and closed her eyes.

'I prefer an open-air bathroom.'

She looked up again. Rico had settled himself across from her. 'You mean the sea?'

A door opened before he could reply to her, and a waiter came in with a tray of refreshments for them.

'Thank you,' Rico said, glancing round at the man. 'You can leave them here.'

Zoë blinked. There was champagne on ice, two tall crystal

flutes, a bowl of sweet wild strawberries, some whipped cream and a bowl of chocolate sauce on the tray. 'Now I have seen everything.' She shook her head incredulously.

'You really think so?'

Rico's voice was challenging, and soft. She didn't answer.

Wrapped in fluffy towels, and stretched out on a recliner next to Rico's, Zoë sipped champagne while Rico lay back watching her through half-closed eyes.

'If this is the Cazulas way of thanking people for giving a party, I may have to stay a lot longer than I planned.' Putting her glass down, she relaxed back against the soft bank of cushions and stretched out her limbs in languorous appreciation.

Selecting a plump strawberry, Rico dipped it in rich chocolate sauce. 'Open your mouth.'

He touched it to her lips, and she could smell the warm chocolate sauce. She wasn't quick enough, and it started escaping in runnels down her chin. Leaning over her, Rico licked it off, and then he was kissing her—kissing her deeply.

It was the taste of Zoë that made him greedy. It made him want more, a lot more of her. It made him want everything. But he knew better than that. He knew he had to wait. Pulling back, Rico saw that her eyes were still closed, her lips still slightly parted as she sucked in breath, and there were smudges of chocolate all round her mouth.

'Don't be mean,' she whispered, opening her mouth wider. 'I want more.'

Smiling wryly, Rico began to feed her again. He kept on until she was begging him for mercy as she laughed; until she couldn't keep up with the chocolate sauce and the cream, and it dripped onto her breasts, and slipped between them. Her lips were stained red with strawberry juice and her eyes were almost as dark as the chocolate. And then he couldn't help himself. He was kissing her again, and she was clinging to him, not caring that her towel had fallen away.

Zoë gasped as Rico's tongue began to lave between her breasts. She had sunk lower and lower onto the recliner, wanting him to continue until every scrap of chocolate had disappeared. Her breasts were streaked with juice and cream, and there was a coating of chocolate on each painfully extended nipple. His tongue was deliciously warm, and rasped against her sensitive skin in a way that was unbearably good.

She wanted more. But Rico was heavily into foreplay— something she had never experienced before. He knew how to tease and torment her; he knew every erogenous zone on her body. Her flesh sang with pleasure as she writhed beneath him, and she could no longer make any pretence at shyness. How could she, with his warm breath invading her ears? She cried out to him, shuddering uncontrollably, but just as she did so he pulled back.

Short of grabbing him by the hair and forcing him to suckle her breasts, she had no idea what to do next. She was getting desperate. 'Shall I feed you now?'

Holding himself up on his fists, Rico looked down at her. 'What did you have in mind?'

There was such a wicked smile tugging at his lips, Zoë couldn't resist it. 'Just this.' Cupping her breasts, she held them out to him.

CHAPTER EIGHT

RICO stared at Zoë's breasts. They were magnificent—a fact he had been trying hard to ignore from the moment he had seen her in a tight top pulling plastic oranges down from the walls. His control had never undergone such a painful test— especially now, when she was warm, soft, and more lovely than ever. But was she ready for this?

He couldn't stop looking at her tight, extended nipples, currently reaching out to him in the most irresistible invitation.

'Wrong colour?' she teased him softly.

'Perfect.' And they were—the most delectable shade of shell-pink.

'Wrong size for you?'

She was still smiling, waiting, her eyebrows arched in enquiry as she stared at him.

'Zoë—' Rolling off his recliner, he hunkered down by her side. 'What would you like me to do, Señorita Chapman?'

'Eat me.'

'Eat you?' He pretended surprise. 'That's very forward of you...'

'Yes, isn't it?'

Taking matters into her own hands, she sat up and locked her hands around his neck to bring him down to her.

Swearing softly in his own language, he pulled back, drawing her with him, staring into her face as he unlocked her hands. Laying her back down on the narrow couch, he took a long, lazy look down the whole lovely, naked length of her. 'Wild cat!' he murmured approvingly.

There was barely an inch of Zoë's body that had been spared the chocolate, the cream, or the sweet red strawberry juice. He applied himself first to the task of cleaning her breasts, using long greedy strokes of his tongue. With each caress she cried out—he might have been inside her, so intense was her response.

Had she never experienced foreplay in her life? He thought not. When he suckled her nipples she moaned rhythmically in time with his actions until he knew he had to stop. He had never known anything like it before; he had never been so aroused before. His senses were on fire and his anticipation of his final possession of her was overwhelming in its intensity. But before he realised what she meant to do she had surprised him.

Scooping up some sticky chocolate sauce, she smeared a handful over his chest. When she began to lick it off, he knew he was in danger of losing control for the first time in his life. Capturing her in his arms, he rolled with her onto a soft rug on the floor, straddling her, and pinning her arms down above her head. Trying to keep her still while she wriggled beneath him was almost impossible. She was moving her head from side to side, laughing and threatening him in the same breath. Finally securing her wrists in one strong fist, he reached for the cream jug with his free hand, and emptied the contents all over her.

Shrieking with surprise, and laughing at the same time, she tried to break away, but when he started lapping at her belly she changed her mind. Meshing her fingers through his hair, she was all compliance, all sensation, as she told him she wanted more. And when he moved lower, nudging her thighs apart, she whimpered with pleasure and angled herself shamelessly towards him.

He stopped just short of where she wanted him to be, making her cry out with disappointment. Before she had a chance to complain any more, he sprang to his feet and swept her into his arms.

The moment had come, Zoë thought, laying her head on

Rico's shoulder. As he carried her across the relaxation room she knew she trusted him completely. By the time they reached the wet room she was shaking with anticipation. She had never been so aroused. This time Rico would make everything right.

Zoë shrieked as she landed with a splash in the hot tub. Moments later Rico was in with her, holding her safe above the water. Reaching for a sponge, he began soaping her down until all the chocolate and cream had disappeared.

He had never been called upon to exert so much control in his life, Rico realised when they'd got out and he had reclaimed his sanity beneath an icy cold drench shower. And he had never had so much fun with a woman.

Wrapping a towel around his waist, he stared at Zoë drying her lush red-gold hair. She looked more beautiful than ever. Her cheeks were still flushed from their seductive play-fight, and her eyes were gleaming as if her zest for life had suddenly increased. She was starting to trust him, Rico knew, and they could never make love until she did. He only had to touch her, to kiss her, to look at her, to know how inexperienced she was. And it troubled him to think what might have happened to her in the past.

She was humming softly to herself, staring clear-eyed into the mirror as she arranged her hair like a shimmering cape around her shoulders. When he walked up to her, and she looked at him, he could feel his heart pounding so hard in his chest it actually hurt.

It seemed that whatever ghosts there were in her past, or in his, they had no power when they were together. He felt a great swell of happiness inside him. It was a dangerous development, and one that made him feel unusually vulnerable.

Dropping a kiss on Zoë's shoulder, he went to get his clothes. He felt a lot more than lust for her. Her innocence had touched him deeply. Was this love?

When he was almost dressed she came to him. Standing

close behind him, she placed her hands on his shoulders. He felt her rest her face trustingly against his back. And in that moment he knew the whole world and everything in it was his.

He wouldn't have agreed to spending the night in separate rooms at the castle for anyone but Zoë, Rico realised, calling a halt to his pacing. She might be a successful career woman, but beneath the gloss of achievement he knew she was terribly vulnerable, and it made him feel protective, even responsible for her.

It was unusual—no, unique—to find someone so tender and pure. Gold-diggers disgusted him, and there were so many of them around. He had closed his mind years ago to the possibility of ever finding someone who cared for him, and not for his money. Zoë didn't need his money, but even if she had, he knew she would have been as sickened as he at the thought of using a person's wealth as a measure for their worth. It warmed him just to be thinking about her. This was special. She was special.

Going to the open window, he planted his fists on the sill and leaned out. A silver-pink dawn was creeping up the sides of the snow-capped mountains, and the sight bewitched him. Zoë would be sleeping now. He smiled to think of her curled up in bed, sleeping the deep, untroubled sleep of the innocent.

Gazing along the balcony they shared, Rico noticed that her window was open. Her career absorbed her completely. She had to be exhausted.

He turned to look at the computer screen. There was nothing yet.

Natural caution made him investigate everyone who threatened his privacy. He knew already that Zoë was no self-seeking adventuress, but his night-owl investigator had been on the case since she'd arrived in Cazulas. It was a juggernaut he couldn't stop now. He had keyed in his password, and expected an e-mail at any time. Once his mind was set at ease, he would go and wake Zoë in a way he knew she would enjoy.

Just the thought of rousing her from sleep, all warm and tousled, and kissing her into the new day had been enough to keep him from his bed. He was eager to be with her. Throwing back his head, Rico let out a long ragged sigh of frustration. It was hard to believe that here, in one of the remotest regions of Spain, fate had put him on a collision course with someone as honest and forthright as Zoë. He was tempted to go to her right now, without waiting for reassurance.

He tensed abruptly, all senses on full alert. Pushing back from the balcony, he strode quickly to the door. He stood outside his room, in the corridor, and listened intently. He thought he had heard a cry. But there was nothing. He turned, knowing everyone in the castle was asleep. Some nocturnal animal must have disturbed him.

Going back into his temporary study bedroom, Rico closed the heavy door carefully. That was it! He cursed himself for not thinking of it sooner. The doors in the castle were so heavy no sound could possibly penetrate them.

Walking onto the balcony, he quietened his breathing and listened outside Zoë's window. At first there was nothing aside from the soft swish of fabric as the fine voile curtains billowed in the early-morning breeze. Then he heard her cry out again, and, reaching through the window, he turned the key in the double doors and stepped into her room.

She was just awake, and clearly confused.

'Zoë—what is it?' He knelt down at her side. She was as beautiful as he had imagined, still warm from sleep and more lovely than any woman had a right to be if a man was to remain sane.

'Rico.' She pressed her hands against his chest. 'Rico, I'm fine. I'm really sorry if I woke you—'

'You didn't wake me. I'm still dressed,' he pointed out. 'But as for your being fine—I'm sick of that word. You're not fine.'

'All right. I had a nightmare.'

'A nightmare?' He turned away. 'You cried out, and I was worried about you—'

Her face went bright red, as if it was she who was in the wrong.

'You don't need to worry about me.'

He was amazed to see how quickly she could recover her composure. Then he remembered that she was used to covering up the truth.

'As I told you, Rico. There's really nothing to worry about.'

'How long are you going to lie to me about this, Zoë?'

There was a long silence, and then she said, 'I don't know what makes you say that.'

'I heard you this time. I heard you cry out. And then, as I came into your room, I heard what you said.'

She covered her face with her hands, but he couldn't let it rest now. 'Don't,' he said softly. Gently taking hold of her hands, he lifted them away. 'You were in the throes of something much worse than a nightmare, Zoë. You were crying out, begging—'

'No!' She shouted it at him, and he waited until she grew calm again, holding her hands firmly between his own.

'Begging?' She forced out a laugh. 'You're mistaken, Rico—'

'I am not mistaken. And I'd like to know what made you call out—"Please, don't hit me again."'

'I've told you, you're wrong. I would never say something like that. Why should I?'

'That's what I'm trying to find out.'

She shook her head, and her eyes wore a wounded expression. 'Is that why you were so gentle with me, Rico? Is that why you won't make love to me? Is that why you agreed to stay over in a separate room? You feel sorry for me—'

'Don't be so ridiculous!' He raked his hair in sheer exasperation. 'I don't spend time with women because I feel sorry for them.'

'How many women?'

'Why are you doing this to yourself, Zoë?'

'I tell you, Rico, you're wrong about me.' She scrambled upright with the sheet firmly clutched in her hand. 'You don't need to feel pity for me. It was just a nightmare. Nothing more.' She shook her head, seeing the disbelief in his eyes. 'I'm really grateful you came in to make sure I was all right. You're kind—very kind—and thank you—'

'Don't!' His voice was sharp as he put his hand up. He regretted it immediately, seeing her flinch. 'I would never hurt you.' His voice was just a whisper, but she had already gathered herself into a ball and pulled the sheet up to her chin. 'Don't ever thank me for being kind to you, Zoë. It's the very least one human being can expect from another.' He was consumed with relief when she lifted her head and looked at him.

'Who hurt you, Zoë?'

'No one…'

Her voice was tiny, like a child's, and it hurt him more than anything he had ever heard. 'Is that why you were crying out?' he pressed gently. 'Were you remembering what had happened to you?'

'Rico, please.'

He could feel the anger pumping through him. His hands, balled into fists at his sides, ached with tension. Who could ever hurt her? It was inconceivable to him that anyone could wish to harm one hair on her head. He wanted to protect her—but how could he when she insisted on pushing him away? 'Won't you trust me enough to tell me, Zoë?'

'I can't. I just can't.'

'Please, don't shut me out. I want to help you, but I have to know the truth—'

'The truth?' Zoë made a short incredulous sound. She hated herself as it was for her weakness. How could she know she would cry out when she was sleeping? 'Do *you* always tell the truth, Rico? Do you?'

He couldn't answer her. How could he when he had been staring at a computer screen half the night? They were both victims of the past in their own way. Suspicion was branded on his heart, but Zoë was damaged too, and her wounds had been carved far deeper and more cruelly than his.

Standing up, he moved away from the bed, carrying the image of Zoë in his mind. Her hair was like skeins of silk, gleaming in the moonlight, and her skin was so soft and warm. The room was filled with the scent of the orange blossom she always wore. As he turned, she turned too, and their eyes locked. He longed to tell her everything. He wanted nothing more in all the world than to take her in his arms and keep her safe for ever. But he could not. Instead, he would go back to his own room and maintain his vigil until the information he had asked for came through.

'Goodnight, Zoë.' He walked onto the veranda, closing the doors softly behind him.

Throwing his head back, with his eyes tightly shut, he let out a heavy sigh. For the first time in his life the price he had to pay for being Rico Cortes was far too high.

CHAPTER NINE

CLUTCHING the receiver between neck and shoulder while she scooped up her discarded nightwear from the floor, Zoë listened patiently. There was an opportunity to do a live interview with a national television show—a roving reporter had just arrived with a camera crew. Could she make it in time?

She looked like hell after her disturbed night. She felt like it too, especially remembering what had happened with Rico. But this was work, and there was nothing on her face that make-up couldn't fix. Her heart was another matter, but that would have to wait.

She was curious, and she was tempted too. The publicity would be great for the series—and she was interested to find out why someone from such a well-known show had come all the way to Cazulas to speak to her. Of course the last series had been a big success, and it had generated a lot of media interest. That had to be it.

'Of course I'll do it,' she said, decision made. 'Half an hour suit you? OK, fifteen minutes,' she conceded. 'But get Marnie and the girls up here right away with the war paint.'

Philip had told her there would be a chance for a run-through first, so there would be no surprises and nothing for her to worry about. It was just what she needed to take her mind off Rico... He must have gone by now. There wasn't much to keep him at the castle. But she still had her career. The thrill of the places it took her to, and the amazement that she had made something of herself after all, in spite of her ex's assurances that she never would, had not diminished. She hoped they never would.

She had to stand under a cold shower to try and put Rico

out of her mind. Finally, reasonably focused on work and totally frozen, she rubbed herself down vigorously with a towel.

There was a bad feeling niggling away inside her, Zoë realised as she dressed. It made no sense. She had done this sort of thing lots of times before, and knew that nothing was left to chance. It might all appear impromptu at home, but the groundwork had already been covered so that none of the questions came out of the blue. And yet...

'To hell with it,' she murmured, spritzing on some perfume. She was a seasoned campaigner and there was nothing to worry about.

Seasoned campaigner or not, she hadn't factored quite such a bubbly young presenter into the equation. The latest in a long line of glamorous young women with an incisive mind, she was the type of person that Zoë found wearing, but fun in short bursts. They talked through the questions, and decided on the best strategy to adopt to promote the show. Zoë was confident she could keep things moving forward smoothly. They were going to film outside, with a backdrop of mountains behind them, and went on air almost immediately.

'So, Zoë, how does it feel to be here in such a fabulous location, as opposed to being stuck in an overheated studio?' The girl fanned herself extravagantly and smiled, as if this made them comrades in adversity.

Her openness made Zoë laugh. 'It feels great, Lisa—but it's hot outside here, as well as under the lights. Don't forget this is Spain—'

'You've got quite a glow going on there, Zoë.' The girl cut across her, facing the camera to address the viewers. 'Could this be something more than a suntan? I hear the Spanish men around here are quite something. Or *man*, rather,' she added as Zoë stared at her. 'Come on, you can tell us—we won't tell a soul, will we?' she exclaimed, turning again to include several million viewers.

'Let's talk about the programme first.' *And last,* Zoë thought, keeping a smile on her face while her mind raced. They hadn't planned to touch on anything other than her new television series. In fact she had made a point of insisting there would be no delving into her personal life. The past was just that—behind her. That was what she and the young reporter had agreed on.

'You're right, Zoë. Let's talk about your programme. That's what we're here for.'

Zoë stalled. The look on the girl's face was open, inviting… Inviting what? There was just enough guile in her eyes to churn Zoë's stomach. 'I think this series is going to be my best yet—'

'You only *think*? Don't tell me Zoë Chapman's become a shrinking violet?'

'Sorry?'

'You're not going to turn coy on us now, Zoë, are you? Disappoint the viewers?' The girl turned to camera and made a moue, but there was a shrewd gleam in her eyes when she looked back. 'After spending the night as the prize of a wealthy man?'

She had just managed to leave out the word *again,* Zoë thought, feeling the blood drain from her face.

'That's right, isn't it, Zoë?' The girl's lips pressed down as she shrugged and managed to look ingenuous for the camera. 'I've seen the footage.' Her eyes opened really wide and she stared around, as if seeking confirmation that her reportage was absolutely accurate from some unseen source.

Zoë's gaze iced over as she waited for the bombshell to fall. After all, the camera never lied…

'Half-naked men wrestling beneath the stars in this sultry Mediterranean climate—and the champion, El Paladín, also known as Alarico Cortes, claiming you as his prize for the night.' She stretched, showing off her taut young belly as if she had all the time in the world to deliver her *coup de grâce*. 'Mmm, sounds pretty hot to me. *He's* pretty hot!'

'That was just an item.' Zoë tried to laugh it off and put on a good-humoured smile for the camera. Inwardly she was seething. The girl's agenda was obvious. This wasn't about her series. There was still mileage in the old scandal.

'Just an item!' The girl cut her off with a short, incredulous laugh. 'OK, Zoë, let's cut to the chase. You bagged Alarico Cortes for one glorious night. I'm only quoting the age-old tradition here in Cazulas, Zo—no need to look at me like that. Alarico Cortes, if you don't know of him at home, is only *the* most eligible bachelor in Spain—a billionaire, and a good friend of the Spanish royal family. So, what was it like? How does it feel, mingling with the aristocracy? And were you really just a prize for the night? Or is this love?'

Alarico Cortes? Aristocracy? Billionaire? Zoë was stunned. If what the young reporter said was true... The last way she would have wanted to hear it was like this.

'I was lucky enough to be invited to take part in a traditional celebration that has been upheld here in Cazulas for centuries. It was great fun—nothing more than that. I'm really sorry to disappoint you.' She finished with a good-natured shrug towards the camera. Game, set, and match, she thought, seeing the girl's face turn sulky.

'Well, you heard it here first, folks.' The reporter quickly recovered. 'The most beautiful celebrity chef on the circuit has something really special in the pipeline for all of us. Don't miss Zoë's new series, or you'll miss those yummy men— and we're talking drop-dead gorgeous in the case of Alarico Cortes, girls. Thank you, Zoë, for sparing us these few precious minutes away from your show.'

'My pleasure,' Zoë said, with a last cheery smile to the viewers. 'Thank you all for your time.'

She even thanked the girl again when the cameras had stopped rolling. They both knew who had come out on top, and Zoë was determined to remain professional to the last. But she couldn't quite believe she had allowed herself to be set up. It had been two years since the scandal broke. Two years to learn caution. She'd thought she was too wary to be trapped like this—but apparently not.

And Rico Cortes, all round good-guy and local one-man protection agency, had been lying to her all along: his *friend's* castle, his *friend's* horses, the down-homey camaraderie of the flamenco camp—and he was a Spanish grandee. Why wasn't she surprised? It all made sense now. He had been lying to her ever since that first meeting, pulling the wool over her eyes, confusing her with his sweet talk and worthy notions. And wasn't she a chump to have thought him any better than her ex? Rico Cortes was one smart operator.

'Great job, Zoë!'

Zoë looked at Philip blankly as he clapped her on the back.

'Our ratings will soar if you keep this up.'

'That's fantastic.' She was already running towards the castle. She had no idea if Rico would still be there. Inside the castle—*his* castle!

Pausing for a moment in the middle of the courtyard, she looked around. Rico's castle. His village, his horses, his spa, his kitchen, his bed, his office. Shading her eyes, she stared up at the balcony they had shared, and in that moment she hated him.

Zoë walked straight into the study bedroom where Rico had been sleeping. At least now he was gone she could use the computer to let her far-flung family members know the interview would be repeated on breakfast television throughout the morning.

'Rico!' Zoë's heart lurched as she saw him, and her eyes filled with tears as he moved away from the computer screen. 'I thought you would have gone by now.'

'I came back.'

'What are you doing?'

'Don't you knock before you enter a room?'

The situation had an element of farce. He was looking at her with a face full of mistrust and anger when *she* was the one who had been wronged. Rico had been lying to her all along—misleading her, pretending to be a local man when he was... She didn't even know who he was.

'I still hold the lease on the castle. Technically this is my room, Rico.'

Tension stretched between them. Whatever he had on the screen, he didn't want her to see it, Zoë realised. 'I'd like to use the computer now, if you don't mind.'

'There's some data on here I can't afford to lose.'

'So save it. My mails are urgent too.'

'Is something wrong?'

'Plenty. But right now I want to contact my family, because I've just done an interview for TV—' She stopped as he made a contemptuous sound. 'What's wrong with you?'

'An interview?' The look he threw her was full of disdain.

'Yes, an interview, Rico—for my new cookery series. Now, if you don't mind—'

'Nothing else?'

Zoë looked at him. 'What are you getting at? Are you worried I might have talked about you, Rico? Let the world know I bagged myself a really rich man—a billionaire? A real live Spanish grandee and good friend of the King?'

When he said nothing, it was Zoë's turn to make a low, angry sound. 'Have you finished with the computer yet?' she demanded, planting her hands on her hips.

'Help yourself,' he said, moving away from the screen.

She didn't need to read the tall, bold letters on the monitor. They had been branded on her mind two years ago. They were lies. Everyone who knew her, who cared about her, knew that. Facing up to them was the only way she knew to snuff out their power.

Star Sells Sex.

Turning to look at Rico, Zoë could read his mind. He had believed the truth about her, and now he believed the lies. And his pride wouldn't allow him to accept that he had been so wrong about her. He believed she had sold herself for money. The thought turned Zoë cold, drained her of feeling. As Rico thought so little of her, perhaps he had her pegged as a gold-digger, after his money, all the time. Perhaps he had even set up the interview to shame her in public… He couldn't believe he had been so mistaken about someone. Neither could she, Zoë realised sadly.

'Are you expecting a reaction from me, Rico? Heated denials—hysterics, possibly?' She could see he was surprised she was so calm. 'This all happened a long, time ago.'

'Two years ago, to be precise.'

'Well, it feels like a lifetime to me.'

Time flew, Zoë reflected. Two years since her ex-husband had tried to destroy her career. She had been so set on rebuilding her life she had hardly noticed how quickly the time had passed. She could still remember the burn of shame when she'd first read the headline. How could she have known then that the old adage would prove true? There was no such thing as bad publicity; this morning's interview had only proved it yet again.

It was two years since her notoriety in the 'Star Sells Sex' scandal had put her name on everyone's lips. Almost immediately her cookery programme had begun to break every ratings record. Her next step had been to form her own company, and that had led to even greater success.

These days the headline was hardly ever mentioned, and on the few occasions when it was people laughed with her, as if it had all been nothing more than a rather clever publicity stunt. She knew the truth behind the headline, and it couldn't hurt her now. Only Rico could do that, if he believed the lies.

'So you've nothing to say in your defence?' he said. 'No explanation to offer me at all?'

'Am I supposed to ask for your forgiveness?'

'The whole scandal blew over quite quickly.' He shrugged. 'That's why I couldn't place you at first.'

'True.' Zoë smiled sadly at him. 'Did you hope I was hiding something, Rico—so that you and I could be quits?'

A muscle worked in his jaw; other than that there was nothing, until he said, 'Do you blame me for being defensive?'

A short sound of incredulity leapt from Zoë's throat.

'If I had told you who I was from the first moment we met—'

'I wouldn't have thought any more or any less of you.'

They stared at each other in silence for a moment, and then, leaning in front of Zoë, Rico clicked the mouse and cleared the screen.

Straightening up, he gazed at her. 'My full name is Alarico Cortes de Aragon. I have many business interests, but flamenco is my passion, and Castillo Cazulas, as I'm sure you have already worked out, belongs to me.'

'When were you going to tell me, Rico? After we'd slept together?'

'Don't speak like that, Zoë. You must understand I have to protect my position.'

'*Your* position? And I have nothing worth protecting—is that it? I was nothing more than an entertaining diversion while you toured your estates in Cazulas?'

'Zoë.' Rico reached out to her, and then drew back. 'Try to understand what it's like for me. I have to know who I'm dealing with.'

'What are you trying to say, Rico?' Zoë said softly. 'A man as important, as rich and influential as you, has to be cautious about the type of woman he takes to bed?'

'It's a lot more than that, Zoë, and you know it.'

'Do I?' She smiled faintly. 'I'm afraid I must have missed something.'

'Can you imagine my shock when I read this headline?'

'It must have been terrible for you.'

'Don't be sarcastic.'

'How do you expect me to be? You tell me you have to protect yourself from me as if I'm some piece of dirt that might tarnish your lustre.'

'Don't say that. I asked for this information before I knew you, Zoë.'

'And now you do know me,' Zoë said bitterly, glancing at the screen. 'You must be glad that you took that precaution.'

'You don't know me very well.'

'I don't know you at all.'

The coldness in her voice, the bitterness in her eyes cut right through him. He wasn't sure about anything any more, Rico realised. He had spent most of his adult life protecting himself from the gutter press. It was ironic to think that it was their common bond. He focused on her face as she spoke again, and was shocked to see the pain in her eyes when she gazed unwaveringly at him.

'I don't have anything concrete like a headline to shake the foundations of my belief in you,' she said. 'All I have are candles, a romantic night in a beautiful luxury spa, and the horrible suspicion that maybe you arranged all that because you wondered if you had what it took to seduce a frigid woman.'

'How can you say that?'

'You seem shocked, Rico. Why is that? Because I'm getting too close to the truth?'

'No!' The word shot out of him on a gust of loathing that she could even think such a thing. 'It isn't true. I don't know what's happened to you in the past, but you're not frigid. And I don't need the sort of reassurance you seem to think I do!'

'You lied to me.' Her voice was low, and cruelly bitter. 'You made assumptions about me, Rico. You invaded my privacy—that same privacy that's so precious to *you*, El Señor Alarico Cortes de Aragon! *You had me investigated.*' She ground out each word with incredulity, and then gazed up at the sky to give a short, half-sobbing laugh. 'And while that was going on you tried to get me into bed. And then—' She held up her hand, silencing his attempt to protest. 'Then you sold me out to the tabloids for some type of sick revenge.'

'Zoë, please—'

'I haven't finished yet!' She shouted the words at him in a hoarse, agonised voice, leaning forward stiffly to confront him, her face white with fury. 'To cap it all, you turn all self-righteous on me—pretending it matters to you that someone else hurt me, used me as a punch-bag—as if you care any more than he did!'

'You've gone too far!' He couldn't hold back any longer. 'How dare you compare me with that—that—'

'What's the matter, Rico? You think of him and you see yourself? Even you can't bring yourself to admit what you are.'

'And just what am I?'

'A deceitful, lying user!'

'User?' He threw his hands up. 'Who's using who here, Zoë?'

'That's right—stay up in your ivory tower, where you're safe from all the gold-diggers, why don't you, Rico? Only I don't want your money—I never did. I can manage quite well on my own!'

'And that's what you want, is it, Zoë—to be on your own?'

'What do you think?' she said bitterly.

'Then I'd better leave.'

'That would be good.'

'You signed the lease on the castle. You can stay until it runs out. Do whatever the hell you want to do! I'll see myself out.'

CHAPTER TEN

HE'D been thrown out of his own castle. That was a first. Rico looked neither left nor right as he strode purposefully across the courtyard towards his Jeep. Throwing himself into the driver's seat, he slammed the door, breathing like a bull. The knuckles on his hands turned white on the steering-wheel.

They wanted each other like a bushfire wanted fuel to sustain it. They were burning so hot they were burning out— burning each other out in the process. He had seen her muscles bunched up tight across her shoulders. And she wanted to believe him—that was the tragedy of the situation. They wanted each other, they wanted to believe in each other, to be with each other and only each other—but they were tearing each other apart. They needed each other—but she didn't need him enough to tell him the truth. She didn't trust him. Maybe she would never trust him. Could he live with that?

The answer was no, Rico realised as he gunned the engine into life. Some of it he'd worked out for himself—the rest he could find out. But that wasn't what he wanted. He wanted her to tell him. She *had* to tell him if there was anything left between them at all. If she was the victim, not the architect, of that newspaper headline, why the hell didn't she just come out and say so? Maybe there was a grain of truth in it—maybe that was why she couldn't bring herself to explain.

Her accusers were guilty of making a profit out of the scandal—but newspapers were in business to make money, not friends. He had been shocked when he'd read the torrid revelations, but he had to admire her. She was a fighter, like him. But was she fighting to clear her name or to put up a smokescreen? Would he ever know?

Trouble was, he cared—he really cared—and it made him mad to think that all the money in the world couldn't buy him the whole truth. Only Zoë could give him that.

Rico's eyes narrowed and his mouth firmed into a flat, hard line. Thrusting the Jeep into gear, he powered away. She was entitled to stay on at the castle—he had no quarrel with that. He had always rattled round the place. Though it was certainly a lot more lively these days, he reflected cynically, flooring the accelerator pedal.

He eased the neck of his collar with one thumb. He was restless, frustrated—even a little guilty that he hadn't stayed to fight it out with her. He shouldn't have left with so much bitterness flying between them. He should have finished it or sorted it. But how could he when she had made such vicious accusations? The very idea of losing control to the extent that he'd hurt anyone, let alone a woman, revolted him. And then to accuse him of setting up that interview. He made a sound of disbelief. Didn't she know how deep his resentment of trash journalism went?

Rico frowned, gripping the wheel, forcing himself to breathe steadily and wait until he had calmed down. Gradually the truth behind the furious row came to him, as if a mist was slowly lifting before his eyes. He could see that the level of Zoë's passion was connected to the level of pain she had inside her. The legacy of her past had just played out between them. Instead of being hurt and offended by her accusations, he should be relieved that she had finally been able to vent her feelings, and that she had chosen to do it in front of him.

She was right. They both needed space, time to think. When he was with her his mind was clouded with all sorts of things that left no room for reason. He had never felt such a longing for anything or anyone in his life. Just the thought that some-one—some man—some brute—had hurt her made him phys-ically sick. So why wouldn't she let him in? Couldn't she see that he would take on the world to make things right for her again? Why wouldn't she trust him?

Swinging onto the main road, Rico channelled his frustration into thoughts of exposing all the bullies in the world to public ridicule. It would be too easy to use strength against them; strength of mind was more his speciality, and a far better tool to drag Zoë back from the edge of the precipice that led straight back to her past.

As he settled into his driving he suffered another surge of impatience. It was so hard to be patient where Zoë was concerned. He had to remind himself that she was worth all the time in the world, and that he hadn't made his fortune by acting on impulse. And, yes, she was right. He had expected an emotional response from her when she saw the screen full of huge letters, each one of them condemning her. He respected that. The headline was more than two years old, but he couldn't believe she had ever reacted to it in any other way. It took real courage to handle it so well.

But he had seen her lose control later. Was it his betrayal that had forced her over the edge even when she could keep her cool under fire from the tabloid press? If so, did that mean there was something really worth fighting for growing between them?

Quite suddenly the newspaper article seemed ridiculous. Zoë had forged a successful career for herself; she had no need to sell anything other than her talent. But where sex was concerned she was seriously repressed. He had firsthand experience to back that up…

Remembering, Rico grimaced. He felt like hell. What had he done? What had he done to Zoë? He should have been there for her. He should have made allowances. He should have proved to her, as well as to himself, that he understood how complex she was. She wasn't like other women, she had been right about that—but not in the way she thought. Her past had left her damaged, and instead of trying to help he had trampled her trust into the ground. There wasn't a brazen bone in her body, and if he had to delve deeper into her past to find out the truth and make things right for her, then he would.

Why was it so important to her that Rico Cortes knew the truth? Zoë wondered as she closed the door on the study bedroom after sending her e-mails. She had been so sure she wouldn't care, so certain she would brazen it out if he looked at her with scorn and contempt. He had done neither, but still the matter wasn't resolved in her head. She had to see him at least once more to sort it out. She had thought she could treat him like anyone else—if he believed the lies, so be it; if he didn't, so much the better. But now she knew she wouldn't rest until he knew the truth.

Her ex had planted the headline—though Rico couldn't know that. He had taken his revenge when she'd left him after years of abuse. She had refused to accept the public humiliation two years ago, and she wasn't about to let it get to her now.

What hurt her far more was the fact that Rico Cortes was a man she might have loved, and that he had deceived her into believing he was nothing more than a local flamenco enthusiast. She could accept his need for caution; Rico was a very rich man indeed—and an aristocrat, according to the search engine on the computer. But he was a self-made man for all that; he had started with nothing but a title.

As she pushed open the kitchen door and walked inside Zoë made a sharp, wounded sound. She was just Zoë Chapman, marital survivor and cook—hardly an appropriate match for a billionaire aristocrat.

She had allowed herself to develop feelings for a man she could never have. Right now she wished she'd never come to Spain, had never met El Señor Alarico Cortes de Aragon, because then he couldn't have broken her heart.

*   *   *

Arriving back at his beach house, Rico tossed the keys of the Jeep onto the hall table and smiled a greeting at his butler.

'A package arrived for you, sir, while you were out.'

'Thank you, Rodrigo.' Rico scanned the details on the well-stuffed padded bag as he carried it through to his study.

Before opening it he pulled back the window shutters so that brilliant sunlight spilled into the room. His whole vision was filled with the shimmering Mediterranean, and he drew the tang of ozone deep into his lungs. Simple things gave him the greatest pleasure. These were the real rewards of extreme wealth: the rush of waves upon the sand, the seabirds soaring in front of his windows, and the matchless tranquillity.

Opening the package, he tipped the contents onto his desk. There was a log of Zoë's everyday life back in England, along with diaries, tapes, transcripts of interviews, photographs, press-cuttings… Rico's hand hovered over the disarray, and then he pushed it all away.

He didn't want to read what someone else had to say about Zoë. He didn't care to acknowledge the fact that his pride and his suspicion had demanded such an invasion of her privacy. He felt dirty, and disgusted with himself, as if the contents of the package somehow contaminated him.

If he cared to look, he knew that whatever he found in the newspaper cuttings would be a sensationalised account. Even the most respected broadsheet had to succumb to such tactics in a marketplace where fresh news was available at the click of a mouse.

Coffee was served to him, and taken away again without being touched. The crisp green leaves of a delicious-looking salad had wilted by the time he absent-mindedly forked some up.

Pushing the plate away to join the rest of the detritus on his desk, he stood up and stretched. Walking over to the window, he was not surprised to see how low the sun had dipped in the sky. The colours outside the window were spectacular, far richer than before, as if the day wanted to leave behind a strong impression before it gave way to the night.

He would not let Zoë go. He could not. If she told him to go again, then he would still let her stay on at the castle as long as it suited her. It was a hollow, unlovely place without her.

After a quick shower and a change of clothes, he didn't wait for the Jeep to be brought round to the front. Sprinting down the steps, he jogged down the drive towards the garage block and, climbing in, switched on and powered away.

He found her in the kitchen, eating with the crew. They were relaxing in the way only good friends could relax—some with their feet up on the opposite chair, men with their shirts undone, sleeves rolled back, and girls with hardly any make-up, and real tangles rather than carefully tousled hair. The table was littered with the debris of a put-together meal, and when he walked in a silence fell that was so complete it left the walls ringing. There was the sound of chairs scraping the floor as everyone stiffened and straightened up. He could sense them closing in around Zoë like a protective net.

Her lips parted with surprise as she stared at him. She was wearing nightclothes—faded pyjamas—with her hair left in damp disarray around her shoulders. She looked to him as if the day had been too much for her and she couldn't wait to get it over with and go to sleep. Someone at the table must have talked her into joining them for a light meal.

It was the enemy camp, all right. Every gaze except for Zoë's was trained on his face. These were the people who had stood by her, who had stayed with her when she'd made the break from the television company run by her ex-husband. That much he'd learned from the Internet. These were the people who had put their livelihoods on the line for Zoë Chapman.

He waited by the door, and she half stood. But the girl sitting next to her put a hand on Zoë's arm.

'You don't have to go, Zo.'

'No, no… I'll be all right.' She pushed her chair back from the table and looked at him. 'I have to get this sorted out.'

He went outside, and she followed him. 'Will you come with me?' He glanced towards the Jeep.

'I'm not dressed.'

If that was the only reason, he'd solve the problem for her. Striding quickly back into the castle, he plucked a shawl down from a peg. As he came out again he threw it round her shoulders. 'You'll be warm enough now.'

'It's not that, Rico. I'm not sure I want to come with you.'

She took a step away from him. Folding the shawl carefully, she hung it over her arm, as if she wanted time to put her thoughts back in order.

'Please.' He wasn't good at this, Rico realised. He could negotiate his way in or out of anything to do with business. But feelings—needs—they were foreign to him, an emotional bank accessed by other people. He was a man of purpose, not dreams—but quite suddenly he realised that purpose and dreams had become hopelessly intertwined. 'Just give me an hour of your time. Please, Zoë. That's all I ask.'

'Will you wait in the Jeep while I get changed?'

He would have waited at the gateway to hell if she had asked him to.

Rico's knuckles were white with tension by the time Zoë emerged from the castle. She hadn't kept him waiting long, and now he drank her in like a thirsty man at a watering hole in the desert. She was wearing her uniform of choice: jeans and a plain top. She looked great. She was so fresh, so clean, and so lovely, with her red-gold hair caught up high on the top of her head in a band so that the thick fall brushed her shoulders as she walked towards him.

'Are you sure we can't talk here—or in the garden?'

'I'd like to show you something,' he said, opening the passenger door for her.

After a moment's hesitation she climbed in. He felt as if he had just closed the biggest business deal of his life. Only this was better—much, much better.

'What a fabulous place,' she said, when they turned in the gates at the beach house. 'Whose is it?'

Her voice tailed off at the end of the question, and he knew she had already guessed. Sweeping through the towering gates, Rico slowed as they approached the mansion. Even he could see it was stunning now he saw it through Zoë's eyes.

'It's all very beautiful,' Zoë said, when they were inside.

He watched her trail her fingers lightly over the creamy soft furnishings as they walked through the main reception room. Everything looked better to him too now she was here. He could see how well the cream walls looked, with smoky blue highlights provided by cushions and rugs, and the occasional touch of tobacco-brown. The walls had been left plain to show off his modern art collection.

'Chagall?' She turned to him in amazement.

He felt ashamed that he took such things for granted. Not for him the colourful poster prints that had adorned his mother's home and made it so cheerful. He liked the real thing, and he could afford it now—Hockney and Chagall were just two of his favourites. He envied the expression on Zoë's face. He wanted to recapture that feeling. He wanted to remember how it had felt to attend his first fine art auction sale, where he had vowed one day he would be bidding.

Zoë turned back to the picture again. She had never seen anything like it outside a museum. The picture showed a handsome man embracing a woman with long titian hair. They were both suspended in an azure sky, with the head of a good-natured horse sketched into the background. A happy sun shone out of the canvas, turning the land beneath it to gold.

'It's genuine, isn't it? This isn't a print?'

'That's right.' He felt shame again. Such things were meant to be shared. When was the last time he had brought anyone into his home?

'I saw a Chagall in Las Vegas—a man and woman, head to head—' Zoë stopped talking, realising they were standing head to head too, and that Rico was smiling down at her.

'You know what I mean.' She waved her hand and moved away, going to stand by an open window. 'Rico, why am I here?' she said, still with her back turned to him.

'I know everything about you.'

'Oh, do you?' she said, managing to sound as unconcerned as if they had been discussing a new style of drapes.

'Zoë, please, can't we talk about it?'

'Why should we? What purpose would it serve?' She turned round to stare at him.

'Will you come with me?' he said.

Something in his expression made her walk towards him.

This must be his study, Zoë realised. It was a pleasant, airy room, but small on the scale of other rooms in the mansion. It was cosy, even a little cluttered. This was the hub around which the rest of his life revolved, she guessed.

'Please sit down,' he said, holding out a chair for her across from his own at the desk.

'I'd rather stand.'

'Please.'

She didn't want to make a fuss.

'Why didn't you tell me?' Rico said, sitting across from her.

'Tell you what?'

'That all that nonsense in the newspaper was a pack of lies?'

'Because I don't feel the need to defend myself.'

'Nor should you.'

Glancing down at the desk, Zoë realised that all the papers

she had thought were Rico's were, in fact, her own history in print. 'So now you know.'

'I only wish I'd known about it sooner. Why didn't you tell me?'

'Because it's none of your business. And because I don't want, or need, anyone's misplaced sympathy.'

'Misplaced?' Rico sprang to his feet and planted his fists on the desk, leaning so far over it their faces were almost touching. 'A man who is supposed to love you beats you up, and you call my sympathy misplaced? You build a whole new life for yourself, and a successful career, only to have that—that—' Rico stopped, the words jamming in his brain as he searched for something to properly describe what he thought of Zoë's ex-husband.

'I finally left him when he tried to sell me to someone he owed money to.'

All the emotion was gone from her voice. He wanted her to rail against her fate, to show some emotion.

'It was just a night of sex, to pay off the debt…'

'Just! Zoë, Zoë—' Rico passed his hand across his eyes, as if it would help him to make some sense of what she was telling him. Walking around the desk, he drew her to her feet. 'Come with me.' He took her to the open window. 'Look out there. Tell me what you see.'

'It's night-time—'

'It's nature, Zoë—pure, harsh, and lovely. Here at my beach house, and at the castle in Cazulas, I escape from the world when I need to. That's why I was so protective of my privacy when you arrived. Why I still am so protective—but now I want you to have the same. I don't want you to live with a nightmare stuck in the back of your mind. I can't bear to think of you trapped like that, in the past.'

Wrapping her arms around her waist, Zoë inhaled deeply, and then turned away from the window to face him. 'I got away, in case you're interested. I could see the man's heart wasn't in it. False bravado brought him to me after a few drinks with my ex-husband. I just explained it was a bad time for me—that there had to be some mistake. He didn't lose face. There was no unpleasantness. I think I handled it well.'

Handled it well? The words tumbled around Rico's head as if someone was knocking them in with a hammer. He wanted to drag her into his arms right then, tell her it would be all right from now on, that he would be there for her, to protect her from harm. He wanted to promise her that she would never have to face such a monstrous situation in her life again—but she was already walking towards the door.

'Will you take me back to the castle now?'

'I'll do anything you want me to.'

She smiled faintly at him, as if to acknowledge his understanding without necessarily accepting that it helped or changed anything for her.

The call came when Zoë had just climbed into bed, and for the second time that night she rushed to pull on her jeans. This time she tugged a sweater over the top of her tee shirt. She didn't know how long she would be, or what might be involved. She just knew she had to be prepared. A phone call from Maria in hospital was serious. Snatching up her bag and some money, along with her car keys, she hurried downstairs.

Zoë felt as if there was a tight band around her chest until the moment she reached the small private room and saw Maria sitting up in a chair beside the bed with a rug over her knees. 'Thank God you're all right,' she said, crouching down at her side. 'Is it serious?' She reached for Maria's hand. 'I've been so worried about you. Will it affect your dancing?'

Maria lifted her other arm from beneath the blanket, revealing strapping. 'Thankfully just a sprain—nothing more. The X-rays have confirmed it. I'm sorry if I frightened you, Zoë. I just couldn't stand the thought of being here all night, and I have such a thing about taxis—'

'No. You were absolutely right to call me. I'm so relieved. I don't know why, but I thought you might have injured your leg.'

'My fault. I should have explained, instead of just saying I had fallen. I can see now that my legs would be the first thing you thought of.'

'Has anyone told Rico? If he hears you are in hospital he'll be very worried.'

'I tried him first,' Maria told her. 'But he wasn't at home.'

No, he was taking me home, Zoë thought, feeling doubly guilty knowing Maria had probably rung Rico to take her to the hospital. And she had been so lost in her own thoughts on the way back to the castle she hadn't spoken a word to him.

'The main thing is that no permanent harm has been done,' Zoë said, returning to practical matters. 'Can you leave now, or must we wait for a doctor?'

'The doctor has to formally discharge me before he goes off duty for the night. But we can talk until then.' Maria stopped and viewed Zoë with concern. 'You look exhausted, Zoë, is something wrong?'

'No.' Zoë forced a bright note into her voice. 'Nothing.' Nothing apart from the fact that Rico knew the whole sordid truth about her now and she would probably never see him again. He'd been sympathetic enough, but, remembering how he had deceived her about his identity, she couldn't help wondering if his sympathy had just been an act too.

She refocused as Maria started to speak again.

'Are you sure that son of mine hasn't said something to upset you?'

'Your son?'

'Rico?' Maria prompted.

'Rico!'

Zoë turned away. Why hadn't she thought of it? Why hadn't she seen it before? Rico's defensive attitude towards

Maria when she had first wanted to approach her… She had thought it pride on his part that she, a stranger, had dared to expect such an artist to put her talent on show for commercial gain. And the attention he paid Maria, his obvious pride in his mother's cultural heritage. All this should have told her. But how could it be? He was not Rico Cortes, local flamenco enthusiast, but El Señor Alarico Cortes de Aragon, a grandee of Spain.

'I don't understand.' She turned back to Maria.

'It is very simple—'

'You don't have to tell me,' Zoë said quickly. 'It's none of my business.'

'I'm not ashamed of what I did. Rico's father was the local landowner. His wife was dead, and we loved each other. We never married, but I gave him a son.' She smiled.

'But how did Rico inherit the title and the castle?'

'There were no other heirs. His father insisted the title must be passed to Rico. They were very close. It was just the title— his money went to the village.'

'But what about you?'

'I was proud—maybe too proud.'

'But Rico was a success?'

'A huge success,' Maria agreed with a wry laugh. 'Rico has always supported me, and eventually he made enough money to buy back the castle. As his father suspected, Rico didn't need his money—he was quite capable of making his own fortune.'

'You must be very proud of him.'

'I am,' Maria assured her. 'And now Rico cares for the village just as his father used to do.'

Maria's glance darted to the door. She was growing anxious, Zoë realised. 'I'll go and find the doctor, and see if I can hurry him up.' Another thought struck her. 'Did you try Rico on his mobile?'

'Yes,' Maria said, her dark eyes brightening as she looked towards the door.

CHAPTER ELEVEN

HAD Maria planned this? Zoë wondered. She couldn't see how that was possible—unless Rico had said something to his mother, and then Maria had put in a call to both of them, using her misfortune as a mechanism to bring them together.

Her heart was hammering louder than Maria's shoes had ever thundered on a floor as Rico moved past her to draw his mother into his arms. Pulling back, he spoke to her quickly in Spanish. Having received the answer he hoped for, he smiled and kissed her cheek before turning to Zoë.

'Thank you for coming, Zoë.'

How could I not? Zoë wondered. 'I was only too pleased I could help. But now you're here I'll leave you with your mother—'

'No.' Rico touched her arm. 'It's late, Zoë. You should not be driving home alone.'

'I'll go and find the doctor before I leave, and send him in to you.'

'No.' This time he closed the door. 'I'm taking you back with us, and that's final. You've had a shock too, and the roads can be dangerous at night.'

No more dangerous than they had ever been, Zoë thought. But Rico's expression was set, and she didn't want to make a fuss in front of Maria.

They settled Maria into her cosy home in the centre of the village, and then got back in the Jeep.

'It really was good of you to go to the hospital for Maria,' Rico said as they moved off again.

'I'd do anything for her,' Zoë said honestly, resting back against the seat.

'I can see you're tired. I'll take you straight back.'

'Thank you.'

So much for Maria's machinations. If it had been a plan at all, nothing was going to come of it. And of course she was relieved...

Clambering into bed and switching off the light, Zoë sank into the pillows, shot through with exhaustion. It had been quite a day. Her body was wiped out, but her mind refused to shut down. Turning on the light again, she thought about Rico, and about Rico and Maria being mother and son. And then she ran through everything Maria had told her about Rico.

Swinging her legs out of bed, she poured herself a glass of water. Rico had set out on a mission to reclaim his inheritance, to preserve everything he believed in, just as she had. They had both succeeded. They were both proud and defensive—you had to be when you'd fought so hard for something. She always felt as if everything she had achieved might slip through her fingers if she didn't hold on tight enough.

Zoë's glance grazed the telephone sitting next to her on the bedside table. She had to decide whether to call him or not. Of course she didn't have to do anything—she could just let him slip away into the past...

Zoë was surprised when the operator found the number so easily. She had imagined Rico would have a number that would be withheld from the public. Instead a cultured voice answered her in Spanish right away. It wasn't Rico's voice, it was some other man—his butler, perhaps. She gave her name, and he asked her to wait and he would see whether it was convenient for Señor Alarico to take her call.

It felt like for ever before Rico came on the line, and then he sounded as if he had been exercising. It was a big house,

Zoë reminded herself, with acres of floor space. 'I'm sorry to trouble you.'

'It is no trouble. What can I do for you?'

'Did I disturb you? Were you sleeping?'

'Sleeping? No. I was in the pool—they had to come and get me.'

'I see. I'm sorry,' she said again.

'Don't be.'

The line went quiet as if he was waiting for her to speak. She couldn't change her mind now. 'We didn't finish our conversation earlier.'

Now it was Zoë's turn to wait, not daring to breathe in case she missed his reply.

'I'll come over tomorrow.'

It was less than she had hoped for, but more in some ways. They were speaking at least.

'Or would you prefer to come here?'

Space from the film crew would be good. They were so defensive on her behalf. She loved them for it, but it made any private discussion with Rico impossible. 'I'm going to see Maria—your mother—in the morning.' She was thinking aloud, planning her day.

'Then I'll pick you up around nine. We'll go and see her together. You can come back here for lunch afterwards...if you like?'

'I would like that.' She smiled. 'Nine o'clock, then.'

'See you tomorrow, Zoë.'

The line was cut before she could reply.

Maria couldn't have made it more obvious that she was pleased to see them. She was already up and about, and insisted on making coffee.

'I'm not an invalid,' she told Rico, brushing off his offer to help. 'And before you say a word, I am returning to teaching today.'

'I forbid it—'

'Oh, you do? Do I dance on my hands, Rico? I still have one good hand with which to direct proceedings. And,' she said, refusing to listen to his argument, 'I am to be collected in half an hour. Before I leave, I have something for you, Zoë—to make sure you never stop dancing.'

'I can't possibly take that!' Zoë looked at the lilac dress Maria was holding up. The one she had worn for her first flamenco lesson. 'It must be worth a fortune.'

'It's worth far more than that,' Maria assured her as she pressed it into Zoë's hands. 'And I want you to have it.'

'It's so beautiful,' Zoë said, resting her face against it.

'Yes, it is—and if you ever need a boost, Zoë, you just look at it and think of us.'

'I'll only need to think of you, Maria,' Zoë said, smiling as she hugged Rico's mother.

It was fortunate Zoë couldn't see his mother's imperative drawing together of her upswept black brows, or the fierce command in her eyes, Rico realised as he took the cue to go, and take Zoë with him. 'We'd better leave you now so that you can get ready for your class, Mother.'

'Yes,' Maria said firmly, clearly relieved that her silent message had been understood. 'But before you go, Rico, you can do one more thing for me.'

'What's that?' he said, pausing with his hand on the door.

'Take this with you,' she said, handing him a camera. 'I want a photograph of Zoë in that dress—to hang in the mountain lodge at the flamenco camp,' she explained to Zoë. 'Then I will be able to see the dress and you, Zoë, any time I want.'

Alongside Beba? Immediately Zoë regretted the thought. Maria just wasn't like that. 'I'm sure you don't want reminding of my pathetic efforts—'

'I most certainly do. You were very good—full of genuine passion,' Maria said firmly. 'Now, take this girl to lunch,

Rico. She looks half starved. And don't forget my photograph.'

'I won't,' he promised, sweeping her into his arms for a parting embrace.

Zoë had her hand stuck up her back when she emerged from Rico's dressing-room. He was sitting on the shady veranda at his beach house, where they had been having lunch. He stood as she approached.

'I can't seem to get the dress right—can you help me?' Maria had been on hand the last time to finish off the fastenings for her.

The setting was superb. There was an archway coated in cerise bougainvillea where she would stand for Maria's photograph, with the sea behind her and some flamenco music playing softly to put her in the mood.

Giving up on the dress, Zoë straightened up. 'Help?' she prompted softly.

'Yes, of course.'

Lunch had been a neutral, emotion-free affair, with delicious food served at a leisurely pace, prepared for them by one of Rico's excellent chefs. Zoë knew they were starting again. They were taking it slowly—each of them feeling their way, each of them strangers to love, each of them determined to put at least a toe in the water.

Rico couldn't have planned anything better than this, Zoë thought as she waited for him to finish fastening her dress. It was a treat just to eat food someone else had prepared. Before she met Rico, she had always taken charge of things in the kitchen. He was right: it was good to kick back and relax from time to time.

'Te gusta el flamenco, señorita?'

''Sí, señor, I like flamenco very much,' Zoë whispered, trying not to respond to the closeness of his body or the tone of his voice as he reached around her waist to secure the

fastenings. Then he murmured, 'Turn around,' and it was impossible, because the warmth of his breath was making every tiny hair on the back of her neck stand erect.

'There—that's done,' he said.

She must have turned too quickly. One silk shoulder strap slipped from her shoulder, and as she went to pull it up again their fingers tangled.

'I'm sorry.' Zoë quickly removed her hand.

'Sorry? What are you sorry for, Zoë?'

His voice was neutral, but his eyes… They were very, very close. His hands were still resting lightly on her waist. 'I didn't give you the chance to explain anything. I just poured out all my own troubles.'

'Stop.' Rico's voice was low, but firm. 'You make it sound as if what happened to you was normal. It wasn't normal, Zoë—and you must never think of it that way or you will come to accept it as normal. You were brutalised—your mind, your body—'

'But I'm all right now.'

'And I'm going to make sure you stay that way.'

'You—'

Rico didn't plan on long explanations. He kissed her so tenderly he made her cry, and he had to catch the tears on her cheeks with his fingertips.

'I feel such a fool.'

'No, you don't,' he assured her. 'You feel wonderful to me.' And, sweeping her into his arms, he walked back into the house.

'What a shame we must take this dress off again,' he said when they reached his bedroom, 'when you have only just put it on.'

He was already halfway down the fastenings as she lay in his arms on the bed. 'Maria's photograph—' Zoë tensed as the last one came free.

'Later.' Rico kissed her shoulder, moving on to nudge her hair aside and kiss her neck.

'But it will be dark later.'

'You will look beautiful by moonlight.'

And then the silk dress was hanging off, and, feeling self-conscious, she wriggled out of it.

Picking it up, Rico tossed it onto a chair by the side of the bed. She wore little underneath it—just a flimsy scrap of a lace thong, not even a bra. There was support built in to the bodice of the dress.

Rico planted kisses as he freed the buttons on his shirt. That followed the dress, and when he kissed her again, and she felt his warm, hard body against her own, Zoë whimpered; she couldn't help herself.

He rested her back against silk and satin, and the linen sheets beneath the covers were scented with lavender. Everything was contrived to please the senses—and it was so easy to slide a little deeper into pleasure beneath his touch.

As Rico looked at the small, pale hands clutching his shoulders, and heard Zoë call his name, he knew she was everything he wanted. Her breasts were so lush, so provocative, the taut nipples reaching out to him, pink and damp where he had tormented her. Her legs moved rhythmically over the bed as she groaned out her need, and now there was just the scrap of lace dissecting the golden tan of her thighs between them.

His gaze swooped up again, lingering on the dark shadow of her cleavage, so deep and lovely. He longed to lose himself in it, to bury his tongue and more besides in its warm, clinging silkiness. But it wasn't just her beauty that bewitched him. He needed her. He had never needed anyone in his life before—he'd made sure of it. But Zoë was different—*he* was different when he was with her, and perhaps that was the most important thing of all.

He watched as she freed the tiny thong and inched it down over her thighs. Had he ever been so aroused? Clamouring sensations gnawed at his control, but he held back. Her trust was too hard won to risk now. How could anyone have abused her? Her skin was as soft and as fragile as the silk upon which she lay. Her eyes were darkening with growing confidence and her lips were parted in invitation. As their eyes locked and she reaffirmed her faith in him, he knew he would defend her with his life.

'Rico…'

As she breathed his name he remembered wryly that foreplay was intended to be an aphrodisiac, not a torture.

He went to pull off the rest of his clothes, but she stopped him. He drew in a deep shuddering breath. He would stop even now if she asked him to.

Scrambling into a sitting position, she touched the belt buckle on his trousers. 'You'll have to help me—my hands are shaking.'

Taking both her hands in his, he kissed each one of her fingertips in turn and then, turning her hands over, planted a tender kiss on each palm.

When Rico finally stood naked before her, Zoë's breath caught in her throat. He was totally unabashed, his dark gaze steady on her face. A lasso of moonlight fell across him, showing the power in his forearms and the wide spread of shoulders. She saw now that his broad chest was shaded with dark hair that tapered down to a hard belly, below which…

She stared into his face, waiting for him to come to her.

Her perfume was intoxicating, drawing him towards her. He stretched his length against her on the bed, not touching her, still holding back. Inhaling deeply, he stroked her thick, silky hair, sifting it through his fingers and enjoying the texture. He loved the way she quivered beneath his touch, eyes closed, mouth slightly open, her breathing nothing more than whispery puffs.

'Rico—'

He kissed her lightly on the lips.

'Kiss me properly.'

'Properly? What do you mean?' His restraint was making her bloom beneath him like a flower that had been too long out of the sun. Her breasts, two perfect globes, were thrust towards him, and her nipples, cruelly neglected, were almost painfully erect. The soft swell of her belly led his gaze down to where she was aching for his attention. Cupping her breasts, he made her gasp. And that gasp soon turned to a whimper as he began to chafe each perfect nipple with his firm thumb pads.

The pleasure was so intense it was almost a pain. He had forgotten how exquisite she was, how sweetly scented, how tender she felt beneath his lips. As he suckled and tugged, and heard her cry out his name, he knew that all he wanted in the world was to keep her safe and love her.

CHAPTER TWELVE

IT WAS so pleasurable, so seductive and intoxicating, fear never entered her head. Zoë wanted to beg Rico to hurry when his firm touch reached her thighs. She had never been so aroused. She cried out with pleasure when his searching fingers finally moved between her legs, and then she begged him not to stop.

Reaching for him, she found she needed two hands to properly encompass him, and he groaned softly beneath her questing fingers until at last she was forced to lift her hands away. Dropping a kiss on her lips, he probed deeply with his tongue, and she pressed against him, searching for the firmer contact she needed so badly.

'Not yet—be patient, *querida*...'

Lifting Zoë's arms above her head, Rico drew her underneath him. As one powerful thigh moved between her legs she shuddered with desire.

'Open your eyes, and look at me, Zoë.'

It was the most exquisite pleasure Zoë had ever known, and the warm, insistent pressure took her to a place where she could only breathe and feel. And then he caught the tip inside her, and it was she who swarmed down the bed to take him deeper. It was so easy, so right, there wasn't a moment of fear or the hint of a painful spasm to wipe out that pleasure.

The pain she had always felt before had been caused by fear, Zoë realised. She wasn't frigid at all. She was just a normal woman who had been waiting for a normal man. And all she wanted now was that Rico took full possession of her body and filled her completely.

She loved this new sensation, the stretching, filling, pulsing.

They started moving together, oblivious to the hungry sounds that escaped their lips, moving firmly until Zoë's fingers bit into the firm flesh of Rico's shoulders and she gave herself up completely to pleasure.

He held her in his arms, stroking her until she was quiet again, and then turned her so that now she was on top of him, straddling him, her legs widely parted. Sweeping the curve of her buttocks with a feathery touch, he tantalised her until she squirmed with delight and longed for him to drag her to him, plunge his tongue deep into the warm secret places of her mouth. But he had more skill than that, and made her wait until she was intoxicated by the raw power burning beneath her.

Feeling the insistent pressure of Rico's erection, Zoë took him deep inside her until she was completely filled. Then she began to move slowly, backwards and forwards, until she felt him take over. Throwing back her head, she closed her eyes, losing herself in sensation while he claimed her breasts, agitating her nipples between thumb and finger until she groaned out her pleasure and begged him for more. He turned her again, bringing her beneath him and using a few firm thrusts to bring on an electrifying climax that went on endlessly until she fell back panting on the bed.

Every part of her was glowing pink in the stunning aftermath of pleasure, Zoë realised, laughing softly with happiness. She had not thought it possible that a man could give himself to a woman so unselfishly. The expression on Rico's face was a fierce mix of passion and tenderness. It made her want him more than ever. She wanted to be the only woman who could put that expression on his face. She wanted his warmth and his strength curled around her for ever. She wanted everything.

As she murmured his name and reached out to him he dragged her close. His drugging kisses, the seductive touch of his hard body was more tantalising than anything she had ever imagined. He knew how to play her, to gently tease her and build her confidence. It was as if they had all the time in the world, and he meant to devote every moment of that time to pleasing her.

His hands were skilled, the look in his eyes commanding. He could order her to new heights of pleasure and she would obey at once. As she enjoyed his warm musky scent, laced with cinnamon and juniper, she felt as if her bones had turned to molten liquid. Her legs moved restlessly on the bed, seeking a cool place and then wrapping around him so he could be in no doubt as to what she wanted.

A great pulse was throbbing between her legs, and yet still he toyed with her, teasing and tempting until she could think of nothing but his firm touch. He must thrust inside her again to the hilt, stretching her wide— 'Please, Rico!'

'So you have not had enough yet?' He sounded pleased.

'Not nearly enough.' She didn't care what he thought of her; all she knew was her need for him. 'Please.'

Rico looked at Zoë, writhing beneath him. More pleasure could be gained by testing themselves to the limit. She must wait. He moved now with an agonising lack of speed, holding away from her until at last he consented to catch just inside her.

Her eyes shot open. 'How can you tease me now?'

'Easily.' He smiled. When she gasped with delight, he slowly brushed the velvet tip against her. 'Is this what you want, Zoë?' He slipped one controlling hand beneath her buttocks.

'You know it is.'

'More than anything?' But she didn't hear him now. Her mind was closed to anything as demanding as speech. She only wanted to feel, and be lost in his arms.

It was late by the time Rico took Zoë back to the castle. He still had work to do, and so did she. The sat in the Jeep like two teenagers who had just discovered each other. They kissed and touched as if every moment might be their last.

Parting from Rico was the hardest thing she had ever had to do, Zoë realised as she climbed out of the Jeep and shut the door. She stood motionless in the courtyard until he had driven away, disappeared from sight, and she couldn't even hear the noise of the engine.

But as she turned she felt as if she was walking six feet off the ground. It was as if the world around her had suddenly come into sharp focus and she had only been viewing it through a veil before. *So this is what happiness feels like,* she thought as she turned her face up to the sky.

Hurrying inside, Zoë couldn't keep the smile off her face. She didn't try. She didn't care if the whole world knew about her and Rico. This was love.

There were five Louis Vuitton suitcases lined up neatly at the end of her bed. Frowning as she dipped down to read the labels, Zoë pulled her hand away as the door swung open behind her.

'Can I help you?'

The voice was young and supercilious. High-pitched. The slight accent suggested she was Spanish.

And very beautiful, Zoë discovered when she turned around. Dressed all in red, the young woman was slender, and shorter than Zoë. The tailoring was Chanel, Zoë guessed from the buttons on her suit jacket, and her glossy black hair was arranged high on her head in an immaculate chignon.

She made Zoë felt scruffy in comparison—scruffy and apprehensive. Her heart was thudding heavily in her chest as she tried not to let her imagination get the better of her. She hadn't a clue who the woman could be. They certainly didn't know each other. This was Rico's castle, yet she seemed perfectly at home. Her mouth was pursed with disapproval, and she was doing a good job of making Zoë feel like the intruder. Zoë was conscious of her own tangled hair, still damp from

Rico's shower. Her face had to be glowing from the aftermath of so much lovemaking, and she knew she was under close inspection.

'What are you doing here?'

'I always stay here,' the young woman said confidently. Crossing to the window, she threw it wide open. She fanned herself theatrically and inhaled deeply, as if its previous occupant had somehow polluted the room.

'I'm sorry—have we met?' Walking up to her, Zoë extended a hand in greeting.

'I'm sure we haven't.'

Dark, cold eyes bored into Zoë's. Fingertips were proffered reluctantly. They were cold too.

'Beba Longoria.'

Zoë couldn't have been more shocked, but she hid it as best she could. *The* Beba? This woman looked nothing like the voluptuous young girl in the poster at the mountain hut. Success had stripped away her bloom, replacing it with an edgy tension. Maybe that was a result of having to defend her position against a constant stream of younger rivals. Yet Maria had remained unchanged...

Zoë pulled herself round with difficulty. 'I'm Zoë Chapman.'

'Ah, so you are Zoë Chapman. I hardly recognised you. You look quite different from the way you appear on television—much older.'

Touché, Zoë thought grimly. She tensed as Beba tossed her handbag onto the bed. The sight of the shiny red pouch clipping the edge of her pillows was the last straw. 'I'm sorry you've had all your things brought in here—someone should have told you I'm using this room. But don't worry. I'll have them transferred.'

'Transferred? What are you talking about?'

'To one of the spare rooms.' Zoë smiled helpfully.

'You clearly don't know who I am.'

'I've seen your poster at the mountain hut—'

'Then Rico must have told you.'

'Rico?' Zoë's confident expression faltered. Inwardly she was in crisis. But she had to try not to jump to conclusions. Rico had brothers and sisters. Beba might be one of them. Longoria could be her married name.

'Alarico Cortes? You do know who I'm talking about?'

'Of course I know him.'

'I see.' One perfectly groomed brow lifted as Beba stared at Zoë thoughtfully, and Zoë realised her hasty response had given away too much. She was on the back foot, cheeks blazing, when it should have been Beba feeling the heat.

'There's an understanding between us.' Beba's voice had dropped to a confidential level, as if she was trying to drop a bomb lightly on Zoë's head. 'Rico and I have been together since we were children. I'm surprised he didn't mention you to me—but then I suppose he can't be expected to remember every woman he meets.'

Turning away, she checked her hair in the dressing-table mirror, picking up Zoë's hand mirror to look at the back.

Zoë could feel the hostile black eyes spying on her through the mirror. But she was determined to hold herself together. 'There's obviously been a mistake.' She shrugged, and kept it pleasant. 'You see, I have taken a lease on the castle, and I'm using this suite of rooms during my tenancy. As you haven't unpacked yet, I'll just call down and have one of the crew come up and help you move to another room—'

'That won't be necessary.'

'I don't want to cause you any inconvenience.' Zoë's anger propelled her into action. She was already freeing the handle on the top of one of Beba's suitcases when she spoke again. 'So of course you are welcome to stay at the castle until you find alternative accommodation.'

'Rico will hear about this!'

'I'm afraid he has no legal rights over the castle until my lease expires. I doubt he can help you.'

'Alarico Cortes wields more power than you could ever understand.' Beba's face was twisted in an ugly mask as she snatched up her handbag from the bed. 'When he hears that I have been insulted—'

'He'll what?'

'Throw you onto the street!'

As Beba swept out of the room Zoë sank down on the bed. Her heart was thundering, but her mind was mercifully empty. She was numb with shock. All she was aware of was the click-clack of heels rattling away down the landing towards the main staircase.

When it was silent again, Zoë found she was shuddering uncontrollably. Burying her face in her hands, she drew her feet up on the bed and curled herself into a tight, defensive ball. Had Rico known about this when they were in bed together? Would Beba have dared to march into the castle and throw her weight around unless they were an item, as she said? Rico had never mentioned another woman. But a man like Rico Cortes with no woman in his life? She really had been living in a dream world!

Was she the type of companion El Señor Alarico Cortes de Aragon would take to the court of the King of Spain? Or would he take Beba—glamorous flamenco star? It was a stark choice between a cook with red hands and wild hair, or someone perfectly groomed, someone fragrant and dainty, with long, manicured fingernails and a musical laugh. She was quite certain Beba had a musical laugh.

Zoë reached for the phone and punched in some numbers. Rico's butler told her Señor Cortes was still out on business. No, he didn't know when he would be back. When pressed, the man admitted Señor Cortes was expected to return before a dinner appointment out, later that evening.

Later that evening! She couldn't wait until later that evening. She had to see him now—speak to him right away—resolve all this. There had to be an explanation.

Rico hadn't mentioned any plans for them, Zoë realised as she cut the line. It had never crossed her mind to ask when they would see each other again—she had taken it for granted. She felt sick, faint. She wanted this to be a nightmare. Because if it wasn't, she was on her way to making a fool of herself for the second time in her life.

She couldn't do anything yet, and it was far better to be busy than to brood, Zoë thought, wheeling the last of Beba's suitcases out of her room. She was hot all over again with the effort of lugging five overweight suitcases into position. She had showered and changed into fresh clothes right after Beba left, and now she would have to shower again, and dry and brush her hair until it shone. She had no intention of wearing her heartbreak on her sleeve. Life went on, with or without Rico Cortes. She was just glad to have a job to pour her energies into, as well as people who relied on her to take the helm.

This time when Zoë left her room she locked the door—something she hadn't felt the need to do since she'd moved into the castle. Hurrying downstairs, she found the team busy working on something in the Great Hall.

Philip swung round when he heard her.

'What's going on?' Zoë could see he was in one of his excitable moods. 'Well, are you going to tell me?' she said, smiling at him as she watched him picking his way over some camera cables.

'Cazulas is one incredible place, Zoë. You won't believe who has turned up now.'

Oh, yes, she would! 'Try me.'

'Only Beba! The best flamenco dancer in all of Spain.'

'Maria is the best flamenco dancer in all of Spain.'

'You know this Beba chick?'

'I've heard of her.'

'Well, you could sound a little more excited.'

'We haven't discussed another feature, Philip,' Zoë said, frowning as she realised what he planned to do.

'What about replacing that footage we didn't like? It's too good an opportunity to miss. Come on, Zoë. We could make this the last and best show of the series.'

He was right. 'So what's the angle? We already have the best flamenco dancer in Spain. That's how we billed Maria.'

'Beba appeals to the youngsters. She's like a pop star in the Latin world. We're talking glamour, we're talking riches, we're talking one sassy lady.'

'Yes, thank you. I think I get the picture.'

'But you haven't heard it all yet. Our audience get Beba—and then you remind the viewers about Maria, the greatest flamenco dancer in Spain! She's agreed to come for the filming, by the way—the old and the new, two for the price of one! What do you say, Zoë?'

'I'd say if I was Maria I'd be pretty insulted.'

'That's where you come in to it. You write the script and make sure she isn't insulted.'

'I can see you've got it all worked out, Philip—but after I write the script what will I cook? You do remember this is a cookery series?'

'Stop worrying, Zoë. I've got it all worked out. We're going to have a café-style setting, with a fabulous selection of food.'

'I see. And where are the ingredients coming from for this fabulous selection of food? And who is going to eat it all?'

'There's a vanload of produce arriving any time now. Come on, Zoë, don't be difficult.'

The thought of having Beba under the same roof for a moment longer than necessary didn't appeal—and Zoë wasn't happy about casual arrangements for food she hadn't picked out herself. But if she agreed she would be so frantically busy there would be no time to think about her personal problems…

'The girls have been round the village already, and everyone is keen to come back and act as extras for the programme, so we have our audience.'

'I do have some stock in the deep-freeze…'

'Don't get hung up on minor details, Zoë. This is going to be a sensational programme and you know it.'

'Food is a pretty large "minor detail" on a cookery show,' Zoë pointed out dryly. But it would prove to Beba—and Rico?—that she had bounced back without causing more than a ripple in her everyday schedule if she could pull it off. 'OK, I'll do it.' And then something else occurred to her. 'Was it you who installed Beba in my bedroom?'

'No, of course not. I didn't even know she had done that.'

His shock was genuine, Zoë realised. 'Don't worry, I moved her out. But you had better see she gets a nice suite of rooms if you want her happy for the programme.'

'She'll have the best.'

'No—I've already got that,' Zoë said, savouring her one small victory. She was starting to fire with enthusiasm. She always did for a new programme. 'I'll need some quiet time to work on the script, then I can get on to the food. When are we filming?'

'Tonight.'

'Tonight!' Get over it, Zoë thought. True, it didn't give her much time. But if they were filming, and Beba was dancing, Beba couldn't be with Rico. That suited her. And if Beba could dance as well as everyone said, it would make great television…

Zoë worked on her script in the bedroom, where she knew she would be undisturbed. She had one call from Philip, to warn her that Beba had insisted on complete artistic control over her performance. Zoë was happy to give it to her. The film would be edited before it was shown. Philip also told her that Beba was now happily installed in one of the grandest suites at the castle. Zoë was relieved to hear she was keeping a low profile, and had been most co-operative. One less thing to worry about, she thought with relief, replacing the receiver.

By the time the food was ready Zoë had to admit the team had done a great job. The Great Hall looked magical. Jewel-coloured tapestries and Persian rugs glowed in the candlelight, and there were colourful floral displays everywhere.

The setting was that of an intimate cellar club, with café tables arranged in groups around a circular wooden stage. People from the village had started to arrive, and were already being shown to their places. Zoë smiled with anticipation. She couldn't help it. This tense air of anticipation for the unexpected was what had drawn her to television in the first place.

But Rico was always there in her mind.

The worry, the uncertainty about him didn't go away. There had still been no word from him. She had tried telling herself it didn't matter, but that was a lie. All she wanted was for him to walk in now, walk up to her, take her in his arms and tell her she had nothing to worry about—that Beba meant nothing to him and never had.

There was no sign of Beba either.

People smiled, and she smiled back, but concern was nagging away at her. He should have been in contact by now. He drove too fast. Surely he hadn't had an accident?

Zoë spun round as the door opened. 'Maria! I'm so pleased you agreed to come.'

'I wouldn't miss this night for the world.'

'Have you seen Rico?'

'No.' She looked at Zoë with concern.

'I'm sorry, Maria, I'm sure he'll be along later. How's your arm?'

'Sore, but mending. I don't need the sling now, and I took the bandage off.'

'That's good.' Zoë could see Maria felt her agitation. So

much for not brandishing her private concerns in public! 'You
are dancing tonight? I'm sorry it's such short notice…'

As Maria touched her arm she smiled warmly into Zoë's
eyes. 'Maybe I will have the chance to dance with you, Zoë?'

I hope not—for the sake of the audience, Zoë thought
wryly—though even that, whether she bodged it or not, would
make good television. 'Do you know Beba well?' she said,
returning to the subject uppermost in her mind.

'Beba?' Maria paused. 'Yes, I know Beba.'

'Was she always so friendly with Rico?'

'You know about that?'

Zoë's heart plummeted. Time to act her socks off. But they
were standing very close, and Maria was very shrewd. 'Yes,
Rico told me all about it. They make a handsome couple.'

'You do know that she used to be my pupil?'

'Your pupil?' Of course. It all made sense now. 'I saw the
poster at the mountain hut.'

'My most celebrated pupil.' There was an odd expression
on Maria's face.

'I see.'

'No, you don't,' Maria assured her, patting Zoë's cheek.

'Is she with Rico now?'

'It would not surprise me.'

Zoë couldn't stop now. 'Have you seen them together here
at the castle—tonight?'

'Stop worrying, Zoë,' Maria said gently. 'Rico will be here.
He will not let you down.'

He already had, Zoë thought.

Her legs felt like lumps of lead as she showed Maria to her
table at the front of the stage. She felt sick and light-headed;
there were icy cramps in her stomach. She really had no idea
how she was going to get through the rest of the evening. But
then the floor manager beckoned to her urgently. She welcomed the distraction. Work had always proved a refuge.
Quite soon Wardrobe and Make-up would want her too, and

she still had to make a crucial addition to her script to explain that Beba had been Maria's star pupil. The news couldn't have come at a more useful time. As far as the show went, Zoë reflected dryly, it couldn't have worked out any better.

Half an hour later the cameras were ready to roll. The main lights had been switched off, and apart from the necessary television lights the only illumination now came from candle-light. It was the most romantic setting imaginable. But as Zoë stood waiting for her cue to introduce Beba she was sure her heart had shrivelled to the size of a nutmeg.

Her sights were firmly fixed on the single spotlight trained on the main entrance. The guitarist was already seated on his stool, and at any moment Beba would appear.

She started when the *tio* from the village touched her arm. She didn't want to offend him by pointing out that the red light would flash on at any second.

'You look worried.' He frowned.

'Always am just before we start recording,' Zoë explained in a whisper. 'Maria's saving you a seat at the front.'

Worried? Concern was eating her up inside. *Was Rico with Beba? How could Rico be with Beba?* The two thoughts were spinning in her mind until she thought she would go mad.

'You must be looking forward to seeing Beba dance?'

'She is a fine dancer.'

Zoë wondered at the *tio's* lack of enthusiasm for the local star. Maria had taught Beba to dance, so surely Beba's success reflected well on Cazulas as well as on her teacher?

A sudden sound made Zoë jump, and with another light touch to her arm the *tio* was gone. Preparing to do her voice-over, Zoë realised the sound she had heard was the rattle of castanets, played by an expert.

There was one more imperative tattoo, and then, wearing a scarlet dress so tight it might have been painted onto her naked body, Beba stepped into the spotlight—on the arm of Rico Cortes.

CHAPTER THIRTEEN

She couldn't break down. Not here—not with everyone to see. Zoë forced her concentration on to the small performance area and cleared her mind of everything but the music—that and her commentary between the various dances.

Beba danced with such purpose, such certainty, it made Zoë shiver. It was as if the young flamenco dancer siphoned up energy from the music and spat it out again in furious movement. Her stabbing heels beat faster than a hummingbird's wings, and there was such passion in her dance that inwardly Zoë recoiled from it. The swirling skirts of Beba's tight scarlet dress shattered the air into smothering perfumed waves.

The dance ended on a crashing chord. The proud head tilted down and Beba's fierce black stare found Zoë's face. At the same moment Zoë knew Rico was making his way discreetly around the back of the hall towards her. After a brief moment of silence the thunderous applause came. She took the chance to move away, but someone caught hold of her arm.

'Maria!' Looking round, Zoë saw the *tio* was talking to Rico. They were trying to hold a conversation above the cheers, the shouts and the stamping feet—the *tio* had his hand cupped to his ear.

'Do you hear that?' Maria whispered in her ear.

How could she not? Zoë thought, forcing a smile. The noise was deafening.

'Do you hear *duende*?' Maria persisted.

'No,' Zoë admitted. She could hear, *'Olé! Brava! Eso es!'*

She really wanted to go. She couldn't bear this any longer. What difference could one word make?

'Now you will hear *duende*!' Maria's voice was commanding as she thrust the beautiful lilac dress she had been holding over her arm into Zoë's hands.

'Are you mad?' Zoë looked down at it in amazement. 'I could never follow that.'

'I can.' Maria's eyes were twinkling again. 'Let us go now, and change into our performance clothes.'

'No!'

'Would you let me down, Zoë? Would you?' she said again, when Zoë remained silent. 'I have told your director; he knows all about this. He says it will be the perfect final sequence for your series.'

Zoë shook her head, thinking of Rico and how he would view her dancing right after Beba's spectacular display. She felt bad enough about the situation. How much humiliation could she take? 'No, Maria. I don't want to let you down, but I can't do it.'

'Yes, you can,' Maria insisted fiercely. 'Whatever happens on that stage, it will make good television.'

'Maria, please—'

'And I need you to help me into my dress. My arm, as I already told you, is still a little sore…'

Zoë made a sound of despair. She couldn't refuse. And now the *tio* had finished talking to Rico, and he was making fast progress around the hall towards her. 'All right,' she agreed tensely. 'I just hope you know what you are doing.'

'Of course I do,' Maria said firmly, pushing Zoë in front of her with her good arm.

Zoë would never know quite what happened on stage that night. She only knew that concern for Maria took her there, and the thought of how Rico had betrayed her supplied the passion.

Maria performed as she always did as if she had absorbed the emotional energy of every person in the audience and released it in breathtakingly fluid moves, and by the time the finale came Zoë hardly cared that Beba had joined them on stage.

'Do you hear it now?' Maria whispered in Zoë's ear.

Zoë listened. She had been so absorbed in her dancing she was hardly aware that it had come to an end, and that now the three of them were standing side by side, acknowledging the gratitude of the audience.

The cries of *'Duende!'* were coming from all around her, Zoë realised incredulously. She could hardly believe it, and then Rico was on stage too, and her mind was reeling as he seized her hands and raised them to his lips.

'You did it, Zoë! You did it!'

He seemed pleased...even proud. And he looked so handsome, with his seductive mouth curving into a grin. She couldn't bear it, and turned her face away. But he cupped her chin and brought her back so she had nowhere to look but into his eyes.

'You have just earned the ultimate accolade in the world of flamenco, Señorita Chapman.' Then he raised her arm and the crowd went wild.

Why didn't you tell me about Beba? Why didn't you warn me? Why did you make love to me when you knew she would be here? Was I just something to fill a gap in your schedule before you had to meet her?

All Zoë's pleasure had drained away. She was like a rag doll, limp and unresponsive. Rico hadn't noticed. He was already moving away from her to embrace his mother. Then finally he took Beba's hand, and Zoë saw the way the dancer looked at him, her dark eyes shining with adoration as he raised her arm in a victory salute.

As another great roar went up Zoë felt her eyes fill with tears. She hated herself for the weakness and could think of nothing but getting away—out of the spotlight, out of Cazulas, and out of Spain. Everyone was happy to see Rico and Beba together again—of course they were. And she was a fool if she thought El Señor Alarico Cortes would choose a cook over his very beautiful, very gifted fiancée.

She could never stand by and see the man she loved with another woman at his side. She had built a new life, won back her self-respect. Making herself available whenever Rico had an itch to scratch was not for her. Smiling brightly at the cameras for the last time, Zoë seized the chance to slip away.

When the knocking started up on her bedroom door, Zoë clutched the sheet to her chest and stayed motionless, listening.

'Zoë, it's me,' Rico called to reassure her. 'Open the door.'

She tensed. Was Beba with him? No—even Rico would not go that far. But Maria was right; the Cortes family did move in sophisticated circles. Rico might think they could make love all day, and again at night, with Beba sandwiched in between. She would not open the door, no matter how much he knocked...

But he didn't knock again. Zoë frowned. She couldn't help but be disappointed that he had given up so fast.

She turned to the window. 'Rico!'

'You should lock these doors at night,' he said, stepping into the room from the balcony.

'I always do.'

'Well, tonight you forgot.'

Instinct made her gaze past him, just to make sure he was alone.

'Who are you expecting?' he said quizzically.

'I didn't think Beba would want to be left alone.'

'Beba is never alone.' Rico laughed as he bent to switch on the light.

'Do you mind? I'm asleep.'

'No, you're not—unless you talk in your sleep.' He smiled as he sat down beside her.

'What do you think you're doing?'

'I'm taking my shoes off. I don't usually wear them in bed.'

'You're not getting into bed with me!'

'Why not?'

'Rico. I can't—'

'You can't what, Zoë?' He brushed a strand of hair back from her face. 'I thought we'd got past this.'

Even though every fibre of her being was filled with longing she pushed his hand away. 'Please—don't.'

'What's happened, Zoë?'

'Beba happened.'

'Beba?'

'You went to her after you slept with me.'

'She wanted to see me.'

'You don't even bother to deny it?' Zoë stopped. She could hear the hysteria rising in her voice.

'No. Why should I?'

This wasn't how it was supposed to be. She had intended to be brisk and to the point, to confront him with facts, hear him out, and then tell him to go. But life was never that clear-cut, or that simple. She should have known. 'I can't do this, Rico—this is never going to work for me.'

'What isn't going to work for you, Zoë? Are you afraid of me? Is that why you're pushing me away?'

She *was* afraid of him, but not in the way he thought. She didn't have what it took to sustain a relationship. A career, yes—she had proved that—but for some reason it seemed she wasn't meant to find happiness with a man. 'I can't believe you misled me again, Rico.'

'About Beba?' He stood up and looked down at her, the proud angles of his face harshly etched in the lamplight.

'She told me—'

'She told you what?'

'That you and she were an item.'

'Then she lied.'

'You never cared for each other?'

'I didn't say that.'

Zoë didn't want to hear any more; she couldn't bear to. 'If you'll excuse me,' she mumbled. Swinging her legs over the opposite side of the bed, she hurried to the bathroom. She closed the door and leaned back against it. Everything she had rebuilt before coming to Spain was in danger of collapsing, thanks to Rico.

But when she had calmed down a little she knew the answer didn't lie in hiding away from him. Grabbing her robe down from the back of the door, she threw it on, belting it tightly. She went into the bedroom again, and switched on the main light.

'Sit down, Rico.' She pointed to the elegant sofa positioned to take in the view from the balcony. 'We really need to get everything out in the open.'

'I'm all right—you sit down. You've had quite a night.'

She searched his face for irony; there was none. 'You can't have us both, Rico.' Standing stiffly, facing him, Zoë raked her hair until it stood around her head like a wild golden-red nimbus.

Rico's gaze never wavered. 'I don't want anyone but you, Zoë.'

How she wanted to believe him. How she wanted to close the small gap between them, throw her arms around his neck and tell him she would stay with him for ever, and under any circumstances. But that would only lead to bitterness and resentment in the end.

'Is there an understanding between the two of you?'

'There was.'

Spain was a traditional country; this was a very traditional part of Spain. Zoë couldn't imagine such 'understandings' were embarked upon lightly.

'I can see you must need an appropriate wife…'

Yes, he had thought that at one time, Rico remembered. When he was younger. When he'd made his first fortune he had been brim-full of arrogance—partly because he hadn't been sure what was expected of a young aristocrat with a huge amount of money in the bank. Now he realised it didn't matter how much money you had, or what your title was. The only thing that mattered was that you made your corner of the world a little better. His mother Maria had done that, without a fortune or a title, and she was his only benchmark for success.

'I don't *need* a wife at all. Do you want me to tell you what Beba's doing at the castle?'

Suddenly she wasn't sure that she did, Zoë realised. If she was going to leave Spain in one piece emotionally, she didn't want to hear another word. In fact, this was the moment she should tell Rico to get lost.

He didn't give her that option. In a couple of strides he had her arms in his grasp. 'I listened to you, Zoë, and now it's your turn to listen to me.'

Zoë tensed. Rico's gaze was frightening in its intensity.

'Or are you just too scared to risk your heart again?'

Scared? She was scared of nothing. She stopped fighting him and clenched her jaw.

'You've built walls so high around you, Zoë, you can't see what's happening outside your own stockade.'

'That's not true!'

'Isn't it? Oh, you're safe enough in there, but you're not going to have much of a life.'

'Just tell me this—are you engaged to Beba?'

'Beba was my fiancée.'

'Was?' Zoë made a short humourless sound. 'She certainly didn't give me the impression she was in the past tense. Oh, I'm glad you can smile about it!'

'I can smile where Beba's concerned—that's just the point. She doesn't change. That's why we're not together now— whatever she might think, or might have told you.'

'So what is the position between you? Did she just turn up

in Cazulas out of the blue—to help me make a television programme, perhaps?'

He ignored her sarcasm. 'Beba? Helping others? That's more in your line, Zoë. Beba was the star in my mother's dance class. We became lovers around the same time I heard I was going to inherit my father's title.'

'Do you think that was a coincidence?'

'I don't think anything is a coincidence where Beba is concerned. I was young, and I thought we were in love. I thought we loved each other. Then Beba discovered that my inheritance was just a title and nothing more—no money, no castle. She hadn't expected that. I explained that it was only a matter of time before I rebuilt the family fortune, but she couldn't wait. I can't blame her. She had talent. She could earn her own money. I was all fired up. It never occurred to me that Beba might not share my enthusiasm for the long years of poverty that lay ahead. She broke off our engagement and went to Madrid to seek her fortune.'

'Which she found,' Zoë murmured.

'I never wanted to hold her back, and I'm delighted that she has been so successful. I was equally determined that I would earn the right to be called El Señor Alarico Cortes de Aragon.'

'Which you did.'

'Yes.'

'And now Beba has returned to Cazulas for the one thing she doesn't have yet, and that's you.'

'Another trophy to add to the others.' Rico smiled wryly at her. 'I would have explained all this to you if I'd known what Beba planned to do in advance, and if my business meeting hadn't gone on for so long. When I arrived at the castle and found she was here it was already too late.'

'But you met with her?'

'I had to talk to her. I had to tell her how I feel about you.'

'About me?'

There was no such thing as dipping your toe in the water with Rico. It was total immersion or nothing. It was the sort of commitment Zoë feared above anything else. Staying safe inside her stockade, as Rico put it, had kept her sane since her divorce. The closest she had ever come to letting go was with him, and she didn't know if she had what it took to let go completely.

'It was only right to escort Beba onto the stage when she asked me to,' Rico went on. 'I knew that playing the tragic heroine suited her purpose. That sort of thing always puts her in the right mood for the dance. But I have no ambition to become an emotional punch-bag. She's just not my type of woman.'

'Are you sure about that?'

'Of course I'm sure. Didn't you notice all that anger and aggression? It has to come from somewhere, Zoë. Beba uses people. She sucks them dry and spits them out—they're just the fuel for her dance.'

'You make her sound so callous.'

'So lonely. That's why she came here to find me—to see if there was any chance of us getting together again.'

'And you refused her?'

'Of course I refused her. Beba and I don't love each other—we never did. I asked her to marry me because I thought I should, and she agreed to marry me—well, you know why. Circumstances pushed us together when we were too young to know any better, but we each had our own very different road to travel.'

'And now those roads have crossed again?'

'I want a wife who will travel the same road as me, Zoë. I don't want a woman who is trawling the world in search of the next thrill.'

'But if Beba had been different?'

Shaking his head, Rico gave a wry smile. 'Beba couldn't be different. Beba couldn't be you.'

'And Cazulas was too small to hold her?'

'The world is too small to contain Beba. She's only here now because she is in between tours. She feeds on drama. The stage, a new lover—it's all the same to her. There is no doubt in my mind at all, Zoë. It's you I want.'

Foreboding coloured everything Zoë was hearing—everything Rico was saying to her. El Señor Alarico Cortes would one day want a suitable wife—not one who travelled the world to pursue her own career. When that day arrived would she be expected to stand aside and spend the rest of her life in the shadows? Rico's father had been a Spanish grandee too. He'd given Maria the flamenco dancer a son, but hadn't married her. Was that par for the course? Was his proud, complex son now offering her his love along with the promise of future pain? Was that what she wanted? Passion with all the heat of flamenco that would burn itself out until it only existed in her memory like a few fast-fading chords?

'Won't you come downstairs to join the party?' Rico pressed, relaxing now he believed he had set everything straight. 'Maria and the *tio* are waiting to see you—to congratulate you on your success.'

It was the end of an intensive stretch of work for the crew. It was churlish of her to stay in her room. Rico didn't need to know that her mind was made up: she was leaving Cazulas for good.

Zoë actually flinched as the thought hovering in her mind became reality. Just outing it gave it clarity, gave it purpose, set it in stone. It was easier than she had imagined. She *was* leaving Cazulas for good. And not because she didn't believe Rico about Beba, but because she did. He really loved her, he really wanted her; she could see that now. But she had nothing to offer him in return. She didn't have anything left inside her. She didn't have the courage it took to risk her heart again, to risk the pain he could cause her. She had been safe feeling nothing…

'Zoë, look at me—don't shut me out.'

The look in Rico's eyes was so intense she felt dizzy, bewildered, disorientated. And then he took her hand and she felt the power he wielded, the force of his will, his strength, his passion flooding into her.

Escape for one more night. Physical pleasure so intense she could shut off the part of her that knew there must be consequences—Rico could offer her that. They could have one last night together, and then she would retreat inside that stockade he'd talked about—her stockade, where not even the memory of their affair would be able to reach her.

'If I put on the lilac dress again, would you take that photograph for Maria?'

'You know I will. Shall I wait outside while you change your clothes?'

'Do you mind?'

'Not at all.'

Zoë watched Rico until he left the room. After all the intimacy they'd shared it seemed bizarre to have such reserve spring up between them now. He respected her, and if she had been content to be his mistress without having to give her love she had no doubt he would have protected her. But it wasn't nearly enough.

When she was ready, Rico escorted Zoë downstairs again.

'I'm wearing the dress so Rico can take that photograph you wanted,' she said when they found Maria.

'You make it sound as if you're leaving us, Zoë.'

There was an expression in Maria's eyes that made Zoë look away. She could lie to herself—she had perfected the art. But she could never lie to Maria.

'Rico.' Beba came over the moment she spotted him. 'We were all wondering where you had got to.'

Her cold dark gaze lingered on Zoë's face, and Zoë was glad when Rico drew her arm through his own.

'I had some important business to attend to,' he said.

'So I see. Well, if you will excuse me…' She turned away, then swung back again. Seizing Zoë's hand, she clasped it in her own. 'I wish you luck.' She slanted a hostile glance at Rico. 'You're going to need it.'

Sour grapes? Zoë wondered. Or sound advice?

She could see the crew already starting to clear up some of the equipment. The hall was emptying fast. Once the series was in the can no one hung around; they had all been away from home too long as it was. She knew they would work through the night if necessary, just to be able to catch the first flight back. She would leave the castle shortly after them, though Rico didn't need to know that.

The arrival of Beba had shaken her. Rico had reassured her where Beba was concerned, but what happened when he wanted a wife? She couldn't give up the independence she had won at so high a price to become a rich man's mistress… But she could have one more night.

'Rico?'

Something in her voice told him what she wanted, and his eyes darkened with desire. 'Are you ready to go to bed now?'

'If you still want me.'

They said their goodnights quickly. And as their fingers intertwined Zoë could think of nothing but the next few hours as Rico led her towards the stairs.

CHAPTER FOURTEEN

ZOË'S lips slipped open beneath the gentle pressure of Rico's mouth. Deepening the kiss, he stripped off the lilac dress while his tongue sought out the dark, secret places in her mouth.

It was as if they had never made love before, her hunger for him was so great. He was inside her before they reached the bed with her legs locked around his waist and her arms secured round his neck, her fingers meshed through his hair. He supported her easily, with his strong hands beneath her buttocks, and the reassurance of feeling him hard and deep inside her was almost unbearably good.

She had to remember this moment for a lifetime, Zoë thought, as Rico lowered her onto the edge of the mattress.

They made love there, with no preliminaries and with no thought of seeking the luxury of the well-sprung bed. Zoë cried out her encouragement as Rico tipped her at an angle, resting her legs over his shoulders to increase satisfaction for them both. And all the time he moved inside her he murmured her name, and told her how much he loved her, and how he wanted to be with her for ever...

This was for ever, Zoë thought. For her, at least.

Zoë stopped waving as the last van disappeared out of sight. She could feel her colleagues' hugs still imprinted on her skin, and hear their words of encouragement and good wishes ringing in her ears. None of them knew how she felt inside. They would never know.

Rico had left her at dawn. It really couldn't have worked

out any better. He had some business to attend to back at the beach house, and so she had been spared a painful parting.

She had slept fitfully in his arms all night, dreading the morning, dreading the moment when she would tell him she couldn't stay in Cazulas. Her idea of sleeping with him one last time, making love with him half the night in the hope of keeping the memory alive, had been a terrible mistake. Instead of leaving her with tender memories to carry forward when she left Spain for good, it had left her with guilt and unbearable loss.

She had learned nothing from the past. She was betraying Rico just as she had been betrayed. Her ex-husband had won the final battle now she had completed the circle of violence. There was no physical violence, of course, but she was violating Rico's trust. She had taken his love and was letting it slip through her fingers because she didn't have the guts to hang on to it. She was still scared of commitment, still scared to risk her heart. She was brave enough to take the pleasure now—just not brave enough to take the consequences.

The best thing for Rico, the best thing all round, would be if she left without a fuss. Her suitcases were already packed, and she intended to drive to the station around noon.

It was strange being alone in the castle. Even Beba had packed up and gone, and it was a quiet, lonely place now. She couldn't bear the thought of leaving her friends in the village, but she didn't belong in Cazulas any more than Beba. Her life revolved around a television programme, and it was time to return to reality.

Back in the kitchen, Zoë could hardly bring herself to look at the collection of local pottery on the table. She was taking all of it back to England. She was quite sure Rico wouldn't want any reminders of her visit. The crew had left some empty packing cases for her, and a removal van was due to arrive before she left for the station. All the heavy equipment for the show that wouldn't fit into the vans had to be shipped back to the UK, and the pottery would be delivered to her London home at the same time.

She had been packing and wrapping for some time when she heard the music. Leaving the kitchen, she hurried into the hall.

'Good morning, Zoë.'

'Rico!'

He was sitting cross-legged on a stool in the centre of the floor, one hand caressing the neck of his guitar, the other hovering over the strings. She had thought it would be possible to get used to the idea of living without him, but in that instant Zoë knew she was wrong.

Turning back to his guitar, he started to play again, as if she wasn't there. The music held her transfixed. He stopped playing quite suddenly. His slap on the side of the guitar echoed around the empty hall. Laying the guitar down carefully on the floor, he stood, reminding her how tall he was, how commanding.

'When were you going to tell me you were leaving?'

Zoë stared at him. There was nothing she could say to justify her actions.

'Don't you think you owe me an explanation?'

'I'm sorry—'

'You're *sorry*?' he said incredulously.

'I need my work—'

'And?'

Zoë's voice was barely above a whisper. It was as if she was talking to herself, trying to convince herself and not him. 'I can't let anyone take over my life again.'

'Take over your life? What the hell are you talking about, Zoë?' He made no attempt to close the distance between them.

'It's all I've got. It's what I do.'

'It's all you had,' he said fiercely.

'You don't understand, Rico. I just can't be there for you.'

He turned away, but not before she saw the hurt in his eyes. 'That's different.'

His voice was hoarse, and he didn't look at her when he spoke. They might have been standing on separate ice floes, drifting steadily apart. But this was what she wanted, wasn't it—this final break between them? She just hadn't imagined doing it face to face. In her usual cowardly way she had been going to bury her head in the sand somewhere far away from Spain.

'You can't be there for me?' he repeated bitterly. 'So what was I, Zoë? Some type of experiment? Just a random male you could use to exorcise your ghosts?'

'Don't say that, Rico.'

'Why not? Because it's true?' He laughed, and it was a hard, ugly sound. 'You should be happy.'

'Happy?' Zoë could hear incredulity approaching hysteria in her voice.

'At least you know you're not frigid now.'

'Stop it!' She covered her ears.

'No, you stop it!' Rico said with an angry gesture. 'You come here to Cazulas. You seek help for your show, which I give to you freely. We make love—at least I did. Yes, I love you, Zoë,' he confirmed fiercely. 'But you just used me. You're no better than Beba!'

'Rico!' Through her shock, Zoë knew what he was saying was true. She reached out to him. 'Rico—don't go yet. Can't we talk?'

'Why shouldn't I go? The only reason I can think of for you wanting me to stay is that you need some more reassurance in bed. And frankly, Zoë, I'm not in the mood.'

The stool was kicked over as he snatched up his guitar, and then he went to the door. Halting with his hand on the heavy iron handle, he turned to her. 'You might as well have this.'

Zoë started towards him, but she was too late.

Putting an envelope on the table by the door, he walked out.

The castle was like a deserted shell. There was no life, no sound, nothing. Zoë's footsteps echoed on the stone-flagged floors as she completed her final check. Even the towering walls seemed to have grown cold and unfriendly. She was glad when she finally closed the heavy oak door behind her; an empty castle was a lonely place.

The removal van had taken the last of her things away, and the few bits and pieces she had found now could be loaded into the car. There was nothing for her to stay for. But before she left Cazulas for good there was one more stop she had to make.

Maria ushered her into the cottage. 'It's very good of you to see me,' Zoë said.

'Rico told me you were leaving.'

'Now I'm here, I don't know where to begin…'

'At the beginning?' Maria suggested gently. 'But first you must sit down. You look worn out.'

'No, no, I'm fine.' Rico's face flashed into her mind, and then the contents of the envelope he had left behind. She bit her lip. 'Truthfully, Maria, I'm not fine.'

'I can see that. Come and sit here with me at the fireside. You take this chair across from mine.'

The overhead fan was whirring. It was almost midday. The shutters were closed and it was hot in the small room. But the fireside was a symbol to Zoë—a symbol of Maria's happy, well-ordered life.

And as she talked things through with Maria it was as if Zoë saw everything clearly for the first time. She saw how she was pushing Rico away each time he got close, grabbing at excuses to justify her actions. She understood the bewilderment she had felt at discovering that having the most wonderful sex with him hadn't been enough to exorcise her demons, after all. She had to stop holding back before that could happen, but she was still terrified of risking herself in a relationship again—so terrified she hadn't even paused to consider how Rico might feel.

And now she was ashamed. She was particularly ashamed in front of Maria, who had given so much of herself so generously—to Rico, to his father, and to the village of Cazulas. If Maria hadn't prompted her so gently, encouraged her so warmly, Zoë knew she would never have had the confidence to pour her heart out as she did.

When she had finished, she gave Maria the envelope Rico had left at the castle.

Maria hesitated, holding it in her hands.

'Please read what's inside,' Zoë prompted.

Maria read the papers, and then put them carefully back into the envelope.

'My son must love you very much. Did you doubt him?'

'Before I met Rico I couldn't see beyond what had happened to me in the past.'

'And after you met him?'

Zoë turned away, unable to meet Maria's candid stare.

'Since he inherited his father's title Rico has been prey to fortune hunters and the press. You have a mutual enemy in the paparazzi, Zoë.'

'Yes, I can see that now.'

'Rico was furious when he returned from his travels to discover that his land agent had leased Castillo Cazulas to a television company. But then he fell in love with you—'

'And made me a gift of the castle.'

'Don't look so surprised. He wanted you to have a Spanish headquarters; the castle is perfect. It is far too big for a family home. Imagine what a film set it will make. Rico must have been on the point of asking you to marry him.'

'Marry him? No, you're wrong about that, Maria.'

'Why else would he have done this? The castle was your wedding present.'

'He would never marry me.' Zoë tried to reason it out. She wanted nothing more than to accept that what Maria had said was true, made sense—but her mind just wouldn't accept it. Deep down she still believed she wasn't good enough. 'I could never—' She stopped, remembering Maria's history.

'Be his mistress?' Maria finished for her. 'As I was to his father? No, don't look so embarrassed, Zoë. You haven't offended me. I made my choice, and now you must make yours. But I can assure you Rico isn't looking for a mistress. He saw how unhappy it made his father. Yes.' She put her hand up when Zoë started to interrupt. 'Rico's father always wanted to marry me. He insisted my fears about our differing backgrounds were unfounded. He was ahead of his time; I was not. I know Rico loves you, Zoë. He wants you with him. He must have known how you would feel about such a life-change. He wanted you to keep your independence, your company—even your own accommodation, if that was what would make you happy.'

'A castle?' Zoë said wryly.

Maria sighed. 'Rico never does things by halves—and, after what you have told me today about your past, I think he wanted to protect you from uncertainty, do everything he could to reassure you. I think he loves you very much.' Maria's soft brown eyes bathed Zoë's face in compassion. 'And now you think it is too late. That is why you have come to me. You think you need my help.'

As their gazes locked, Zoë realised she had never needed anyone's help as much as she needed Maria's. 'I don't know what I can do to put things right,' she admitted huskily, 'or if it's possible to put things right.'

'You are strong enough to know what is right. You just

can't see it yet. You don't need me or your television company to cling to. You're a survivor, like me, Zoë. You know what you have to do.'

Zoë found Rico walking barefoot at the water's edge in front of the beach house. His jeans were rolled up and a soft breeze was lifting his blue-black hair as he faced the wind with his hands shoved deep inside his pockets.

She didn't have to see his face to know how much he was hurting—how much she had hurt him. There could be no more hiding inside the stockade. No more hiding, full stop. Reaching out, putting her heart on the same line as his, was exactly what she wanted to do.

'Zoë?' Rico whirled round with surprise. 'I thought you would have left for the airport by now.'

'Rico.' Zoë's heart lurched when she saw the weariness in his eyes. 'Can we talk?'

'Why not?' Opening his arms, he gestured around. 'There are only seabirds to hear us.'

Digging into the back pocket of her jeans, she pulled out the envelope. 'You didn't expect me to walk away after you left this at the castle?'

He didn't answer. He just folded his arms and stared at her.

'I've come to give it back to you.'

'That's a pity.' He looked at the envelope and turned it over in his hands. 'I grew up believing it was my destiny to own Castillo Cazulas. But when I brought it back into the family again I discovered it was just a large, empty building.'

'That's exactly what I thought when I locked it up just now.'

'When you were there the whole place was transformed.' Holding her gaze, Rico shook his head and smiled a smile that didn't quite make it to his eyes. 'Your programme, your team—you brought it back to life, Zoë. It was exactly what the old place needed.'

'Chaos?'

This time they both smiled.

Straightening the envelope he had tightly clenched in his fist, Rico held it out. 'When Castillo Cazulas was first built a whole community thrived there, not just one family. I want the castle to live again through you. Take it, Zoë. Castillo Cazulas is nothing without you. I'll probably sell it.'

'You can't give me a castle,' Zoë said incredulously. 'Rico, that's ridiculous.'

'That's what I keep telling myself.' He shrugged as he thrust the envelope into her hands.

Zoë shook her head. The only sound was the wind, and the sea pounding on the shore at their feet. 'I couldn't be in Cazulas, knowing I might see you, bump into you.'

'I don't want Castillo Cazulas for the very same reason,' Rico admitted. 'I could never see the castle now without thinking of you.'

'I'm sorry—this was a mistake. I should never have come.'

Turning, Zoë began walking quickly back across the sand towards the road, where she had left the car.

'Zoë—'

Rico's voice wavered on the wind, and then sank beneath the noise of the surf. Was this what she really wanted? Zoë wondered, her steps faltering. A lifetime of wondering, *What if*? A lifetime of running away from the past? A life without Rico in it? Hadn't the time come to stop running—to face up to life—to face him?

They both turned at the same moment.

Zoë didn't know who took the first step. She only knew that she was running with the wind at her back, and then Rico tasted of salt and sunshine, and when his arms closed around her she knew it was the only reassurance she would ever need.

The lease for Castillo Cazulas lay forgotten on the sand, and then the breeze picked it up and carried it away out to sea.

'You can't leave Cazulas, Zoë,' Rico said, pulling away

from her at last. 'We need you here. I need you. The village needs you. You're good for all of us. We love you. I love you. Please tell me you'll stay.'

'How can you ask me that when I've been so selfish—when I've hurt you so badly?'

'You haven't been selfish,' Rico assured her. Bringing her hands to his lips, he kissed them passionately. 'You were knocked down to the ground, Zoë. It takes time to grow straight again, to grow tall. But I'll wait for you for ever, if that's what it takes.'

Zoë was touched, dazed—even shamed by Rico's declaration. He saw so much where she had been blind. But her eyes were wide open now. This proud, passionate man was every bit as vulnerable when it came to love as she was.

Reaching up, she traced his cheek with her hand. 'I love you with all my heart, Rico. You've shown me what love should be, and I'll never leave you.' And she never would, Zoë realised; with or without his ring.

'I'm not asking you to give up anything, as long as you promise to leave some space in your life for me.'

'You've got it,' Zoë assured him. 'But it's a rather big space, if that's all right with you?'

'That's just perfect.' He dragged her close. 'Now, who shall we have to cater for the wedding?'

'The wedding?' Zoë stared incredulously into Rico's face as he heaved a mock sigh.

'I suppose you should have the night off on your wedding day.'

'Rico, what are you saying?'

'I'm saying the caterers will have quite a lot to live up to—'

'Rico!'

'Did I forget something?'

'You know you did!'

'Will you marry me, Zoë?' he said, growing suddenly serious. And when she just stared at him he knelt down in the wet sand and reached for her hand.

'You'll ruin your jeans—'

'Then say yes quickly, or I'll have to take them off.'

'Then it will take me a very long time indeed to accept your proposal.' Kneeling in front of him, Zoë put her hands in his. 'Yes, I'll marry you, Rico. And I'll love and honour and cherish you for ever—'

'There's just one condition for the wedding,' he cut in, drawing her close.

'Oh?' Zoë murmured against his mouth. 'What's that?'

'No cameras, *mi amor*.'

EPILOGUE

CAZULAS had never seen a wedding like it, the village *tio* assured Zoë excitedly. And they both agreed that it must be true when the King of Spain and his beautiful Queen attended the marriage ceremony—along with all of Zoë's friends and what seemed like half of Spain.

The dapple-grey horses that drew her wedding carriage had bells and ribbons bound through their glossy manes, and everything she wore for the wedding had been bought in Paris, where she had enjoyed a 'pre-marriage honeymoon', as Rico had insisted on referring to their trip.

Events had moved swiftly after that late afternoon together on the beach. It was the way they had both wanted it.

Breakfast in Madrid, lunch in Paris: Zoë discovered such things were commonplace in the life of El Señor Alarico Cortes de Aragon and his wife-to-be. To put the seal on their new life together, Rico never mentioned the little notebook Zoë took everywhere with her to jot down ideas for her new television series.

'Everyone in Cazulas can see that El Señor Alarico Cortes of Aragon has met his match,' the *tio* exclaimed, reclaiming Zoë's attention. 'Rico is very much in love.' He tapped the side of his nose in the familiar gesture.

'And I get to take the photographs,' Maria exclaimed, snapping away furiously.

'Are you really happy, Zoë?' Rico asked her later, when they danced together.

'Yes, I'm utterly, completely and totally happy. And as for this—' She gazed around at the glittering throng of friends and family Rico had assembled to celebrate their wedding day. 'This is *duende* for me—how about you?'

Rico drew her a little closer. 'Every moment I'm with you, Zoë, is a whole lot better than that.'

THE SOUTH AMERICAN'S WIFE

KAY THORPE

CHAPTER ONE

SOFT but insistent, the sound of her name drew Karen out of a dreamless sleep. She opened her eyes to gaze for a blank moment or two at the unfamiliar, sun-filled room, her mind struggling to orientate itself.

Her eyes dropped to the lean, brown masculine hand covering hers where it lay on the white bed cover, travelling slowly up the length of a bronzed muscular arm to reach the face of the man seated at the bedside: a vital masculine face beneath thick black hair, short-cropped to control its curl.

'So you're back with us at last,' he said in heavily accented English.

Mind still fogged, Karen eyed him in perplexity. 'I don't understand,' she murmured, surprised to hear how weak her voice sounded. 'What happened? Where am I?'

Some nameless expression flickered across the dark eyes. 'You were involved in an accident and suffered a concussion,' he said. 'You're in hospital here in Rio.'

The fog deepened. 'Rio?'

'Rio de Janeiro.' He paused, brows drawing together. 'Do you not remember?'

Karen stared at him in total confusion. Rio de Janeiro? That was in Brazil, wasn't it? The farthest she'd ever been from home was Spain!

'I don't understand,' she repeated helplessly. 'Who are you?'

There was no immediate answer; the expression on the hard-boned face was disturbing. When he did speak it was in measured tones. 'I'm Luiz Andrade. Your husband.'

She froze, eyes wide and dark, mind whirling. 'I don't have a husband,' she got out. 'What kind of game is this?'

The hand still covering hers tightened as she tried to draw it away. 'The concussion has confused you. Relax, and everything will come back to you.'

'No, it won't, because it isn't true!' She pressed herself upright, wincing as pain shot through her head, but in no frame of mind to give way to it. 'I'm Karen Downing! I live in London! I've never been to Rio de Janeiro in my life, and I'm certainly not married—to you or anyone!'

'Hush! You must not agitate yourself this way.' Looking concerned, he reached for the bell-push on the bedside table. 'The doctor will give you something to calm you. When you waken, everything will be clear again.'

'No!' She tore her hand free, shrinking as far as she could get from this stranger, now on his feet and towering over her. 'It's all lies!'

'Why would I lie?' he asked. 'For what possible reason would I claim to be your husband if it were not the truth?'

'I don't know!' she flung back. 'All I do know is that I never saw you before in my life!'

As if on cue, the door opened to admit a uniformed nurse. Looking from one to the other, she said something in a language totally foreign to Karen's ears, answered by the man claiming to be her husband in what appeared to be the same language.

'What did you tell her?' she demanded as the woman exited again.

'To fetch a doctor,' he said. 'You're obviously suffering from a temporary amnesia.'

'There's nothing temporary about it!' she claimed. 'Whatever this is about, you can forget it!' She glanced down at the white hospital smock she was wearing, then wildly about her. 'Where are my clothes?'

'The ones you were wearing at the time of the accident have been disposed of,' he said. 'Others will be brought when you're deemed fit to be discharged.'

'I want to go now!' she shot back at him. 'You can't keep me here against my will.'

Powerful shoulders lifted. 'To where would you go? You know no one in Rio.' A muscle jerked in the firm jawline as if he'd clamped his teeth together on some addition to that statement. 'Be patient,' he went on after a moment, 'and everything will be all right.'

He turned as the door opened again, this time to admit a white-coated doctor, addressing him in the same language he'd used with the nurse. Portuguese was the language spoken in Brazil; Karen knew that for a fact. She felt trapped in a never-ending nightmare.

The fight went out of her suddenly. She subsided on to the bed, unable to summon the strength of either mind or body to protest when the doctor produced a syringe. Sleep would be a welcome release from the turmoil in her head.

She opened her eyes again to soft lamplight, and for a moment imagined herself safe in her own bedroom, having fallen asleep reading as she often did.

Only it wasn't her room, and it hadn't been a dream, because the same man was seated at the bedside.

'How are you feeling now?' he asked.

Her voice came out low and ragged. 'Afraid.'

Face expressionless, he said, 'Do you know me?'

Karen shook her head, too demoralised by the realisation that the nightmare hadn't ended to summon any semblance of spirit.

'So what exactly *do* you remember?' he asked.

'I'm Karen Downing,' she said. 'I'm twenty-three years old, and I share a flat in London with a friend who works for the same firm. My parents were killed in a plane crash four years ago.'

That memory alone was enough to pierce her fragile control. She swallowed on the lump in her throat, recalling the agony of those days, weeks, months it had taken her to come to terms with her loss.

'This much I already know,' Luiz Andrade returned. 'What appears to have happened is that your mind has somehow blanked out the past three months of your life. The three months you've spent here in Brazil as my wife.' He paused again, as if gathering himself. 'We met at the hotel where you were spending a holiday. We were married within the week.'

'That's impossible!' Karen burst out. 'I'd never...'

She broke off, biting her lip. If she couldn't remember, how could she be sure of *what* she might have done? But three months! Three whole months missing from her life! It didn't seem possible!

'How did I get to Rio?' she asked, forcing herself to calm down a little. 'I couldn't afford a holiday in Brazil on my earnings.'

'You told me you had won a sum of money on your

lottery, and decided to see something of the world out-side of Europe while you had the opportunity.'

'So you didn't marry me on the assumption that I was rich,' she murmured, trying to make sense of the story.

The strong, sensual mouth slanted briefly. 'It was your beauty that attracted my eye, your personality that captured my heart.' He registered the expression that crossed her face with another humourless smile. 'You looked much the same way the first time I made my feelings clear to you—as if you doubted your power to stir a man to such a degree. Only when we made love did you begin to believe in me.'

Warmth rose beneath her skin as her eyes dropped involuntarily down the length of his body to the lean hips and long legs clad in close-fitting white jeans, the stirring deep down in the pit of her stomach no fluke of imagination.

'You were a virgin,' he went on softly. 'That in itself would have been enough to seal my fate. It was fortunate that you felt for me too, because I would not easily have let you go.'

It had to be true, Karen thought desperately. As he'd said before, what possible reason could he have to lie? If only she could find even the slightest kink in the blanket cloaking her mind!

'You said we were married within a week of meeting?' she ventured.

'Just five days, to be precise. For me, it would have been sooner, but there were necessary formalities to be observed. We travelled to my home in São Paulo the following day.'

Karen's brows were drawn in the effort to recall,

but there wasn't even a glimmer. 'You're saying I never went back home at all?'

'There seemed no need when you had so little to return for. Your friend was contacted, and your place of work.'

'But my things!'

'Most of which you had with you. The apartment apparently was rented. The few items you did express a desire to have were despatched by your friend.'

Karen absorbed the information in silence for a moment, trying to imagine Julie's reaction to the news. 'It must have been a tremendous shock for her,' she said at length.

'I imagine it was. You're still in touch with her, if you feel the ring you wear isn't verification enough.'

Karen raised her hand slowly to gaze at the wide gold band, shaking her head in numb acceptance. 'I believe you. I *have* to believe you! It's just so difficult to take in.'

'It must be.' Luiz leaned forward to ease his position, lips twisting as she flinched. 'You have nothing to fear. Retribution is farthest from my mind.'

Karen felt her heart jerk. 'Retribution?' she got out. 'For what?'

It was apparent from the expression in the dark eyes that he regretted having said what he had. 'There are matters perhaps best left alone for the present,' he declared. 'The problems are many already without adding to them.'

'I want to know what you meant,' she insisted, every nerve in her body on edge. 'I have a right to know!'

The hesitation was brief, the lift of his shoulders signifying resignation. 'Very well. You came to Rio in the company of a man named Lucio Fernandas, with whom you had apparently been carrying on an affair. I followed you in order to bring you back, but the accident happened before I even reached the city. Perhaps fortunately,' he added on a harder note, 'or I may have been driven to measures that would have done none of us any good.'

Karen had difficulty finding any words at all. An affair? She'd been having an affair!

'Are you sure?' she asked faintly.

The firm mouth acquired a cynical slant. 'Why else would you have run away with the man?'

'I don't know,' she admitted. And then with a flash of spirit, 'But if it is true, why on earth would you have wanted me back?'

'What is mine remains mine.' The statement was all the more compelling for its lack of force. 'There has never been, nor ever will be, a divorce in the Andrade family—no matter what the provocation.'

Karen felt a sudden shiver run down her spine. She made a valiant effort to regain control of herself.

'So where is he, this Lucio Fernandas?'

'Vanished, like the coward he is!' The contempt was searing. 'You were alone when the medics reached you.'

'Reached me where?'

'At the road outside the airport where you were hit by a car. It was fortunate that your bag wasn't stolen while you lay unconscious. Once your identity was proven, news was relayed to our home, then passed to me on landing.' His jaw contracted. 'You were unconscious for almost two hours. It was feared that your skull was fractured.'

Karen considered the foregoing, feeling ever more

confused. 'You said the news was passed to you on landing?'

'I set out after you the moment I became aware of your departure this morning,' Luiz acknowledged. 'You'd taken your passport, but I doubted that you would have gone straight to the international airport in case of pursuit. I was right. Unfortunately, I was fifteen minutes too late to catch you at Congonhas. I took the next flight to Rio. Having first checked that Fernandas was on the plane too,' he added, anticipating the question hovering on her lips. 'There was no mistake.'

'I'm…sorry.' It was totally inadequate, but all she could come up with for the moment.

The dark head inclined. 'I'm the one who should be sorry. I shouldn't have told you all this so soon.' He got to his feet, body lithe as a panther's. 'You must rest. I'll see you again in the morning.'

Stranger or not, she didn't want him to go. At least while he was here she could keep on asking the questions crowding her mind—keep on hoping for that breakthrough.

'I can't stay here!' she exclaimed on a note of desperation.

'You have to stay.' His tone brooked no argument. 'At least until we can be sure you suffered no deeper damage. Perhaps a night's sleep will restore you.'

He didn't believe that any more than she did, Karen reckoned. Whatever the reason for her memory loss, it was going to take more than a night's sleep to restore it. In the meantime, she had no other recourse but to do as he said.

Thankfully, he made no attempt to touch her in any way, but simply lifted a hand in farewell. She watched him go to the door, appraising the tapering line from broad shoulder to narrow waist and hip. A fine figure of a man in any language. She had lain in his arms, known the intimate intrusion of his body. How could any woman forget that? How could any woman forget *him*?

The nurse who came in after he'd gone was different from the one before, but kindness itself. She insisted on helping Karen across to the *en suite* bathroom. A welcome hand, Karen found when she stood up.

There was a full length mirror on the back of the bathroom door. The face looking back at her was pale, throwing into sharp contrast the purpling bruise at the temple. The wide-spaced green eyes looked bruised too, the soft, full mouth vulnerable. There was some grazing across cheek and jawline, though superficial enough to make any scarring unlikely.

If nothing else had convinced her of the passage of time, the couple of inches her hair had grown since she last recalled looking at it would have done so. Natural silver-blonde in colour, it fell curtain straight to her shoulders.

Luiz would be in his early thirties, she calculated. The kind of man most women would find devastatingly attractive, she had to acknowledge. She could well imagine the impact he would have had on her at first sight: an impact deep enough to make her willing to give up everything she'd ever known just to be with him.

Which made the idea of her having had an affair with another man within three months of marrying him even harder to believe.

The nurse waiting outside knocked on the door. 'You are well?' she called.

Karen gathered herself together. There was nothing to be gained from standing here grappling with matters she had no knowledge of. All she could hope for was eventual enlightenment.

A sleeping pill gave her a good night's rest, but morning brought no change. Awake at five-thirty, with little of yesterday's physical unsteadiness left, she got up to take a shower and wash her hair. She had no make-up to hand, and nothing but the gown left by last night's nurse to put on, but at least she felt bodily refreshed.

Where she went from here she had no clear idea. She was married to a man she not only didn't remember, but whose trust she had apparently betrayed. Even if he was prepared to take her back, could she bear to go with him?

Yet what other choice did she have when it came right down to it? She had neither home nor job to return to in England, even if she still had the means left to get there.

Back in the bedroom, she drew the window blind to look out on a picture postcard view of sparkling white skyscrapers and green parks stretching down to a sea the same deep blue as the great bowl of sky above it. Rising from a jutting peninsula, the conical shape of Sugar Loaf Mountain was recognisable from a multitude of travelogues.

Built up here in the foothills of the backing mountains, this was no common or garden hospital, Karen realised—something she should have known already from the standard of both furnishings and facilities. Luiz Andrade was obviously a man of some means.

She dismissed the idea that that might have had something to do with her readiness to marry him. If the very thought of it turned her stomach now, it would certainly have done the same then.

Breakfast was brought by yet another nurse, who spoke no English at all. Karen picked at the fruit and cereal, mind still going around in circles. Physically she was surely well enough to leave the hospital today, which made it imperative that she come to terms with her predicament.

Luiz Andrade was her husband. That much she had to accept. What concerned her the most at present was what he might expect from her. She had no idea of a wife's rights here. For all she knew, he could be within his in demanding an immediate resumption of marital relations, regardless of her condition. There had been an element of ruthlessness about him last night when he'd spoken of what he might have done had he caught up with her missing lover. It wasn't beyond the realms of possibility that she might have suffered some form of retribution herself before being dragged back to wherever it was that they lived.

She was in a state bordering on panic by the time Luiz put in an appearance. He was wearing the same white jeans and shirt—both items freshly washed and pressed from the look of it.

'I brought no change of clothing,' he said, correctly interpreting the unspoken question. 'There was no time. The hotel where I spent the night provides laundry facilities.' He studied her, dark eyes revealing nothing of his thoughts. 'How do you feel now?'

'Much the same,' she acknowledged, fighting the

urge to throw a wobbly. 'Mentally, at any rate. Physically, I don't think there's a great deal wrong with me.'

'We'll allow the doctors to decide that.' He moved to take a seat on the edge of the bed itself, registering her involuntary movement with a narrowing of his lips. 'You certainly look more yourself this morning. Apart from the bruising, of course. Is your head very painful still?'

'Only if I move it too sharply.' Karen was doing her best to maintain a stiff upper lip, vitally aware of the warmth radiating from the well-honed body. 'I'd feel a whole world better for a touch of lipstick!'

'You have no need of cosmetics to enhance your looks,' he declared. 'Your hair alone is colour enough.'

'I washed it,' she said, desperate to keep the conversation on an inconsequential level. 'It was filthy.'

'Hardly surprising after being dragged in the dust.' Luiz put up a hand to tuck a still damp strand back from her cheek, refusing this time to be put off by her jerky movement. 'Is my touch so obnoxious to you?'

'It's an automatic reflex,' she said. 'Nothing personal. I just can't get my head round this whole situation.'

'I find it difficult myself,' he admitted. 'You gave no indication that you no longer found my attentions desirable. Our lovemaking the very night before you left was—'

'Don't!' Karen was trembling, the muscle spasm high in her inner thighs a hint that her body might remember what her mind did not. 'Can't we talk about something else?'

'What would you suggest?' he asked drily.

She cast around. 'Your home?'

'*Our* home,' Luiz corrected. 'The home to which we shall be returning.' He shifted from the bed to the chair he had occupied the night before, face expressionless again. 'São Paulo is many kilometres from here, the city the largest in Brazil, the state one of the richest. Guavada is a cattle ranch lying to the northwest of the city.

Nothing of what he was telling her meant anything. A cattle ranch!

'You're a manager or something?' she hazarded.

About to answer, Luiz broke off as the door opened to admit the same white-coated doctor from the night before, getting to his feet to greet the man.

The latter came to examine the bruise on Karen's temple, shining a torch into each eye before finally pronouncing himself satisfied with her condition.

'You are fortunate,' he said, 'that the damage was no worse.'

'I don't see amnesia as a light matter,' she retorted. 'Have you any idea how long it might last?'

The man hesitated, obviously reluctant to commit himself to a prognosis. 'Your memory could return at any time,' he said at length. 'Shock can do many things to the mind. You must be patient and try not to worry about it.'

Easy enough to say, Karen reflected hollowly. How could she *not* worry about it?

Luiz walked with the man to the door, returning to announce that she was cleared to leave the hospital.

'Your bag will be brought for you to select fresh clothing,' he said. 'Shall you need help in dressing?'

'No!' The denial came out sharper than she had intended, drawing another of the cynical smiles.

'I was thinking of a nurse's assistance, not my own.'

'I'm sorry.' She made a helpless little gesture. 'It isn't that I don't trust you.'

'Is it not?' he asked softly. 'Can you truly claim to believe that every word I've spoken is the truth?'

'I have to believe it,' she said. 'I don't have any other choice.'

'No,' he agreed, 'you don't. Just as I have no other choice.'

He had gone before Karen could summon the strength for any further exchange. Not that there was a great deal left to say. She was going with him because she had nowhere else to go. To what exactly she had still to discover.

The leather suitcase that arrived a few moments later was accompanied by a leather handbag, neither of which she recognised. She rifled swiftly through the contents of the latter, finding a passport in her married name, along with a wallet containing a wad of foreign currency.

She had no idea of the worth. Nor did it make a great deal of difference to the present state of affairs. What she did wonder was just what plan she and this Lucio Fernandas had supposedly made.

There was nothing in the handbag to provide an answer to that question. She opened the suitcase, disconcerted by the jumble of clothing inside. Packed hastily and with little regard to content from the look of it, which suggested a decision made bare minutes before departure rather than a planned exit. Stuck in the middle of it all was a framed photograph that brought a lump to her throat. It had been taken on a camping holiday bare months before her parents had been killed. They were laughing together, holding up the tiny fish her mother had just caught in the river flowing behind them. A handsome pair, with everything to live for.

Julie would have sent it through along with the other things she'd asked for, Karen concluded, blinking the tears from her eyes. It would have been the last thing she'd have left behind, for certain.

She sorted out a pair of lace panties and matching bra, topping them with a white skirt and sleeveless cotton top she'd never to her knowledge seen before. There were only two pairs of shoes. She chose the pale beige sandals that were the only ones with a highish heel. At five feet six she was far from short, but she needed the boost to face a man over six feet in height with any degree of confidence at all.

The handbag yielded a pouch containing a pale pink lipstick, smoky eye-shadow and a mascara wand. No surprises there: she'd never used a lot of make-up. She donned the touch of lipstick she'd spoken of, and ran a comb through her dried hair. The bruising looked worse than it had the night before, as did the grazes on her cheek and jaw, but she had more to think about than her appearance.

Her last clear memories were of attending a leaving party for a workmate, followed by dinner out with a group from the office. Julie had been out herself when she had got back to the flat. She'd made a hot drink and gone straight to bed.

That had been the twelfth of September. The day before yesterday, so far as her mind was concerned. Luiz had said they'd been married three months, but that didn't tell her the date now.

He supplied an answer to that question on his return. 'It's the twenty-seventh of January,' he said. 'More than halfway through our summer. The temperatures on the plateau are milder than here on the coast. While the days are hot at this time of the year, the humidity is low, the nights refreshingly cool.'

'It sounds good.' Karen was doing her utmost to stay on top of her emotions.

Luiz came to close and lock the suitcase she'd left open on the bed, hoisting it effortlessly up. 'I have a taxi waiting to take us to the hotel.'

'Hotel?' she queried.

'I think it better that the two of us spend some time together before returning to Guavada,' he said. 'We have a great deal to discuss.'

Karen forced herself into movement, reluctant to abandon the only bit of security she knew right now. Luiz went ahead to open the door for her, falling into step at her side to traverse a short, beautifully tiled corridor to a bank of lifts.

The one that arrived silently and smoothly in answer to his summons was empty. They descended without speaking, to emerge in a luxuriously appointed lobby. The receptionist on duty at a central desk bade them a smiling farewell, expressing what Karen took to be good wishes for the future. A forlorn hope indeed while the past months remained a blank.

Although it was still only a little after nine-thirty, the temperature outside was already soaring. Karen was glad to dive into the air-conditioned taxi-cab. With the suitcase stowed, Luiz slid in beside her. His thigh lay next to hers, the firm muscularity clearly defined beneath the fine cotton of his jeans when he moved.

Stripped, he would be magnificent, came the unbidden thought, bringing a sudden contraction deep down in the pit of her stomach. She would have seen him like that for certain—as he had no doubt seen her. She wondered how she, so unpractised in full-blown love-making, had managed to satisfy a man who would certainly have been no virgin.

They drove down through a city humming with workaday energies to a luxury hotel overlooking a superb crescent of white beach that was already heavily populated. Sugar Loaf reared now to the left, outlined against a sky beginning to cloud over a little.

'Is it going to rain, do you think?' Karen asked, turning from the balconied window—more for something to say than through any real interest in the weather. 'Summer is the rainy season out here, isn't it?'

Watching her from across the superbly furnished and decorated room, Luiz inclined his head. 'It is, yes.' His regard was penetrating. 'You recall that much then?'

'Not the way you mean,' she said. 'I must have read it somewhere.'

'Then the view out there means nothing to you?'

Karen's brows drew together. 'I've seen it in pictures.'

'But no more than that?'

'No.' Heart thudding against her ribcage, she added, 'What else might it mean?'

'It's the view you had from your room in this same hotel three months ago,' he said. 'Not the same room, I admit, but a replica of it. I hoped it might strike some spark of recollection.'

'It hasn't.' Her tone was flat. 'I must have won quite a lot to afford to stay in a place like this.'

'Several thousand pounds, I believe. A one-time opportunity to see how the other half lived, was how you excused the extravagance. There would have been little left to take home with you, for certain.'

'Except that I found myself a husband who *could* afford to stay in places like this.' She made a gesture of self-disgust. 'Forget I said that, will you?'

The dark head inclined again. 'It's forgotten.'

Considering his expression a moment ago, Karen doubted it. If she wanted to alienate him any more than he already must be alienated, considering the reason he'd followed her to Rio, she was going the right way about it.

He was leaning against a chest of drawers on the far side of the queen-size twin beds. Karen could only be thankful that there were two of them—although the thought of sharing even a room with him was daunting.

'I have the room next door,' he said, reading her mind with an ease she found daunting in itself. 'I've no intention of pressuring you into anything you find distasteful.'

'I'm sorry.' Karen scarcely knew what else to say. 'It isn't that I find you...unattractive.'

'A start, at least.' His tone was dry. 'Patience is no particular virtue of mine, but it seems I must learn to employ it. Perhaps sight of our home will help.'

'Perhaps.' Karen hesitated, reluctant to put the idea in his mind if it wasn't there already, yet needing reassurance. 'You don't think I'm pretending to have lost my memory, do you?'

His expression underwent an indefinable alteration. 'What might cause you to do such a thing?'

She lifted her shoulders. 'Fear of retribution, perhaps.'

'You see me as a wife-beater?'

'I don't know what you're capable of.' She was beginning to wish she'd kept her mouth shut. 'It isn't true, anyway. If I were capable of putting on that kind of act, I'd belong on the stage!'

'I believe you would.' His shoulders lifted. 'There have been moments in our relationship when you've sorely tried me, I admit.'

Karen eyed him in silence for a moment. 'We had rows?'

'We had some differences of opinion. You're a strong-willed young woman.'

'Where I come from, *all* women have minds of their own,' she claimed.

'As do Brazilian women—except that they are rather more subtle in their employment of it.' The pause was brief, the sudden change of tone emphatic. 'We have to put this behind us, and begin again.' He held up a staying hand as Karen started to speak. 'I'll arrange a hire car and show you the sights—the way I did when we first met. Perhaps then things will start to come back to you.'

He straightened away from the chest, turning towards the door. 'Come to the lobby in half an hour.'

Karen stood where she was for several moments after he'd left the room, mulling over everything that had been said. There were still so many questions to be answered, and only Luiz to supply those answers.

But was what he told her the whole truth? Why had she felt the need to turn to another man at all?

CHAPTER TWO

THE limousine Luiz had hired was already waiting for them outside when she went down. He put her into the front passenger seat before going round to slide behind the wheel.

He had shown her the sights this way when they'd first met, he'd said upstairs. If the hotel itself, plus the view from the window, had failed to stir her memory, it was unlikely that this was going to work either, but it was worth a try, Karen supposed. Anything was worth trying!

They headed for the mountains backing the city, leaving the congested streets to enter a world of tropical rainforest where thick lianas hung like pythons from tree branches furry with moss. The tangled canopy far above filtered out the sunlight, casting an eerie green glow over writhing creepers and huge tree ferns. There were flowers in abundance, their colours jewel-like among the foliage.

Karen was mesmerised, hardly able to believe that they were still within the city limits.

'It's like another planet!' she exclaimed, viewing a begonia bush bursting with bright yellow blossom and smothered in bees. 'What's making all the noise?'

'Monkeys,' Luiz advised. 'We invade their territory. This is the Terra da Tijuca, Rio's national park. It spreads over a hundred or more square miles.'

'It's wonderful!'

He cast a swift sideways glance at her rapt face. 'But in no way familiar?'

'No.' The enthusiasm faded as reality reared its head again. 'To the best of my knowledge, I've never seen any of this before.'

She sank back into her seat, head against the rest, eyes closed. 'I feel I'm living someone else's life!'

'I can assure you you're not,' Luiz responded. 'Your memory will return when you're ready to remember.'

Karen stole a glance at the hard-edged profile, feeling the fast-becoming-familiar tension in her lower body. 'Supposing that's never?'

His jaw compressed momentarily. 'Then we accept matters the way they are and live our lives accordingly.'

'I'm not sure I *can* accept it,' she said, and saw the compression come again.

'There's no other way.'

It was obvious that any further protest on her part would be a waste of time and breath, Karen acknowledged silently. Whatever she'd done, she was his wife and she was staying his wife.

Topped by the towering white statue of Christ, the granite peak of Corcovado afforded a panoramic view over both city and coastline. The skyscrapers below were reduced in size to toytown dimensions, the beaches of Copacabana and Impanema to curving crescents of white dotted with ants. Karen was overwhelmed by the sheer spectacle.

'You were equally impressed the first time you saw it,' said Luiz, watching her face as she gazed at the scene. 'As you were with everything.'

'Including yourself,' she murmured.

'Including myself,' he agreed. 'As I intended you to be.'

'How long did I hold out?'

Dark brows lifted. 'Hold out?'

'Before you got me into bed with you?'

It was a moment before he answered, his tone quizzical. 'Does it matter to you?'

'Yes,' she said. 'I need to know.'

His shrug was brief. 'We made love on the first night of our acquaintance.'

Karen swallowed. 'You must have thought me the easiest conquest you'd ever made!'

'No such thought entered my mind,' he denied. 'We were two people drawn by the same overwhelming force.'

She couldn't bring herself to meet the dark eyes full on. 'Would you still have wanted to marry me if I'd had previous experience?'

'I would have accepted it, yes.'

Karen looked at him then, oblivious to the other people on the platform. An arm resting against the guard rail, head outlined against the sky, he looked at ease in a way she envied. She had a sudden urge to disrupt that equanimity.

'Tell me about Lucio Fernandas,' she said with deliberation. 'Who exactly is he?'

She gained her wish as his face hardened. 'I prefer not to speak of him.'

'We *have* to talk about him,' she insisted.

Straightened now away from the rail, Luiz studied her for a moment in silence. When he spoke it was in tautly controlled tones. 'There's little enough I can tell you of his background. He was employed by one of my foremen. Had I had any notion...' He broke off, gritting his teeth together. 'Suffice to say he would have been in no fit state to arouse *any* woman's interest!'

Karen's chest felt tight as a drum. Luiz Andrade was a proud man; it didn't take intimate knowledge to be aware of that. The discovery that his wife had been having an affair at all would have hit him hard enough, but for her to have become involved with a mere employee!

'I'm still not convinced it's the truth,' she said defensively. 'What actual proof do you have that there was any affair to start with?'

Amber lights glinted in the depths of his eyes. 'What proof do I need other than that you provided yourself in running off with him?'

'There had to be some prior signs, surely?'

'There apparently were, had I been willing to see them. Beatriz suspected, but failed to warn me.'

Karen put up an involuntary hand to her temple as pain lanced briefly through it. There was an odd buzzing in her ears, a sense of being drawn somewhere she didn't want to go.

Luiz moved swiftly to catch her as she swayed, arms sliding about her to hold her close. She could feel the strong beat of his heart at her breast, the sun-stoked heat of his body.

'I'm all right now,' she managed. 'Just a bit of a dizzy spell, that's all.'

He made no attempt to stop her as she pulled away from him. 'I should have refused to discuss the matter,' he said. 'This isn't the place.'

What attention they'd drawn from those in the vicinity had now been returned to the scenery. Karen tilted her head to let the breeze cool her cheeks, both hands on the guardrail to steady herself.

'Who is Beatriz?'

Luiz made a curt gesture. 'As I said, this isn't the place. We'll return to the hotel.'

She made no protest. The name had meant something to her, that was obvious, but there was no further break in the curtain.

It was well into the afternoon when they reached the hotel again. Luiz accepted Karen's plea that she was tired and needed rest rather than food without demur, simply saying that he would see her later.

A shower was a first priority on reaching her room. She luxuriated for several minutes in the glass-walled cabinet, blanking out everything but the feel of the water streaming over her skin.

Towelled dry, she donned the robe provided and returned to the bedroom to extract fresh underwear from the suitcase. There seemed little point in unpacking fully when she had no idea how long they would be here.

Her throat closed up at the thought of what she would be facing when they did return to the ranch. However much she might want to disbelieve it, all the evidence pointed to the fact that she really had been having an affair with another man.

Where would she have been now, she wondered, if there had been no accident? What kind of life would she have had with a man capable of leaving her lying unconscious in the road? How could she have been drawn to another man at all when she was married to one as charismatic as Luiz Andrade?

Unless Luiz wasn't the man *he* appeared to be either. How could she be sure what their marital relationship had really been like? There had been rows, that much he'd admitted. She only had his word that there had been no serious rift between them.

He left her alone until eight, by which time she had begun to wonder if he had deserted her after all. When he did put in an appearance he was wearing a light linen suit that sat on his frame as if made to measure.

'I felt the need of fresh clothing,' he said. 'You at least have that facility.' He ran an appraising glance over her slender curves in the lilac silk tunic that had been one of the few items in the suitcase she considered suitable for dining out. 'Did you rest well?'

Karen turned away, unable to hold his gaze for long. 'As well as can be expected, considering. What happens now?'

'We have dinner here in the hotel. If we repeat, as far as is possible, the details of our time here together, perhaps it will stir something in your memory.'

'*Every* detail?' she asked after a moment.

'I said as far as is possible,' he responded. 'I make no demands on you.'

'For now,' she murmured, and heard him draw a roughened breath.

'Do you think me so easily able to banish the thought of you with Fernandas from my head? Whenever I close my eyes I see you in his arms!'

Karen made herself look at him, seeing the anger glittering his eyes. 'I'm sorry,' she said wretchedly. 'I wasn't thinking.' She paused, searching for words. 'Do you think you ever will be able to put it aside?'

'If not I must learn to live with it.' He was in control again, though his voice remained taut. 'The marriage will not be dissolved.'

There was nothing she could say to that. Nothing

likely to help the situation. But there were still so many things she needed to know.

'This morning you mentioned someone called Beatriz,' she ventured. 'Who is she?'

Something flickered deep in the dark eyes. 'She's the wife of my brother, Raymundo.'

The latter name struck no chord either. 'Does he work on the ranch too?'

'He and Beatriz have their home there,' came the somewhat ambiguous reply. 'As does my young sister too. Regina was devastated by your leaving.'

Karen sank to a seat, her legs no longer supportive. Just how many people *would* she be facing on her return to the home she had fled?

'How old is Regina?' she asked.

'Eighteen now.'

Green eyes lifted to view the incisive features. 'And Raymundo?'

'Twenty-eight. Four years younger than myself. There was another brother between us in age, but he died some two years ago.'

Empathy came swiftly, born of her own loss. 'I'm sorry.'

'You never knew him.' Luiz moved abruptly, crossing to open a cabinet Karen hadn't attempted to explore. 'I think we're both in need of a stimulant.'

He poured a colourless liquid for them both, bringing both glasses back to where she sat to thrust one into her hand. Not gin, she realised, putting it to her lips, but white rum. The spirit burned her throat, but she finished it, glad of the immediate effect. Alcohol was no solution to her problems, for certain, but it helped take the edge off them.

'What about parents?' she said.

'I lost my father some years ago. My mother married again, and now lives in Brasilia.'

Karen viewed the empty glass in her hand with lacklustre eyes. 'Have we met?'

'Just the once, when I took you to visit her.'

'Did she approve? Of the marriage, I mean?'

'No.' His tone was unemotional. 'She would have preferred that I marry a woman of my own race.'

'That's understandable.'

'It's of no consequence.' His own glass also drained, he took hers from her unresisting hand, depositing both on the nearest surface. 'Enough questions for now. You need to eat.'

Food was the farthest thing from her mind, but she rose obediently to her feet. It would be embarrassing going into a restaurant looking like this, she acknowledged, catching sight of her face in a nearby wall mirror, but there was little to be done about it.

There were others in the lift descending to the ground floor. Karen could feel the glances. If Luiz was aware of them too, he gave no sign. The subdued lighting in the restaurant afforded some comfort. All the same, it was a relief to gain the relative privacy of the alcove table.

There was nothing in the least bit familiar about the plush surroundings. She hadn't really expected there to be. She left it to Luiz to choose her meal, eating what was put in front of her without tasting a thing. The wine he'd ordered went straight to her head. She drank only half a glass, afraid of losing her grip altogether.

'This isn't going to work,' she said bleakly over coffee. She cast a glance at the man seated opposite, senses stirred by his dark masculinity. 'I don't think anything is.'

'There's nothing to be lost by trying,' he said. 'From here we went to a club.' His gaze was on her face. 'And then back to the hotel.'

Karen felt a pulse throb suddenly at her temple, setting her heart pounding in empathy. She tried desperately to grasp the image that fleeted through her mind.

'What is it?' Luiz's voice was low but urgent. 'Do you remember?'

She slowly shook her head. 'Just a feeling for a moment. Nothing concrete.'

'But it meant *something* to you, that was apparent.'

'It seems so.' She studied the vital features, wishing she could tell what he was thinking right now. 'Does everyone know about Lucio Fernandas?'

The glitter sprang in his eyes for a moment, then subsided again. 'Beatriz is the only one with that information.'

'You trust her to keep it to herself?'

'She had better do so. Regina believes you left merely because of dissidence between us. Your amnesia will be difficult enough for her to accept.'

Not nearly as difficult as it was for her, Karen thought. Recollection might not be palatable, but it had to be better than this blankness.

'We could always try keeping it a secret,' she said, and saw his lips thin.

'You find the situation one to treat with flippancy?'

She made a small apologetic gesture. 'No, of course not. It's just…' She paused, swallowing thickly. 'Have you any idea what it's like to sit here and listen to you telling me about people and places and matters I've absolutely no concept of? The person I seem to have become bears no relationship to the person I believe myself to be. It's like looking in a mirror and seeing someone else's reflection!'

Luiz inclined his head, face set. 'Difficult for both of us. To be deceived is bad, but to be forgotten...'

He left it there, lifting a hand to signal to the waiter. Up to now, Karen had been too involved with her own feelings to give any real thought to what he must be going through. She tried to put herself in his shoes, to imagine how it must feel to be wiped completely from her mind after months of living together as husband and wife. What man could handle that with equanimity?

She watched him sign the bill that was brought to the table. Those lean, long-fingered hands would know every inch of her, came the thought, sending a *frisson* the length of her spine. In three months she would no doubt have got over any inhibitions she might have had herself: the way her body was reacting at this moment gave every indication of it. She might not remember loving this man, but she was vitally attracted by him. Whatever had driven her to seek another man's arms, it couldn't have been because Luiz no longer stirred her.

She made an effort to compose herself as the waiter departed, to meet the eyes raised to her. 'What now?' she asked.

'As I said before, we follow the same pattern.'

'You really think it's going to help?'

'Whatever chance there is of stirring something in your memory, we must take,' he stated. He got to his feet, rounding the table to draw out her chair. 'The night is still young.'

It was gone ten o'clock, Karen saw from the thin

gold watch on his wrist as she rose. Handsome, charismatic, obviously not without money, it could be said
that Luiz Andrade was everything any woman could
possibly want. Yet she had left him for a man whose
backbone, it seemed, was so weak he had left her lying
in the road. It didn't make sense.

They took a taxi to what appeared at first sight to
be a large private residence. Luiz handed over a card
in the well-appointed entrance hall, and they were duly
signed in to wander at will through rooms devoted to
various pastimes.

Luiz ignored the crowded casino, leading the way
to a smaller, dimly lit room where couples swayed to
the beat of an excellent four-piece combo. There were
tables set around the periphery of the room, but he
ignored those too, drawing her on to the floor and into
his arms.

Held against the hard male body, Karen concentrated on matching her steps to his. She felt his hand
warm at her centre back, his breath stirring the hair at
her temple. Her mouth was in line with the hollow of
his throat, revealed by the open neckline of his shirt;
the male scent of him tantalised her nostrils.

All sensations of the present not the past, she told
herself. Luiz was a man to whom any woman with an
ounce of red blood in her veins would respond. Perhaps if they actually made love…

She rejected the thought immediately. Even if she
could bring herself to try such an experiment, Luiz
almost certainly wouldn't with the images he'd spoken
of earlier crowding his mind. He had followed her to
Rio with the intention of fetching her back because his
pride wouldn't allow him any other course, but that

wasn't to say he'd have been prepared to make love to her again.

'Could it have worked even if I hadn't lost my memory?' she heard herself ask. 'Forcing me back, I mean.'

It was a moment or two before Luiz answered. When he did speak his tone was unemotional. 'I would have found it difficult to put your transgressions aside, I admit. Trust isn't easily restored.'

'But you still wouldn't have been prepared to finish it?'

'No. Marriage, in my eyes, is for life. The reason why I waited so long to find the woman I could live that life with.'

'Only she let you down,' Karen said huskily. 'I can't tell you how awful it makes me feel to think I'm capable of that kind of behaviour! I still find it hard to believe I *could* be capable of it.'

'There was no mistake,' he said. 'Only the one you made in choosing a man who cared so little for you that he left you sprawled in the dust.'

Karen rode the hurt as best as she was able. 'What's even harder to explain is why a man like that would have abandoned a good job.'

Luiz gave a short laugh. 'Fear of what would happen to him when I discovered the affair would have been incentive enough.'

'In which case,' she pursued, 'why would he have taken the risk in the first place?'

The laugh came again. 'You do yourself an injustice. Few men could remain indifferent to you. You were a virgin when we met only because you'd never known one capable of bringing the fires smouldering within you to life. I could have taken you within minutes of our meeting.'

'So why didn't you?' she challenged.

'Because I wanted more than just your body.' His voice had softened in reminiscence. 'I wanted every part of you.'

All thought suspended, Karen felt heat rising through her from a central core, a spreading weakness in her limbs. Her body moved instinctively against him, pressing closer to his hardness.

'Stop that!' he said harshly.

She came back to earth with a jolt as reality raised its ugly head again, her face flaming as she looked up into the sparking dark eyes.

'It wasn't intentional,' she stammered. 'It just…happened.'

His lip curled. 'The way it just happened with Fernandas?'

'How can I know?' she asked wretchedly. 'How can I know anything for certain? All I have to go on is what you tell me.'

Luiz stopped moving, the spark grown to a blaze. 'Are you accusing me of lying to you?'

'No, of course not. But unless this Lucio Fernandas had money of his own, none of it adds up. The money I had on me almost certainly wouldn't have been enough to take the two of us very far.'

'So why else would the two of you have been on the same flight? Why else, for that matter, would you have been on the flight at all?'

Karen shook her head, feeling ever more desperate. 'I can't answer that. All I do know is…'

'Is?' he prompted as she broke off.

What she'd been about to say was that she simply

couldn't visualise walking out on someone who could make her feel the way he'd made her feel just now, but she wasn't ready to go down that particular road.

'Nothing,' she said. 'Can we call it a day? I have a dreadful headache.'

Anger gave way to concern. 'The fault is mine for insisting on continuing the attempt. I'll arrange for a taxi to be called.'

He was solicitousness itself while they waited for the taxi to arrive. Karen hadn't lied about the headache; it felt as if a hammer was beating at the space between her eyes. And this was just the beginning. There was worse to come. Facing the rest of the family would tax her resources to the limit.

It was coming up to midnight when they reached the hotel. Luiz had the receptionist on duty procure some painkillers and a glass of water for her before taking the lift to their floor.

'I trust the headache will soon subside,' he said at her door. For a moment he seemed to hesitate, his eyes on her pale face, then he said a brief goodnight and moved on to the room next door.

Thankful to be alone at last, Karen shed her clothing and took a shower. The bathroom was lined in mirror glass. She studied herself clinically as she towelled dry. Breasts high, waist slim, hips smoothly rounded, her body was, she knew from past experience, a magnet for male eyes, her face, in normal times, an equal draw. She'd had several short-term romances, but had lost hope of ever meeting any man who could make her want him the way he wanted her.

Until coming here to Rio and meeting Luiz Andrade. The very thought of him sent a ripple down her spine. The mistake she'd probably made then was in confusing lust with love. A mistake she must have realised eventually.

Regardless, she just couldn't imagine herself turning to another man for solace. Especially one like this Lucio Fernandas. Could she possibly have been so desperate that she'd cultivate a relationship with him simply to secure his help in getting away from Guavada?

She was going round in circles again, she acknowledged wearily, and still getting nowhere. The only chance she had of learning the truth was by returning to Guavada. Not that she had any choice in the matter anyway.

Worn out, she slept like a log, awakening to sunlight and a low-pitched ringing that turned out to be the telephone on the bedside cabinet.

'How are you feeling?' Luiz asked.

'Better,' she said, referring to the headache not the inner turbulence. 'What time is it?'

'Gone ten o'clock. You missed breakfast, but I can have something brought to the room.'

She wasn't hungry, Karen started to say, breaking off as her stomach growled a protest. 'Give me ten minutes,' she said instead.

'What would you like?'

'Fruit and coffee will be fine.'

She put the receiver down, wondering how she could speak so calmly and collectedly when her insides were dancing a fandango at the mere sound of his voice. They'd made love the night before her departure, he'd said yesterday. If it was the truth, whatever had gone wrong between them hadn't affected her physical responses even at that point.

Showered, she donned the white robe and went to open up the balcony doors with the intention of eating outside. She closed them again hastily on feeling the sticky heat, glad of the cool blast from the air-conditioning vents. São Paulo was far less humid than this, Luiz had said; she could be glad of that at least.

A knock at the door heralded the arrival of a waiter with a table trolley containing far more than the items she had requested. Luiz followed the man in, despatching him with what appeared to be a whole handful of banknotes. It was unlikely to be payment on the spot in a place like this, Karen concluded, so it had to be a tip. Generous or not, she had no way of knowing.

He was wearing the suit from last night, this time with a black shirt. Opened a little lower at the neckline than the night before, it revealed a fine gold chain bearing a small medal, the latter nestling amidst a curly mat of hair.

'I only asked for fruit and coffee,' she said, pulse rate increasing by the minute. She indicated the cereal, the covered tureen containing who knew what, the rolls and preserves. 'I can't eat all that!'

From the look in the dark eyes, her instinctive move to tighten the tie belt of the robe had not gone unnoted, though he made no comment. 'It's of no consequence,' he declared. 'The choice is there should you change your mind. I'll take coffee with you.'

Feeling distinctly vulnerable, she poured for them both, leaving his black as he'd requested the previous night. Luiz accepted the cup from her to set it down on the small table at the side of a nearby chair.

'I reserved seats on the one-thirty shuttle to São Paulo,' he announced without preamble. 'You were right last night. Attempting to recreate our beginnings is a waste of time and effort. All we can do is return to Guavada and hope for an eventual cure.'

Karen took a couple of deep swallows from her own cup before answering, needing the stimulant. 'What do we tell your sister?'

'She already knows about the amnesia. I spoke to her earlier. She sends her love, and hopes to help in your recovery.'

'And the others?'

'Regina is to pass on the news. If you're concerned for what Beatriz might say, you can rest assured of her silence,' he added hardily.

'You think she won't even have told your brother the real reason I went?'

He hesitated. 'Perhaps that would be asking a little too much. There should be no secrets between husband and wife.'

Karen busied herself slicing a banana into a dish, adding grapes and ready-cut pieces of melon. 'As manager of the ranch, I suppose you hold a lot of authority,' she murmured.

'I don't manage the ranch,' he said. 'I own it.'

Her head came up. 'You *own* it?'

'Why such surprise?' he asked on an ironical note. 'Do I appear a man of small means?'

'No,' she acknowledged. 'Not at all. I just thought…' She broke off, lifting her shoulders. 'I'm not sure what I thought. Is your brother a partner?'

'No.' The statement was unequivocal. 'Are you going to eat the fruit, or simply continue poking at it?'

Karen forked up a piece of banana and put it in her mouth, chewing on it resolutely. Fruit here had a far better taste than back home, she had to admit. Except that England was home no longer, of course. Not for her. She might never even see it again!

'Is it far to the airport?' she asked, shutting out the hovering despondency.

'The São Paulo shuttle flies from Aeroporto Santos Dumont in the city centre,' Luiz returned. The flight itself takes less than an hour, the drive to Guavada considerably longer, but we should be there before dark.'

To meet more people she couldn't remember. People who had known *her* a whole three months. How, Karen wondered numbly, was she to deal with it all?

CHAPTER THREE

THE flight was short and uneventful. Luiz had left a Land Rover at the São Paulo airport on his way out, prompting Karen to wonder how she and this Lucio had got there themselves. If in a car, it must still be parked here somewhere.

She didn't care to broach the subject. Any mention of Lucio Fernandas was like waving a red rag before a bull.

By four o'clock they had left the city suburbs well behind and were driving through a landscape of grassy, tree-dotted plains broken by isolated low ranges. As Luiz had promised, the climate up here, some two thousand feet above sea level, was far pleasanter than Rio's.

Karen recognised nothing. Not that she'd expected to. The closer they came to the home she had abandoned just a few days ago, the worse she felt. Beatriz may be the only one to know the real reason she had flown, but the others were hardly going to see a supposed disagreement with Luiz as an adequate reason. There was every chance that her partial amnesia would be suspect to them, if not to Luiz himself. It was, she had to acknowledge, a very convenient method of avoiding responsibility for her actions.

'Are you feeling unwell?' Luiz asked, shooting her a glance. 'Do you wish to stop?'

Karen shook her head, pulling herself together. 'Just nervousness. How are they likely to react?'

He gave a faint smile. 'If I know my sister, she will throw her arms about you and commiserate. She blames me for driving you away with my domineering manner.'

'Are you?' Karen ventured. 'Domineering, I mean?'

'No more than I have to be to maintain your respect. We come from different cultures. There were adjustments to be made by each of us. I believed we had achieved a balance.'

'When I ruined everything by going off with another man,' Karen said hollowly. 'I still can't imagine how I could have done that. To leave…'

'To leave?' Luiz prompted as she let the words trail away.

Like the night before, she'd been about to say, To leave a man like you, but it still sounded too much like sycophancy. 'Without even a word,' she substituted. 'The whole thing was shameful!'

It was a moment before Luiz responded, his expression austere again. 'We must put it behind us.'

'*Can* you, though?' she asked.

'As I've said before, I have no choice.'

There was little comfort in the answer. Karen hadn't really expected any. It was still difficult to accept that the person she had been—the person she still felt herself to be inside—could have behaved in the manner ascribed to her. As if someone else had taken over her body during the lost months.

'Tell me about the ranch,' she said after a moment or two, desperate for something to break the silence between them.

Eyes on the road, Luiz lifted his shoulders in a brief shrug. 'What can I tell you? Guavada produces beef for the export markets. It was founded in my grandfather's day, the land area increased over the years to become what it is today.'

'You own a third share then?'

'As the eldest son, I inherited outright ownership.' His lips slanted when she failed to comment. 'I sense disapproval.'

Karen stole a swift glance at the hard-cut profile. 'It seems a bit unfair, that's all. In England all the children would be entitled to a share—male *and* female.'

'This is not England,' came the short response. 'Raymundo is no pauper. He could found businesses of his own. As to Regina, she bears the name only until she marries.'

'Is that imminent?'

'Regina has yet to meet someone capable of retaining her interest for longer than a few weeks.'

'Well, at eighteen she has plenty of time. After all…'

'After all, *I* waited long enough to find the right person,' he finished for her on a sardonic note as she broke off.

'What you obviously believed was the right person at the time,' she said, gathering her resources once more. 'We can all make mistakes.'

'Especially when judgement is clouded by a lovely face and body.'

'I doubt that you'd have allowed your libido to rule you to such an extent.' Karen kept her tone level with an effort. 'Any more than I would myself.'

Luiz made no reply. He looked remote again. Karen leaned back against the seat rest and closed her eyes, willing herself to stay in control. Whatever happened from here-on-in, she could only go along with it.

They drove through a sizeable township bright with

greenery, turning off the road on to a narrower one some fifteen minutes later, to pass beneath a tall wooden archway with the name carved into its surface.

Fencing stretched to either hand as far as the eye could see, though with no sign of either cattle or habitation. The latter proved to be hidden behind a large clump of trees a half mile or so ahead.

Anticipating something akin to the ranch houses seen in cowboy films, Karen was totally thrown by the lovely colonial-style building that came into view. Fronted by beautifully landscaped lawns, its white walls glinting in the late afternoon sunlight, it had verandas running the whole way round.

The girl who came out from the house as the car drew to a standstill was an Andrade through and through, her waist-length hair darkly luxuriant about her vibrant young face, her figure, clad casually in shorts and sleeveless top, lithe and lovely. As Luiz had predicted, she gave no quarter to the amnesia, descending the steps with open arms and a radiant smile.

'So wonderful to have you home with us again!' she declared. 'But your poor face! How it must pain you!'

'Not any more,' Karen assured her. 'And the marks will soon be gone too.' She found a smile of her own, overcoming the awkwardness of the moment by sheer willpower. 'Perhaps my memory will have returned by then.'

The shadow that passed across her sister-in-law's face was come and gone in an instant. 'It will! I'm sure of it!'

'I think refreshment would be a priority at present,' said Luiz with a questioning look at Karen. 'A cold drink, perhaps?'

She hesitated. 'I don't suppose tea would be available?'

'Of course.' His tone was tinged with humour for a moment. 'You insisted on it. Too much coffee, you said, was bad for the health.'

Mood lifting a little, she tried a lighter tone herself. 'Not very tactful in a coffee-producing country!'

'I like tea too,' claimed Regina. 'I'll have some prepared immediately.' She held out an inviting hand. 'Come.'

Karen accompanied her indoors to a wide hall. A wrought-iron staircase rose from the centre to branch off left and right to open galleries. Plant-life abounded, spilling from standing pots, from hanging baskets, from the galleries themselves.

The woman who appeared in an archway under the curve of the staircase was in her mid-twenties. Unlike Regina's, her hair was a dark blonde; her striking features were formed from a totally different mould, her figure voluptuous. There was no welcome in the tawny eyes, just a cold watchfulness.

She spoke in Portuguese, drawing a sharp admonishment from Luiz.

'We will all of us speak only English when Karen is present. The way we did when she first came to Guavada.'

'Does that mean I learned to speak Portuguese myself?' Karen asked, picking up on the nuances.

'You acquired a fair grasp,' he confirmed.

She found that difficult to take in. She'd shown little aptitude for compulsory French in school, much less other languages.

On the other hand, she'd never lived in a foreign speaking household before.

'You expect us all to believe this claim of yours?' demanded the newcomer, who could only be Beatriz.

'What you believe is your affair,' Luiz cut in hardily before Karen could form an answer. 'What you *say* in this house is mine. Where is Raymundo?'

'He had to go out.' Beatriz both looked and sounded resentful of the warning, but obviously wasn't prepared to make an issue of it. 'Some problem.'

'Then we'll see him at dinner. Have the tea sent up,' he added to his sister.

He took Karen's arm to guide her up the iron-balustraded staircase, creating havoc with her hard-won equilibrium. She was torn between two opposing fires when he released her at the top of the stairs, a part of her relieved to be free of his touch, another, deeper, part yearning for even closer contact.

The room to which he led the way lay towards the end of the open gallery. It was large and airy, the carved dark wood furnishings relieved by white walls and lush fabrics. The panelled windows were shuttered in slatted wood.

The wide bed drew Karen's eyes. It would, she reckoned, sleep four with ease. She had shared that bed with the man at her side—made love with him in the dark of night. The thought alone made her quiver.

'Your bathroom lies through there,' said Luiz, indicating a door in the far wall. 'The other door gives access to my room.' He registered her expression with an ironic slant of his lips. 'A matter of tradition still sometimes upheld in our culture—although we made little use of it.'

He was standing close. Karen had a sudden mad urge to turn and put her arms about his neck, her lips to his; to seek a way back to what she had lost. Only the fear of rejection kept her from giving way. It would take time, he'd admitted, to put the images of her in another man's arms aside. She could hardly blame him for that.

Her suitcase was brought by a young man dressed in dark trousers and white shirt, whom Karen could only assume was a servant. He gave her a curious glance, but said nothing, depositing the suitcase on a stand at the foot of the bed and departing. No doubt, she reflected wryly, to speculate with others on the return of the errant wife.

Luiz had moved to a window, standing with hands thrust into trouser pockets, gazing out on to landscaped grounds lush with foliage.

'We must find a way,' he said. 'There can be no going back, only forward.'

'I know.' Karen's voice was husky, her throat tight. 'It isn't going to be easy for either of us.'

He swung to look at her, lips twisting as he took in the pallor of her face, the shadows beneath her eyes. 'You dread the thought of renewing our relationship?'

'I dread the thought of living with this blankness for the rest of my life,' she prevaricated.

'It may not come to that. The doctor told me you could recover your memory at any moment.'

He would also have told him that the longer the amnesia went on the less likely it was to end, Karen suspected. She gazed at him in silence, willing him to take the first step towards the renewal he had spoken of. He still wanted her; she could sense that much in him. It could be a way back. It might be the *only* way back.

The arrival of the tea, borne this time by a young woman, put paid to any move he might have made.

'I'll leave you to refresh yourself in peace,' he said. 'Dinner is at nine. I'd suggest you take advantage of the time to rest. You look exhausted.'

She felt it. Both emotionally and physically. Lonely too, when he'd gone. She had been mistress of this household for a whole three months. A role she would be expected to take on again if the marriage was to continue in any sense at all. The very idea was daunting.

Drained though she was, sleep was farthest from her mind at present. She drank the tea gratefully, then took a look in the bathroom, finding it equipped with every luxury.

The cabinet above the ornate vanity unit held an array of expensive feminine toiletries, the brand name the same as the ones she had found in her suitcase back at the hospital. She closed the door again, faced by her reflection in the mirror fronting it. The grazes were already beginning to heal, the bruise at her temple to lighten a little in hue. In another few days—a week at the most—there would be no outward sign of the accident left, her looks fully restored. For what that was worth.

Back in the bedroom, she tentatively tried the connecting door, finding it locked. According to Luiz, he'd spent little time in there, but he would almost certainly be doing it tonight. For how many other nights remained to be seen. Whatever else had been lost, the physical attraction between them was still strong. It was all she had to cling to.

A walk-in closet held a variety of garments. She fingered through them, looking for something—*anything*—recognisable. There was nothing. She could only think she must have acquired a whole new wardrobe for her trip to Rio.

The surface of the highly polished dark wood dressing table was bare. Tucked away in a drawer, she at last found some familiar items: the silver-backed hair brushes her parents had given her on her eighteenth birthday; two ballet dancer figurines; the antique silver box she used to hold tissues. None of them worth a great deal in monetary terms, but sentimentally irreplaceable.

There must be other things somewhere—these, and the photograph of her parents, couldn't be all she had asked Julie to send—but they sufficed to give her some feeling of home.

Someone must have been in here and cleared them away, she reflected. Hardly the kind of thing the servants would take it on themselves to do, and she doubted if either Regina or Raymundo was the culprit. Which left only Beatriz.

The woman's animus had been only too apparent. Considering what she knew, it was hardly unexpected. Hardly so surprising either that she might suspect her of fabricating the amnesia in order to protect herself from Luiz's anger.

Weariness finally overcame her. With almost three hours to go until dinner, there was plenty of time to take the sleep Luiz had advised. She was going to need all the stamina she could muster to get through the evening.

The room was lamplit when she opened her eyes, the shutters closed on the outside world. She hadn't undressed before lying down on the bed, but someone had still seen fit to cover her with a light throw. Luiz? she wondered.

It was just gone eight, she saw from the clock on the bedside table. Her head felt heavy when she sat up, her eyes filled with grains of sand. She had to force herself to her feet.

A shower went some way towards refreshing her, although she'd left herself with no time to wash and dry her hair as she would have liked to do. She used a tortoiseshell clip she found in a drawer to pin it back into her nape.

Going by the style of clothing she had found, dress here was more casual than formal. She donned a swirly skirt in mingled colours, along with a white top scooped low at the neckline, viewing her image with a spark of interest. A very different look from her normal, or what had been normal, style, but she had to admit it suited her.

With no further excuse to linger, and with the time approaching the set hour, she nerved herself to leave the room. The man standing in the wide hall below looked up as she paused at the gallery rail, the expression that crossed his face at the sight of her too swiftly come and gone for analysis.

The resemblance between him and Luiz was too marked for him to be anyone other than the brother. Karen drew a steadying breath.

'You must be Raymundo.'

Dark head tipped back, he viewed her for a long moment in silence. 'So it's true,' he said at length. 'You have no memory of me.'

'Not of anyone,' she confirmed. 'I'm…sorry.'

'A dreadful thing to happen.' He sounded genuinely sympathetic. 'Are you coming down?'

Cheered a little by the lack of censure—assuming his wife had told him about Lucio Fernandas—she

moved to the staircase and descended to join him. He
was shorter than Luiz by an inch or two, she judged,
though no less fit.

He said something in Portuguese, shaking his head
as if in recollection. 'It's good to have you back,' he
amended softly. 'Soon you'll be speaking our language again.'

'I can't imagine it right now, but I'll do my best,'
she returned, sparking a sudden smile.

'We'll all of us do that.' He extended an arm. 'You
will allow me to guide you?'

He meant to the dining room, of course. She had,
Karen acknowledged, not the slightest idea which of
the doors leading off the hall it might lay behind.

'Thanks,' she said gratefully.

They found the rest of the family already seated in
a room which, though well appointed, was very much
smaller than she would have anticipated in a house of
this size and stature. The table itself was round, and
would seat no more than six.

'This is where we eat as a family,' Raymundo explained, as if sensing her confusion. 'The dining room
is only used for more formal entertaining.' His eyes
were on his brother, who had risen from his place.
'Karen was lost. She needed to be shown the way.'

Face unrevealing, Luiz moved to pull out the chair
at his side in mute invitation. Karen slid into it, feeling
anything but comfortable, aware of Beatriz's eyes on
her from across the table. She didn't need to look to
know what they held. The enmity was searing.

Raymundo took his own seat between the two of
them, with Regina closing the circle.

'You look so much less tired than when you arrived,' exclaimed the latter warmly. 'The rest has been good for you.'

'You slept deeply,' said Luiz. 'You failed to stir even when I closed the window shutters.'

'It's been a long day.' Karen made the comment as light as possible. It was going to seem an even longer night, she judged, but it had to be endured. It all had to be endured. Beatriz wasn't going to make life easy for her for certain.

Hungry by now, she ate her fill of the delicious seafood stew that constituted the main part of the meal. *Moqueca*, Regina told her it was called. She refused both the coffee that ended the ritual and the tea that was offered, finishing off her wine instead. She longed to retire to the privacy of her bedroom again, yet at the same time dreaded the thought of the lonely hours to come.

Luiz had said little at all during the meal. Karen could see his hand on the periphery of her vision as he lifted the coffee cup to his lips. Her husband: the man she had married with what appeared to be scarcely a moment's real thought about what she was doing. Even while she could appreciate how bowled over she would have been by him on sight alone, it had been an utterly mad impulse to follow. She hadn't known him any better then than she knew him now. Not in any proper sense.

Julie must have thought she was utterly crazy. *She* certainly would have if the positions had been reversed. Except that Julie would never have got herself into such a situation. Her feet were far too firmly on the ground.

If she'd stayed in touch with her it was possible that she'd told her what was going on. The only way to find out was to put Julie in the picture regarding her memory loss and ask, although she shrank from the thought.

'Your head hurts?' Luiz asked, bringing her to the sudden realisation that she had a hand to her temple.

'It aches a little,' she admitted truthfully.

'Then you must rest again.' He got to his feet, coming behind her to draw back her chair. 'Sleep is the best healer.'

For the body, perhaps, she thought. It made little difference to her mental state.

'I'll say goodnight then,' she proffered to the table at large, avoiding any direct contact with Beatriz's gaze.

'Tomorrow,' said Regina purposefully, 'we will renew your acquaintance with La Santa.'

'The town we passed through,' Luiz supplied.

'It's market day tomorrow,' Regina continued. 'You like the market.'

Karen could imagine. She always had liked them. She smiled at the girl. 'I'll look forward to it.'

Expecting to be left to find her own way back to her room, she was disconcerted when Luiz accompanied her.

'You don't need to do this,' she said in the outer hall. 'I'll be quite all right.'

'You look far from all right,' he returned shortly. 'I'm in need of rest myself, so you've nothing to fear from me tonight.'

'I don't fear you,' she denied. 'I just…' She spread her hands in a helpless little gesture. 'It's so hard to know *what* to say!'

'Then say nothing,' he advised. 'Only time will tell

whether our marriage can be made good again. But be assured, good or not, it will continue.'

There was nothing she *could* say to that, Karen acknowledged painfully.

CHAPTER FOUR

AWAKE at seven-thirty, Karen was downstairs by eight, to find Luiz and Raymundo had already breakfasted and gone about whatever business they had. What time they might return was apparently anyone's guess.

The meal was served out on the veranda at the rear of the house. Eating the fruit that was all she had appetite for, Karen felt pinioned beneath Beatriz's steely gaze. She was grateful for Regina's efforts to lighten the atmosphere.

The day was already warm, with a promise of higher temperatures to come. It would have been October when she had first arrived: a brand new bride, too head-over-heels in love with the man she'd known bare days to view her new world through anything but the most rose-tinted of glasses.

How long, she wondered, had it taken for reality to kick in? How long before she'd begun to regret abandoning everything and everyone she knew to settle in a country totally alien to her? Life here was so different from what she'd been accustomed to. Had she ever really adjusted to it?

'You mentioned reintroducing me to La Santa today,' she said to Regina, doing her best to ignore Beatriz's heavy presence. 'Do you still feel like it?'

'Of course.' The girl hesitated a moment. 'You realise word of your amnesia will already have spread.'

'It would be a difficult secret to keep,' Karen

agreed, trying to be practical about it. 'At least I shan't be expected to recognise people on sight.'

Silent up until now, Beatriz said something short and sharp beneath her breath, then rose abruptly to her feet to stalk indoors. Karen caught Regina's eye and gave a helpless little shrug.

'Pay no attention,' the younger girl advised. 'She was always jealous of you. You took the position she would have occupied herself had Luiz been willing. Raymundo is my brother too, and I love him dearly, but he can never be more than second best in Beatriz's eyes.'

Taken aback, Karen sought a response. 'That's a big assumption to make.'

'I make no assumption.' Regina's tone was emphatic. 'She has no real love for him. She even refuses to give him a child!'

'You can't possibly know that,' Karen felt bound to protest.

'Then why has she not fallen pregnant in three years of marriage? Raymundo yearns for children!'

Luiz must want them too, came the thought. Or a son at least. Yet she hadn't fallen pregnant either. A failure on her part, or on his?

'It sometimes happens that way,' she said, blanking out the question. 'Three years isn't all that long.'

'It is for the Andrades. You had only been married to Luiz for four weeks when you discovered your pregnancy.' The dark eyes widened in sudden dismay at the shock expressed in the green ones opposite. 'Luiz did not tell you?'

'No.' Karen's voice seemed to be coming from a long distance away, almost drowned by the drumming in her ears. 'What happened?'

'You miscarried.' Regina was distressed, obviously at a loss as to how to proceed. 'I'm so sorry! I thought…I believed…'

It took Karen everything she had to keep herself from crumbling. A baby! She'd been going to have a baby! How could she not have known that?

'I suppose Luiz thought I had enough to deal with at present,' she got out. 'How…far gone was I?'

'Almost two months.' The distress was growing by the moment. 'He will be furious with me for telling you. How can I have been so dense?'

'I had to know some time.' Fighting to stay on top of her chaotic emotions, Karen drew a deep breath. 'Do you know what caused me to miscarry?'

'The doctors could find no organic reason for it. And they said there was no cause to fear it might happen again.' Regina was eager to repair at least some of the harm she had done. 'You will have many healthy babies, I'm sure of it!'

She broke off once more in recollection of the present circumstances, pulling a rueful face. 'I speak before I think again. Can you ever forgive me?'

Karen forced a smile. 'There's nothing to forgive.' Her hesitation was brief, the need to know outweighing the reluctance to ask. 'Did Luiz blame me for it?'

'Blame you?' Regina sounded shocked. 'Of course not! He was devastated, of course, but his concern was mostly for you. He loves you so much, Karen. You must believe that!'

'He told me we had disagreements.'

It was Regina's turn to hesitate. 'Well, yes. He can be a little imperious at times. But there was never any serious disunity, until—'

'Until I suddenly upped and went,' Karen finished for her.

The younger girl nodded. 'It was a shock to all of us, but to Luiz most of all. Whatever he'd said or done to make you do such a thing, he was utterly distraught. It was fortunate that he returned early to the house. You had been gone no longer than an hour or two when he set out after you.'

Karen's brows were drawn together in an effort to break through the barriers. 'How could he know where I was heading?' she asked, only just stopping herself from saying we.

'You had taken your passport, as if your intention was to return to England, but if so you could have gone there direct from São Paulo. I believe you went to Rio because he had made you unhappy, and you just wished to teach him a lesson.'

As a mere gesture, it would have been a little over the top, Karen reflected. Better that Regina retained the notion, though, than know the truth. Whether Lucio Fernandas would have told anyone else about the affair there was no way of knowing, although fear that Luiz would find out should surely have been enough to keep his mouth closed.

She still found the affair itself so difficult to accept. The way she felt about marital infidelity now was the way she'd always felt—the way her parents had felt. She'd read somewhere that losing a baby could affect a woman in more ways than just the physical. Was it possible that her loss had triggered a whole change of character?

'The car you took was fetched back from the airport yesterday,' Regina continued, intent on filling in the pieces for her.

Distracted, Karen said blankly, 'I can drive?'

'Of course. How else could you have got there? Luiz taught you himself. It meant we no longer had to call on Carlos. I hold a licence too now, but I'm happy to direct you.'

Karen shook her head, mind whirling. 'If I can't remember being able to drive, I can hardly just set off. I wouldn't even know *how* to change gear, much less when!'

'The car you drive is an automatic,' Regina answered, 'but I understand your reluctance. Perhaps it will come back to you quickly when you do try.'

Karen couldn't imagine it. If she knew what time Luiz might be back she would stay and face him with what she had just learned, but sitting around waiting for him to put in an appearance would only serve to increase the anger boiling up inside her. He should have told her about the baby! How could he *not* have told her? What else was he keeping from her?

'What should I wear?' she asked, desperate to stop herself from dwelling on it all. 'To go to town, I mean.'

'We dress very casually on most occasions,' Regina advised. 'Especially in the summer. You must wear what you find the most comfortable.' She gave a sigh. 'It's difficult to remember how little you know of our ways. You became so much a part of us.'

'I was never homesick?'

'Perhaps a little at times, but Luiz could soon bring a smile back to your lips. You told me once that he was the only man you had ever loved.' She glanced at the watch encircling her wrist. 'We should go while the morning is still young.'

Karen went up to her room and changed the dress

she'd slipped on for a pair of light cotton trousers and a shirt, similar to what Regina herself was wearing. The wad of notes was still in the wallet. She still had no idea of the value, but there would surely be ample should she fancy buying anything. Not that shopping was of any interest right now.

Only on opening another section did she find the platinum credit card bearing her name. She must have been relying on that as a means of obtaining more money, she thought painfully. It was more than likely that Lucio Fernandas had been relying on it too, hence the disappearing act when she was knocked down. The last thing he would have wanted was to be around when Luiz came on the scene.

The whole concept was intolerable. What spell had the man cast on her?

Fairly minor though it was, the town offered a variety of shops, restaurants and places of entertainment. Bathed in a glow of gilt, the church was a baroque magnificence. The market was held in a tree-shaded square, a collection of gaily coloured awnings covering stalls selling everything and anything.

Wandering through them at Regina's side, Karen was aware of sideways glances and whispered comments from one or two of the vendors. She did her best to ignore them. Fretting about it wouldn't help anything. She simply had to learn to live with it.

The woman Regina greeted by one of the stalls made a valiant effort to show no discomfiture. She was in her early thirties, face and figure comfortably rounded.

'This is Dona Ferrez,' said Regina. 'She and her husband, Marques, are close family friends.'

'I'm sorry to be like this,' proffered Karen with a

smile before the other could speak, determined to grasp the nettle firmly.

'The fault is far from yours,' Dona assured her in stilted English, looking a little more relaxed. 'We were all of us desolated to hear of your accident. You must be finding matters very difficult.'

'It certainly isn't easy,' Karen agreed. 'I feel like a fish out of water!'

'It would be best for you to meet with all the people who know you at the one time,' the other suggested. 'I will arrange a barbecue for this coming Sunday.'

Unable to see a way out of what threatened to be a pretty overwhelming experience, Karen could only smile and nod. 'That's very thoughtful of you. I'll look forward to it.'

'It won't be so very bad,' Regina comforted as they moved on. 'The people who will be there will be only too anxious to put you at your ease. You are regarded very highly by all our friends.'

'I've met them often?'

'On many occasions. We socialise a great deal. Unlike Rio, it can become quite cold at times here in winter. Our entertainment then takes place indoors.'

Karen had always believed Brazil to be hot everywhere all year round but, covering such a vast area, she supposed there had to be variations in climate. She preferred the idea of some seasonal change in temperature. It made it seem more like home.

Home. The wave of nostalgia that swept her was grievous. Would she ever see England again?

The desire to confront Luiz had subsided to some extent by the time they returned to the house. The sight of him lounging on the veranda, seemingly without a care in the world, brought it all surging back.

Wearing dark jeans and T-shirt, his feet clad in leather boots, he looked very different from the man who had brought her here yesterday. His working gear, she guessed, although someone in his position would hardly be called on to perform any manual labour.

'How long have you been waiting?' asked Regina a little tentatively.

'Perhaps an hour,' he said. His eyes were on Karen, appraising the spots of colour burning high on her cheekbones. 'You enjoyed the market?'

'I didn't recall anything, if that's what you really want to know,' she answered shortly.

Her tone brought a sudden narrowing of the dark eyes. 'You sound hostile,' he observed. 'Is there something you have to say to me?'

'It's my fault.' Regina looked as though she would prefer to be anywhere but where she was at this moment. 'I thought Karen knew about the baby.'

'Which I would have, if you'd had the decency to tell me about it yourself!' Karen cut in. 'Don't blame Regina for taking it for granted you would have done!'

'Regina should have had the sense to realise how far from ready you were for such a disclosure,' he returned, directing an angry glance at his sister. 'You have enough to contend with.'

'I'm the best judge of what I can or can't deal with,' Karen flashed, and saw his lips slant.

'How would you know whether or not you're able to deal with matters in advance of the information being imparted? I made the judgement I thought best for you.'

'Then stop it!' She was trembling, but too fired up to withdraw. 'If I'm to have any hope at all of regaining my memory I need to know everything there is to know about these past months. So anything else you're holding back I'd—'

'There's nothing more.' The interruption was terse. 'If there was, we would not be discussing it here and now. I think it might be best if you took some time to calm yourself before we discuss anything at all.' He held up a staying hand as she started to speak. 'I said that's enough!'

Karen subsided with reluctance, not quite up to meeting the challenge. Regina had said he could be imperious; she had certainly been right!

Maddening though she found it now, and would almost certainly have found it then, she doubted all the same if it would have been enough on its own to send her careering into another man's arms. There *had* to be something more! Something he still wasn't telling her.

A flicker of movement from the doorway drew her eyes. Whoever had been standing there had gone, but she had a strong feeling that it had been Beatriz. If what Regina had told her was to be taken seriously, the woman's dislike of her was easier to understand, if not appreciate. She felt sorry for Raymundo.

'I think I might go and lie down for an hour,' she said, suddenly weary of it all.

Luiz inclined his head, his expression giving little away. 'By all means.'

'You will come down for lunch?' asked Regina. 'We eat at two.'

It was only just twelve. 'I'll be there,' Karen confirmed, more to please her sister-in-law than through any desire for food.

She made her escape before anything else could be said. Gaining the bedroom, she stood for a moment or two trying to gather herself. The weariness was more mental than physical. She felt totally drained.

There was little comfort to be gained by lying down. Sleep had never seemed further away. She put her hands to her smooth abdomen, still finding it difficult to believe that she'd carried a child for two months. Had it been a boy or a girl? Had she miscarried here, or in hospital? The questions kept piling up, whirling like dervishes around her brain. There was so much she needed to know.

The gentle knock on the door came as some relief. Regina might be in the dark regarding the reason she had left Guavada, but she could provide at least one or two more answers.

Except that it wasn't Regina who came into the room at her invitation, but Luiz himself, tautening her throat afresh.

'I came to apologise,' he said unexpectedly. 'I should have warned Regina to keep her own counsel on the matter until you were better able to withstand the shock. The blame is mine, not hers. I can only hope you suffer no lasting harm from learning the news so precipitately.'

Propped on an elbow, Karen regarded the firmly controlled features with eyes suddenly opened to the realisation that she wasn't the only one who'd undergone the loss. His loss, in fact, was twofold: not just his child, but his wife too.

'It can't have been easy for you either at the time,' she said softly.

The dark head inclined. 'No, it was not—though the assurance that there was no reason to fear it happening again was some consolation.'

'Did we try for another baby?' Karen ventured.

'No. I believed it best to take a little time to ourselves first. If I'd realised…' He broke off, jaw tensing. 'What can't be altered must be endured.'

'If you believe I began this affair with Lucio Fernandas some way back, it seems odd that Beatriz was the only one to suspect anything,' Karen got out with difficulty.

'The two of you were obviously very circumspect in your meetings. Beatriz herself became suspicious only a matter of days before you left.'

'I'd have thought she would have tried to warn you.'

The shrug was dismissive. 'If she had, I might have thought she was simply attempting to cause trouble between us. She never approved of the marriage.'

Considering what Regina had told her earlier, Karen could understand that. What she still couldn't understand was how on earth she and this Lucio had managed to keep the affair so secret. If it weren't for the fact that Luiz had verified the names on the passenger list to Rio that day, she might even suspect Beatriz of making the whole thing up in order to discredit her in his eyes.

'I'm sorry,' she proffered miserably. 'I know I keep saying that, but it's all I *can* say. I hate to think of what I've done to you—to our marriage. I only wish I could somehow put things right again.'

Dark eyes travelled the length of her body, revealing a hunger that stirred her to the depths. When he moved it was with purpose, coming across to sit down on the edge of the bed and draw her up into his arms.

Karen met the kiss hesitantly at first, not at all sure if this was what she wanted right now: a hesitancy dispersed in seconds by the emotions sweeping through her. Her arms lifted of their own accord to slide about his neck, her fingers tangling in the crisp thickness. Her breasts were pressed against the hardness of his chest, springing the nipples to vibrant life, her nostrils filled with the male scent of him. There was a dampness between her thighs, an aching need she could barely sustain. If her mind failed to recall what fulfilment felt like, her body had no such problem.

Without removing his lips from hers, Luiz reached between them to unbutton her shirt, sliding his hand inside to seek the firm curve of her breast. Karen caught her breath as his fingers enclosed the sensitive, tingling tip, moaning deep in her throat at a sensation so close to pain yet so infinitely pleasurable.

She was bereft when he withdrew the hand and put her from him to rise abruptly to his feet again.

'I'll show you round the ranch after lunch,' he said without looking at her. 'I have other matters to attend to for now.'

Karen eased herself to a sitting position as the door closed behind him, reaching with numbed fingers to fasten the buttons he had opened. She had wanted him to make love to her so badly, but the spectre of Lucio Fernandas still loomed too large. Perhaps there would come a time when he was able to put the images that haunted him from his mind. If they were to make anything at all of this marriage of theirs, he would have to. They would both have to.

Beatriz was missing from the lunch table. She had gone to visit a friend, Raymundo advised. Karen could only be grateful for the woman's absence. There were questions only Beatriz could answer for her, but she was reluctant to ask them for fear of what she might hear.

Whatever Luiz had been feeling earlier, he appeared to have recovered from it. Conversation was light throughout the meal. Regina greeted the news that he was to take Karen on a tour of the ranch with pleasure, obviously reassured that things were working out between them.

They went by Jeep, to Karen's relief. She had never, to the best of her knowledge, ridden a horse in her life. The corrals she had originally expected to see lay some half a mile from the house, backed by barns and other outbuildings. There were several ranch hands around employed on various jobs. Luiz stopped to speak with one of them who appeared to be in charge, leaving Karen to fidget beneath the covert glances cast by those in the vicinity.

If Lucio Fernandas had lived and worked with these men it seemed unlikely that none of them had known of his affair with the wife of their employer, yet it seemed equally unlikely that if any of them *had* known they would have kept totally quiet about it. Her memory loss would be the reason for the glances. There probably wasn't a solitary soul within a hundred mile radius who hadn't heard about *that*!

'I'm beginning to feel a regular freak,' she commented wryly when they were on their way again. 'It was the same in town this morning. Everyone staring and whispering!'

'It will soon be forgotten,' Luiz answered, giving way to a smile at the realisation of what he'd just said. 'An unfortunate turn of phrase in the circumstances.'

Karen smiled too, heartened by the humour. 'But hopefully true.' She paused, looking for some non-contentious subject. 'We met someone called Dona Ferrez in town this morning. She offered to arrange a barbecue on Sunday in order for me to get all the meetings over with at the one time.'

'Thoughtful of her.' Luiz directed a glance. 'How do you feel about it?'

'Nervous,' she admitted. 'But there's no point crying off. At least none of them…'

'None of them will know why you were in Rio to begin with,' Luiz supplied levelly as she let the words peter out. 'A question I may be called on to answer myself.'

'You could say I was shopping,' she suggested after a moment, and saw his lips twist.

'There's nothing you could buy in Rio that couldn't be obtained in São Paulo city, but then, there's no accounting for a woman's whim.'

He brought the Jeep to a halt as a party of riders appeared round a bend in the trail. The leader approached the vehicle without dismounting, his attitude respectful. A good-looking man in his thirties, lithe and fit in his working gear of denims and shirt, much like those Luiz himself had been wearing earlier.

Karen kept her eyes front as the two men conversed. If this man was the ranch foreman, as seemed likely, he had been the one to employ Lucio Fernandas. Obviously, Luiz accorded him no blame. But then why should he? The man could hardly have foretold what was to happen.

'I think I'd like to go back now,' she said dully when the men departed. 'I have a headache coming on.'

It was no out and out lie, though Luiz's immediate solicitude made her feel guilty of deception.

'Of course,' he said. 'I should have realised that the Jeep would prove too jolting a ride for you.'

The Jeep had nothing to do with what was ailing her, but it sufficed as an excuse. Karen closed her eyes as he turned back along the track, hoping he would take the hint and not attempt to talk. She felt so utterly debased.

Luiz despatched her to rest again when they reached the house. She went without protest, needing some time alone to try pulling herself together.

The dull ache behind her eyes was no aid to clear thinking. Not that clarity of thought had any bearing when it came to pondering the imponderable. While her mind refused to release the memory of these past months she had to accept the situation as it appeared, regardless of how much she deplored it.

She was sitting at the window watching the sun slowly sink beneath the horizon when a knock came at the door. Expecting Luiz, she was surprised to see Beatriz enter the room in answer to her invitation.

The older woman closed the door and stood with her back to it, gazing hard-faced across the distance between them.

'What do you hope to gain by this act?' she demanded harshly.

'It's no act.' Karen was hard put to keep her voice from revealing her inner turbulence. 'I don't remember anything that happened these past months. Why should you doubt it?'

'Because I know how devious you are,' came the taut reply. 'If you hope...'

She broke off, biting her lip as if about to say something she hadn't planned on saying. 'Luiz was a fool for ever marrying you!' she spat.

'It was probably a foolish move on both our parts.' Karen drew a steadying breath, reluctant to ask the question yet unable to refrain from it too. 'Luiz tells me you suspected I was…seeing Lucio Fernandas.'

The expression that flickered across the other face was difficult to define in the lowering light. When the answer came it was in a subtly altered tone. 'Yes.'

'So why didn't you tell him?'

The pause was brief. 'Because I had no proof and feared his reaction. I had no choice but to tell him when you left.' Her tone hardened again. 'He should have let you go! You were never worthy to hold the name of Andrade!'

'So it seems.' Karen made a valiant effort to hang on to some semblance of self-respect. 'Unfortunately, Luiz doesn't believe in divorce.'

'But neither can he keep you here against your will.'

The light was almost gone. Karen reached out a hand to the table at her side and switched on the reading lamp, gazing across at her sister-in-law with drawn brows.

'You're suggesting I should leave again anyway?'

'The only honourable course,' came the answer. 'How can Luiz be expected to feel anything but disgust for you after what you did? What kind of life are you condemning him to by staying?'

'What kind of life would *I* have to look forward to if I did as you say?' Karen asked, doing her best to stay in control of her emotions. 'I've no home, no job. I'm not even sure I have enough, if any, money of my own left to get me back home to start with.'

'I could help you there.'

The offer came too pat to be anything but premeditated. Swept by a disgust of her own, Karen got to her feet, better to face the woman.

'For what purpose?' she shot back. 'Divorced or not, Luiz would never turn to you for solace.' She shook her head emphatically as Beatriz made to speak. 'This has gone far enough. I want you to leave. And in case there's any doubt left in your mind, *I'll* be staying.'

The striking features opposite were for a moment suffused with a fury that turned them almost ugly, tawny eyes glittering with hatred. When she moved it was abruptly, the door slamming in her wake.

Karen sank back into the seat she had vacated, the anger that had driven her to her feet overridden by shame that she had allowed herself to be goaded into retaliation.

Tomorrow was Saturday. The best time to catch Julie at home—once she'd discovered what the time difference between here and London was. Reluctant though she felt to put the question, she had to know what her friend might have been told. Only if she heard it from Julie's lips could she really start to believe there had been an affair.

CHAPTER FIVE

TIME differences in Brazil apparently differed by region. São Paulo was only three hours behind GMT, Luiz advised at dinner when asked. If she rang around eleven in the morning, she'd catch Julie at breakfast, Karen calculated. In the meantime, there was another night to be got through.

Luiz made no move to accompany her when she took her leave barely an hour after they finished eating. He seemed distant. Hardly to be wondered at, Karen supposed. He was still having difficulty coming to terms with their altered circumstances. How long it might be before he managed to set the knowledge of her apparent betrayal aside was anyone's guess. It might be never. Only if she could prove that there was no truth in it did they stand a chance of restoring all they'd lost—and how did she do that when all *she* had to go on was instinct?

She was still awake when he came to bed himself; she heard the movement from the next room. She'd tried the connecting door earlier and found it now unlocked, but she doubted if he had been the one to do the unlocking. Regina, at a guess. Her young sister-in-law would probably try anything to get the two of them together again.

A part of her wanted desperately to get up and go to him, but the fear of rejection was stronger. It had to be up to him to make the first move. For now, all she could do was deal with the need churning her whole body as best she may.

Morning brought rain. A downpour that lasted more than an hour and stopped as suddenly as it had begun. Viewing the still heavy skies from the veranda after breakfast, Karen wondered if there was more to come.

'It will clear,' Luiz told her. 'In a little while the sun will break through and the land will begin to steam. At least here the humidity remains at a bearable level. Rio is like a sauna in the rain.'

'It was bad enough even without it,' Karen returned, recalling the impact when she'd emerged into the open for the first time back at the clinic. 'I can't imagine how anyone manages to work in that kind of heat!'

'The offices are air-conditioned, the ones who work outdoors are accustomed to it,' he said. 'Do you plan to telephone your friend today?'

'As soon as I think she'll be up and about.' Karen stole a glance at him, uncertain of his mood. 'You don't object?'

The bronzed features remained impassive. 'Why should I object? Perhaps she will be able to shed some light on your memory.'

Having given the possibility some thought overnight, Karen doubted that she would have told Julie she'd been having an affair, in the certain knowledge of what her friend's reaction would be. All she could hope for was that there might be something Julie *could* tell her that would fire a spark.

The rest of the family had dispersed, leaving the two of them alone. Beatriz had had little to say for herself this morning, though her attitude certainly hadn't altered. Karen dismissed the woman from her mind. Right now, she had more important concerns.

Seated in one of the lounging chairs, legs thrust out before him, Luiz looked relaxed on the surface, but she could sense the tension in him. He was dressed casually in lightweight trousers and cotton shirt.

'Are you free all day today?' she asked tentatively.

'I'm free whenever I wish it,' he answered. 'My foremen need no supervision.' His head turned her way, gaze sliding over her face to linger for a heart-thudding moment on the vulnerable curve of her mouth. 'Your injuries are fading fast. Not that they could detract from your beauty even at their worst. I can blame no man for wanting you, but I'll kill any other who attempts to take you from me—as I would Lucio Fernandas should I ever catch up with him.'

The tone was almost conversational. Only in the depths of the dark eyes did the ferocity show. Karen drew a shallow breath.

'If I chose to have an affair with him, then the fault is just as much mine.'

'You say *if*?' Luiz's tone had hardened. 'For what other reason would the two of you have been travelling together? For what other reason would you have left at all?'

'I don't know,' she said wretchedly. 'According to what you told me back in the hospital, everything appeared normal with our marriage right up until the night before I left, but I'm sure it wouldn't have been if I'd been…sleeping with another man.'

'Meaning you would have been unable to respond to me physically?' Luiz slanted a lip. 'You give me little credit.'

Karen felt warmth rise under her skin beneath the sardonic gaze, a stirring deep in the pit of her stomach. Whatever the circumstances, he would have no difficulty at all in arousing her. He was doing it now without even trying, making her yearn for what she couldn't even remember.

'I meant in other ways,' she got out. 'There must have been *something*!'

The hesitation was brief. 'You've seemed withdrawn at times these last weeks, I admit. I assumed the moodiness was due both to the loss you'd suffered and the normal female cycle, but perhaps I was simply deluding myself.' He straightened abruptly, getting to his feet. 'Whichever, it's past and gone. What we have to deal with is the present. I'll leave you to make your call.'

It wasn't nearly time, she could have said, but she refrained, reluctant though she was to be left with only her thoughts for company. She watched him stride indoors, feeling the fast-becoming-familiar contraction in the region of her groin at the supple movement of his hard-packed thighs. The hunger in her owed nothing to memory, everything to instinct. She ached in every fibre.

She was still aching when Raymundo joined her some twenty minutes or so later, dropping into the chair vacated by his brother.

'You should not be left alone to brood,' he said. 'Not in your condition.'

Karen turned a blank look. 'Condition?'

'Your memory loss. It must be difficult for you.'

'It has to be difficult for everyone,' she returned, following it up with a faint smile. 'Apart from Regina. She won't allow it to be.'

'My sister adored you from the moment you arrived at Guavada,' he claimed extravagantly. 'As did everyone.'

Karen allowed herself an edge of sarcasm. 'Everyone?'

Raymundo gave a wry shrug. 'Sadly, my wife allows jealousy to impair her judgement. Until your arrival, she was the...'

'Queen bee?' Karen supplied as he hesitated over the term.

His smile was a little discomfited. 'Mistress of the household, I believe you would call it. Handing over that charge to you was hard for her.'

'She must have known Luiz would marry some day,' Karen protested, wondering if Raymundo could possibly be as blind to his wife's true feelings as Regina had made out.

'But perhaps to someone content to allow things to stay the same.'

'Which I obviously wasn't.'

The smile came again, wry this time. 'No. Nor, I think, would Luiz have been happy had you been. He loved your spirit as well as your beauty. He...'

He broke off, shaking his head in rueful recollection. 'I speak in the past tense. Luiz loves you still, I'm sure of it.'

'I take it Beatriz made no mention of her suspicions to you either?' Karen said after a moment.

'No.' He looked discomfited again. 'She told no one until Luiz found you gone. He was angry with her for keeping it from him, but all she had was suspicion.'

'Odd, that no one else appears to have had any notion.'

'Women are renowned for their intuition,' he said with a certain reserve.

Karen left it there, sensing that she wasn't going to get any further. The more she heard, the more she suspected that Beatriz might have somehow set her up. Proving it was another matter, but at the very least it gave her some hope.

Dubious though she was that Julie could be of any help, she still needed to speak to her. She was the only contact she had with home. It was only half past ten, but she could wait no longer.

'I have to make a phone call,' she said, getting up. 'Can I dial direct to England?'

'Providing you know your country code,' Raymundo confirmed. 'You may have some difficulty getting through. The lines are often busy.'

'I'll manage.'

She made her escape, heading back indoors. She reached her bedroom without running into anyone, closing the door before crossing to the telephone on the bedside table. So far as memory went, she'd last spoken to Julie the day before she'd woken up in the hospital. In reality, she had no idea just how long it had been.

As Raymundo had warned, it took a little time and effort to get the call through. Even when the connection was made, an age seemed to pass before the receiver was lifted. The voice on the other end of the line sounded sleepy.

'Can't a body have a lie in on a Saturday morning, for heaven's sake? It's not even eight!'

'Julie, it's me,' Karen said swiftly. 'Sorry about the time.'

'That's okay.' She sounded wide awake now, though still far from her normal vibrant self. 'How are you, Karen? It's been ages! My fault mostly, I have to admit. I changed my job. Just never got round to answering your last call. Anyway, how's it going? Still madly in love with that gorgeous Brazilian hunk?'

'Of course.' It was all Karen could say. It was obvious that she'd passed nothing at all on to the other girl, which meant there was little to be gained from telling her about her memory loss, with all the subsequent explanations, 'I just thought I'd give you a call,' she tagged on lamely. 'I must have miscalculated the time difference.'

'You're forgiven.' Julie was fast recovering from the guilt she apparently felt over her tardiness in making contact. 'What's the weather like over there? It's raining cats and dogs here!'

'Fine.' The last thing Karen felt like was an exchange of weather details. 'A good move, was it, the new job?'

'Sure was! I've met the most wonderful man! Not a patch on your Luiz, of course, but it's given to few of us to be quite *that* lucky in love! I must say, I thought you'd gone utterly mad when you rang to say you were never coming back, but then I thought you were utterly mad spending all your winnings on a trip to Rio in the first place. I'm just so glad it's all turned out so well.'

There was a pause, as if in anticipation of some response, a slight change of tone. 'Everything *is* all right, isn't it?'

If there had been any hesitation left in Karen's mind, it was banished now. 'Of course,' she said. 'Couldn't be better! I'm really happy you've found someone yourself, Julie. I hope it works out.'

The two of them chatted a while longer about general matters, parting on the promise to keep in more regular contact from now on. Karen replaced the receiver with a heavy heart, suspecting that the friendship would continue to slide. Not that she blamed Julie for neglecting to call. She had her own life to lead: a very full one, by all accounts.

What *she* had to concentrate on now was attempting to rebuild the relationship she'd destroyed by running away—whatever her reason for doing it. According to Raymundo, Luiz still loved her, but how could he know that? Luiz was unlikely to have confided his innermost feelings.

Without proof, there was no way she was going to convince him that there had been no affair; she couldn't be wholly convinced herself, if it came to that. So all she could do was try to wipe out the hurt. If that meant putting her pride on the line and risking rebuff, then so be it. One way or another, she was going to get this marriage back on track.

She went through the day in a fever of anticipation mingled with apprehension. The way Luiz made her feel, there was no physical barrier: desire, it seemed, transcended memory loss. She wanted his lovemaking, wanted desperately to be reminded of how it felt to be nude in his arms, to have his hands exploring her body, his lips seeking hers.

Just how deep her feelings had gone, there was no way of knowing, though it seemed unlikely that she'd have married him for sex alone, however wonderful.

On the other hand, even if her suspicions regarding the supposed affair turned out to be right, she still had to find a reason why she had left him.

She was getting nowhere with this, Karen decided wryly. If she didn't want to drive herself mad, she had to put the whole thing aside and start again from here.

With both Beatriz and Raymundo out for the evening, dinner was a more relaxed occasion—or would have been if she hadn't been on tenterhooks over her plans for later. The temptation to shelve everything and wait for Luiz himself to make another approach was great.

Keyed up, she knocked over her water glass, cascading liquid across the table.

'You seem tense,' Luiz remarked when the mopping up was done and order restored. 'Is your head troubling you again?'

'No, it's fine,' Karen assured him. 'I was just clumsy, that's all.'

'I've done the same thing myself on occasion,' chimed in Regina. 'At least it was only water.' She gave a girlish giggle. 'I once tipped a whole glass of red wine over a guest. She was most annoyed.'

'Understandably,' her brother returned drily. 'Her clothing was ruined.'

'Only because she refused to allow me to practise the remedy I read about and throw white wine over the stains,' came the unperturbed reply. 'One is supposed to bleach out the other. Have you heard of that, Karen?'

'Actually, yes,' Karen agreed. 'Although I can't say I've ever tried it.' She smiled at the younger girl, grateful for the intervention she suspected was designed to switch Luiz's attention. 'We'll have to experiment some time just in case.'

'What time shall we be expected at this barbecue tomorrow?' she added, looking for more diversion.

'Any time from noon onwards,' Regina answered. 'People arrive when they feel like it. The food will be cooking all day. You must not worry about seeing everyone. They will all do their utmost, I'm sure, to be at ease with you.'

Easier said than done from both sides, Karen reflected. Rather worse for herself, considering she would have a whole lot of names to fit to faces. Hopefully, everyone would speak at least some English, because her grasp of Portuguese showed little sign of returning as yet.

She could feel Luiz's eyes on her, penetrating her defences. Without glancing in his direction, she was vitally aware of his lean length, his breadth of shoulder and depth of chest. The tailored trousers he was wearing enclosed the essence of his masculinity: the part of him that had been a part of her, that had sown the seed from which the baby she had lost had begun to grow. It felt so strange to know that yet have no physiological concept of it.

Once again, Luiz simply said goodnight when she announced her intention of retiring around eleven. Karen went to her room still in a state of flux. It was only a bare four days since she had woken up to all this in the clinic. There was no denying the desire Luiz aroused in her, but was it enough on its own? Had it ever been enough?

While reluctant to believe that she might have married him on the crest of that particular wave, the possibility had to be faced that it was the lack of any deeper emotion that had caused her to make a break for freedom.

That the same reason might be given for seeking an affair was something she refused to contemplate. Whatever Lucio Fernandas had been doing on that plane, he hadn't been with her, she was certain of it.

She was in bed, though far from sleep, when Luiz

entered the next room. She lay listening to the faint
sounds, waiting for the silence that would tell her he
was in bed himself.

Even then, it was another half an hour before she
finally forced her limbs into movement, closing her
mind to the misgivings. Something had to be done;
they couldn't go on like this. If she hadn't loved him
with any depth before, she could learn to do it now.
In three short months, she'd hardly given it a chance.

She eased the door open as quietly as possible. The
room beyond was in darkness, the bed on the far side
lit only by a stray gleam of moonlight. Karen hesitated
on the threshold, fighting the urge to turn back. She
stifled a gasp when Luiz rolled over and sat up.

'What is it?' he asked. 'Are you ill?'

'No.' Her voice sounded thick. 'I thought…I
wanted…' She drew in another breath as he put out
an arm with the obvious intention of reaching for a
lamp switch. 'Don't put the light on, please!'

His arm fell back. Highlighting the white linen sheet
covering the lower half of his body, the moonlight left
the rest of him in shadow. Only when he leaned forward a little did she see that he was naked from at
least the waist up. Eyes adjusting, she viewed the dark
curls of hair across his chest with a leap in an already
racing pulse rate, feeling her nipples peak in what
could only be anticipation.

'You wanted?' he prompted after a moment.

'You,' she said before she could lose it altogether.
'I want *you*, Luiz!'

There was no immediate reaction. His skin looked
like oiled silk in the moonlight. Face still partially
shadowed, he gazed across at her. When he did speak
it was in low, controlled tones.

'Why?'

Karen's mind grappled with the unexpected question. Surely the answer was obvious.

'Because it's driving me crazy!' she burst out. 'Because I can't bear another minute of feeling the way you make me feel without doing something about it! I realise how difficult it must be for you believing I've been with another man, and I know you're not going to believe me when I say *I* know I haven't.'

'*How* do you know?'

'I just do,' she said. 'Call it instinct. Call it what you like.'

The pause was lengthy, his expression—what she could see of it—giving nothing away. 'You're suggesting that Beatriz was lying?' he said at length.

About to confirm, Karen bit the words back, settling for a compromise instead. 'Or simply mistaken.'

'Then how would you explain Fernandas's name on the passenger list?'

'I can't,' she admitted. 'I can't explain what *I* was doing on that plane, much less him! I suppose it's possible we'll never know, but if I'm to stay here—'

'There's no question of anything other,' came the harsh interruption.

Karen spread her hands. 'Fine. I accept that. Only we both have to make the effort to put things right between us. If you turn me down now...'

'You think me capable of it?'

He threw back the sheet, revealing his nudity all the way down. He was already fully and heart-jerkingly aroused. Karen felt her stomach muscles contract, the heat rush through her.

'You're right,' he said on a softer note. 'Our only recourse is to wipe the past from mind. Come.'

Heart thudding like a trip hammer, every nerve-ending in her body on fire, she reached the bed.

'Take off your gown,' Luiz instructed, still in the same tone. 'Let me see you.'

Karen reached for the thin straps with fingers that felt nerveless, sliding them down over her shoulders to let the heavy silk glide to the floor at her feet. She felt no reticence in revealing herself to him, only gratification at the look she saw in the eyes scanning every inch of her body.

He said something in his own language, the words foreign to her ears yet somehow understandable. When he held out a hand to her, she went willingly into his arms.

She had longed to feel those supple hands of his on her body, and he left no part of her untouched. She writhed in ecstasy beneath his caresses, opening herself to him with a wantonness she would never have believed herself capable of, clutching in a frenzy of sensation at the lowered dark head as he penetrated her innermost being.

She felt no reticence either in returning the caresses, pressing lingering, teasing kisses down the muscular length of him to bring him almost to the point of climax with the wicked use of tongue and teeth.

When he finally turned her under him, her legs wrapped themselves almost of their own accord about his hips, her whole body arching to the incredible feel of him sliding inside her, carrying her with him on a roller coaster ride to sheer heaven. She climaxed only a bare moment before he did, her cries mingling with his deep down groans.

'Has it always been like that between us?' she whispered when she could speak at all, hardly able to believe her own overwhelming passion.

Luiz lifted his head, eyes fathomless pools in the dim light. 'Perhaps not quite the same.'

'Meaning you had to teach me how to…respond?'

'Only in the sense of releasing you from the inhibitions covering your true nature.' He lifted a hand to smooth the tumbled damp hair back from her face, lingering to caress the smooth line of her cheek. 'The first time I took you was an experience I will never forget. You were so anxious to please me, so apologetic for your lack of experience, so unaware of what it means to a man to be the first to make love to a woman. You offered me your beautiful tempting lips to kiss, your lovely body to do with as I would.'

'When did you decide you wanted to marry me?' Karen murmured.

He gave a brief smile. 'I was captivated for life the moment I set eyes on you.'

'You really would have wanted to marry me even if I hadn't proved to be a virgin?'

'As I already told you on Corcovado, yes. The virginity was, as the Americans would say, the icing on the cake.'

'You're American yourself,' she said.

'*South* American,' he corrected. 'A world of difference!' His tone softened again as if in reminiscence. 'I only discovered your lack of experience when you revealed it in fear that you would be unable to satisfy me.'

Karen was silent for a moment or two, trying to break through the fog in her mind, giving up because it was a hopeless exercise. She brought her own hand up to lightly trace the lips that had given her so much pleasure, registering the desire building in her again without surprise. Whether what she felt for this man had been more than just a physical need before her memory loss, she still couldn't say, but what she was feeling right now surely went beyond it.

'There's no way I could ever have turned to another man while I had you!' she declared with passion. 'You have to believe it, Luiz!'

'We agreed to put the matter aside,' he returned on a resolute note. 'Until your memory returns, there is no other way.'

If it didn't return the question would never be answered, whispered a treacherous little voice at the back of her mind. Affair or no affair, *something* had moved her into taking flight.

She blanked the thought out as Luiz bent his lips to hers once more.

It was apparent from the way Regina regarded the two of them at breakfast that she had noted a difference in attitude this morning. Judging from the looks Beatriz directed their way, she was aware of it too, and not at all happy about it.

Karen forced herself to ignore the glances. She and Luiz might only have achieved a partial reconciliation last night, but it was a vital part. Recovering her memory could even be a bad thing in the long run, came the thought. What she didn't know couldn't hurt her.

'I must get down to learning the language again,' she declared. 'I obviously didn't find it too difficult before.' She gave a laugh. 'I bet I'm one of the few people to have to do it twice!'

'Very possibly the only one,' Luiz returned. 'You may even find your ear already attuned.'

'I'll help all I can,' offered Regina eagerly. 'Good morning is *bom dia*, good afternoon *boa tarde*, although you—'

'I think Karen may have already worked out the basics for herself,' her brother interjected drily.

Regina lowered her head, the quirk of her lips belying the apparent humility. '*Desculpe*,' she murmured. '*Me perdoe*, Karen.'

'There's nothing to be sorry for,' Karen answered, taking a guess at the meaning. 'Any help at all is welcome.'

'I was just going to say that you need no formal address to greet people who already know you,' her sister-in-law returned, casting a sly glance in Luiz's direction. '*Oi* will be sufficient.'

Meaning hello, Karen surmised, doubtful if she could produce quite the same sound. She still felt daunted at the thought of meeting these people Regina was speaking of, but it had to be done. At least none of them would be aware of what she'd really been doing in Rio.

She shelved *that* thought before it could get going.

Neither Raymundo nor Beatriz showed any interest in attending the barbecue. Karen felt more than a little impatient with her brother-in-law, who seemed totally under his wife's thumb. The antithesis of Luiz in character if not in looks.

The Ferrez home was a sprawling, single-storey villa set in grounds which for the most part appeared to have been left to prolific nature. There were already a dozen or more people there when the three of them arrived, the women dressed casually in shorts and sun tops as Regina had advised Karen to dress.

There was some awkwardness, but Karen had expected that. It was impossible for anyone to face a situation such as this with equanimity. She had mingled with these people for three months—had no doubt been hostess to similar gatherings at Guavada—yet not one face or name meant anything to her. Not everyone spoke English either, which didn't help.

Luiz stayed close at first. She did her best to cope when one of the men stole him from her side to discuss some matter or other, but she could feel the panic building inside her. These people were total strangers to her. How could she be expected to handle the situation on her own? Half the time she didn't even understand what they were saying!

In danger of losing what composure she still retained, she sought a few minutes respite in a quiet corner of the gardens. The sky was clear overhead, though cloud was gathering on the horizon. She found a seat on a stone bench, lifting her face to the sun, eyes closed against the glare. Her head felt as if it were packed with cotton wool.

'You have no drink,' said a voice.

Karen opened her eyes again with reluctance to view the man holding a wine bottle and two glasses. He had, she assumed, followed her. She sought her immediate memory for a name. Jorge Arroyo, if she had it right. Around Luiz's age, and good looking in a flashy way, he had struck her as a man with a pretty high opinion of himself. A man Luiz himself had little time for, she'd gathered.

'I've had enough to drink, thanks,' she declined. 'I just needed a little time on my own.'

The hint went unheeded. 'I sympathise with you,' he said. 'Even more so with Luiz. He was the envy of us all when he first brought you here, but he would, I think, as soon have lost you to another man than be cast so completely from mind.'

Convinced for a heart-jerking moment that he was referring to Lucio Fernandas, Karen only just stopped herself from blurting out a denial. She was hearing innuendo where none existed, she thought wryly.

'At least we're still together,' she said.

'But can it ever be the same for you?'

She lifted her shoulders, trying to keep a level head. 'As I can't remember what it was like before, that's hardly a question I can answer. Your English is excellent,' she added in an effort to steer him away from personal probing.

'We were able to converse in Portuguese just a short time ago,' he returned. 'The mind plays strange tricks.'

The 'we' disturbed her in its intimation that the two of them had shared many such conversations. There was something about the man that roused an instinctive wariness.

Luiz emerged from the shrubbery, taking in the little scene in one rapier glance.

'I've been searching for you,' he said tautly. 'Have you eaten?'

Karen shook her head, aware of his anger, and resenting it. 'Not yet.'

'Then you'll come now.'

She got to her feet, casting an uncomfortable glance in passing at the man who might not be there at all for what notice Luiz was taking of him.

'Why did you leave the others?' he demanded as they headed back along the path.

'I needed a respite,' she answered, equally shortly.

'Jorge followed you?'

Karen winged a glance at the set features, reluctant

to go on the defensive yet sensing a need to clarify the situation. 'I didn't ask him to accompany me, if that's what you're thinking.' She hesitated a moment before adding, 'Do you have something specific against him, or is it just a general antipathy?'

'It's enough for you to know that he isn't a man to be trusted,' was the short response.

She was going to get no more than that for certain, Karen acknowledged. She wasn't sure she wanted to know more anyway.

If anyone else had noted her absence, nothing was said. Food was both plentiful and excellent, the steaks the biggest she'd ever seen. She wondered if the meat came from Guavada.

'Most goes for export,' Luiz confirmed when she asked. 'But yes, we supply the surrounding areas. There's a small abattoir in the town.' Her involuntary wince drew a dry smile. 'A fact of life. The meat apart, the very sandals you're wearing owe their existence to animal hide.'

'I know,' she said. 'I know it's silly to be squeamish about it too, but I—'

'But the English love of animals extends itself to all species.' He paused a moment, viewing her with enigmatic eyes. 'Perhaps you'd like a pet of your own?'

Conscious of the tension still existing between them, she was taken aback by the offer. 'I'd love a dog,' she admitted. 'My parents always had one.'

'Then I'll see what can be arranged. Although you would have to teach it to stay away from the river. Alligators make no exceptions.'

'If there are alligators in the river, I'll make darn sure *I* stay away from it,' she said with feeling, realising just how much she had to relearn about her life here. 'What else do I need to look out for?'

'Cougars, rattlesnakes.' Luiz smiled again briefly at the look on her face. 'I tease you. Few people are faced with any heart-racing encounters.'

A foot lifted casually to rest on the edge of a wooden flower tub, shorts drawn taut across muscular thigh, he was heart-racing enough himself. Karen felt desire rising in her. She wished they were alone. Only then might they stand a chance of recapturing last night's togetherness.

'I think it's time we went home,' he said on a softer note.

Suggesting that he recognised her need was clear to him. That he was ready to set aside whatever doubts he still entertained to indulge his own need was also apparent. Not that she had any intention of denying either of them.

'What about Regina?' she asked.

'Someone will bring her.'

Dona Ferrez made no protests over their early departure, accepting Karen's plea of tiredness at face value. They had travelled here in the spacious leather-upholstered saloon that had brought them from the airport so few days ago. Head cradled against the rest as they headed back through the town, Karen contemplated the coming hour or two with growing fervour. Whatever else was missing from the marriage, nothing could take this away from them. Nothing!

CHAPTER SIX

WHILE the amnesia showed no sign of lifting in the main, Karen found herself picking up the basics of the language a great deal faster than she would have anticipated. Brazilian Portuguese was different from the European version. It was enriched by local Indian dialects, as well as African languages brought over in the past by slaves.

'Did I ever manage to get my tongue round the vowels?' she asked Luiz one evening, frustrated by her efforts to produce the right sound.

'Not quite,' he admitted. 'But it will come in time.' His expression had darkened a fraction. 'Everything becomes easier in time.'

Apart from the one thing they could neither of them put completely aside, Karen acknowledged.

'It might have been better for both of us if I'd never won that money,' she said wryly. 'If we'd never met.'

Luiz shook his head. 'I see no use in speculation of that kind. What we have, we live with.'

Brushing her hair at the dressing table, Karen watched him in the mirror as he slid into the bed. He always slept in the nude, and insisted that she did too. Not that she objected.

They'd made love every one of the past ten nights. Tonight would be no exception. Her period had to be due some time soon, she realised. It had always been around the middle of the month—although pregnancy might have altered her cycle.

Luiz hadn't mentioned the subject again, and she'd hesitated to bring it up herself. She wondered who the baby would have looked like. Had it been a boy or a girl?

Pregnancy. It was the first time she'd given a thought to the fact that Luiz never used any form of protection—and she certainly didn't. The brush suspended in mid-stroke, she considered the implications, her emotions too confused to be separated.

Propped against the pillows now, Luiz eyed her speculatively.

'Is there something you have to say?'

Her voice sounded husky. 'You think another baby would bring us closer again?'

'I think it could do no harm,' he returned without missing a stroke. 'There's no physical reason to wait.'

'We could have discussed it,' she said. 'You'd no right to make that decision on your own!'

Expression enigmatic, he said, 'You don't want a child?'

She caught herself up, biting her lip. 'That's not the point.'

'Then what is?'

'This whole situation!'

'The situation is what we make of it from now,' he returned. 'We agreed to a fresh start. Are you saying you no longer want that?'

'Of course I'm not! I just…' She broke off, lifting her shoulders in a wry shrug. 'I think it might be better to wait a while, that's all.'

'I disagree.' The tone was unequivocal. 'Are you coming to bed?'

Anger flared in her, jerking the words from her lips. 'Not just to provide you with a son and heir!'

She regretted it the moment she'd said it. Luiz hadn't moved, but his silence spoke volumes. She flung down the brush and got up to go to him, sinking down on the bed edge to lay her cheek against his chest. 'That was unfair,' she whispered.

He slid a hand into her hair to caress the nape of her neck, but she could feel the rigidity in him. 'If you don't feel ready,' he said.

'I do.' She lifted her head to look at him, putting everything she had into convincing herself as well as him. 'I want us to get back to where we were in the beginning. Anyway,' she added, trying for a lighter note, 'it could already be an accomplished fact. No use shutting the stable door after the horse has bolted!'

The smile that curved his lips failed to strike an answering spark in his eyes. 'No use at all,' he agreed.

Karen put her lips to the broad chest, allowing her instincts full sway as she kissed her way down to where the sheet lay across his hipline, thankful to feel his response. He was right. They had to carry on with their lives the way they would have done if there had been no disruption. Children were part and parcel of a marriage.

She could only hope the doctors had been right in their assessment of future risks.

The puppy Luiz brought in a couple of days later was a bit of a mixed variety with its roly-poly body, long tail and over-sized paws, but Karen was entranced from the word go. She named the little creature Samson to compensate for his lack of stature.

Beatriz, naturally, found everything wrong with having an animal of any kind loose in the house, although she tended to keep her opinions low-key when Luiz was within hearing.

'She just looks for faults to find,' Regina declared, enraptured herself with the new addition. 'Luiz said Samson was one of a litter of five. Perhaps I could have one of the others for myself.'

That would really give Beatriz something to complain about, Karen reflected.

'Would *you* ask Luiz?' Regina added ingenuously. 'He can refuse you nothing.'

Karen doubted that. Their relationship out of bed was nowhere near as clear-cut as it was in it.

'I'll try,' she promised. 'But don't count on anything.'

His response when she did put Regina's request that night wasn't immediately encouraging. His sister had never shown any interest in animals as pets before this, he said. It would just be an impulse on her part.

'If it did turn out to be, I'd happily be responsible for both animals,' Karen declared. 'But I think you're doing her an injustice.'

'You mean she's unlikely to change her mind?' he asked on an ironic note. 'There are a number of past occasions which would give the lie to that.'

'There's a big difference between passing fancies in boyfriends and this,' Karen protested.

'You believe so?' He studied her, his expression difficult to read. 'Regina idolises you. You must realise that. Where you lead, she will follow. A responsibility in itself.'

'I love her too.' Karen could say that with truth. 'Let her have the pup, Luiz. She'll look after it, I'm certain.'

He inclined his head. 'I'll leave it to you to tell Beatriz.'

'Coward,' she taunted lightly, and saw a glint spring suddenly in his eyes.

He took a swift step forward and swung her up in his arms, carrying her across to dump her face down on the bed, holding her there with a hand between her shoulder blades. 'Apologise, or pay the price,' he threatened.

Karen held up her hands in mock surrender. 'I apologise, I apologise!'

He turned her over but didn't let her up, humour giving way to a more potent emotion as he surveyed her lovely laughing face. It would have been like this in the beginning, Karen thought yearningly, meeting his lips: so different from the trials and tribulations of the past weeks.

Lying sated but sleepless later, she wondered if a psychiatrist might help her break through the block in her memory. Or even a hypnotist.

Yet did she really want to know the truth? came the sneaking thought. Whatever it was that had sent her careering off to Rio, it was in the past, and probably best left that way.

Luiz stirred, the arm curved about her waist drawing her closer against him. The very feel of him was a stimulus. She ran her fingertips along one taut thigh, feeling the muscle tense to her touch. He opened his eyes as she found him, his response immediate.

'I believed you satisfied,' he said softly.

'That was then,' she responded, 'this is now. It's your own fault. You shouldn't make it so fantastic!'

He gave a low laugh and rolled on top of her, joining the two of them together again in one fluid movement. 'You may live to regret your boldness,' he declared.

She may live to regret a lot of things, but never this! she thought.

Predictably, two healthy, lively pups left a certain amount of havoc in their wake. The household staff took a tolerant view, Beatriz anything but. More than once it was on the tip of Karen's tongue to suggest that she and Raymundo find a home of their own if this one no longer suited, but it was Luiz's place to make that decision, not hers.

The despondency she felt on receiving proof that she wasn't pregnant went deeper than she would have anticipated. Luiz appeared philosophical about it, but she sensed his disappointment.

'Supposing it never happens again?' she said. 'Supposing I can never give you a son to take over Guavada?'

'Better the positive than the negative outlook,' he returned. Eyes veiled, he drew her to him to kiss her. 'There's no shortage of time.'

Certainly no shortage of effort, Karen reflected, wondering how he was going to cope with several celibate nights, wondering how *she* was going to cope, for that matter.

It proved no problem because Luiz wouldn't allow it to be. There were pleasure zones still to be explored, she found. If she had one wish, it would be for them both to be able to say the words that really meant something, but there were too many unanswered questions for it to be likely. How could there be love where there was no trust?

* * *

March brought slightly cooler, though still pleasant temperatures, along with a sharp decrease in rainfall.

It was exactly six weeks since she'd woken up in that hospital bed, Karen realised one morning, checking the date; some four and a half months since she'd won the money that had totally changed her life.

The major part of that time was still a great big blank. She'd accepted the probability that it always would be. She still suffered the occasional nostalgic pang at the thought of what she'd left behind in England, but she had to admit that there was no comparison between the life she had led there and what she had here.

Her only real complaint was that she saw so relatively little of Luiz during the day. Apart from the time he spent out on the ranch, he had an office right here in the house equipped with enough technological paraphernalia to keep several businesses going. Unlike Raymundo, who was happy to sit back and allow others control of his affairs, he preferred full involvement.

'Maybe I could help out in some way?' she suggested one evening. 'I'm conversant with computers, and all that.'

Luiz laughed. 'I don't doubt your intelligence, but it isn't necessary.'

'Meaning you don't want me meddling in your affairs?' she responded on a note that drew a sudden line between the dark brows.

'Meaning I prefer to work alone. You surely have enough to occupy you. Especially now that you're driving again.' He studied her, the frown deepening. 'You find your life here boring?'

'No, of course not,' she denied. 'It's just so different from what I'm used to.'

'Your old life is almost six months past and gone,' he returned.

'Not to me,' she said. 'Or had you forgotten?'

She regretted the retort the moment the words left her lips, seeing his jaw harden. 'Joke!' she added in an attempt at humour that fell miserably flat.

'A very poor one,' he remarked. '*I* can forget nothing!'

'Luiz, I'm sorry!' Karen caught his arm as he made to turn away. 'I realise how hard it is for you too. I just…'

'You needed to hit out,' he finished for her as she broke off. 'I know the feeling well.' His lips slanted at the expression that sprang in her eyes. 'Not physically. You never had anything to fear from me in that sense.'

'I know,' she said, and saw the sardonic smile come again.

'You can't *know* anything about those three months.'

'I'm sure I'd sense it if I'd ever had cause to be afraid of you.' She was desperate to undo the harm she'd done. 'The same way I'd sense having been with any other man but you!'

For a lengthy moment he didn't move, searching her face feature by feature with an intensity that pierced her. Karen reached up to kiss him on the lips, putting everything she'd learned these last weeks into persuading the firmness to soften.

'I want you!' she whispered, abandoning all other trains of thought in the swift flaring of passion.

There was no verbal reply, just an answering flame in the dark eyes. Karen clung to him as he lifted her to carry her to the bed. This wasn't the answer to everything, but right now it was enough.

The pups showed signs of outstripping all expectations with regard to ultimate size. Banned from the house when Beatriz finally won the day after the pair of them ripped up a couple of rugs, they were given a new home in the grounds, complete with outside run and a kennel equipped, at Karen's demand, with heating against the chill of the coming winter nights. Regina had to a large extent lost interest in the animals, although she did play with them on occasion.

'I won't say I told you so,' Luiz remarked on finding Karen walking the two of them on her own one afternoon.

'You just did,' she returned. 'So you were right. It's no big problem.'

'It seems it might become a very big problem,' he said, assessing the difficulty she was having in controlling the pair. 'They're too strong for you now. How will you cope when they're fully grown?'

'They'll be trained by then,' she declared with more hope than faith. 'All it takes is perseverance.'

'Yes, I can see how well they're learning to obey you.'

The mockery lit a spark in her eyes. 'We can't all be despots!'

Dark brows lifted in sardonic amusement. 'A tyrant, am I?'

She had to smile. 'All right, so it was a bit over the top. Don't give Regina a hard time though. She'll think I've been complaining about her.'

'So you should,' he said. 'She puts too much reliance on your good nature.' He indicated that she hand over the leads. 'I'll walk them back to the compound and save a little wear and tear on your arm muscles.'

Karen obeyed, not in the least surprised when both animals followed the same impulse, falling into docile step at his side.

'You're not going to suggest Bruno goes, I hope,' she said tentatively. 'Samson would be lonely without him.'

'He can stay if you agree to let Carlos take the pair of them in hand.'

'Not if he's going to beat obedience into them. I won't have them cowed!'

'I'll make sure he treats them well.' There was a pause before he spoke again, his tone subtly altered. 'I have to go to Brasilia.'

'To see your mother?'

'I'll call on her while I'm there, but I have other business to attend to.'

Karen shot him a glance, drawn by some instinct she couldn't explain. His expression gave nothing away.

'How long will you be gone?' she asked.

'Two days, perhaps three. No more than that.'

'When?'

'Tomorrow.'

She swallowed on the sudden dryness in her throat, wondering if she was coming down with something. 'I'll miss you.'

His smile was brief. 'By night at least.'

It was a moment before she could find the words. 'You think sex is all I care about?'

'I think it plays a major part in our relationship,' he answered levelly. 'And always did.'

Karen forced herself to continue walking. 'You're saying I never felt any more than that for you?'

'I believe you convinced yourself that you did. I convinced myself for a time.'

'Until the day I proved otherwise by running out on you.' Her tone was as flat as his. 'You still believe I went off with Lucio Fernandas, don't you?'

'I can find no other reason,' he admitted. 'He left that same day without telling anyone he was going.'

She shook her head emphatically. 'There's no way I could have been drawn to a man of his type!'

'Many other women were. He was renowned for his conquests.'

'You've been making enquiries about him?'

'I needed none. His reputation was well-known.'

'But you still kept him in your employ.'

'Providing he does the job he's paid to do, a man's private life is his own.'

'Unless it encroaches on yours, of course!'

The sarcasm left him unmoved. 'True. Medical opinion appears to be that partial amnesia of the kind you're suffering from is the mind's way of blocking out what it doesn't want to remember. If the blockage is permanent, the only way I can ever be sure there was nothing between the two of you is to have him tell me so himself.'

'And how do you propose doing that, when you don't know where he is?'

'I've employed someone to try and trace him.'

Karen felt more than a flicker of apprehension. It was all very well to tell herself she wouldn't have gone near a man of the kind Lucio Fernandas appeared to be, but how could she be certain? How could she be certain of *anything*?

'I hope they succeed,' she said, knowing it was only a half-truth.

Luiz left the subject alone after that, but it was obvious that it was never going to stop preying on his mind. It had begun preying on her own again. Lucio Fernandas had been on the same flight on the same day after walking out on his job without a word to anyone. What other explanation was there?

They had people coming to dinner that evening. Nothing too formal, just a gathering of friends. Karen chose a slub silk skirt and sleeveless top, sliding her feet into high-heeled sandals. With the pups to exercise several times a day, she'd become accustomed to wearing flats. It felt good to stand tall again.

Her prowess in the language made socialising a great deal easier. If anyone felt any awkwardness over her amnesia these days, they hid it well.

Even Beatriz made some effort to conceal her feelings in company. Watching her surreptitiously as she conversed with the man seated next to her, Karen thought how different she looked when she smiled. There was no chance, she knew, of them ever becoming friends. She had the man Beatriz had really wanted. Nothing was going to change that.

Raymundo might appear to be oblivious of his wife's preference, but he couldn't be totally unaware. She often felt like telling him to stand up for himself when Beatriz was in one of her moods and finding fault with everything he said or did, but she held it back. Luiz had simply shrugged when she brought the subject up, and said it was up to Raymundo to command some respect. Beatriz certainly took no liberties with him.

Seated at the head of the table, the pure white silk of his shirt a foil for the olive skin of his face and throat, he made her ache. He was so wrong when he said sex was the driving force in their relationship. A vital force, yes, but there was so much more to the emotions he aroused in her now.

If she'd felt as deeply as this for him before, wild horses couldn't have dragged her away from him, she was sure. So what had made the difference?

With the night-time temperature a little too cool now for coffee out on the veranda, the party adjourned to one of the spacious living rooms. Conversation went on apace. Karen did her best to keep up, but her mind wasn't really on it. She didn't even know what time Luiz was planning on leaving tomorrow, she realised.

Regina came to sit beside her, her lovely young face lit by an inner glow.

'So what do you think of him?' she asked eagerly.

Karen brought her thoughts back to the here and now, wrinkling her brow in query. 'Think of whom?'

'Miran, of course. Miran Villota!'

Karen turned her attention to the young man in question. Miran was in his mid-twenties and extremely good-looking, with a dashing air about him scheduled to appeal to any girl. He was visiting the Ferrez's, hence his inclusion in tonight's invitation.

'He seems nice enough,' she pronounced.

'Nice!' Regina looked affronted. 'Is that all you can say?'

Karen kept her face straight with an effort. 'What else would you like me to say? I've only spoken with him a couple of times. Hardly enough to make an evaluation.'

'*I* find him excellent in every way,' Regina claimed. 'He lives and works in São Paulo, but he travels a great deal too. He knows so much of the world!'

'Is that what you'd like yourself?' Karen asked. 'To travel, I mean?'

'Of course. There are many places I want to see. I could do that with Miran.'

Karen held up a staying hand. 'Whoa a minute! You only just met him!'

'You told me you knew the moment you saw Luiz that he was the one,' came the rejoinder. 'I feel the same way about Miran.'

Nonplussed, Karen said cautiously, 'But does he feel the same way about you?'

The dark eyes glowed. 'He tells me so.'

'When did he do that?'

'When we were together at the table. He said I'm the most beautiful girl he's ever seen. He said he has never felt such an instant rapport before with anyone!'

Karen hardly knew what to answer. She'd noticed the two of them talking together once or twice, but had been too involved in the conversations going on around her to pay much attention.

'All the same, it's a bit soon to be thinking along the lines you're thinking,' she ventured.

'Why?' Regina demanded. 'It happened for you and Luiz, why not for Miran and me? I was never so certain of anything as I am of this!'

'You were certain you wanted a puppy not so long ago,' Karen pointed out, instantly regretting the remark. 'Sorry, that was unfair,' she apologised.

'Yes, it was.' Regina's chin was up, her eyes sparkling. 'Miran is not to be compared with a pet animal!'

'Of course not.' Karen hesitated, still not sure how

best to tackle the situation. 'I believe he'll be here for several days?'

'Four more days,' Regina confirmed. 'We're to meet tomorrow in La Santa for lunch together.'

It was hardly fair to dismiss her sister-in-law's feelings for Miran Villota out of hand, Karen decided. His either, for that matter. As a friend of the Ferrez family, he surely had to be trustworthy.

'I'll look forward to hearing more tomorrow then,' she said.

It was almost two in the morning before everyone left. Karen saw Regina and Miran exchanging meaningful glances on his departure, although there was no physical contact between them.

'I think it a good thing Miran will only be here for a few days,' Luiz commented as they prepared for bed, proving he hadn't been blind to the exchange either. 'He's no unseasoned youth.'

'He can't be all that much older than I am,' Karen murmured.

'In years, perhaps. In experience...' He left the sentence unfinished, his tone enough.

Definitely *not* the time to tell him what Regina had in mind, Karen reflected wryly. He might have gone overboard himself at one time, but he was unlikely to view Regina's captivation in the same light.

'Men tend to be, don't they?' she said, trying for a humorous tone. 'More experienced, I mean. You certainly were.'

He gave her an ironic glance. 'How can you be sure of that?'

She laughed. 'You wouldn't try claiming I was the first for you too?'

'Perhaps not. But I was always selective.'

'Perhaps Miran Villota has been too,' she said.

Luiz studied her thoughtfully. 'Why do you feel it necessary to defend him?'

'I'm just suggesting that you could be wrong about him, that's all.'

'An opinion based on a few minutes conversation?'

'I'm going on instinct,' she claimed. 'Feminine instinct.'

'Not always dependable.'

'What time will you be leaving in the morning?' Karen asked, wishing she'd kept her mouth shut.

It was obvious from his expression that he found the change of subject questionable, but he responded. 'My flight is at noon. I must leave here no later than eight-thirty.'

It was half past two now, which gave them a good five hours before they need get up, Karen calculated. She thrust all other thoughts aside as she slid into the bed alongside him, heart racing as always in anticipation when he turned to her. Little more than a brushing of his lips, the kiss left her high and dry.

He was asleep within moments, to judge from his breathing. Lying there in the darkness, Karen took herself to task for feeling deprived. So it was the first time he'd failed to make love to her in one way or another. There had to be a first time. With a lengthy drive to the airport ahead of him, he needed to be alert.

There was more to it than that, she knew. He hadn't liked her seeming defence of Miran. She'd been doing it for Regina's sake, but he wasn't to know that. In his eyes, the interest was hers.

She considered waking him to tell him it was nonsense, but it was probably best to let the whole thing lie. By the time he returned, Regina would hopefully have come to her senses, and Miran Villota could be forgotten by all.

It was a long time before she slept, and already well gone nine when she awoke. There wasn't much point rushing around in the hope that Luiz hadn't yet left, she acknowledged disconsolately. The house already felt empty.

Regina greeted her eagerly when she finally went down. She was still over the moon with regard to Miran, still convinced that she had found the love of her life.

'Today I tell him what I feel for him,' she declared happily.

Karen wondered just what his reaction would be. Everything Regina had told her he had said to her last night was no more than any man might say to any woman he was attracted to. Any Latin, at any rate. Yes, he'd asked to see her today, but it didn't add up to all that much. So far, they hadn't even kissed!

Regina was still starry-eyed when she returned from the lunch date, although a little disappointed that Miran had declined her invitation to come back with her. He had business to take care of, she said. They hadn't actually discussed the future yet. They'd had so much else to talk about.

'He is so wonderful!' She sighed. 'I told him how you and Luiz knew instantly that you were meant for each other too.'

'What did he say to that?' asked Karen tentatively.

'He thought it very romantic. As it was, of course. As it is now for the two of us!'

'So when are you seeing him again?'

'He is to telephone me to make the arrangement.'

Hardly the action of a man reluctant to be parted

from his loved one for longer than absolutely necessary, Karen reflected, though who was she to judge?

'You realise Luiz is unlikely to approve?' she said.

'Luiz can't stop me marrying Miran,' came the un-
daunted response.

He'd certainly have a darn good try, Karen thought.
Not that she was convinced it was any of it more than
pie in the sky as yet. The only way to find out what
Miran's feelings really were was to ask him outright,
and at the earliest opportunity.

How to get in touch was the problem. She could
telephone the Ferrez home and ask to speak to him,
but considering Luiz's attitude last night, and the possibility of his discovering she had made the call, that
might not be a good idea. Lucio Fernandas still
loomed too large in their lives.

The problem was resolved when she was called to
the phone herself that evening. Expecting it to be Luiz
on the line, she was nonplussed when the call turned
out to be from Miran.

'I have to talk with you,' he said urgently. 'About
Regina?' Karen asked.

'About Regina, yes,' he said. 'I can't discuss the
matter now. Someone might hear. Will you meet with
me?'

She hesitated, already suspecting the truth. 'You
should speak with Regina herself.'

'I can't do that. Please! I beg of you!'

Short of refusing point-blank, she was left with little
choice, Karen accepted resignedly. She should have
told Luiz what was going on last night and let him
sort it all out.

'All right,' she said. 'Where and when?'

'I have commitments in the morning, and for lunch,

but I'll be free by half past three. I'll wait at the market square. I must go now,' he added before she could answer.

Karen replaced the receiver feeling anything but happy with the arrangement. There was no market in town tomorrow, but there would still be plenty of people around the square. She was pretty sure what Miran was going to say. Regina had gained entirely the wrong impression, and he didn't know how to tell her.

Which meant she was probably going to get the job.

'Was that Luiz?' Beatriz asked.

Karen forced herself to turn without haste to view the woman standing a few yards away. 'Yes,' she said, realising she would have a hard time explaining if Luiz happened to ring while they were standing here. 'He had a good journey,' she added lamely.

Beatriz curled a lip. 'That is all he had to say to you?'

'No.' Karen was hard put to it to keep a civil tongue in her head. 'The rest is between husband and wife.'

'You can hide from the truth, but you can't escape it for ever!' Beatriz spat after her as she started to turn away.

It was something in her tone as much as the words themselves that pulled Karen up. The shaft of pain lancing her head was reminiscent of that day back on Corcovado when she'd first heard Beatriz's name mentioned. She swallowed thickly on the sudden blockage in her throat.

'What are you talking about?' she managed to get out.

The malice in the amber eyes was soul-searing. 'You think the business Luiz has in Brasilia concerns

Guavada. If you wish to remind yourself of what it does concern, you'll find the proof in his office desk.'

Karen stood rooted to the spot for several moments after Beatriz left her. Her head was gripped by a vice, her mind spinning in endless circles out of which no coherent thought emerged. When she did eventually move it was like an automaton obeying a programmed instruction.

She had only been in the office a couple of times these past weeks. Standing in the doorway, she surveyed the room with eyes blanked of all expression.

The big dark wood desk was by the window, flanked by others bearing various pieces of equipment. She crossed to it, ignoring the papers spread across the surface to start rifling through the drawers.

She found what she wasn't even sure she was looking for in one of the bottom ones. Face ravishingly lovely beneath gleaming coils of black hair, the girl portrayed was no more than eighteen. She held a child on her lap: a boy of perhaps two years old, his dark curly hair and emerging features only too recognisable.

The photograph gripped in her hand, Karen sank nervelessly into the chair as the fog finally lifted...

CHAPTER SEVEN

TALL and lean, shoulders broad beneath the close fitting white T-shirt, he drew every female eye in the vicinity. Karen was no exception. The lurch in the pit of her stomach as she took in the planes and angles of his face beneath the pelt of curly black hair needed no explanation. There was no shortage of good-looking macho males in Rio, but he was the first to have this effect on her on mere sight.

He paused in the restaurant doorway, surveying the crowded room without haste. Karen shifted her gaze back to her plate as his eyes came to rest on her, feeling the increase in her pulse rate. In a country where most women were dark-haired, her colouring alone made her stand out. She'd been subjected to several unwelcome approaches since she'd arrived in Rio. The price to be paid by a woman travelling alone.

Her stomach muscles jerked again as the *maître d'* appeared at her elbow.

'We have a problem, *senhorita*,' he said deferentially. 'This is the only table with a seat not taken. Would you allow Senhor Andrade the use of it?'

Karen didn't need to look beyond him to know who Senhor Andrade was. She could sense his presence. There was only one response she could make without appearing churlish—and churlishness was farthest from her mind right now.

'Of course,' she said.

The smile her new companion gave her as he slid

into the chair directly opposite was devastating. She could only hope her expression was as unrevealing as she tried to make it.

'This is very accommodating of you,' he said in excellent though heavily accented English. 'You're here on vacation?'

'Holiday,' she corrected lightly. 'In England we say holiday. And yes, I am.'

'Alone?'

Her chin tilted, green eyes acquiring a faint spark. 'Yes.'

'Rio is no place for a woman like you to visit alone,' he declared. 'Your hair alone is a beacon.'

'Maybe I should consider dyeing it,' she said with deliberate flippancy.

'That would be a crime in itself.'

He took the menu from the waiter who had just appeared and ran his eyes down it, reeled off the name of a dish and handed it back with a request for the wine waiter to attend.

'You will join me in a glass of wine?' he asked.

Be a bit of a tight fit, it was on the tip of her tongue to retort; she bit it back because humour of such an infantile kind was unlikely to be appreciated.

'Thank you, but I'm quite happy with the water,' she said, with a sudden notion that she was going to need to keep a steady head.

Dark as night, his regard gave her palpitations. She wanted to look away, but she couldn't, mesmerised by the tiny amber sparks deep down in the blackness.

'My name is Luiz,' he said. 'The management will vouch for me if you find it necessary.'

'Why might I find it necessary?' she asked, and saw

the firmly moulded mouth take on a curve that set her pulses racing all over again.

'Why indeed?' The pause was brief. 'You still have to tell me your name.'

'It's Karen Downing.'

'Karen.' His voice caressed the word. 'You're very beautiful. Too much so to be alone by anything but choice. Is there no man in your life?'

Not until now, came the unbidden thought.

'I'm footloose and fancy free,' she quipped, trying to keep a grip on herself. 'To travel alone is to travel fastest!'

'Have you been long in Brazil?'

'Just three days. I've wanted to visit Rio ever since I first saw it in a travelogue.'

'And does it meet with your expectations?'

'The scenery certainly does. I went up Sugar Loaf yesterday. The view is tremendous!'

'The view from Corcovado is even more spectacular,' he said. 'I'll drive you up there this afternoon through the rainforest.'

Karen gazed at him with lifted brows, fighting the mad inclination to just go along with anything he suggested. 'You're taking rather a lot for granted.'

'No more than my senses tell me should be taken.' The tone was soft, his gaze spellbinding. 'You'd deny the attraction between us?'

'We only just met,' she protested faintly.

'But we were destined to meet,' he said. 'I've waited many years for this moment—this certainty. You feel it too.'

Right now, Karen wasn't sure *what* she felt. Her head was spinning. He was right about the attraction—

her every sense was fired by it—but giving way to it was another matter.

'I really don't think—' she began.

'Then don't think,' he cut in. 'Just follow what your heart tells you. You want what I want. *Everything* I want! I see it in your eyes.'

Coming from any other man, she would have called that the most supreme egotism, but what he said was too close to the truth to be dismissed that way. She'd been attracted to men on occasion, but never physically aroused as she was right now. Her skin felt as if ants were crawling over it, her insides turned fluid.

Go with it, an inner voice urged. Live dangerously for once!

She gave a slightly shaky laugh. 'As a line, I have to admit it's a good one!'

'I speak no line. Only what I feel. You stir me the way no other woman ever stirred me.'

'Why?' she queried helplessly.

'Your beauty alone could be reason enough, but I sense a great deal more to you than that. Fate brought you here to Rio for a purpose.'

'A lottery win brought me here,' she said on as pragmatic a note as she could manage. 'I could never have afforded it otherwise. It will almost all be gone by the time I get home, so if it's money you're after...'

She broke off as amusement danced in his eyes. 'You think I appear in need of money?' he asked.

'No,' she admitted. 'I just thought I should make it clear.'

'I take due note.' Amusement still gleamed. 'The allure is more than sufficient as it stands, I assure you.'

Gazing at him, Karen knew a sudden devil-may-

care surge. Luiz Andrade was like no other man she
had ever met—like none she was ever likely to meet
again. Practised in the art of seduction for certain, yet
she somehow trusted him.

'Shall I need to change?' she asked. 'For the drive,
I mean.'

Viewing the sleeveless lemon top outlining firm
breasts, he shook his head. 'You're perfect just as you
are.'

Karen had enjoyed seeing Rio on her own, but not
nearly as much as with Luiz for a guide. She found
herself telling him just about her whole life story, and
hearing many details of his.

After completing the business that had brought him
to Rio, he had decided to take a few days to himself
before returning home, moving into the hotel that very
morning. A man of some means, she gathered, reading
between the lines. Wealthy enough to have little need
of finding a rich woman to fleece, for certain.

'You must have thought me very gauche to come
out with an accusation like that,' she said ruefully at
one point.

'I found your lack of conceit in suspecting money
might have a bearing on my interest utterly delightful,'
Luiz returned. 'You have no real concept of the effect
you have on a man, have you?' he added.

They were alone on the highest of the Corcovado
platforms, immediately beneath the towering figure of
Christ. Karen felt her throat dry as he slid a hand beneath her hair to tilt her face to his.

The kiss was gentle at first, almost playful, lips
brushing, nibbling, teasing hers apart. She was lost to
everything but the feel of him, the masculine scent of
him, the warmth spiralling through her body.

The silky touch of his tongue sent a shudder rippling down her back, inciting a response she couldn't, and didn't want to, control. She slid her arms about his shoulders, fingers seeking the curl of hair at his nape. Somewhere in the back of her mind she regretted her lack of high heels to bring the lower half of her body into closer contact with his: a need fulfilled when he drew her up to him.

He was aroused himself, but still in control, the proof of that in his failure to take further advantage of her inflamed emotions. Karen came back to earth with a thud as he put her firmly from him.

'Tonight we dance together,' he murmured.

'You're taking a lot for granted again,' she got out.

A wicked sparkle lit the dark eyes. 'I speak of the Samba. In Rio, everyone dances the Samba!'

Karen had to smile. The Samba might come first, but she knew where the day was going to end—knew where she wanted it to end. What happened after that she couldn't find the will to care.

It was already approaching eight o'clock when they returned to the hotel. Back in her luxurious room, she took a shower and donned a simple blue sheath of a dress for the evening, adorning it with the single strand of small cultured pearls that had been her mother's.

Falling from a central parting, her hair framed the pure oval of a face too familiar to her to be viewed with any overriding vanity. It appealed to Luiz. That was all that mattered. She only hoped she didn't disappoint him too much in other ways when the time came.

They ate dinner in one of the hotel restaurants, continuing on from there to a private club. Devastating in a white tuxedo, Luiz guided her through a whole selection of Latin American dances, creating havoc with a tango that had her moulded to his body like a second skin.

'If they could see me now!' she quipped breathlessly when the music stopped.

'If who could see you now?' Luiz asked, still holding her close.

'Friends back home. They'll never believe I did that!' She gave a laugh, eyes sparkling up at him. 'I can hardly believe it myself! It was so...'

'Sensual?' he supplied as she searched for the right word. 'It's meant to be. The prelude to lovemaking.' His voice was low, his gaze intent on her face, his expression leaving nothing to doubt. 'I want to make love to you. I ache for it!'

'Me too,' she whispered, abandoning what little emotional control she had left.

He kissed her then, ignoring the others on the floor. Karen returned it without reserve. She knew no embarrassment on feeling knowing eyes on them as he led her from the floor. So what if people did guess where they were heading? It happened the world over.

It was almost one o'clock when they reached the hotel. By silent consent they went to her room. Karen knew a momentary misgiving as Luiz quietly closed the door, but it vanished as he took her in his arms to kiss her with overriding passion.

He undressed her with dexterity, caressing each freshly exposed portion of her body. Her breasts filled his palms, nipples small and pink. She cried out at the exquisite sensation when he took them between his lips.

Stripped himself, he was everything she had imagined: skin taut over smoothly honed muscle, chest lightly covered in curling black hair, hips lean and hard, the proud manhood shortening her breath. She wished desperately that she was experienced in love-making, knowledgeable in the sexual arts.

'Is it possible that this is your first time with a man?' he asked softly, sensing the constraint in her.

'Yes,' she confessed. 'I'm sorry to disappoint you.'

'Disappoint me!' He added something in his own language, eyes charged with those sparkling amber lights. 'That you could never do. Surrender yourself to me! Let me show you the way!'

From that moment time dissolved. All she knew was sensation after rippling sensation as Luiz introduced her to erogenous zones she hadn't even known her body possessed. Reticence withered and died beneath the skilful caresses, a sensuality she had never dared acknowledge before prompting her to answer in kind. Exploring him as he was exploring her, to fetch the breath hissing through his teeth and glory in the power.

When the moment came, she was so aroused she felt barely any pain at all as he carved a passage to the molten centre of her body. The feel of him inside her went beyond anything she had ever imagined, filling her, claiming her. She almost passed out at the peak, body arching as spasm after spasm shook her.

Supporting himself on bent elbows, Luiz looked down into her drowned face with gratification.

'You belong to me now,' he said. 'For all time! I'll allow no other man to know you. We'll be married as soon as it can be arranged.' He smiled as her eyes flew open in shock. 'You must know what I feel for you. What you feel for me. There can be no other way.'

'I'm only here for two weeks,' she whispered, unable to believe he really meant it. 'My home is in England.'

'You have no family to draw you back there.'

'I have friends.'

'And they mean more to you than what exists between us?'

'This is just…physical,' she got out. 'I'm sure you've felt the same way over other women.'

Dark eyes blazed in repudiation. 'Never! Neither can you have ever felt this way for another man, or you would have already given yourself.'

He put his lips to hers again, robbing her of the ability to think straight—even to think at all. His tongue slid silkily into the softness, making her quiver as passion rose in her once more.

'You see,' he murmured when the world had stopped spinning again. 'We belong together. Can you deny the strength of our feelings?'

Karen couldn't, and had no desire to. What kind of fool would she be, she asked herself, to turn her back on the only man she'd ever met who could make her feel this way? A man who wanted far more than just her body. What did she really have back home to return to? Friends might miss her for a while, but they had lives of their own to get on with.

Luiz read the response in her eyes, his own registering a depth of emotion that shook her to the core. She drew him down to her to kiss him with tremulous intensity, closing out the reservations nibbling at the corners of her mind.

There were moments during the days following when those reservations surfaced again, but one look at Luiz was enough to push them back under. He was so much the macho male. She felt protected, cared about—all the things she'd missed so much these past four years since her parents had gone.

The phone call home to tell her flatmate she wouldn't be returning was received with initial disbelief. How could she possibly marry a man she'd known such a short time, and a foreigner at that? Julie demanded. What about her job, her belongings, her whole life?

Apart from certain mementos, nothing was important compared with Luiz, Karen told her, refusing to acknowledge even the faintest doubt.

If Luiz entertained any doubts of his own, he gave no sign of it. They spent the days doing all the things Karen had planned to do: visiting the sights, lounging on the famous beaches, swimming in the warm blue sea. At night they made love, each time better than the last. For Karen it was a dream world where nothing could intrude. She floated on air.

The wedding, a civil ceremony, took place just a week after her arrival in Rio. There would be a church blessing when they were home in São Paulo, Luiz had promised.

He wanted it this way, he said when she asked why they didn't wait until they got to São Paulo to get married, which made her suspect him of presenting a probably disapproving family with a *fait accompli*. Not that she allowed the suspicion to affect her. She was marrying the man, not the family.

Only on completing the formalities did it strike home that she'd really and truly burned her boats. Karen Downing was no more. In her place stood

Senhora Andrade, wife of a man still a stranger in many ways.

'Do your brother and sister know about the wedding yet?' she asked that night after their tumultuous love-making.

'They do,' Luiz confirmed.

'But they didn't want to be here for it?'

'Regina wanted to come,' he admitted, 'but I forbade her to travel alone.'

'And your brother?' she said after a moment.

There was a brief pause before he answered, his tone dispassionate. 'Raymundo allows himself to be ruled by his wife's opinions.'

Karen kept her tone light. 'Something you'd never do!'

'Ruled, no,' he agreed. 'Beatriz might form some respect for her husband if he began making his own decisions.'

'I take it, then, that your sister-in-law is the fly in the ointment,' she said.

His laugh was dry. 'If that means she is the one least likely to offer you a welcome, then yes. Not that you must allow her to undermine your position. You will be head of the household.'

'Under you, of course,' she murmured in mock humility.

He rolled on to his back to pull her on top of him, eyes glinting up at her as he fitted her to him. 'Not always,' he said.

Karen gave herself over to the exquisite sensations, loving his mastery. No regrets, was her last fading thought.

She would have preferred a little more time with

Luiz on his own, but he didn't give her the option. They travelled to São Paulo the following day.

After the heat and humidity of Rio, the drier, milder climate of the São Paulo plateau was a wonderful relief.

'Happy?' Luiz asked as they drove away from the airport in the car he'd left there on his departure.

'Blissfully!' she said. She hesitated before adding, 'I'll be even happier once I've got the meeting with your family over.'

'They'll love you,' he declared. The glance he turned her way was heart-warming. 'They can do no other!'

'You're biased,' she teased.

Luiz looked her way again, eyes skimming her glowing, sun-bronzed face, the silver fall of her hair, the smooth line of her throat revealed by the open collar of her cream silk shirt.

'I adore you,' he said. 'Every inch of you!' The wicked sparkle danced in his eyes. 'And I *know* every inch of you!'

She could verify that, Karen thought, senses fired by the mere memory of last night's excesses. She had believed they'd already reached the pinnacle, but he'd proved her wrong. She watched his hands on the wheel, lean and long fingered, the nails trimmed short and smoothly filed, wrists supple. Those hands alone had afforded her more pleasure than she had ever thought possible.

Tonight they would share a bed again, but first she had to contend with meeting her new relatives. From what Luiz had said, his sister-in-law was the only one unlikely to extend a welcome, but the marriage would have been a shock for them all. She could hardly blame Regina and Raymundo if they held back too.

Expecting more of a village than a town, she found La Santa enough of a surprise, but the house and landscaped grounds took her breath away. Knowing Luiz was no pauper was one thing, realising that the ranch probably formed only a part of his assets quite another. She was married to a man of means way beyond her imaginings.

Regina greeted her with open arms, her lovely young face lit with pleasure and excitement.

'Luiz said you were beautiful,' she exclaimed, 'but never have I seen hair the colour of yours before!'

'Inherited from my mother,' Karen told her, warmed beyond measure by the reception. 'I always wanted a sister. Now I have one!'

'And a brother,' said Raymundo, coming forward to kiss her on both cheeks. 'Welcome to Guavada!'

He seemed genuine too, Karen thought, smiling back at him. Odd that someone who looked so much like Luiz could leave her totally unstirred.

The woman at his back made no attempt to offer an embrace. Her striking features were expressionless.

She said something in Portuguese, drawing a frown from Luiz.

'Karen has no knowledge of the language yet,' he said. 'We'll all of us speak English alone in her company for the present.'

'I want to learn the language,' Karen protested.

'Which you will,' he said. 'In time.' His smile was for her and her alone. 'We have a lifetime ahead of us.'

A lifetime in a country she knew next to nothing about, with a man she knew little more about, came the thought, pushed hastily to the back of her mind where it could do least harm.

Her spirits lifted again in the privacy of the bedroom when Luiz took her in his arms to welcome her home his own way. *This* was what counted the most, she told herself.

She clung to that thought during those first days. Adjusting to a lifestyle totally different from what she was accustomed to proved far from easy. She suffered badly from homesickness at times.

With a manager to oversee the day-to-day running of the ranch, Luiz hardly needed to be involved in any physical sense himself, but he was often out riding the range with the men—even turning his hand to manual labour on occasion.

'I enjoy it,' he said simply when Karen questioned the necessity. 'It fulfils me. A different kind of fulfil-ment,' he added, seeing the expression in her eyes. 'Not to be compared.'

'I should hope not,' she said, doing her best to be rational about it.

He laughed, gathering her to him to kiss her with undiminished ardour. 'As if anything could possibly compare with the pleasure you give me!'

Maybe not in the same way, came the thought, but she was still only a part of his life.

He had been the focus of hers back in Rio, blinding her to everything else. Here at Guavada, she was be-ginning to realise the enormity of the step she had taken. Abandoning the country of her birth to live a life totally alien to her with a man she barely knew had been utterly crazy.

Not that the emotions he aroused in her were any

less intense. He only had to turn those glittering dark eyes on her to have her on fire. In his arms it was easy to convince herself that just being with him made everything worthwhile. As a lover, he was all she could ever have wished for.

A draw though his masculine assertiveness had proved in the beginning, and still was to a degree, there were times when she found it just a little overpowering too. Accepting his offer to teach her to drive instead of opting for proper lessons proved a less than sensible move.

'I read somewhere that driving lessons can spell death to a marriage,' she remarked on one occasion, trying to inject a little humour into a particularly heated exchange.

'Call me what you just called me one more time, and it's certainly death to this!' Luiz threatened, obviously not in the least amused. 'I'm not one of your English wimps!'

And I'm not one of your Brazilian doormats, it was on the tip of her tongue to retort. She bit it back because she'd not only yet to meet a woman here who could be termed a doormat in any sense, but had to admit that he had some cause for complaint over the invective she'd used just now.

'I just lost my temper for a moment,' she said placatingly.

'Then you had better learn to keep it,' he responded, the anger still glittering in his eyes.

Humour came to her rescue again, lowering her eyes in mock humility. 'I beg forgiveness,' she said.

There was no immediate response. She peeped at him from beneath her lashes, to see his mouth take on a somewhat unwilling curve.

'You,' he said, 'have no respect. I must teach you some.'

They were parked in the centre of town, with people thronging the pavements either side. Karen widened her eyes at him. 'Here?'

'Later,' he promised, unable to sustain his displeasure in the face of the emerald sparkle. 'We'll continue with *this* lesson for now.'

Lesson number one in handling her Brazilian, Karen reflected drily, putting the car into motion again: always make allowances for dented male pride, even if it did go against the grain.

Her relationship with Regina progressed by leaps and bounds. At seventeen, her sister-in-law was a romantic who found her brother's marriage in total accord with the novels she read so avidly. The heroes and heroines always finished up living happily ever after, Karen gleaned. She hoped that could be true of her and Luiz too eventually.

Attempts to get through the barriers Beatriz had erected against her met with little success. The woman treated her with open contempt when Luiz wasn't around.

'Does Raymundo have no assets of his own?' she asked Regina once.

'Of course he does,' the girl responded. 'He was left well provided for. He loves Guavada too much to make his home elsewhere.' She slanted a glance. 'Luiz would make him go if you asked it.'

'I wouldn't dream of it,' Karen denied.

'Not even to have Beatriz gone too?'

Karen gave a wry smile. 'A temptation, I admit. Why does she hate me so much?'

'Can you not guess? She would have liked to marry

Luiz herself. She took advantage of Raymundo's feelings for her to secure at least the name. Deep down, he has to know it, but she still has him in her grip.'

If that was true, and not just the product of Regina's fertile imagination, it would certainly explain a lot, Karen reflected. If it *was* true, she could feel some sympathy for Raymundo. He might be weak, but he deserved better than to be used.

With that in mind, she went out of her way to be nice to him. Away from Beatriz, he was a different person, with a sense of humour Karen delighted in drawing out.

'You and Beatriz don't really seem to have all that much in common,' she commented lightly one time when the two of them were on their own.

'No,' he agreed on a wry note. 'I can never be everything Beatriz desires.'

'You're happy to accept that?' Karen queried tentatively after a moment.

'I have no choice,' he said. 'Luiz would never sanction divorce.'

It isn't up to Luiz, Karen wanted to say, but she held it back. 'You must have loved her when you married her,' she ventured.

'I was possessed by my craving,' he admitted. 'I knew even then that it was Luiz she really wanted, but I believed I could satisfy her. It…' He broke off, expression rueful. 'I shouldn't be saying such things to you.'

'You obviously need to let it out to someone,' she said. 'Does Luiz know how you feel?'

'No.' Raymundo looked alarmed. 'You must say nothing to him!'

'I won't,' she assured him. 'But you should.'

'To what purpose?' he asked. 'I know what his answer would be.'

'That you've made your bed and must lie on it?'

A faint smile flickered at the corners of her brother-in-law's lips. 'Perhaps not in quite the same words, but the message would be the same.'

'It's *your* life, not his!' Karen was incensed. 'He has no right to tell you what you can or can't do!'

'He has the right to insist that I leave Guavada,' came the reply. 'And that I would hate.'

He closed up after that, obviously regretting having confided in her to such a degree. Karen felt both sorry for and impatient with him. Luiz may be a bit of an autocrat in some respects, but she doubted if he'd react the way Raymundo feared, regardless of his views.

Although La Santa wasn't lacking in entertainment, their social life tended to be centred more around friends and neighbours. While most appeared friendly enough on the surface, it was apparent that the marriage was looked upon with disfavour by some. Not everyone in the area spoke English, which didn't help. With her grasp of Portuguese still in its infancy, Karen was only too happy to find someone other than the Andrades themselves to converse with at one of the frequent gatherings.

Jorge Arroyo was a man of independent means, from what she could gather. He had a studio in La Santa where he dabbled in the arts, to put it in his own words. Some two or three years younger than Luiz, he had an appealingly free and easy attitude to life.

'Luiz's return with a bride ruined many hopes,' he said. 'He could have taken his choice from those still unwed. Not that any could have matched you. I yearn to capture you myself! On canvas, of course,' he added with a devilish sparkle in his eyes.

'Of course,' Karen echoed, smiling herself. 'What does one of your portraits cost?'

'There would be no sale,' he said. 'I would keep it for my eyes alone.'

'I don't somehow think Luiz would go along with that,' she responded, still in the same light vein.

He gave a mock sigh. 'I think you may be right. Luiz has little appreciation of my talents. He won't like it that you speak with me.'

Green eyes acquired a sudden spark. 'It's up to me to decide who I talk to!'

'Then I look forward to many other conversations,' he said.

He was stirring it, she thought, catching the devilish look in his eyes again as he turned away to answer some question put to him by one of the other men. Whatever his reason, she shouldn't have allowed him to provoke her.

Luiz was with a group of people a short distance away. She went to join him, slipping her hand into his, and aiming a general smile at the others. They would have been conversing in Portuguese of course, she realised, as the pause stretched.

'Do carry on,' she invited, determined not to show any discomposure. 'It's the only way I'm going to learn the language.'

'It would help you to take proper tuition,' said one of the women, not unkindly.

'I suppose it would,' Karen agreed. 'What do you think, Luiz?'

'It could do no harm,' he returned.

Karen looked at him swiftly, registering a certain

terseness in his voice. It was possible that Jorge was right, she thought, noting the tension in his jaw: he'd seen her talking with the man, and hadn't liked it. If so, it was unfortunate. She might regret what she'd said to Jorge, but she stood by the sentiment.

Luiz waited until they were home and in the privacy of the bedroom before confirming her guess. 'You'll avoid any further association with Jorge Arroyo,' he said flatly the moment the door was closed.

Half prepared though she was, Karen bristled instinctively at the tone. 'Why?' she demanded.

'It should be enough that I say so.'

'Well, I'm afraid it isn't. All I was doing was talking with the man!'

The glance he gave her was lacking its usual warmth. 'You were not just talking with him, you were flirting with him.'

'*He* was flirting,' she retorted.

'With your encouragement.' Luiz held up a hand as she made to speak. 'I want no debate.'

'Don't treat me like some second rate citizen!' she flung back. 'Where I come from, we have equality!'

He lifted a sardonic eyebrow. 'Where you come from, men have given up their right to be called men. I expect my wife to do as I ask.'

'You're not asking me,' she shot back, 'you're *telling* me!'

'So, I'm telling you.' He hadn't even raised his voice. 'You're to stay away from Jorge Arroyo.'

He turned away to head for the bathroom, leaving her seething.

She was in bed with her back turned to the centre when he returned to the room. He always slept in the nude, and she'd learned to do so too. Donning a night-dress was a gesture meant to convey her rejection.

He slid into the bed behind her without speaking. Furious though she still was, mind had little control over matter she found as his hand slid around her to seek her breast.

'Leave me alone!' she said between her teeth. 'I don't want you!'

If he'd been angry with her a few minutes ago, it obviously no longer reckoned with him. The feather-light pressure of his lips down her spine made her tingle.

'I think you lie to me,' he said softly.

She attempted to stay the movement down the length of her body to the hem of the nightdress, but he simply laughed and continued, sliding up beneath the material to find the moist centre of her being.

'Other men may desire you, but no other will ever know you this way,' he declared. 'You belong to me, and only to me!'

Body on fire, she could summon no further resistance when he drew her around to remove the gown. His lips were passionate, driving every extraneous thought from mind.

It was only afterwards, lying sleepless in his arms, that she gave way to the little voice that had been nibbling at the corners of her mind for some time. Luiz didn't love her. Not the way she'd imagined he did. She was just another possession.

CHAPTER EIGHT

ATTENDED by family and close friends, the blessing of the marriage took place at the town's magnificent church. The civil ceremony had been binding in the legal sense, but this one tied an even tighter knot. Not that she had anything to complain about, Karen acknowledged. With a wonderful home, no financial worries, and a sex-life most women would give their right arm for, she could be said to be in clover.

Confirmation of her pregnancy brought mixed emotions. It had been odds on that it would happen, of course, as no steps had been taken to stop it, but she somehow hadn't given it a thought up to now.

Luiz greeted the news with gratification. 'This won't be our only child!' he declared.

'I wouldn't want it to be.' Karen made an effort to sound as uplifted as he so obviously was. 'If this one is a boy, I'd hope the next one would be a girl.'

He laughed and shook his head. 'Two sons first. *Then* you may have a daughter.'

'I realise you're pretty strong-minded,' she returned with a slight edge, 'but some things even you can't govern!'

Luiz smiled the slow intimate smile that never failed to stir her. 'I can but try.'

Regina was delighted about the baby too, though also a little despondent.

'I think I'm destined never to meet a man I can love!' she declared soulfully.

'You're only seventeen,' Karen returned. 'You've plenty of time. Someone will come along one day and sweep you off your feet!'

'The way Luiz did with you! How did you know he was the one?' the younger girl insisted. 'What made him different from other men?'

Karen sought a light response. 'He's Brazilian.'

Her sister-in-law pulled a face. 'Now you joke with me!'

'Only a little.' Karen kept the smile going. 'I suppose it was his looks, his manner, the things he said.'

'What kind of things?'

'You'll find out for yourself one day.'

Regina laughed. 'I look forward to it! I look forward to the baby too,' she added with renewed enthusiasm. 'Shall you choose English names?'

'I doubt if your brother would go along with that.'

It was more than likely true, Karen reflected. She was married to a Brazilian, the child would be a Brazilian. Luiz had already suggested that she apply for citizenship herself, but she had dismissed *that* idea out of hand. The last thing she intended giving up was her nationality.

He'd accepted the refusal with good grace, she had to admit. But then, that was one thing he couldn't lay down the law about.

Reluctant though she'd been to give way to his demand, she'd steered clear of any further one-to-one encounters with Jorge Arroyo, though it proved impossible to avoid him altogether.

'I believed you had more spirit,' he said sadly when they came face to face in La Santa one morning.

'It's called diplomacy,' she defended, seeing no

point in pretending not to know what he was talking about.

'It's called submission,' he countered. 'If you have any independence left at all, you will take coffee with me.'

About to refuse, Karen knew a sudden insurgence. He was right: it was time she showed Luiz she had a mind of her own still.

'All right,' she said.

Jorge gave an approving smile. 'That's better.'

The café he took her to was already well-populated. Karen recognised one or two familiar faces, and knew word would get back to Luiz, but she refused to let it concern her.

'What is it that Luiz has against you, anyway?' she asked when they were seated.

Jorge gave a rueful shrug. 'Regina became attracted to me last year. He believes I encouraged her.'

'And did you?'

He put on a hurt expression. 'I wanted only to paint her. The rest was in her mind only.'

'Tell me about it,' Karen invited.

'There is little to tell,' he said. 'She came to my studio just the three times. I had no notion of her feelings for me until she declared herself. It was difficult to know what to do. I'm not accustomed to dealing with the emotions of teenage girls. Luiz made her tell him what was making her so unhappy. He threatened to kill me.'

'People say all sorts of things under pressure,' Karen responded, trying to view the situation impartially. 'I gather he didn't know about the painting?'

'I hadn't realised that Regina had kept it a secret,' Jorge defended.

Karen studied him for a lengthy moment, uncertain whether to believe him or not. Sixteen was an impressionable age, she had to admit: she'd developed a crush on one of her teachers herself back then.

'I suppose all's well that ends well,' she said at last. 'Regina obviously recovered, and you're still here to tell the tale.'

'It's no tale,' he insisted. 'She held no appeal for me other than as a subject. Perhaps I should have sought Luiz's approval before asking her to sit for me, but I gave it no thought.'

'Whether or not, I think there's enough bad blood between you and Luiz without adding to it,' she said. 'I shouldn't have agreed to this.'

Jorge looked at her scornfully. 'I have no fear of him, but you must do as you see fit, of course.'

It wasn't fear that prompted her, Karen could have told him. She'd accepted the challenge in a belated gesture of defiance against Luiz's dictate, but if he believed Regina had been encouraged by the man, she could understand the objection. If he'd told her why at the time, she would have accepted it.

Only that wasn't Luiz's way, was it? Why should he bother explaining anything?

She could feel eyes following her as she left the café. People who knew both Luiz and Jorge would be aware of the rift between them, even if they didn't know the reason for it. Her being here with the latter had to give rise to speculation.

Regina greeted her reproachfully when she got back to the house.

'I would have come to town with you if I'd known you planned a trip,' she said.

'If you'd been here when I decided, I'd have asked you,' Karen returned mildly. 'Where did you get to?'

'I was helping Carlos change a wheel on the Mercedes,' she said. 'I may have need of such knowledge when I have my own licence next year.'

'Nothing to do with Carlos being such a hunk, of course,' Karen teased.

About to launch an indignant denial, Regina caught her eye and settled for a grin instead.

'He is, isn't he? You won't tell Luiz? He'd get rid of him if he thought I was becoming enamoured.' She sounded suddenly wry. 'I did something very stupid last year, and allowed myself to be dazzled by a man many years older than me. It was fortunate that Luiz found out and put a stop to it, before it became any more than an infatuation on my part.'

It was so strange, Karen thought, that Regina should choose to tell her all this on the same day she'd heard it from Jorge. From the way she *had* told it, it seemed he'd probably been lying through his teeth.

The only way to be sure was to question her further, and the other looked as if she might already be regretting the confidence.

'We've all of us done stupid things at times,' she said comfortingly. 'The best thing is to put it out of mind.'

'It would be easier to do that if I no longer saw him at all.' Regina made an effort to lift her spirits again. 'Have you felt the baby kick yet?'

Karen had to laugh. 'It's far too early for that.'

'But you will let me know the instant it happens?'

'Providing it's not in the middle of the night.' She waited until she was safely in the bedroom before giving way to the impulse that had almost overtaken her downstairs, splaying her fingers across an abdomen still flat and taut. She would be twelve weeks gone or more before there were any really noticeable signs, the gynaecologist had told her. It was barely seven weeks yet, so the stirring she felt had to be in her imagination.

Luiz was turned on by the way she looked now: body slender and supple, breasts high and firm. Would he feel the same way when all that changed?

She whipped her hands away as the door opened. Luiz gazed across at her with quizzically lifted brows.

'You look startled,' he said.

'I was miles away,' she prevaricated. 'I didn't realise you were home.'

'I've been at work in the office for the past two hours. Regina said you'd returned.' He paused, in obvious expectation of some response, gaze sharpening when she failed to make it. 'Is something wrong?'

'You'd better hear it from me before you hear it from someone else,' she said. 'I had coffee with Jorge Arroyo this morning.'

The muscles about the strong mouth tautened ominously. 'I told you—'

'I know what you told me.' Karen kept her tone even. 'I also know *why* you don't want me associating with him. If you'd told me about Regina to start with, I'd have understood.'

Luiz closed the door, face expressionless now. 'I saw no reason to explain my motives.'

'In other words, it should have been enough just to say it.' Karen drew a deep breath, battening down her temper. 'Well, it wasn't.'

'Apparently.' He was angry, but in control of it, the only indication in the slight pinching of his nostrils.

'As I'd doubt that Jorge would have told you about it himself, I gather Regina did.'

'Yes. Although Jorge had already…' Karen broke off, biting her lip.

Luiz gave her a humourless smile. 'Had already claimed to be the innocent victim of a young girl's infatuation, is that what you were about to say?'

'More or less,' she admitted. 'Not that I believed him.'

'That's *something* to be grateful for.'

'There's no need for sarcasm,' she flashed. 'I'm trying to be straight with you. I don't have the slightest interest in Jorge Arroyo!'

'You had coffee with him simply to prove a point?'

'Yes.' She lifted her chin. 'Stupid, I know.'

He surveyed her, lean features relaxing. 'Misguided, perhaps.'

Karen made no move as he came over to her. He took her face between his hands, the way he so often did, tracing the curve of her lips with the ball of his thumb, eyes searching hers. 'No regrets?'

'No regrets,' she echoed.

It was far from the truth. She regretted so many things: winning the money that had brought her here to Brazil in the first place; allowing herself to be overcome by lust; marrying a man she'd known just a few days on the strength of that lust. Because that was all it had ever really been for her, when it came right down to it. She'd been caught up in a fantasy of her own making.

'What is it?' There was a line drawn between the dark brows.

Karen shook herself. Regretted or not, the marriage was a fact. Even if Luiz had been willing to have it dissolved before, he certainly wasn't going to do it now, with the baby on the way.

'I'm feeling a bit homesick, that's all,' she said.

'*This* is your home!' he declared. 'If you return to England at all, it will only be to visit.'

And not for a long time, she thought, reading between the lines.

His kiss drew its usual response from her. That at least hadn't altered. Hopefully it never would.

Luiz's announcement the week before Christmas that they were to visit his mother in Brasilia came as something of a surprise.

'I rather gathered the impression that you were estranged,' Karen said.

'We were for a time,' he admitted. 'She remarried too soon after my father's death for propriety.'

'But you've forgiven her?'

The shrug was brief. 'She's my mother. What else could I do?'

'What about her husband?' Karen asked.

'He's a good enough man. He travels extensively on business, so we may not see him.'

'Your mother does know about me though? I mean, that I'm not Brazilian?'

'She knows.'

They left for Brasilia the following day. It was the first time in several weeks that Karen had been further than a few miles from the ranch.

Driving to the airport, she thought about the journey out when she was still on cloud nine, convinced that she'd found the love of her life. In the physical sense, she probably had, but no matter how fantastic, sex wasn't the be all and end all of a relationship. If she'd never met Luiz she would be waking up in the London flat right about now, with Julie just the other side of the wall and a familiar routine ahead.

'You're very quiet,' Luiz commented, slanting a glance. 'Are you feeling ill?'

Karen seized on the excuse. 'Just a little.'

'Do you wish me to stop the car?'

She shook her head. 'It will pass.'

'Perhaps I should have waited a little longer before making this arrangement,' he said after a moment. 'We can turn back now, if you wish.'

Not looking forward to the coming meeting, she was tempted, but it was best to get it over and done with, she supposed.

'We can't mess your mother around at the last minute,' she said. 'Anyway, it's going off already.'

Luiz winged a smile. 'Women are very resilient.'

Karen suffered a guilty pang. So far she had yet to undergo morning, or any other time of day, sickness. 'We have to be to put up with you men,' she returned, adopting a flippant note.

He laughed. 'Such martyrdom!'

She studied him from the corner of her eye, stirred as always by the sheer masculine impact. She knew his body the way he knew hers, but that was all she really knew of him. It was probably all she would ever really know of him.

'Isn't it though?' she said.

His glance was sharper this time, though he made no comment. Karen could almost hear him putting the brittleness he'd obviously caught in her voice down to her condition. Some of it perhaps was. She felt trapped.

Spread over several square miles, Brasilia was al-

most surrounded by a vast artificial lake. Luiz's
mother lived in a sector of residential dwellings built
along the southern end of the lake. The house was set
within spacious, landscaped grounds. Long and low,
it looked far too large for two people.

The gates were electrified. Luiz spoke briefly into a
box set in the side wall, driving through as they
opened to bring the hired car to a stop on the wide,
stone-laid circle fronting the house.

'What did you say your stepfather does for a living?' Karen asked.

'I didn't say,' Luiz answered. 'He's a cabinet minister, dealing with foreign affairs. Mother met him
when she came to Brasilia to visit with friends some
weeks after my father's death. They were married
within the month.'

'Like mother, like son,' Karen thought, only realising she had actually murmured the words out loud
when Luiz stopped in the act of getting from the car
to give her a suddenly hardened look.

'There's no comparison!'

'I know.' She made a contrite gesture. 'Our circumstances were completely different.'

The dark eyes failed to soften. 'I'm glad you realise
it.'

A man dressed in the dark trousers and white shirt
that signified serving staff came from the house. Luiz
slid from his seat to answer the respectful greeting,
coming round to assist Karen from her place as the
man opened the boot to extract their bags.

Karen restrained the urge to say she wasn't yet far
enough along to need assistance. Her emotions regarding the baby were still in a state of flux, one min-

ute anticipatory, the next downbeat. Hormones, she supposed.

The house inside was built to the American open plan, with coolly tiled floors winging away in all directions. The furnishings were a little over-elaborate for Karen's tastes, but obviously no expense had been spared. Beyond the sliding glass doors fronting the vast living area could be seen a broad covered lanai, and beyond that a free-form swimming pool complete with waterfall.

Cristina Belsamo rose from a brocade chair. Considering Luiz's age, she had to be in her fifties, yet she looked no more than the mid-forties. She was both beautiful and elegant in her designer dress of cream silk, her luxuriant dark hair piled high, but the smile on her lips was not reflected in her eyes.

She greeted her son in Portuguese, switching to a somewhat formalised English to address Karen herself.

'You are very lovely, but I would have expected no less. You must be weary from the journey. You would no doubt like to rest before dinner.'

It was more of a command than a suggestion, Karen thought. Not much of a welcome anyway. It was on the tip of her tongue to say she'd much prefer to take a swim, but she bit it back. She hadn't a suit with her, in any case, and this was no place to go skinny-dipping.

'That's very considerate of you,' she said instead.

'You have the blue suite,' Cristina told Luiz, adding something in Portuguese too fast for Karen to even take a guess at translation.

He made no answer in either language, simply indicating that Karen should accompany him. His expression was unrevealing, though she sensed something simmering beneath the surface.

The guest suites lay down a side corridor. Three of them, counting the doors beyond the one Luiz opened. Blue was certainly the colour: carpet, drapes, bedspreads, all toning shades against off-white walls. Twin beds, Karen noted: Cristina's way of expressing her feelings about the marriage, perhaps. She at least had married another Brazilian, not a foreigner.

Their bags had already been deposited on stands at the foot of each bed. Had they not been locked, Karen suspected they would have been unpacked too by now.

'Leave that,' Luiz said as she made a move towards her own bag. 'You need to rest.'

'I'm not in the least tired,' she retorted. 'Will you please stop treating me like an invalid?'

'I have no intention of treating you like an invalid,' he denied levelly. 'Now, or at any other time. You must naturally do as you feel able.'

Karen caught herself up, already regretting the tartness. 'Sorry,' she said. 'That was uncalled for. I just…' She broke off, spreading her hands in a helpless gesture. 'Maybe I am tired.'

His expression relaxed a little. Coming forward, he tilted her chin with a finger to receive his kiss.

'I'll be with you shortly,' he said. 'My mother wishes to speak with me.'

To express her disapproval face to face, no doubt, Karen reflected. Not that there was anything the woman could do about it.

She unpacked both bags while Luiz was gone. With no clear idea of how long they would be staying, or what they might be doing, she had allowed for all eventualities. If Edigar Balsamo was away, it was unlikely that Cristina would be entertaining friends. That would be a relief in itself. Dealing with her attitude was going to be bad enough. Facing others of the same viewpoint she could do without.

The sun went down in a blaze of glory, backlighting the clouds spreading out from the horizon. Beyond the pool and outlying grounds lay an uninterrupted view of the lake's southern reaches. Cabinet Ministers must be pretty well-paid to afford a place like this, Karen reflected. Of the two, she much preferred Guavada.

Luiz looked distinctly rattled when he eventually returned. Karen forbore from asking the obvious question. Assuming that dinner would be at the same time as Guavada, there were still a couple of hours to go. She knew one sure way of passing the time pleasurably for them both.

A smile overcame the tension about the strong mouth as he read the message in her eyes.

'You,' he said, 'are a rare woman!'

'For an Englishwoman, you mean?' she murmured as he drew her to him and heard his low laugh.

'For any nationality!'

The lovemaking was incredible as always. Luiz never rushed things, nor allowed her to do so. As always, when she was in his arms, she wanted to be nowhere else. When she was in his arms, the whole world could go to hell for all she cared. In his arms, she had no inhibitions: teasing him with caresses that drew him to the very brink; offering herself to him with wanton abandonment when he in turn aroused her to fever pitch.

'I heard that pregnancy can turn a woman against sex in the initial stages,' he murmured when they lay entwined after a climax that robbed them of just about every ounce of energy. 'I can only be thankful for my good fortune.'

He lifted his head to look into her eyes, the amber lights deep in the darkness of his drawing her in. 'You fulfil my every desire!'

At this moment perhaps, she thought. 'And you mine,' she murmured back, because it was expected of her. 'You're a lover without equal!'

His smile was brief. 'You have no comparison. Nor will you while I draw breath,' he added on a suddenly fiercer note. 'You're mine, and mine alone!'

Possession, not love, came the fading thought as he claimed her once more.

They were in Brasilia just three days in total. Three days that seemed more like three months. Cristina was courteous, but no more than that. Nor was she likely to soften, Karen judged. In her view, Luiz had betrayed his race by marrying out of it.

A handsome man in his early sixties, Edigar Belsamo put in a brief appearance that first evening. Although he made an effort to extend a welcome, he obviously found the situation difficult. Karen was unsurprised when he announced that he had to leave again the following morning. She only wished she could do the same.

Luiz spent the whole of the next day showing her round the capital with its ultra modern plazas and buildings. Karen would have preferred to explore on foot, but with temperatures in the lower eighties and little shade, few people walked anywhere.

'I'd hate to live here,' she said over lunch at one of the city's top hotels. 'It's so huge!'

'So is London,' Luiz returned, 'but you lived there.'

Nostalgia swamped her for a moment, totally disregarding the times she'd wished she could swap city living for somewhere in the countryside. 'It's not the same,' she said.

He regarded her quizzically. 'Apart from the architecture, in what way is it different from any other city?'

'It has soul. A history that goes back hundreds of years, not just a few decades! If you'd ever visited it, you'd know what I'm talking about.'

'You must give me the guided tour.'

Karen gazed at him in silence for a moment, unable to decide whether he meant what he seemed to be implying, or was just making noises.

'When?' she asked, opting for the former.

His shrug was easy. 'Perhaps in a year or so when the child is old enough to be left.'

If he had his way, she would probably be pregnant again by then, she reflected, recalling what he'd said about this not being their only child. Not that she had any quarrel with that. She'd have loved siblings of her own.

The best thing might be not to go back at all. What was the point? Her life was here now. Perhaps not quite as perfect as she had first envisioned, but hardly a bad one.

'What are your thoughts?' Luiz asked curiously, watching the play of expressions across her face.

'I was wishing we were home,' she said impulsively, surprising herself because it was the first time she had thought of Guavada in that light. 'I'm sure your mother would have no objection if we leave tomorrow.'

Something flickered deep down in the dark eyes. 'I have matters I must attend to tomorrow.'

He made no attempt to enlarge on that statement. Business matters, Karen supposed. The thought of spending the day alone with her mother-in-law was far from appealing.

Cristina had an engagement herself in the morning. Karen spent it out on the lanai with a book. Luiz hadn't said how long his affairs might take. She hoped he'd be back before his mother returned.

He wasn't. Cristina came in around one-thirty, and the two them ate lunch together. Conversation was minimal, the atmosphere frigid. Karen could finally stand it no longer.

'I realise you totally disapprove of me as a suitable wife for your son,' she said, 'but I'm *his* choice. Can't you accept that?'

There was no softening of expression in the older woman's eyes. 'I will never accept it!' she stated. 'He did this to punish me!'

Karen looked at her in some bewilderment. 'Punish you?'

'For the insult I gave to his father's memory.'

'Oh, come on!' Karen could scarcely believe she was serious. 'He'd hardly go that far!'

'You think you know my son better than I do myself?' Cristina gave a short, humourless laugh. 'You have a lot to learn about him. He could have had his choice of bride from among those fit to bear the name. Why else, if it were not to hurt me, would he choose one he knew I could never approve?'

'He told me his father died some years ago,' Karen returned. 'Why would he wait this long to get back at you?'

The laugh came again. 'He had first to find someone who fulfilled his physical needs too.'

It could quite possibly be true, Karen thought, feeling a dull ache in the pit of her stomach. She already knew that Luiz didn't love her—at least, not what she called love. But then, she didn't love him either.

Yes, you do, whispered the small voice at the back of her mind. Stop hiding from it!

She swallowed thickly, searching for something—*anything*—to say to the woman.

'You're entitled to believe whatever you want to believe,' she got out. 'The fact remains, I'm Luiz's wife and I'm carrying his child. Your first grandchild.'

'You think so?' Cristina's expression registered derision. 'As I said, you have a lot to learn.'

Karen studied her uncertainly, grappling with the implications. 'What are you trying to tell me?'

For a moment the older woman seemed to hesitate, then she lifted her shoulders. 'You believe Luiz is conducting some business affairs today, but you are wrong. He is visiting his son.'

How long Karen just sat there she couldn't have said. Her mind was in turmoil. 'You're lying,' she whispered at length.

'Why would I lie about such a thing?' the other woman demanded. 'Do you think I am any more proud to have a bastard grandchild than I shall be to have one of mixed blood?'

'Why...' Karen cleared her throat and tried again. 'Why didn't he marry the mother?'

A shutter came down suddenly in her mother-in-law's eyes. 'She is not of our class. I refuse to discuss the matter further,' she added flatly. 'He does duty by the child, that is all you need to know.'

And what did he do for the mother? Karen wondered. She hurt as though she'd been kicked. She got to her feet, unsurprised by the shakiness in her limbs. 'I'm going to take a siesta.'

The expression that flitted across Cristina's face could have been shame, though Karen doubted it.

'If you are wise, you will say nothing to Luiz of this,' the woman said.

If she were wise, she wouldn't be in this position to start with, Karen could have answered. She didn't because the words would have stuck in her throat.

The bedroom was cool and dim, the window blinds slanted against the sun's rays. She lay down on her bed fully clothed, gazing blindly at the shadowed ceiling.

Her hand moved of its own accord to caress her abdomen. Not Luiz's first child after all: that honour belonged to a boy born the wrong side of the blanket through no fault of his own. Under English law, he would have the same claim as any legitimate issue, but this wasn't England.

Not of our class, Cristina had said of the mother. Marriageable she may not be in Luiz's eyes too, but she would certainly be good-looking. There was every chance that the two of them were in bed together right now.

The pain went deep. What she was going to do she couldn't begin to think—didn't want to think. It was all too much to cope with.

Emotionally drained, she finally fell asleep, waking with a jerk when Luiz came into the room.

'Are you feeling unwell?' he asked concernedly.

Karen made a valiant effort to pull herself together as memory came flooding in. 'Just tired,' she said. 'What time is it?'

'Ten minutes past five,' he answered, glancing at his watch. 'I'm sorry to have been away so long.'

The time to fling accusations was now, but the words wouldn't come. 'Busy day?' she said instead.

'Very,' he agreed. 'I've told my mother we'll be leaving in the morning.'

'Good.' She faked a yawn, unable to stand much more for the moment. 'Do you mind if I go back to sleep for a while?'

He came over to the bed, dropping to sit on the mattress edge to bend and put his lips to her temple. 'You look pale,' he observed. 'Are you sure there's nothing wrong?'

Another opportunity, but she couldn't bring herself to take it. She steeled herself when he ran the back of his fingers gently down her cheek. Even knowing what she knew made little difference to her responses. She wanted him the way she had always wanted him. No doubt he had the same effect on his mistress.

'I told you, I'm just tired,' she said, trying to keep a level tone.

He considered her for a moment, obviously not wholly deceived, then he patted her cheek again and got to his feet. 'Have all the rest you need, of course. I'll take a change of clothing to another room so that I don't disturb you.'

She watched through slitted lids as he gathered what he needed, letting out a pent-up breath on a long-drawn sigh when he went from the room. She should have faced him with what she had learned, she knew. She hadn't because deep down she didn't want to hear him admit it, didn't want to see the guilt in his eyes.

He would have counted on his mother keeping her own council, considering her feelings towards his illegitimate son. Cristina was unlikely to confess her betrayal, so why rock the boat? For the sake of the child growing inside her, if nothing else, she had to put the whole affair aside.

CHAPTER NINE

THE journey back to Guavada was passed for the most part in silence. His conversational overtures unproductive, Luiz ran out of patience in the end.

'Do you find pregnancy such a toil that even words are too much of a burden?' he asked in the car. 'I accept—as I accepted last night—that there will be times now when you feel too physically tired for love-making, but you can surely summon the strength to talk!'

'I didn't think what you were saying just now called for any in-depth response,' Karen retorted, drawing a narrowed glance.

'I doubt if you were even listening to what I was saying just now. You've been in a strange mood all day, in fact.'

'I'm a woman,' she returned, trying to make light of it. 'We're a moody species. You men just have to learn to live with it, I'm afraid.'

'Not this man,' came the less than humorous reply. 'If you have some grievance I prefer to hear it.'

The accusation trembled once more on her lips, but was held back by a stronger instinct. 'What grievance could I possibly have?' she said instead. 'You give me everything a woman could want.' She forced herself to reach out a hand to touch his thigh, to put a smile on her lips. 'Sorry for being such a grump.'

The answering smile was somewhat restrained. 'You're forgiven. Just don't let it happen too often.'

Karen kept a tight rein on the tart retort. If she let fly now it would all come out, and what good would it do in the end? She could demand that he give up all physical contact with the other woman and her child, but it was unlikely that he'd agree never to see his son again.

While it pained her to know that the baby she carried wasn't his first-born, she could somehow stomach that more easily than the probability that he still had a relationship with the other woman. She'd turned from him last night because she couldn't rid herself of the images. Images that still persisted, although what excuse she would use tonight she had no idea.

The sun was already setting when they reached Guavada. Regina greeted them with her customary enthusiasm. She'd so missed her companionship, she told Karen.

'How did you find my mother?' she asked when the two of them were alone for a few minutes.

Karen kept her tone as easy as she could. 'I doubt if we'll ever be great friends.'

'I was afraid of that.' Regina sounded rueful. 'She had what she believed would be the ideal wife for Luiz already chosen years ago. There have been others too, but Luiz favoured none of them. You must not allow her rejection to hurt you. She would have been the same over anyone he'd chosen for himself.'

Perhaps not so much if he'd chosen one of his own countrywomen, Karen reflected. Right now, her mother-in-law's feelings weren't of importance to her. She had far more pressing matters on her mind.

Unable to cast those matters aside, she slipped out on to the veranda after dinner for a breath of fresh air. The night air was deliciously cool on her skin. Seated on the swing couch, she contemplated the moonlit landscape. Guavada had grown on her, she had to admit that now. If it weren't for what she knew, she could even consider it home. If she truly didn't love Luiz, none of what she'd learned would hurt as much, she was sure. The question was, how did she cope with that hurt?

'I was speaking with Cristina earlier,' said Beatriz from the doorway. There was an odd note in her voice. 'She tells me you know about the boy.'

Karen didn't turn her head. 'So I know about the boy.'

The pause was lengthy, the atmosphere charged. 'Are you going to tell Luiz that you know?' Beatriz finally asked on the same odd note.

'I see no reason to.' Karen kept her tone level with an effort. 'It happened before we met.'

'You are very tolerant. More than I would be myself in such circumstances.' The other woman sounded almost sympathetic.

'We're very different people,' Karen returned, not trusting the sympathy for a moment. 'Concentrate on your own marriage, and leave me to deal with mine.'

'*My* marriage is secure in every way,' retorted her sister-in-law, dropping back into character. 'Yours is dependent on the way you look. Luiz is a man to whom a woman's looks are all important. Should she lose them, he would have little interest left.'

She was telling her nothing she didn't already suspect, Karen acknowledged. If she didn't look the way she did, Luiz would never have even noticed her that day in Rio. It boded ill for the future.

Beatriz disappeared back indoors, leaving her to contemplate that future with growing despondency. It took the gathering ache in her lower back to bring her back to the present. She eased her position, but the ache remained, spreading now to her abdomen and increasing in intensity to a gripping pain.

The realisation of what was happening struck her with mind-numbing force. She clutched herself, as if it might be stopped by application of pressure, knowing it was a useless gesture. Nature held the upper hand.

'So here you are!' Luiz exclaimed, appearing round the corner of the veranda. 'I was beginning to—'

He broke off abruptly as he took in her position and drawn expression. 'What is it?'

'The baby,' she got out through clenched teeth. 'I'm losing the baby!'

Things happened in a blur from there. Luiz carried her into the house, an ambulance was called, and she was transported to the nearby clinic, where vain attempts were made to stay the process. Karen suffered through it all in silence, the sense of loss too deep for words. She knew Luiz was there with her, but there was no comfort to be found.

He was at the bedside when she awoke from a sedated sleep, strain etched deep on the olive features.

'I'm sorry,' she said tonelessly.

He took her hand, raising it to his lips. There were no amber lights in the dark eyes. 'If the fault lies with anyone at all, it must be mine for taking you on an unnecessary journey.'

'Do the doctors say that?' she asked.

'No,' he admitted. 'They tell me it just happens this way sometimes for no apparent reason.'

But not to his mistress, she thought. He should have married her, if only for his son's sake. The boy had more right to the Andrade name than any child she might have had.

'They also tell me,' he went on, 'that there's no reason why you shouldn't carry a child to full-term in the future.'

'Nothing to stop us trying again then.'

'But not immediately.' His tone was steady. 'You need time to recover.'

'Whatever you think,' she said. She took her hand from him to push back the sheet and press herself upright. 'I just want to get out of here.'

Christmas came and went quietly. With the miscarriage almost two weeks behind her, Karen insisted that celebrations for the New Year were not curtailed.

Open to all and sundry, the Guavada barbecue was renowned. It began at midday, to finish when the last reveller departed. Not even the hour-long summer rainstorm could dampen the party spirit. People either took shelter until it passed over, or simply stood around in it, depending on age. With the temperature hovering in the mid-eighties, there was little danger of catching a chill.

Luiz took over one of the grills himself after the rain stopped. Karen watched him as he doled out sizzling steaks to the seemingly never-ending line, exchanging repartee. Devastated though he'd been by the miscarriage, he'd proved a tower of strength the past two weeks. It was difficult to equate the man he appeared to be with the man she now knew him to be. 'The master cooks well for us,' said a voice she didn't recognise.

She turned to view the man who had spoken, the smile ready on her lips fading a little as she met bold dark eyes. One of the ranch hands, judging from his clothing, she guessed. Young and good-looking, he appraised her in turn, his expression only too easily read.

'Yes, he does,' she replied in the same language. 'You work for him?'

He inclined his head, his gaze discomfiting. 'I am Lucio Fernandas. You are even more beautiful than it is said. Luiz is a lucky man!'

With her command of the language still in its infancy, and his speech fast, Karen had a struggle to translate but she got the gist. The words themselves were innocuous enough, the look accompanying them far from it.

Dona Ferrez came to her rescue, drawing her away before she could summon any kind of reply.

'What was he saying to you?' asked the older woman.

'Nothing much,' Karen answered, reluctant to make any fuss over what amounted to no more than a leer. She'd been treated to worse than that back home in England.

'Luiz would not like it that he speak with you,' Dona declared.

'Then we won't tell him,' Karen said lightly. 'Do you think anyone will think it rude of me if I take a bit of a siesta?'

'Of course they will not! You must not tire yourself. I will tell Luiz where you are.'

Karen turned for the house as Dona headed for the grills, almost running into Beatriz. The other made no attempt to speak, her regard narrowed as if in contemplation. Whatever was brewing in the woman's head, Karen was past caring. All she wanted at present was to lay her head on a soft pillow and sleep.

She awoke to the feather-light touch of lips on hers. Luiz smiled at her bemused expression.

'I thought it time to come and check on you,' he said.

'How long have I been asleep?' she asked.

'More than two hours. Some of our guests have already left, but the rest seem prepared to stay out the rest of the day. Do you feel strong enough to rejoin them, or shall I ask them all to depart?'

'Don't do that.' Karen sat up, swinging her legs to the floor as Luiz rose to his feet. 'Give me fifteen minutes to have a shower and change my clothes, and I'll be down.'

'You're sure you feel up to it?' he insisted.

She felt anything but, only she wasn't about to admit it. 'Quite sure,' she said.

Luiz drew her to her feet and into his arms, holding her close for a moment or two. 'There can be other babies,' he consoled. 'There's no haste. For now, we'll rest content with each other.'

Until he felt moved to visit the woman who *had* provided him with a child, thought Karen hollowly.

The last of the revellers finally weaved their way homewards around ten, by which time even Regina had had enough.

'I would like my birthday celebration at Café Lamas,' she declared, naming the town's top restaurant. 'Eighteen is a very special age.'

'It is indeed,' agreed Luiz. 'I'll make the arrangements.'

'And a car of my own?' she suggested.

He smiled. 'Reaching the age of authority to hold a licence is only a beginning. When you know how to drive a car, I may consider it.'

'You can teach me, the way you taught Karen.'

'When exactly *is* your birthday?' Karen asked, forced to smile herself as she caught Luiz's dry glance.

'The thirteenth of January.' Regina pulled a face. 'Not a nice date on which to be born.'

Hardly an unlucky one for her, considering what she'd been born into, Karen reflected. A life of leisure until she married, and even then it would be to a man rich enough to keep her in the style to which she was accustomed.

Not that she had anything to complain about in that sense herself.

She left Luiz to share a nightcap with his brother. Beatriz followed her from the room.

'I saw you with Lucio Fernandas earlier,' she said. 'As did others. It was fortunate that Luiz did not.'

'Why?' Karen asked. 'Are the ranch hands considered too far down the social scale?'

'For his wife to exchange banter with, yes.'

Karen opened her mouth to deny the allegation, cutting off the words in the certain knowledge that Beatriz would pay little heed. 'Your concern does you credit,' she said instead, and continued on her way.

She was in bed, though far from sleep, when Luiz came up. He had exercised the utmost forbearance since the miscarriage, although it couldn't have been easy, she knew, for a man of his appetites to hold himself in check for so long.

Watching him as he undressed, she wanted him again, desperately enough to override everything else. She reached for him the moment he slid into the bed, bringing him to instant arousal.

Even then, he restrained himself long enough to

take measures against conception. Karen made no protest. The last thing she wanted was another pregnancy.

Listening to his steady breathing later, feeling the muscular strength of his arms about her, she could almost feel sorry for the woman who would only know this on infrequent occasions. Sorry too for the boy who would grow up barely knowing his father at all. She might not have everything she desired herself, but she had so much. Could she begrudge the two of them so little?

The days slid by. Regina's birthday came and went with all the appropriate observance. Karen gave her a course of professional driving lessons to go with the sleek little sports model Luiz came up with despite all he'd said.

Life went along much the same as it had before the trip to Brasilia. A good life in most respects. Without Beatriz around, it might have been possible to come to terms with the situation, but the woman lost no opportunity to taunt her with the knowledge they shared whenever they were alone together.

Had she no pride, that she'd stay with a man who led a double life? she would jeer. Did she really believe he had any real depth of feeling for her?

Karen didn't believe it, but it still hurt to hear it put into words. Perhaps Beatriz was right, she told herself. She should have more pride. She still had enough left from the lottery win to pay her passage back to England. All it took was the will.

If she hadn't been so emotionally off-balance she would have seen what a crazy idea it was—that the only realistic course was to bring the whole affair out into the open—but it continued to fester at the back of her mind.

It took the photograph Beatriz showed her of mother and son to precipitate matters. Karen had known the woman would be beautiful, but she had expected a woman, not a teenage girl who could surely have been no more than sixteen when she had become pregnant.

How could Luiz live with himself? she thought numbly. How could *she* continue to live with him after this?

He'd left early without waking her that morning. Mind blanked of everything but the urge to get away, she left Beatriz and went upstairs to throw a few things haphazardly into a suitcase. Her passport was to hand. She stuffed that into a bag, along with what ready cash she could find. It wouldn't be enough to get her where she was going, and she'd never bothered with a cheque book, so she'd just have to use the credit card Luiz had provided her with to purchase a ticket home. What she would do when she got there, she didn't even think about.

Beatriz had disappeared. Regina had gone to visit a friend, and Raymundo was out somewhere too. Even the staff seemed to have vanished. She took the car she'd first learned to drive in, keeping her gaze fixed straight ahead as she headed out past the house that had been her home for the past months. That part of her life was finished with.

The drive to São Paulo was the longest she had undertaken on her own. The realisation, on reaching the Congonhas airport at last, that it only handled domestic flights, was dismaying. It meant retrieving the car from the car park where she'd left it, and driving many further kilometres to the international airport on the other side of the city.

She could take a bus to Guarulhas, a helpful counter

clerk advised her. He even offered to check if there were any London flights scheduled, although he didn't hold out much hope of securing a seat at such short notice.

He was right about that. All London flights were booked solid for the next three weeks. There was one seat going spare on a flight from Rio at seven, he said, consulting the computer readout once more. He could get her on the three-thirty shuttle, which should give her plenty of time to cross to Rio's international airport.

Still in the grip of the same compulsion, Karen was ready to do whatever it took. She paid for both flights with the platinum card. An expensive detour, but Luiz could afford it.

It was a lengthy wait for the shuttle. The plane was full, the noise from a crowd of excited schoolchildren overpowering. Karen closed her eyes as they lifted off, only now beginning to come to her senses a little. Luiz wasn't going to just let her go like this. She was his wife, his property. Wherever she went, he'd find her, there was little doubt of that.

Well, let him! she thought resolutely. Once out of the country, she'd be safe from any attempt to force her back. If he wouldn't divorce her, she'd divorce him, however long it took.

The man occupying the seat at her side said something unintelligible and got to his feet, allowing someone else to slide into the seat. Some kind of mix up, she supposed.

'Fortune smiles on me!' declared the newcomer.

Karen opened her eyes to view the man in startled recognition, unable to believe that Lucio Fernandas was on the plane too.

'What are you doing here?' she asked blankly.

He flashed his teeth in a grin. 'Like you, I go to Rio. I have money. Much money! I can give you a good time.'

'Not in a thousand years!' she said in English.

If he didn't understand the words, he understood the meaning. The smile disappeared. Karen had no idea what his response was, although it certainly wasn't polite. She was thankful when he returned the seat to its original occupier.

She turned her attention to the window in order to avoid the man's obvious curiosity. The coincidence apart, there was something very odd about Fernandas being on the plane at all. She had no idea what the Guavada hands earned, but would have doubted it was enough to allow vacations in one of the most expensive cities in the world.

It was none of her business, anyway, she concluded. She had more important things on her mind.

Up to now she hadn't given a thought to what she was going to do on landing in London. Finding somewhere to stay would be a first priority. If Luiz cancelled the credit card—which was a possibility she hadn't taken into account—she'd be in real trouble. She could hardly turn up at Julie's door like some waif and stray.

It would be far more sensible to turn back and sort the whole thing out at source, she acknowledged, but common sense had played no part from the beginning of her whole relationship with Luiz. For better or for worse, she'd made her choice.

She took care on landing to steer well clear of any further encounter with Lucio Fernandas. Buses ran to the international airport but she'd be best taking a taxi, the counter clerk had told her. With two and a half hours still to go before the London flight, she should be fine, providing she could get transportation fairly quickly.

There were people milling around outside the concourse. Confused, Karen hesitated on the edge of the busy service road. That must be the taxi rank across there, she thought, catching a flash of yellow through the press. If she stepped lively...

CHAPTER TEN

KAREN caught sight of her watch as she slid the photograph back into the drawer where she had found it. She felt quite numb at present.

The money Lucio Fernandas had boasted of could only have come from Beatriz: she must have sent the man off post-haste to back up the story she had given Luiz. It suggested pre-planning: counting on the effect the photograph would have on a mind already primed. Considering the circumstances, she couldn't possibly have known about the Rio flight—that must have been his own idea—but it had certainly lent credence to the story.

Luiz was probably with his mistress right now. At this hour, his son would be in bed, leaving the two of them to catch up on the long weeks since their last meeting. It was back to square one, facing the problem her mind had solved once by returning her to a time before the lottery win that had begun it all. As that was unlikely to happen again, she had to deal with it this time. How, she couldn't even begin to think.

There was no sign of Beatriz when she emerged from the office. Not that she'd expected her to be hanging around. In no frame of mind to face anyone, she headed for the privacy of the bedroom.

It took sight of the bed she'd shared with Luiz these past weeks to unlock her emotions. When she thought of the way she'd gone to him that night—begged him to make love to her—she almost retched. To be disillusioned once was bad enough, but to go through it twice!

She was sitting by the window, still fully dressed, when Regina came up to find out what had happened to her.

'Are you feeling ill?' she asked anxiously.

'Just a bit off-colour, that's all,' Karen assured her.

'Do you think you might be pregnant again?' her sister-in-law ventured.

'No!' she snapped, immediately regretting it as she saw the expression on the younger girl's face. 'I doubt it,' she amended on a milder note. 'Sorry for being such a bear. I've got a really bad headache. Would you mind fetching me a couple of painkillers?'

Regina made for the bathroom with a readiness that made Karen ashamed, returning with the pills and a glass of water. 'If there is anything else I can do for you, you know you have only to ask,' she said.

'I know.' Karen forced a smile. 'Thanks.'

The headache was real enough, though she doubted if the aspirin would have any effect. Alone again, she tried to come to some kind of decision about where she went from here, but she was too weary in spirit. Luiz had said he'd be gone two or three days, so there was no immediate pressure.

She spent a restless night, getting up heavy-eyed and depressed. With no appetite, she went down to breakfast only to set Regina's mind at rest.

The others were already at the table. Beatriz looked unusually subdued. Probably realising the danger she'd placed herself in by allowing her animus to overcome her last night, Karen reflected. Luiz would be merciless when he knew she'd lied about Lucio Fernandas.

If he believed it, that was. She had no actual proof that Beatriz had plotted the whole thing.

'You're evil, do you know that?' she accused the other woman when she got her alone. 'Stupid too. If you'd left things the way they were, I might never have known what you were capable of!'

'A mistake, I admit,' Beatriz returned without remorse. 'Although regaining your memory really changes very little when I come to consider. The fact that Lucio was on the same plane is still enough to condemn you.'

'Not if I can prove that you paid him to follow me,' Karen flashed back, bringing a sneer to her sister-in-law's lips.

'And how would you do that?'

'Luiz has someone out searching for him. He'll get to the truth!'

That gave Beatriz pause for a moment, but only for a moment. 'First he has to find him,' she said. 'What should concern you more is the secret he's kept from you all these months. How does it feel to know that he's with Margarita and Maurice this moment?'

It felt, Karen thought, like a sword through her chest!

'I'll deal with that in my own time and my own way,' she said. 'I'll leave *him* to deal with you.'

Beatriz eyed her with a certain calculation. 'Will telling Luiz you recovered your memory really gain you anything?'

Nothing at all, she was bound to admit. It would still be her word against Beatriz's with respect to Lucio Fernandas, with the fact that they'd both been on the Rio flight, coincidence though it must have

been, weighing against her. And she would still have
to face his duplicity.

'Why not just leave things the way they are?'
Beatriz pursued, sensing her hesitation. 'Do you think
Luiz will cast Margarita and her son aside for you?
You have his name. That is what matters.'

'To you, maybe,' Karen returned.

'To any woman.' Beatriz paused. 'We might even
become friends ourselves in time. Think on it.'

She moved away before Karen could reply. Not that
she was in any doubt about her answer. She'd as soon
put her trust in a rattlesnake!

The day dragged on interminably. Regina was like
a cat on hot bricks waiting for Miran to call. She grew
ever more despondent as the hours passed. With a
good idea of what was coming, Karen had little desire
to keep the appointment she'd made with the man herself.

She told no one she was going out after lunch.
Miran was waiting at the corner of the central square
in La Santa. He got into the car quickly, enabling her
to drive on almost without stopping.

'It's good of you to come,' he declared. 'I'm concerned that Regina may have taken my attentions to
mean more than I intended them to mean.'

'What makes you think that?' Karen asked cautiously.

'The things she said at luncheon yesterday. She
spoke of you and Luiz, and the way the two of you
knew immediately that you wished to spend the rest
of your lives together. She said that Luiz could have
no complaint that we felt the same way about each
other.' He spread his hands. 'I gave her no cause to
believe such a thing!'

'You paid her a lot of attention the other night,' Karen responded, shelving her own problems for the present in sympathy with her sister-in-law's coming disillusionment.

'No more than I would pay any beautiful girl!' he protested. 'It was never my intention to suggest anything more than admiration for that beauty. You think she may have spoken with Luiz already?' he added anxiously.

Karen gave him a disgusted glance, aware now of the main concern.

'Luiz is in Brasilia,' she said. 'He knows nothing of this.' She paused, marshalling her reserves. 'I think you should be more careful of what you say and how you say it in future. I also think you should have had the decency to make your feelings clear when you met yesterday, instead of allowing Regina to go on imagining you shared her emotions.'

The handsome features took on a piqued expression. 'You would have had me embarrass her that way?'

'You could have found some way of letting her down gently if you'd really tried, instead of relying on someone else to put her straight. That's what you are relying on, isn't it?'

'It's best that she hear it from someone close to her who can offer comfort,' he agreed shamelessly.

Karen curled a scornful lip. 'Best for you, you mean. I think it might be a good idea if you go back to São Paulo today. I'm sure you can find some adequate excuse.'

'Perhaps so,' he said. He studied her for a moment, taking in the pure lines of her face, the silken sheen of her hair, his expression altering to one she was only too familiar with. 'You're very beautiful yourself.'

Karen turned a deaf ear. 'I'll take you back to the square.'

She was glad to have shut of him. Regina was going to suffer when he failed to get in touch again, but she'd get over it. The way *she* would have got over Luiz if she'd had the sense to return home all those months ago.

It was almost five o'clock when she got back to the house. Walking into the hall to see Luiz descending the stairs was a shock that left her momentarily lost for words.

'You look as if you'd seen a ghost,' he commented drily.

'I wasn't expecting to see you for another couple of days,' she managed.

'My business was completed in less time than anticipated.' His appraisal too keen for comfort, he added, 'I arrived home over an hour ago. Where have you been?'

'Just driving around,' she said. 'If I'd known, of course—'

'You would have been here to greet me,' he finished for her. The dark brows lifted as she continued to stand there. 'So, do I not get a welcome now?'

She went to him reluctantly, steeling herself for his kiss. Her toned down response drew a speculative look.

'I think there are things we need to discuss,' he said.

'About what?' she asked.

His lips twisted. 'About the fact that I did you an injustice where Miran Villota is concerned. I'd seen you watching him during the evening. When you appeared to defend him later, I believed you were drawn to him.' He held her close again, pressing his lips to her temple. 'I can't bear for you to be drawn to *any* other man!'

But it was all right for him to want another woman, she thought. Even more than one, for all she knew! She should do what she should have done weeks ago, and expose him for the hypocrite he was!

She didn't because she couldn't. Because, in spite of it all, she admitted wryly, he still exercised the same power. Just being here close to him now, she wanted him. When it came to matter over mind, it was just no contest.

'I've no interest in Miran Villota,' she said.

'I know that now. I must learn to curb my possessiveness.' He kissed her again and released her, his smile a caress in itself. 'I have much to make up for.'

He'd expect to do that tonight in bed, of course. That gave her five or six hours to come to some final decision. Either she faced him with the truth, or she did as Beatriz had suggested and settled for what she had.

The evening stretched interminably. Regina was so unusually quiet Luiz was drawn to ask if she was suffering some ailment. He looked unconvinced when she denied it, though he didn't pursue the subject.

A little on edge to begin with, Beatriz relaxed as time went on, contempt in her eyes when she looked Karen's way. She was assuming too much too soon, Karen could have told her; the decision was still to be made.

Regina singled her out at the first opportunity, her lovely young face downcast.

'Miran didn't call,' she said. 'Do you think I should call him?'

Karen hesitated, not at all sure she was capable of

handling other problems in addition to her own right now.

'I think it would be best to wait and see,' she advised at length.

Her sister-in-law's face clouded even further. 'You think I was too hasty, don't you?' she said miserably. 'That I took his interest in me for more than it was?'

It was sometimes necessary to be cruel to be kind, Karen reflected, and took the plunge. 'It's possible, yes. Men like Miran are not the kind to put any trust in.'

'But he was so wonderful to me!' Regina burst out. 'If he felt nothing for me, why did he allow me to believe he did?'

'I'm sure he did feel something for you.'

'But not enough.' Tears were threatening. 'Why did he not stop me from making a fool of myself!'

'Perhaps he just couldn't find it in himself to hurt you,' Karen murmured.

Regina dashed the back of her hand across her eyes. 'The hurt is no less now than it would have been then. I'll never trust any man again!'

'They're not all the same,' Karen comforted, wishing she could be convinced of that herself. 'You've all the time in the world to find the right one.'

She'd thought Luiz engrossed in conversation with his brother. Looking up to find his gaze fixed on the two of them was disconcerting. He would naturally want to know what Regina was upset about, but his sister would be even more mortified than she already was to have him know about it.

Regina compounded speculation by eating little at dinner. She excused herself with a plea of tiredness the moment the meal was finished, and departed for bed. Karen toyed with the idea of following her up to offer more comfort, but decided that she was probably best left alone for now.

She had her own troubles still to deal with anyway. As time crept on, she grew ever more uncertain of which way to go. Her heart almost broke through her ribcage when Luiz suggested it was time they retired for the night.

'Why was Regina weeping?' he asked as they mounted the stairs.

'It's private,' Karen answered. 'Woman to woman.'

Luiz gave her a shrewd glance 'Nothing to do with Miran Villota?'

'I thought *I* was the one supposed to be interested in him?' she responded.

'A mistake for which I already apologised,' he said without inflection. 'I don't need to be reminded of it. I trust the distress has no physical basis?'

Further denials were useless, Karen decided resignedly. 'Of course not,' she said. 'Regina would never allow herself to be taken in that far.'

'It can happen.' They had reached their door. Luiz opened it, ushering her through ahead of him. 'I believed she had learned to be a little more selective.'

He was referring to the affair with Jorge Arroyo, Karen guessed. Something Regina could have told her about since the memory loss, of course, but she refrained from comment.

'You wish to use the bathroom first?' he asked, already unbuttoning his shirt.

She seized on the chance to extend the decision time, knowing she was only putting off the inevitable.

She always took a shower before going to bed. Tonight, there was no stimulation to be found.

Her mind was going round in circles. She couldn't ask Luiz to give up his son, but she could demand that he give up any sexual relationship with the child's mother. Always providing one still existed. She still had no proof of it.

Recalling the girl in the photograph, she felt no reassurance. Luiz was a lover of beauty in women, and Margarita's looks left nothing to be desired.

She was still standing there under the flow when the cabinet door slid open. Luiz stepped in at her back, hands sliding around her to seek the firm curve of her breasts, lips nuzzling her nape, exposed by the shower cap she was wearing.

'You were gone too long,' he breathed against her skin. 'I could wait no longer for you!' He smoothed a slow passage down the length of her body to seek her inner softness, bringing her to quivering life. 'You fill my every waking thought—even my dreams! No other woman could ever match you!'

If it weren't for the last, she would have succumbed without a struggle. She stiffened in his grasp, fighting the urge to let go with the invective clamouring for release.

'Would it ever occur to you that I might not be in the mood?' she asked with what control she could muster. 'Or is it taken for granted that wives have to be permanently on heat?'

For a moment there was no reaction at all. When he moved it was abruptly, stepping away from her as though he'd been stung. Karen's legs felt weak, her whole body shivery. She'd hit him where it would reckon the most, but there was little satisfaction in it.

He was sitting in a chair wearing a silk robe when

she eventually emerged from the bathroom. He viewed her towelling cover-up with cynical eyes.

'You need have no fear. I've no intention of forcing you into fulfilling your duties.'

'It hadn't occurred to me that you would,' she said. 'I'm entitled to refuse on occasion.'

The muscles around his mouth tautened. 'You're entitled to refuse any time you wish, but there are ways of doing it that—'

'That don't undermine your pride?' Her tone was scathing. 'Why should yours be any more important than mine?'

Regard narrowed, he said softly, 'I think there's more to this than a simple lack of desire. Something happened to you while I was away.'

If ever there was a time, that time was now, but the words wouldn't form.

'Perhaps I just came to my senses at last,' she heard herself saying instead. 'Perhaps I realised that being married to you isn't such a bed of roses after all.'

'I've heard no complaints before this.' The level tone was belied by the glitter in the dark eyes. 'On the contrary, in fact.'

'That was then, this is now.' She was getting in deeper and deeper, yet she couldn't stop herself, the need to hurt paramount. 'I want out!'

Luiz came to his feet in one rapid movement, crossing the room in a stride to take hold of her. The kiss was scorching, his arms like iron bands across her back. Karen staggered a little when he released her.

'There will be no divorce!' he gritted.

'Even if it turned out to be true after all about Lucio Fernandas?' she said with the same heedless compulsion.

The glitter in his eyes became a blaze, smothered in seconds by sheer force of will. 'Even then,' he declared. 'You signed a contract with no escape clause.'

He turned away from her, heading across the room to the communicating door. Karen watched him go in numb acceptance. There was no going back from here. She'd made her decision; now she had to live with it.

Regina seemed to have recovered much of her usual spirits in the morning. The resilience of youth, Karen thought wryly, feeling anything but herself.

Luiz wasn't at breakfast. He'd gone out early, she said when Beatriz asked where he was. The woman suspected something amiss, that was obvious, although she made no comment. Karen would have loved to wipe the smug expression from her face, but it was too late for that.

She went out on to the veranda after the meal. Raymundo followed her, eyeing her with some concern as he took a seat.

'Have you and Luiz had a disagreement?' he asked with a delicacy that might have been amusing in normal circumstances.

'Something like that,' she said. She gave him a smile. 'It will soon blow over.'

He looked unconvinced. 'Luiz can sometimes be a little too assertive, I know.'

Like laying down the law about his own situation, she thought. She opened her mouth to commiserate with him, closing it again with the realisation that what he'd told her about his marriage had been before her memory loss. It was difficult to recall exactly what had happened when. One mistake could expose her.

So what? asked the small voice of reason. Things

could hardly be any worse than they were right now. If nothing else, it would help explain last night's episode.

Why bother? another part of her mind asked. Even if they came to some kind of agreement over Margarita and her son, Luiz would never forgive the things she'd said to him. Like Raymundo himself, she'd made her bed and must lie on it.

'I suppose I'm a bit too assertive myself at times,' she said, trying to inject a touch of humour. 'If Luiz had wanted a wife with no spirit, he would have chosen one,' Raymundo answered. 'He loves you the way you are. I only wish—' He broke off, looking uncomfortable. 'I must be going. I'm sure you will soon be friends again.'

His married life was certainly no bed of roses, Karen reflected as he went back indoors. Beatriz treated him like dirt. His own fault, maybe, but love was notoriously blind in its early stages. She should have remembered that herself.

Luiz didn't come back for lunch either. Karen took the pups for a walk, then retired on the pretext of taking a siesta, though sleeping was the last thing she felt like doing.

She tried to concentrate on a book, but the words made no sense. Eventually, she gave up and just sat there waiting. Luiz had to return some time.

The afternoon was drawing towards evening when he finally put in an appearance. Dressed in his working gear, he came straight to the room she was occupying, face rigid as he regarded her.

'So you had no interest in Villota!' he jerked out. 'Don't try to deny it! You were seen with him in La Santa!'

It had been on the cards, Karen supposed. The possibility had simply been pushed to the back of her mind by everything else.

'I wasn't going to deny it,' she said resignedly. 'We were together no more than fifteen minutes.'

Luiz curled a lip. 'Long enough.'

'Not for what you're thinking.' She came to her feet, shaky but not cowed. 'I was hoping not to have to tell you, but it seems I've no choice. Miran asked me to meet him to talk about Regina. He was afraid she'd taken his interest in her a little too seriously, and didn't know what to do about it.'

Fury leapt in the dark eyes. 'Don't you dare bring Regina's name into this!'

'It's true.' Karen tried to keep her tone level. 'The reason she was so unhappy last night was because Miran had failed to contact her. I thought it best to simply let the whole thing fade away. Miran will be back in São Paulo by now, so she's unlikely to see him again.'

Luiz regarded her with scepticism. 'You expect me to believe you were acting purely in Regina's interests?'

'Not really.' Karen drew a shallow breath, starting to lose her grip. 'You believe me guilty of having the affair with Lucio Fernandas. Why should you trust my word now? I spent several minutes in private conversation with your brother this morning. Perhaps I've designs on him too!'

'That's enough!' Luiz clipped.

'No, it isn't!' She was past caring what she let out. 'If you really want to know why Lucio was on the plane, ask your sister-in-law! Not that I'd expect you to take my word against hers, of course, but if you'd taken the trouble to check your credit card statement for January, you might have seen that I only paid for *one* ticket to Rio, and the same to London. Oh, I saw him on the plane—he was bragging about having lots of money—but he wasn't with me!'

Luiz was gazing at her in dawning realisation. 'You recovered your memory!'

'Every last detail! I suppose I should be flattered that you abandoned your mistress and son to get back to me yesterday—especially when you see so little of them. It's a pity…'

Karen broke off, struck by the expression on the lean, bronzed face.

'My *what*?' he asked.

'It's no use trying to deny it,' she retorted. 'I've seen the photograph you keep in your office drawer. Your son looks just like you!'

'He looks,' Luiz said levelly, 'like my brother Maurice. He was killed in a road accident more than two years ago, before he could put right the wrong he'd done. Margarita mourns him still. She would consider me no substitute.'

Karen swallowed on the dryness in her throat, her mind in turmoil. 'I'm sorry,' she got out. 'I didn't…know.'

'Obviously.' Luiz indicated the chair she'd risen from. 'I think you'd better sit down before you fall down.'

She did so, trying to get her head round it all. 'I don't understand. Beatriz—your mother—they both told me the child was yours.'

'They both lied.' The statement was iron-hard. 'I took over responsibility for Margarita and Maurice as a duty. I visit them when I'm in Brasilia on business, no other time. The photograph was given to me as a mark of gratitude.'

He studied her bewildered face, his own softening a little. 'How long have you been able to remember?'

'Only since yesterday.' She looked at him appealingly. 'What I said to you last night. It wasn't true, any of it. I was eaten up with jealousy. I couldn't stand the thought of sharing you with anyone.'

'I know the feeling,' he said.

'There was no affair. Not with Lucio Fernandas, not with Jorge Arroyo, not with anyone.'

'I believe you.' His tone was wry. 'You were right. If I'd checked the statement it would have proved what you say.' His brows drew together again. 'But that still doesn't explain why you took flight.'

'I'm afraid that was Beatriz too. She showed me the photograph, told me you already had a child. I didn't stop to think things through.'

'You were still suffering the trauma of losing the baby,' he said grimly. 'She will pay dearly for that alone. You believe she paid Fernandas to follow you?'

'She didn't actually deny it when I faced her with it yesterday, just said it would be hard to prove.' Karen made a rueful gesture. 'I let her persuade me that the doubt would still be there in your mind even if I told you I'd got my memory back. I'd almost managed to persuade myself that I could live with things the way they were—until you came to me in the shower. I wanted to hurt you. I wanted to make you feel the way I was feeling. Your pride—'

'Damn my pride!' he said forcefully. 'It was my heart that was shattered! I've never loved any woman before you. I could never think of loving any woman other than you!'

He drew her to her feet again, holding her close, his hands buried in her hair, eyes glowing with an inner fire. 'The moment I saw you, I was lost! I wanted to spend my life with you, to raise a family, to grow old alongside you. I know you don't feel as much for me, but—'

'Perhaps not in the beginning,' she said softly, 'but I do now. I've gone through hell all day thinking about you.' She lifted her hands to his face, tracing the incisive lines with her fingertips. 'It's still hard to believe it's all ended! All the wondering and doubting. I love you so much, Luiz.' She gave a shaky smile. 'Do you think we could go back to where we were last night before I launched that rocket? I've so much to make up for.'

'The fault was never yours,' he said. 'Beatriz is responsible for most of what we've both gone through, but my mother must share the blame.'

He kissed her tenderly on the lips, then put her from him, jaw hardening. 'We'll go back to where we were, never fear, but first I have to deal with my brother and his wife.'

'Raymundo doesn't know what she's been up to,' Karen defended. 'He'll be devastated!'

'He'll be more than that. They'll both of them be gone within the hour, I can promise you!'

'You can't throw your brother out,' she protested as he started for the door. 'He loves Guavada!'

Luiz looked back at her with a frown. 'Are you suggesting I allow Beatriz to get away with what she's done?'

'No.' Karen could say that without hesitation. 'I hate her for it! But let Raymundo stay. He'll be only too happy to be free of her. I know he's been weak—

he knows he's been weak—but give him a chance. There are times when divorce is the only path left to take.'

'There have been times when such a heartfelt plea on behalf of another man—even my own brother—would have been incentive enough to be rid of him,' came the reply after a moment. 'I'll let him decide for himself whether he stays or goes, if it makes you happy.'

'Not just me,' she said. 'You lost one brother, you can't afford to lose another. And Regina needs you both.'

Luiz came back to where she stood to take her in his arms again, lips cherishing hers.

'You are everything a woman should be,' he said gruffly. 'Don't go away.'

Karen had no intention. She watched him go out of the door, loving every masterful, masculine inch of him. She could almost feel sorry for Beatriz, who was going to get the shock of her life. Raymundo would opt to stay, for certain. Eventually he'd meet someone who was right for him.

In the meantime, she and Luiz had a family of their own to build. Starting the moment he returned.

She could hardly wait.

EPILOGUE

'MY WAIST is a whole three inches bigger than it was when I married you,' Karen complained, checking the tape measure.

'One for each baby,' Luiz returned easily. 'Some sacrifices have to be made.'

'And what exactly have *you* sacrificed?' she asked in mock indignation.

He laughed. 'I gave up my freedom for you. The biggest sacrifice a man can make! Are you coming to bed, or do I have to come and fetch you?'

Green eyes sparkled. 'You'll have to catch me first!'

She gave a yelp as he shot from the bed at the speed of lightning to sling her up across his shoulder, pummelling at his bare back with both fists. 'Unfair advantage! I wasn't ready!'

'I am,' he said, dumping her on the pillows.

He wasn't lying. Karen melted beneath him, aroused as always by the muscular strength of him, the oiled smoothness of his skin, the masculine scent. Thirty-eight, and still not one ounce of surplus flesh on his frame.

He took it slowly, making her wait—trailing feathery kisses down over her fluttering stomach muscles to linger for endless, tantalising moments before bestowing the most intimate of kisses. She writhed in ecstasy, fingers tangled in the thicket of black curls.

He never tired of making love to her, never left her

185

unsatisfied. A man in a million! she told herself eons later in the lazy, hazy aftermath.

Six years! It had passed so fast. Edmundo had been born almost exactly nine months after Beatriz's hasty departure, with Joana eighteen months later, and Maria Teresa just last year. Edmundo looked more and more like his father every day, while the girls took after her. Exactly how it should be, Luiz had declared.

Life couldn't be better than this, Karen thought contentedly. Each and every day she thanked her lucky stars. Without that lottery win, she would never have come to Brazil, never have known Luiz, never have given birth to these three particular children. It had to be kismet!

Luiz had never revealed exactly what passed between him and his sister-in-law that afternoon, but she'd been gone, as he'd promised, within the hour. Raymundo had not been held entirely blameless, but he'd been allowed to stay on at Guavada. The divorce had gone through eventually, though he hadn't found another wife yet. Once bitten, twice shy, Karen supposed.

Regina had been married two years to a man Luiz knew and trusted. No children so far, but there was time. Margarita was married too now, which meant Luiz no longer had sole responsibility for his brother's son, although he still saw the boy when he visited Brasilia.

Although Cristina had claimed sincere remorse for the harm she'd done, Luiz had never really forgiven her. Karen doubted if she and her mother-in-law would ever have a good relationship.

'Not asleep yet?' asked Luiz softly, bringing a smile to her face in the darkness.

'Maybe you could sing me a lullaby,' she said.

He laughed. 'I think I might have a better remedy than that.'

'And you call *me* insatiable,' she accused as he drew her on top of him.

'I thought we might try for another inch on that waistline of yours,' he said. 'Another boy would be nice.'

Karen arched her back, relishing the feel of him deep inside her. Another baby of any description would be nice, she thought happily.

'Perhaps you could manage twins this time,' she said. 'One of each. Five sounds a good number to finish on. On the other hand, all things being equal, we could go for a whole football team. Five a side, girls against boys! Just think of—'

Luiz was laughing; she could feel it right the way through her. He reached up to draw her down to him, cutting off the words with a kiss that drove whatever she had been about to say from her mind.

Not that it mattered.

LET'S TALK
Romance

For exclusive extracts, competitions
and special offers, find us online:

 facebook.com/millsandboon

@MillsandBoon

@MillsandBoonUK

Get in touch on 01413 063232

For all the latest titles coming soon, visit
millsandboon.co.uk/nextmonth